A QUIET FLAME

A QUIET FLAME

Philip Kerr

Quercus

First published in Great Britain in 2008 by

Quercus
21 Bloomsbury Square
London
WC1A 2NS

A CIP catalogue reference for this book is available
from the British Library

ISBN 978 1 84724 356 0 (HB)
ISBN 978 1 84724 357 7 (TPB)

10 9 8 7 6 5 4 3 2 1

Typeset by E-Type, Aintree, Liverpool
Printed and bound in Great Britain by Clays Ltd, St Ives plc.

Para el desaparecido

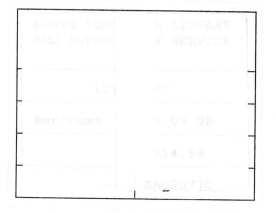

ONE

BUENOS AIRES. 1950.

The boat was the SS *Giovanni*, which seemed only appropriate given the fact that at least three of its passengers, including myself, had been in the SS. It was a medium-sized boat with two funnels, a view of the sea, a well-stocked bar, and an Italian restaurant. This was fine if you liked Italian food, but after four weeks at sea at eight knots all the way from Genoa, I didn't like it and I wasn't sad to get off. Either I'm not much of a sailor or there was something wrong with me beyond the company I was keeping these days.

We steamed into the port of Buenos Aires along the grey River Plate and this gave me and my two fellow travellers a chance to reflect upon the proud history of our invincible German navy. Somewhere at the bottom of the river, near Montevideo, lay the wreck of the *Graf Spee*, a pocket battleship that had been invincibly scuttled by its commander in December 1939 to prevent it falling into the hands of the British. As far as I knew this was as near as the war ever came to Argentina.

In the North Basin we docked alongside the Customs House. A modern city of tall concrete buildings lay spread out to the west of us, beyond the miles of rail track and the warehouses and stockyards where Buenos Aires got started – as a place where cattle from all over the Argentine Pampas arrived by train and were slaughtered on an industrial scale. So far, so German. But then the carcases were frozen and shipped all over the world. Exports of Argentine beef had made the country rich and transformed Buenos Aires into the third largest city in the Americas after New York and Chicago.

The three-million population called themselves *porteños* – the people of the port – which sounds pleasantly romantic. My two friends and I called ourselves refugees, which sounds better than fugitives. But that's what we were. Rightly or wrongly, there was a kind of justice awaiting all of us back in Europe and our Red Cross passports concealed our true identities. I was no more Doctor Carlos Hausner than Adolf Eichmann was Ricardo Klement, or Herbert Kuhlmann was Pedro Geller. This was fine with the Argentines. They didn't care who we were or what we'd done during the war. Even so, on that cool and damp winter morning in July 1950, it seemed there were still certain official proprieties to be observed.

An immigration clerk and a customs officer came aboard the ship and, as each passenger presented their documents, they asked questions. If these two didn't care who we were or what we'd done, they did a good job giving us the opposite impression. The mahogany-faced immigration clerk regarded Eichmann's flimsy-looking passport and then Eichmann himself as if both had arrived from the centre of a cholera epidemic. This wasn't so far from the truth. Europe was only just recovering from an illness called Nazism that had killed more than fifty million people.

'Profession?' the clerk asked Eichmann.

Eichmann's meat cleaver of a face twitched nervously. 'Technician,' he said, and mopped his brow with a handkerchief. It wasn't hot but Eichmann seemed to feel a different kind of heat from anyone else I ever met.

Meanwhile the customs official, who carried the odour of a cigar factory, turned to me. His nostrils flared as if he could smell the money I was carrying in my bag and then he lifted his cracked lip off his bamboo teeth in what passed for a smile in that line of work. I had about thirty thousand Austrian schillings in that bag, which was a lot of money in Austria but not such a lot when it was converted into real money. I didn't expect him to know that. In my experience, customs officials can do almost anything they want except be generous or forgiving when they catch sight of large quantities of currency.

'What's in the bag?' he asked.

'Clothes. Toiletries. Some money.'

'Would you mind showing me?'

'No,' I said, minding very much. 'I don't mind at all.'

I heaved the bag onto a trestle table and was just about to unbuckle it when a man hurried up the ship's gangway, shouting something in Spanish and then, in German, 'It's all right. I'm sorry I'm late. There's no need for all this formality. There's been a misunderstanding. Your papers are quite in order. I know because I prepared them myself.'

He said something else in Spanish about the three of us being important visitors from Germany, and immediately the attitude of the two officials changed. Both men came to attention. The immigration clerk facing Eichmann handed him back his passport, clicked his heels, and then gave Europe's most wanted man the Hitler salute with a loud 'Heil Hitler' that everyone on deck must have heard.

Eichmann turned several shades of red and, like a giant tortoise, shrank a little into the collar of the coat he was wearing, as if he wished he might disappear. Kuhlmann and I laughed out loud, enjoying Eichmann's embarrassment and discomfort as, snatching back his passport, he stormed down the gangway and onto the quay. We were still laughing as we joined him in the back of a big black American car with a sign displayed in the windscreen that read VIANORD.

'I don't think that was in the least bit funny,' said Eichmann.

'Sure you don't,' I said. 'That's what makes it so funny.'

'You should have seen your face, Ricardo,' said Kuhlmann. 'What on earth possessed him to say that, of all things? And to you, of all people?' Kuhlmann started to laugh again. 'Heil Hitler, indeed.'

'I thought he made a pretty good job of it,' I said. 'For an amateur.'

Our host who had jumped into the driver's seat, now turned around to shake our hands. 'I'm sorry about that,' he told Eichmann. 'Some of these officials are just pig-ignorant. In fact, the word we have for pig and public official are the same. *Chanchos*. We call them both *chanchos*. I wouldn't be at all surprised if that idiot believes Hitler is still the German leader.'

'God, I wish he was,' murmured Eichmann, rolling his eyes into the roof of the car. 'How I wish he was.'

'My name is Horst Fuldner,' said our host. 'But my friends in Argentina call me Carlos.'

'Small world,' I said. 'That's what my friends in Argentina call me. Both of them.'

Some people came down the gangway and peered inquisitively through the passenger window at Eichmann.

'Can we get away from here?' he asked. 'Please.'

'Better do as he says, Carlos,' I said. 'Before someone recognises Ricardo here and telephones David Ben-Gurion.'

'You wouldn't joke about that if you were in my shoes,' said Eichmann. 'The soaps would stop at nothing to kill me.'

Fuldner started the car and Eichmann relaxed visibly as we drove smoothly away.

'Since you mentioned the soaps,' said Fuldner. 'It's worth discussing what to do if any of you is recognised.'

'Nobody's going to recognise me,' Kuhlmann said. 'Besides, it's the Canadians who want me, not the Jews.'

'All the same,' said Fuldner. 'I'll say it anyway. After the Spanish and the Italians, the soaps are the country's largest ethnic group. Only we call them *los Russos*, on account of the fact that most of the ones who are here came to get away from the Russian Czar's pogrom.'

'Which one?' Eichmann asked.

'How do you mean?'

'There were three pogroms,' said Eichmann. 'One in 1821, one between 1881 and 1884, and a third that got started 1903. The Kishinev Pogrom.'

'Ricardo knows everything about Jews,' I said. 'Except how to be nice to them.'

'Oh, I should think the most recent pogrom,' said Fuldner.

'It figures,' said Eichmann, ignoring me. 'The Kishinev was the worst.'

'That's when most of them came to Argentina, I think. There are as many as a quarter of a million Jews here in Buenos Aires. They live in three main neighbourhoods, which I advise you to steer clear of. Villa Crespo along Corrientes, Belgrano, and Once. If you think you are recognised, don't lose your head, don't make a scene. Keep calm. Cops here are heavy-handed and none too bright. Like that *chancho* on the boat. If there's any kind of trouble they're liable to arrest you and the Jew who thinks he's recognised you.'

'So, there's not much chance of a pogrom here, then?' observed Eichmann.

'Lord, no,' said Fuldner.

'Thank goodness,' said Kuhlmann. 'I've had enough of all that nonsense.'

'We haven't had anything like that since what's called Tragic Week. And even that was mostly political. Anarchists, you know. Back in 1919.'

'Anarchists, Bolsheviks, Jews, they're all the same animal,' said Eichmann, who had become unusually talkative.

'Of course, during the war, the government issued an order forbidding all Jewish emigration to Argentina. But more recently things have changed. The Americans have put pressure on Perón to soften our Jewish policy; to let them come and settle here. I wouldn't be surprised if there were more Jews on that boat than anyone else.'

'That's a comforting thought,' said Eichmann.

'It's all right,' insisted Fuldner. 'You're quite safe here. *Porteños* don't give a damn about what happened in Europe, least of all to the Jews. Besides, nobody believes half of what's been in the English language papers and on the newsreels.'

'Half would be quite bad enough,' I murmured. It was enough to push a stick through the spokes of a conversation I was starting to dislike. But mostly it was just Eichmann I disliked. I much preferred the other Eichmann. The one who had spent the last four weeks saying almost nothing, and keeping his loathsome opinions to himself. It was too soon to have much of an opinion about Carlos Fuldner.

From the back of his well-oiled head I judged Fuldner to be around forty. His German was fluent but with a little soft colour on the edges of the tones. To speak the language of Goethe and Schiller, you have to stick your vowels in a pencil sharpener. He liked to talk, that much was evident. He wasn't tall and he wasn't good-looking, but then he wasn't short or ugly either, just ordinary, in a good suit with good manners and a nice manicure. I got another look at him when he pulled up at a level crossing and turned around to offer us some cigarettes. His mouth was wide and sensuous, his eyes were lazy but intelligent and his forehead was as high as a church cupola. If you'd been casting a movie you'd have picked him to play a priest, or a lawyer, or maybe a hotel manager. He snapped his thumb on a Dunhill, lit his cigarette, then began telling us about himself. That was fine by me. Now that we were no longer talking about Jews Eichmann stared out of the window and looked bored. But I'm the kind who listens politely to stories about my redeemer. After all, that's why my mother sent me to Sunday School.

'I was born here, in Buenos Aires, to German immigrants,' said Fuldner. 'But, for a while, we went back to live in Germany, in Kassel, where I went to school. After school I worked in Hamburg. Then, in 1932, I joined the SS and was a captain before being seconded to the SD to run an intelligence operation back here in Argentina. Since the war I and a few others have been running Vianord, a travel agency dedicated to helping our old comrades to escape from Europe. Of course, none of it would be possible without the help of the President and his wife, Eva. It was during Evita's trip to Rome to meet the Pope, in 1947, that she began to see the necessity of giving men such as you a fresh start in life.'

'So there's still some anti-Semitism in the country, after all,' I remarked.

Kuhlmann laughed and so did Fuldner. But Eichmann remained silent.

'It's good to be with Germans again,' said Fuldner. 'Humour is not a national characteristic of the Argentines. They're much too concerned with their dignity to laugh at very much, least of all themselves.'

'They sound a lot like fascists,' I said.

'That's another thing. Fascism here is only skin deep. The Argentines don't have the will or the inclination to be proper fascists.'

'Maybe I'm going to like it here more than I thought,' I said.

'Really,' exclaimed Eichmann.

'Don't mind me, Herr Fuldner,' I said. 'I'm not quite as rabid as our friend here wearing the bow-tie and glasses, that's all. He's still in denial. To do with all kinds of things. For all I know he still holds fast to the idea that the Third Reich is going to last for a thousand years.'

'You mean it isn't?'

Kuhlmann chuckled.

'Must you make a joke about everything, Hausner?' Eichmann's tone was testy and impatient.

'I only make jokes about the things that strike me as funny,' I said. 'I wouldn't dream of making a joke about something really important. Not at the risk of upsetting you, Ricardo.'

I felt Eichmann's eyes burning into my cheek and when I

turned to face him his mouth went thin and puritanical. For a moment he continued staring at me with the air of one who wished it was down the sights of a rifle.

'What *are* you doing here, Herr Doctor Hausner?'

'The same thing as you, Ricardo. I'm getting away from it all.'

'Yes, but why? Why? You don't seem like much of a Nazi.'

'I'm the beefsteak kind. Brown on the outside only. Inside I'm really quite red.'

Eichmann stared out the window as if he couldn't bear to look at me for a minute longer.

'I could use a good steak,' murmured Kuhlmann.

'Then you've come to the right place,' said Fuldner. 'In Germany a steak is a steak, but here it's a patriotic duty.'

We were still driving through the dockyards. Most of the names on the bonded warehouses and oil tanks were British or American: Oakley & Watling, Glasgow Wire, Wainwright Brothers, Ingham Clark, English Electric, Crompton Parkinson, and Western Telegraph. In front of a big open warehouse, a dozen rolls of newsprint the size of hayricks were turning to pulp in the early morning rain. Laughing, Fuldner pointed them out.

'There,' he said, almost triumphantly. 'That's Perónism in action. Perón doesn't close down opposition newspapers or arrest their editors. He doesn't even stop them from having newsprint. He just makes sure that by the time it reaches them the newsprint isn't fit to use. You see, Perón has all the major labour unions in his pocket. That's your Argentine brand of fascism, right there.'

TWO

BUENOS AIRES. 1950.

Buenos Aires looked and smelled like any European capital city before the war. As we drove through the busy streets, I wound down the window and took a deep, euphoric breath of exhaust fumes, cigar smoke, coffee, expensive cologne, cooked meat, fresh fruit, flowers, and money. It was like returning to earth after a journey into space. Germany, with its rationing and war damage and guilt and Allied tribunals, seemed a million miles away. In Buenos Aires there was lots of traffic because there was lots of petrol. The carefree people were well dressed and well fed because the shops were full of clothes and food. Far from being a remote backwater, Buenos Aires was almost a *belle époque* throwback. Almost.

The safe house was at 1429 Monasterio Street in the Florida district. Fuldner said Florida was the smartest part of Buenos Aires but you wouldn't have known it from the inside of the safe house. The outside was shielded by a carapace of over-grown pine trees and it was probably called a safe house because, from the street, you wouldn't have known it was there at all. Inside, you knew it was there but wished it wasn't. The kitchen was rustic, the ceiling fans just rusty. The wall-paper in all the rooms was yellow, although not by design, and the furniture looked as if it was trying to return to nature. Poisonous, half-decayed, vaguely fungal, it was the kind of house that belonged in a bottle of formaldehyde.

I was shown to a bedroom with a broken shutter, a thread-bare rug, and a brass bed with a mattress as thin as a slice of rye bread and about as comfortable. Through the grimy, cobwebbed window I looked out onto a little garden over-grown with jasmine, ferns, and vines. There was a small fountain that hadn't worked in a while: a cat had littered several kittens in it right underneath a copper waterspout that was as green as its eyes. But it wasn't all bad news. At least I had my own bathroom. The bath itself was full of old books but that didn't mean I couldn't take a bath in it. I like to read when I'm in the bath.

Another German was already staying there. His face was red and puffy and there were bags under his eyes like a naval cook's hammock. His hair was the colour of straw and about as tidy, and his body was thin and scarred with what looked like bullet holes. These were easy to see because he wore his malodorous remnant of a dressing gown off one shoulder, like a toga. On his legs were varicose veins as big as fossilised lizards. He seemed a stoic sort who probably slept in a barrel, but for the pint of liquor in his dressing gown pocket and the monocle in his eye, which added a jaunty, polished touch.

Fuldner introduced him as Fernando Eifler but I didn't suppose that was his real name. The three of us smiled politely but we were all possessed of the same thought: that if we stayed in the safe house long enough, we would end up like Fernando Eifler.

'I say, do any of you chaps have a cigarette?' asked Eifler. 'I seem to have run out.'

Kuhlmann handed one over and helped him get it alight. Meanwhile Fuldner apologised for the poor quarters, saying it was only for a few days and explaining that the only reason Eifler was still there was because he had turned down every job offered to him by the DAIE, which was the organisation that had brought us to Argentina. He said this quite matter-of-factly, but our new housemate bristled noticeably.

'I didn't come half way around the world to work,' Eifler

said sourly. 'What do you take me for? I'm a German officer and a gentleman, not a bloody bank clerk. Really, Fuldner, it's too much to expect. There was no talk of working for a living when we were back in Genoa. I'd never have come if I'd known you people expected me to earn my bread and butter. I mean, it's bad enough that one has to leave one's family home in Germany without obliging one to accept the added humiliation of reporting regularly to an employer.'

'Perhaps you'd have preferred it if the Allies had hanged you, Herr Eifler?' said Eichmann.

'An American noose or an Argentinian halter,' said Eifler. 'It's not much of a choice for a man of my background. Frankly, I would prefer to have been shot by the Popovs than face a clerk's desk at nine o'clock every morning. It's uncivilised.' He smiled thinly at Kuhlmann. 'Thank you for the cigarette. And, by the way, welcome to Argentina. Now, if you'll excuse me, gentlemen.' He bowed stiffly, limped into his room, and closed the door behind him.

Fuldner shrugged and said, 'Some find it harder to adjust than others. Especially aristocrats like Eifler.'

'I might have known,' sniffed Eichmann.

'I'll leave you and Herr Geller to settle in,' he told Eichmann. Then he looked at me. 'Herr Hausner. You have an appointment this morning.'

'Me?'

'Yes. We're going to the police station at Moreno,' he said. 'To the Registry of Foreign Persons. All new arrivals have to report there in order to obtain a *cedula di identidad*. I can assure you it's only a matter of routine, Herr Doctor Hausner. Photographs and fingerprints, that kind of thing. You'll all need to have one to work, of course, but for appearance's sake it's best you don't all go at the same time.'

But outside the safe house Fuldner confessed that while it was true that all of us would require a *cedula* from the local police station, this was not in fact where we were now going.

'Only I had to say something,' he said. 'I could hardly tell them where we're really going without hurting their feelings.'

'We certainly wouldn't want that to happen, no,' I said, climbing into the car.

'And please, when we come back, don't for Christ's sake say where you've been. Thanks to Eifler, there's already enough resentment in that house without you adding to the store of it.'

'Of course. It'll be our little secret.'

'You're making a joke,' he said, starting the engine and driving us away, 'but I'm the one who's going to be laughing when you find out where you're going.'

'Don't tell me I'm being deported already.'

'No, nothing like that. We're going to see the President.'

'Juan Perón wants to see *me*?'

Fuldner laughed just like he'd said he would. I guess my face did look kind of silly at that.

'What did I do? Win an important award? Most promising Nazi newcomer to Argentina?'

'Believe it or not, Perón likes to greet a lot of German officers who arrive here in Argentina, personally. He's very fond of Germany and the Germans.'

'It's not everyone you can say that about.'

'He is a military man, after all.'

'I imagine that's why they made him a general.'

'He likes to meet medical men most of all. Perón's grandfather was a doctor. He himself wanted to be a doctor but instead he went to the National Military Academy.'

'It's an easy mistake to make,' I said. 'Killing people instead of healing them.'

Dropping a couple of ice cubes into my voice, I said, 'Don't think I'm not well aware of the great honour, Carlos. But you know, it's been quite a few years since I plugged my ears with a stethoscope. I hope he's not looking to me to come up with a cure for cancer or give him the gossip from the latest

German medical journal. After all, I've been hiding out in the coal shed for the last five years.'

'Relax,' said Fuldner. 'You're not the first Nazi doctor I've had to introduce to the President. And I don't suppose you'll be the last. Your being a medical man is merely confirmation of the fact that you are an educated man, and a gentleman.'

'When the occasion demands, I can pass for a gentleman,' I said. I buttoned my shirt collar, straightened my tie and checked my watch. 'Does he always receive visitors with his boiled eggs and his newspaper?'

'Perón is usually in his office by seven,' said Fuldner. 'In there. The Casa Rosada.' He nodded at a pink-coloured building that stood at the far side of a plaza lined with palm trees and statuary. It looked like an Indian maharajah's palace I'd once seen in a magazine.

'Pink,' I said. 'My favourite colour for a government building. Who knows? Maybe Hitler might still have been in power if he'd had the Reich Chancellery painted a nicer colour than grey.'

'There's a story why it's pink,' said Fuldner.

'Don't tell me. It'll help me to relax if I can think of Perón as the kind of president who prefers pink. Believe me, Carlos, this is all very reassuring.'

'That reminds me. You *were* joking about being a Red, weren't you?'

'I was in a Soviet prison camp for almost two years, Carlos. What do you think?'

He drove around to a side entrance and waved a security pass at the guard on the barrier before carrying on through to a central courtyard. In front of an ornate marble stairway stood two grenadiers. With tall hats and drawn sabres they looked like an illustration from an old fairy tale. I glanced up at the loggia-style upper gallery that overlooked the court-yard, half expecting to see Zorro show up for a fencing lesson. Instead, I caught sight of a neat little blonde eyeing us with interest. She was wearing more diamonds than seemed decent at breakfast time and an elaborate baker's loaf of a hairstyle. I thought I might borrow a sabre and cut myself a slice of it if I got a bit peckish.

'That's her,' said Fuldner. 'Evita. The President's wife.'

'Somehow I didn't think she was the cleaning lady. Not with all the mints she's wearing.'

We walked up the stairway into a richly furnished hall where several women were milling about. Despite the fact Perón's was a military dictatorship nobody up here was wearing a uniform. When I remarked on this, Fuldner told me that Perón didn't care for uniforms, preferring a degree of informality that people sometimes found surprising. I might also have remarked that the women in the hall were very beautiful and that perhaps he preferred them to uglier ones, in which case he was a dictator after my own heart. The kind of dictator I would have been myself if a highly developed sense of social justice and democracy had not hindered my own will to power and autocracy.

Contrary to what Fuldner had told me, it seemed that the President was not yet at his desk. And while we awaited his much anticipated arrival, one of the secretaries fetched us coffee on a little silver tray. Then we smoked. The secretaries smoked, too. Everyone in Buenos Aires smoked. For all I knew even the cats and dogs had a twenty a day habit. Then, outside the high windows I heard a noise like a lawnmower. I put down my coffee cup and went to take a look. I was just in time to see a tall man climbing off a motor scooter. It was the President, although I would hardly have known that from his modest means of transport or his casual appearance. I kept comparing Perón with Hitler and trying to imagine the Führer dressed for golf and riding a lime green scooter down the Wilhelmstrasse.

The President parked the scooter and came up the stairs two at a time, his thick English brogues hitting the marble steps with a sound like someone working the heavy bag in the gym. He may have looked more like a golfer in his flat cap, tan-coloured, zip-up cardigan, brown plus-fours and thick woollen socks, but he had a boxer's grace and build. Not quite six feet tall, with dark hair brushed back on his head and a nose more Roman than the Coliseum, he reminded me of Primo Carnera, the Italian heavyweight. They would have been about the same age, too. I figured Perón for someone in his early fifties. The dark hair looked like it got blacked and polished every day when the Grenadiers cleaned their riding boots.

One of the secretaries handed him some papers while another threw open the double doors of his office. In there the look was more conventionally autocratic. There were lots of equestrian bronzes, oak panelling, portraits that were still wet, expensive rugs, and Corinthian columns. He waved us to a couple of leather armchairs, tossed the papers onto a desk the size of a trebuchet, and flung his cap and jacket to another secretary, who hugged them to her not insubstantial bosom in a way that made me think she wished he was still wearing them.

Someone else brought him a demitasse of coffee, a glass of water, a gold pen, and a gold holder with a cigarette that was already lit. He took a loud sip of coffee, put the holder in his mouth, picked up the pen and started adding his signature to the documents presented earlier. I was close enough to pay attention to his signature style: the flourishing egoistic capital 'J', the aggressive, showy, final downward stroke of the 'n' of Perón. Based on his handwriting, I made a quick psycholog-ical evaluation of the man and concluded that he was the neurotic, anally retentive type, who preferred people to be able to read what he had actually written. Not like a doctor at all, I told myself with relief.

Apologising in almost fluent German for keeping us waiting, Perón carried a silver cigarette box to our fingers. Then we shook hands and I felt the heavy knob of bone at the base of his thumb that again made me think of him as a boxer. That, and the broken veins under the thin skin that covered his high cheekbones, and the dental plate that was revealed by his easy smile. In a country where no one has a sense of humour the smiling man is king. I smiled back, thanked him for his hospitality and then complimented the President on his German, in Spanish.

'No, please,' Perón answered, in German. 'I very much enjoy speaking German. It's good practise for me. When I was a young cadet at our military school, all of our instructors were Germans. This was before the Great War, in 1911. You had to learn German because our weapons were German and all of our technical manuals were in German. We even learned to goose-step. Every day at six p.m. my Grenadiers goose-step onto the Plaza de Mayo to take the flag down from the pole. The next time you visit, you must make sure it's at that time so that you can see for yourself.'

'I will, sir.' I let him light my cigarette. 'But I think my own goose-stepping days are over. These days it's as much as I can do to climb a set of stairs without running out of breath.'

'Me, too.' Perón grinned. 'But I try to keep fit. I like to ride and to ski when I have the chance. In 1939, I went skiing in the Alps, in Austria and Germany. Germany was wonderful then, a well-oiled machine. It was like being inside one of those great big Mercedes-Benz motorcars. Smooth and powerful and exciting. Yes, it was an important time in my life.'

'Yes sir.' I kept on smiling at him, like I agreed with every word he said. The fact was I hated the sight of goose-stepping soldiers. To me it was one of the most unpleasant sights in the world; something both terrifying and ridiculous that defied you to laugh at it. And as for 1939, it had been an important time in everyone's life. Especially if you happened to be Polish, or French, or British, or even German. Who in Europe would ever forget 1939?

'How are things in Germany right now?' he asked.

'For the ordinary fellow, they're pretty tough,' I said. 'But it really depends on whose zone you're in. Worst of all is the Soviet zone of occupation. Things are hardest of all where the Ivans are in charge. Even for the Ivans. Most people just want to put the war behind them and get on with the reconstruction.'

'It's amazing what has been achieved in such a short period of time,' said Perón.

'Oh, I don't just mean reconstruction of our cities, sir. Although of course that is important. No, I mean the reconstruction of our most fundamental beliefs and institutions. Freedom, justice, democracy. A parliament. A fair-minded police force. An independent judiciary. Eventually, when all of that has been recovered, we might regain some self-respect.'

Perón's eyes narrowed. 'I must say you don't sound very much like a Nazi,' he said.

'It has been five years, sir, since we lost the war,' I replied. 'There's no point in thinking about what's gone. Germany needs to look to the future.'

'That's what we need in Argentina,' said Perón. 'Some forward thinking. A bit of the German can-do, eh Fuldner?'

'Absolutely, sir.'

'If you don't mind me saying so, sir,' I said, 'but from what I've seen so far, there's nothing Germany can teach Argentina.'

'This is a very Catholic country, Doctor Hausner,' he told me. 'It's very set in its ways. We need modern thinking. We need scientists. Good managers. Technicians. Doctors like yourself.' He clapped me on the shoulder.

Two little poodles ambled in, accompanied by a strong smell of expensive perfume, and out of the corner of my eye I saw that the blonde with the Kudamm hairdo and the diamonds had entered the room. With her were two men. One was medium height with fair hair and a moustache and a quiet unassuming way about him. The other was about forty, grey-haired with thick-framed, tinted glasses and a small beard and moustache, but physically more powerful. There was some-thing about him that made me think he might be a cop.

'Will you practise medicine again?' Perón asked me, adding, 'I'm sure we can make that possible. Rodolfo?'

The younger man by the door unfolded his arms and pushed himself off the wall. He glanced at the man with the beard for a moment. 'If the police have no objection?' His German was every bit as fluent as his master's.

The man with the beard shook his head.

'I'll ask Ramon Carillo to look into it, shall I, sir?' said Rodolfo. From the pocket of his beautifully tailored, pin-stripe suit he took out a small leather notebook and made a note with a silver propelling pencil.

Perón nodded. 'Please do,' he said, clapping me on the shoulder a second time.

In spite of his declared admiration for goose-stepping, I found myself liking the President. I liked him for his motor scooter and his ridiculous plus-fours. I liked him for his slugger's paw and his stupid little dogs. I liked him for his warm welcome and the easy way he had about him. And – who knows? – maybe I liked him because I badly needed to like someone. Maybe that's why he was president, I don't know. But there was something about Juan Perón that made me want to take a gamble on him. Which is why, after months of pretending to be someone else who was pretending to be Doctor Carlos Hausner, I decided to level with him about who and what I really was.

THREE

BUENOS AIRES. 1950.

I put out my cigarette in an ashtray as big as a wheel hub that lay on the President's uncluttered desk. Next to the ashtray was a Van Cleef and Arpels jewellery box – the leather kind that looks like it would make a swell gift on its own. I figured the contents of that box were pinned to the little blonde's lapel. She was fussing with the dogs as I started my noble-sounding monologue. It took only a minute to get her attention. I flatter myself that when the spirit moves in me I can make myself more interesting than any small dog. Besides, I guessed it wasn't every day that someone in the President's office tells him he'd made a mistake.

'Mister President, sir,' I said. 'I think there's something I should tell you. Since this is a Catholic country maybe you can call it confession.' Seeing all their faces blanch, I smiled. 'It's all right. I'm not about to tell you about all the terrible things I did during the war. There were some things I'm not happy about, sure, but I don't have the lives of innocent men and women on my conscience. No, my confession is something much more ordinary. You see, I'm not a doctor at all, sir. There was a doctor back in Germany. A fellow named Gruen. He wanted to go and live in America only he worried what might happen to him if they ever found out what he'd done during the war. So, to take the heat off himself, he decided to make it look like I was him. Then he told the Israelis and the Allied War Crimes people where to come and look for me. Anyway, he did such a good job of convincing everyone I was him that I was obliged to go on the run. Eventually I turned for help to the old comrades and the Delegation for Argentine Emigration in Europe. Carlos, here. Don't get me wrong, sir, I'm very grateful to be here. I had a hard job convincing an Israeli death squad that I wasn't Gruen and was obliged to leave a couple of them dead in the snow near Garmisch-Partenkirchen. So you see, I really am a fugitive. I'm just not the fugitive you might think I am. And in particular, I am not, nor ever have been a doctor.'

'So who the hell are you? Really?' It was Carlos Fuldner, and he sounded annoyed.

'My real name is Bernhard Gunther. I was in the SD. Working for intelligence. I was captured by the Russians and was interned in a camp before escaping. But before the war I was a policeman. A detective with the Berlin police force.'

'Did you say a detective?' This was the man with the small beard and the tinted glasses. The one I'd marked down as a cop. 'What kind of a detective?'

'I worked in homicide, mostly.'

'What was your rank?' asked the cop.

'When war was declared in 1939, I was a KOK. A Kriminal Ober-Kommissar. A Chief Inspector.'

'Then you'll remember Ernst Gennat.'

'Of course. He was my mentor. Taught me everything I know.'

'What was it that the newspapers used to call him?'

'The full Ernst. On account of his bulk and fondness for cakes.'

'What happened to him? Do you know?'

'He was Deputy Chief of the Criminal Police until his death in 1939. He had a heart attack.'

'Too bad.'

'Too many cakes.'

'Gunther, Gunther,' he said, like he was trying to shake a thought like an apple from a tree growing in the back of his head. 'Yes, of course. I know you.'

'You do?'

'I was in Berlin. Before the collapse of the Weimar Republic. Studying Jurisprudence at the university.'

The cop came closer, close enough for me to smell the coffee and the cigarettes on his breath, and took off his glasses. I guessed he smoked a lot. For one thing there was a cigarette in his mouth and for another his voice sounded like a smoked herring. There were laugh lines around the grey iron filings that constituted his moustache and his beard, but the walnut of a frown knotted between his bloodshot blue eyes told me that maybe he'd got out of the habit of smiling. His eyes narrowed as he searched my face for more answers.

'You know you were a hero of mine. Believe it or not, you're one of the reasons I gave up the idea of being a lawyer and became a policeman instead.' He looked at Perón. 'Sir, this man was a famous Berlin detective. When I first went there, in 1928, there was a notorious strangler. His name was Gormann. This is the man who caught him. At the time it was quite a *cause célèbre*.' He looked back at me. 'I'm right, aren't I? You are that Gunther.'

'Yes, sir.'

'His name was in all the newspapers. I used to follow all your cases as closely as I was able. Yes indeed, you were a hero of mine, Herr Gunther.'

By now he was shaking me by the hand. 'And now you're here. Amazing.'

Perón glanced at his gold wristwatch. I was beginning to bore him. The cop saw it, too. Not much escaped him. We might have lost the President's attention altogether if Evita hadn't walked up to me and given me a once over like I was a spavined horse.

Eva Perón's was a good figure if you liked women who were interesting to draw. I never yet saw a painting that persuades me those old masters preferred women who were skinny. Evita's figure was interesting in all the right places between the knees and the shoulders. Which is not to say that I found her attractive. She was too cool, too businesslike, too efficient, too composed for my taste. I like a little vulnerability in my women. Especially at breakfast time. In her navy blue suit Evita already looked dressed to launch a ship. Something more important than talking to me, anyway. On the back of her bottle-blonde hair was a little navy blue velvet beret, while over her arm was a Russian winter's worth of sables. Not that any of that caught my eye very much. Mostly my eyes were on the mint candies she was wearing – the little chandeliers of diamonds on her ears, the floral bouquet of diamonds on her lapel, and the dazzling golf ball on her finger. It looked like it had been an excellent year for Van Cleef and Arpels.

'So, we have a famous detective, here in Buenos Aires,' she said. 'How very fascinating.'

'I don't know about famous,' I said. 'Famous is a word for a boxer or a movie star, not a detective. Sure, the police leaders of Weimar encouraged the newspapers to believe that some of us were more successful than others. But that was just public relations to give the public confidence in our ability to solve crimes. I'm afraid you couldn't write more than a couple of very dull paragraphs in today's newspapers about the kind of detective I was, ma'am.'

Eva Perón tried a smile but it didn't stay long. Her lipstick was flawless and her teeth were perfect but her eyes weren't in it. It was like being smiled at by a temperate glacier.

'Your modesty is – shall we say? – typical of all your fellow countrymen,' she said. 'It seems none of you was ever very important. Always it is someone else who deserves the credit, or, more usually, the blame. Isn't that right, Herr Gunther?'

There were a lot of things I might have said to that. But when the President's wife takes a swing at you it's best to take it on the chin like you've got a boiler-plated jaw, even if it does hurt.

'Only ten years ago, Germans thought they should rule the

world. Now all they want to do is live quietly and be left alone. Is that what you want, Herr Gunther? To live quietly? To be left alone?'

It was the cop who came to my aid. 'Please ma'am,' he said. 'He is just being modest. Take my word for it. Herr Gunther was a great detective.'

'We'll see,' she said.

'Take the compliment, Herr Gunther. If I can remember your name, after all these years, then surely you would have to agree that, in this case at least, modesty is misplaced.'

I shrugged. 'Perhaps,' I allowed.

'Well,' said Evita. 'I must be going. I'll leave Herr Gunther and Colonel Montalban to their mutual admiration.'

I watched her go. I was glad to see the back of her. More importantly I was glad to see her behind. Even under the President's eye it demanded attention. I didn't know any Argentine tango tunes but, watching her closely sheathed tail as she stalked gracefully out of her husband's office, I felt like humming one. In a different room and wearing a clean shirt I might have tried slapping it. Some men liked slapping a guitar or a set of dominoes. With me it was a woman's ass. It wasn't exactly a hobby. But I was good at it. A man ought to be good at something.

When she was gone the President climbed back into the front seat and took over the steering wheel. I wondered how much he would let her get away with before he slapped her himself. Quite a bit, probably. It's a common failing with older dictators when they have younger wives.

In German, Perón said, 'Don't mind my wife, Herr Gunther. She doesn't understand that you spoke from—' He slapped his stomach with the flat of his hand. '—Down here. You spoke as you felt you had to speak. And I'm flattered that you did so. We see something in each other, perhaps. Something important. Obeying other people is one thing. Any fool can do that. But obeying oneself, submitting oneself to the most rigid and implacable of disciplines, that is what is important. Is it not?'

'Yes sir.'

Perón nodded. 'So you are not a doctor. Therefore we cannot help you practise medicine. Is there anything else we can do for you?'

'There is one thing, sir,' I said. 'Maybe I'm not much of a sailor. Or maybe I'm just getting old. But lately I've not been feeling myself, sir. I'd like to see a doctor, if I could. A real one. Find out if there's anything actually wrong with me, or if I'm just homesick. Although right now that does seem a little unlikely.'

FOUR

BUENOS AIRES. 1950.

Several weeks passed. I got my *cedula* and moved out of the safe house on Monasterio Street into a nice little hotel called the San Martin, in the Florida district. The place was owned and managed by an English couple called the Lloyds who treated me with such courtesy that it was hard to believe our two countries had ever been at war. It's only after a war that you actually find out how much you have in common with your enemies. I discovered the English were just like us Germans, with one major advantage: they didn't have to speak German.

The San Martin was full of old world charm with glass cupolas, comfortable furniture and good home cooking – if you enjoyed steak and chips. It was just around the corner from the more expensive Richmond Hotel, which had a café I liked enough to make it a regular port of call.

The Richmond was a clubby sort of place. There was a long room with wood panels and pillars and mirrored ceilings and English hunting prints and leather armchairs. A small orchestra played tangos and Mozart, and for all I knew, a few Mozart tangos. The smoke-filled basement was a home to men playing billiards, men playing dominoes and, most important of all, men playing chess. Women were not welcomed in the basement at the Richmond. Argentine men took women very seriously. Too seriously to have them around while they were playing billiards or chess. Either that, or Argentine women were just very good at billiards and chess.

Back in Berlin, during the dog days of the Weimar Republic, I'd been a regular chess player at the Romanisches Café. Once or twice I'd even had a lesson from the great Lasker, who was a regular there too. It hadn't made me a better player, just better able to appreciate being beaten by someone as good as Lasker.

It was in the Richmond basement that Colonel Montalban found me, locked in an end game with a diminutive, rat-faced Scotsman called Melville. I might have forced a draw if I'd had the patience of a Philidor. But then Philidor never had to play chess under the eye of the secret police. Although he almost did. Luckily for Philidor he was in England when the French Revolution took place. Wisely he never went back. There are more important things to lose than a game of chess. Like your head. Colonel Montalban didn't have the cold eye of a Robespierre, but I felt it on me all the same. And instead of asking myself how I was going to exploit my extra pawn to best advantage I started asking myself what the Colonel could want with me. After that it was just a matter of time before I lost. I didn't mind losing to the rat-faced Scotsman. He'd beaten me before. What I minded was the free tip that accompanied the clammy handshake.

'You should always put the rook behind the pawn,' he said in his lisping European Spanish which sounds and smells very different from Latin American Spanish. 'Except, of course, when it is the incorrect thing to do.'

If Melville had been Lasker I would have welcomed the advice. But he was Melville, a barbed-wire sales agent from Glasgow, with bad breath and an unhealthy interest in young girls.

Montalban followed me upstairs. 'You play a good game,' he said.

'I do all right. At least I do until the cops turn up. It takes the edge off my concentration.'

'Sorry about that.'

'Don't be. I like you being sorry. It's a load off my mind.'

'We're not like that in Argentina,' he said. 'It's all right to criticise the government.'

'That's not the way I heard it. And if you ask from whom you'll just prove me right.'

Colonel Montalban shrugged and lit a cigarette. 'There's criticism and there's criticism,' he said. 'It's my job to know the subtle difference.'

'I should think that's easy enough when you have your *oyentes?*' The *oyentes* were what *porteños* called Perón's spies – those who eavesdropped on conversations in bars, on buses, or even on the telephone.

The Colonel raised his eyebrows. 'So, you already know about the *oyentes*. I'm impressed. Not that I should be, I suppose. Not from a famous Berlin detective like yourself.'

'I'm an exile, Colonel. It pays to keep your mouth shut and your ears open.'

'And what is it that you hear?'

'I did hear the one about the two river rats, one from Argentina and the other from Uruguay. The rat from Uruguay was starving so it swam across the River Plate in the hope that it might find something to eat. Half way across it met an Argentine rat swimming in the opposite direction. The Uruguayan rat was surprised and asked why such a well-fed looking rat was going to Uruguay when there was so much to eat in Argentina. And the Argentine rat told him—'

'—I just want to squeak now and then.' Colonel Montalban smiled wearily. 'It's an old joke.'

I pointed at an empty table but the Colonel shook his head and then nodded at the door. I followed him outside, onto Florida. The street was closed to traffic between the hours of eleven a.m. and four p.m. so that pedestrians could inspect the attractively dressed windows of big shops like Gath & Chaves in comfort, but it could just as easily have been so that men could inspect the attractively dressed women. Of these there were plenty. After Munich and Vienna, Buenos Aires felt like a Paris catwalk.

The Colonel had parked off Florida, on Tucuman, outside the Claridge Hotel. His car was a lime-coloured Chevrolet convertible with polished wooden doors, whitewall tyres, red leather seats and, on the hood, an enormous spotlight in case he needed to interrogate a parking attendant. When you sat in it you felt like you should have been towing a water-skier.

'So, this is what the polenta drives in B.A.,' I remarked, running my hand over the door. It had the height and feel of a bar-top in a deluxe hotel. I suppose it made sense. A nice pink house for the President, a lime convertible for his deputy head of security and intelligence. Fascism never looked so pretty. The firing squads probably wore tutus.

We drove west on Moreno with the top up. What was probably a cold winter's day to the Colonel felt pleasantly springlike to me. The temperature was in the low sixties but most *porteños* were walking around wearing hats and coats as if it was Munich in January.

'Where are we going?'

'Police headquarters.'

'My favourite.'

'Relax,' he said, chuckling. 'There's something I want you to see.'

'I hope it's your new summer uniforms. If so I can save you a journey. I think they should be the same colour as the Casa Rosada. To help make policemen in Argentina more popular. It's hard not to like a cop when he's wearing pink.'

'Do you always talk so much? Whatever happened to keeping your mouth shut and your ears open?'

'After twelve years of Nazism it's nice to squeak a little now and again.'

We drove through the entrance of a handsome nineteenth century building which didn't look much like a police station.

I was beginning to understand a little of Argentine culture from a keen appreciation of its architecture. It was a very Catholic country. Even the police station looked like there was a basilica inside and one that was probably dedicated to Saint Michael, the patron saint of cops.

It might not have looked like a police station but it certainly smelt like one. All police stations smell of shit and fear.

Colonel Montalban led the way through a warren of marble-floored corridors. Cops carrying files climbed out of our way as we went along.

'I'm beginning to think you might be someone important,' I said.

We stopped outside a door where the air seemed more foetid. It made me think of visiting the aquarium at the Berlin Zoo when I was a child. Or perhaps the Reptile House. Something wet and slimy and uncomfortable anyway. The Colonel took out a packet of Capstan Navy Cut, offered me one, and then lit us both. 'Deodorants,' he said. 'In here is the Judicial Mortuary.'

'Do you bring all your first dates here?'

'Just you, my friend.'

'I feel I should warn you that I'm the squeamish sort. I don't like mortuaries. Especially when there are dead bodies in them.'

'Come now. You worked in homicide, didn't you?'

'That was years ago. It's the living I want to be with as I get older, Colonel. I'll have plenty of opportunity to spend time with the dead when I'm dead myself.'

The Colonel pushed open the door and waited. It seemed I didn't have much choice but to go inside. The smell got worse. Something wet and slimy and definitely dead, like a dead alligator. A man wearing white scrubs and bright green rubber gloves came to meet us. He was vaguely Indian-looking, dark skinned with even darker rings under his eyes, one of which was milky, like an oyster. I had the idea he'd just crawled out of one of his body drawers. He and the Colonel exchanged a silent mime of nods and head jerks and then the green gloves went to work. Less than a minute later I was looking at the naked body of an adolescent girl. At least I think it was a girl. What usually passed for clues in this department appeared to be missing. And not just the exterior parts, but quite a few of the internal ones, too. I'd seen more obviously fatal injuries, but only on the Western Front in 1917. Everything south of her navel appeared to have been mislaid. The Colonel let me take a good look at her and then said, 'I was wondering if she reminded you of anyone.'

'I don't know. Someone dead?'

'Her name is Grete Wohlauf. A German Argentine girl. She was found in the Barrio Norte about two weeks ago. We think she was strangled. More obviously, her womb and other reproductive organs had been removed, probably by someone who knew what they were doing. This was not a frenzied attack. As you can see, there is a certain clinical efficiency about what has been done here.'

I kept the cigarette in my mouth so that the smoke acted as a screen between my sense of smell and the gutted cadaver that was laid out in front of us like something on an abattoir floor. Actually, the smell was mostly formaldehyde but whenever I caught it in my nostrils it dislodged memories of the many unpleasant things I'd seen in my time as a Berlin homicide detective. There were two things I remembered in particular, but I saw no reason to mention these to Colonel Montalban.

Whatever it was he wanted from me, I wanted no part of it. After a while, I turned away.

'And?' I said.

'I just wondered ... if this might jog any memories.'

'Nothing that ought to be in my photograph album.'

'She was fifteen years old.'

'It's too bad.'

'Yes,' he said. 'I have a daughter myself. A little older than her. I don't know what I'd do if something like this happened.' He shrugged. 'Everything. Anything.'

I said nothing. I imagined he was coming to the point.

He walked me back to the mortuary door. 'I told you before that I studied Jurisprudence in Berlin,' he said. 'Fichte, Von Savigny, Erlich. My father wanted me to be a lawyer but my mother, who is German, she wanted me to become a philosopher. I myself wanted to travel. To Europe. And after my law degree I was offered the opportunity to study in Germany. Everyone was happy. Me, most of all. I loved Berlin.'

He pushed open the door and we went back into the corridor outside.

'I had an apartment on the Kudamm, near the Memorial Church and that club with the doorman who dressed up as the devil, and where the waiters dressed as angels.'

'The Heaven and Hell,' I said. 'I remember it very well.'

'That's right.' The Colonel grinned. 'Me, a good Roman Catholic boy. I'd never seen so many naked women before. There was one show – Twenty-five Scenes from the Life of the Marquis de Sade, it was called – and another called The Naked Frenchwoman: Her Life Mirrored in Art. What a place. What a city. Is it really all gone?'

'Yes. Berlin itself is a ruin. Little more than a building site. You wouldn't recognise it.'

'Too bad.'

He unlocked the door to a little room opposite the Judicial Mortuary. There was a cheap table, a few cheap chairs and some cheap ashtrays. The Colonel drew up a blind and opened a dirty window to let in some fresh air. Across the street I could see a church, and people going in the door who knew nothing about forensics and murder and whose nostrils were filled with something better than the smell of cigarettes and formaldehyde. I sighed and looked at my watch, hardly caring to conceal my impatience now. I hadn't asked to see the body of a dead girl. I was irritated with him for that and for what I knew was surely coming.

'Forgive me,' he said. 'I'm just getting to it now, Herr Gunther. What I wanted to talk to you about. You see, I've always been interested in the darker side of human behaviour. That is why I became interested in you, Herr Gunther. You are one of the reasons I became a policeman rather than a lawyer. In a sense you helped to save me from a very dull life.'

The Colonel drew up a chair for me and we sat down.

'Back in 1932 there were two sensational murders in the German newspapers.'

'There were a lot more than two,' I said sourly.

'Not like these two. I remember reading about them in some lurid detail. These were lust murders, were they not? Two girls similarly mutilated, just like poor Grete Wohlauf. One in Berlin and one in Munich. And you, Herr Gunther, you were the investigating detective. Your picture was in the paper.'

'Yes, I was. Only I don't see what that has to do with anything.'

'The murderer was never caught, Herr Gunther. He was never caught. That's why we're talking.'

I shook my head. 'That's true. But look, it was almost twenty years ago. And several thousand miles away. You're surely not suggesting that this murder might be connected.'

'Why not?' The Colonel shrugged. 'I have to consider every possibility. With the benefit of hindsight, it seems to me that these were peculiarly German crimes. Who was that other fellow who murdered and sexually mutilated all those boys and girls? Haarmann, wasn't it? He bit out their throats and cut off their genitals. And Kürten. Peter Kürten. The Vampire of Düsseldorf. Let's not forget him, shall we?'

'Haarmann and Kürten were executed, Colonel. As I'm sure you must remember. So it can hardly be them, can it?'

'Of course not. But there were other lust murders, too, as I'm sure you remember. Some of them involving mutilation and cannibalism.' The Colonel leaned forward on his chair. 'All right. Here's where I'm going with this. Many Germans have come to live here in Buenos Aires. Before the war, and after the war. And not all of them are civilised people like you and me. Naturally I've been paying close attention to the trials of your so-called war criminals, and it's quite clear to me that some of your countrymen have done some terrible things. Unimaginable things. So here's my theory, if you can call it that. Not everyone who has come to Argentina in the last five years is an angel. Some might be devils. Just like in that old Berlin club, the Heaven and Hell. You will admit that much, surely?'

'Freely. You heard what I said to the President.'

'Yes, I did. It made me think that you might be a man I could use, Herr Gunther. An angel, if you like.'

'I've never been called that before.'

'Oh, I think you have but I'll get to that. Let me finish this particular train of thought. You will also admit, I hope, that many of your colleagues in the SS enjoyed killing, yes? I mean, it stands to reason, doesn't it? That some of these men in the SS were psychopaths. Yes?'

I nodded. 'I can see where you're going with this, I think.'

'Exactly. Take the case of Rudolf Höss, the commander of the Auschwitz concentration camp. He'd murdered before. In 1923. As had Martin Bormann. A man does not become a psychopath because he puts on a uniform, therefore it must be the case that there were many psychopaths who found a congenial home in the SS and the Gestapo as licensed murderers and torturers.'

'I always thought so,' I said. 'You can imagine my pleasure when I was inducted into the SS, in 1940. It comes as quite a shock to spend your whole life investigating murder, then to be sent to Russia and expected to start committing it yourself.'

'Oh I wasn't suggesting you were a psychopath, Herr Gunther. Look, let's say that in 1932 this murderer is not caught. In 1933 the Nazis come to power and he joins the SS where he finds a new, socially acceptable means of satisfying his lust for cruelty. During the war he works in a death camp, killing as many as he wants with total impunity.'

'And then you invite him to come and live in Argentina.' I grinned. 'I take your point, but I don't see how I can help.'

'I should have thought it was obvious. A chance to re-open an old case.'

'I'm not the neat type, Colonel. And believe me there were plenty of other unsolved cases on our books. None of them costs me any sleep.'

The Colonel was nodding but I could see that he still had cards to play.

'Another girl has gone missing,' he said. 'Here in B.A.'

'Girls go missing all the time. Darwin called it natural selection. A girl selects a young man and naturally her father doesn't like him very much, so she runs off with him.'

'So I can't appeal to your social conscience?'

'I hardly know my way around this city. I barely speak the language. I'm a fish out of water.'

'Not exactly. The girl who is missing is of German-Argentine origin. Like Grete Wohlauf. I was thinking you might confine your enquiries to our German community. Didn't I just explain that I have a hunch we're looking for a German? You don't need to speak good Spanish to do that. You don't need to know the city, you need to be a German. And to hunt among the people I want you to hunt among, you need to be one of them. When I said you could be my angel, I meant my black angel. Isn't that what Germans called men who were in the SS? Black angels?'

'Set a thief to catch a thief, is that it?'

'Something like that, yes.'

'They're not going to like that, my old comrades. They have new names, new faces some of them. New names, new faces, and amnesia. I could find myself becoming very unpopular with some of the most ruthless men in South America. Present company excepted.'

'I already thought of a way of handling things so that you don't wind up dead.'

I smiled. He was persistent, I had to give him that much. And I was beginning to have a feeling he had already second-guessed all of my objections. 'I bet you have, Colonel.'

'I've even considered your financial situation,' he said. 'After having converted your money at the Bank of London and South America – the branch on Calle Bartolomé Mitre, wasn't it?'

'So much for banking secrecy in this country,' I said.

'You will have learned that twenty-five thousand Austrian schillings is not such a lot. By my calculations you have about a thousand dollars, which is not going to last you very long in Buenos Aires. A year, maybe less if there are unforeseen expenses. And it's my experience that there are always unfore-seen expenses, especially for a man in your position. On the other hand, I'm offering you a job. Unlike the kind of job Carlos Fuldner will probably offer you, this is a job you would actually be good at.'

'Working for you? In the secret police?'

'Why not? There's a salary, a desk in the Casa Rosada, a car. There's even a passport. A proper one. Not that piece of shit the Red Cross gave you. With a proper passport you could go back to Germany, perhaps. Without having to answer all sorts of awkward questions when you got there. After all, you would be an Argentine citizen. Think about it.'

'Perhaps if I had the original case files it might have been possible.' I shook my head. 'But it was almost twenty years ago. Probably the files were lost during the war.'

'On the contrary. They're here in B.A. I had them sent from Berlin Alexanderplatz.'

'You did that? How?'

The Colonel shrugged modestly, but still managed to look

quite pleased with himself. As well he might have done. I was impressed with him.

'Actually, it really wasn't very difficult. It's the Americans who dislike Perón and the generals, not the Russians. Besides, the Delegation for Argentine Immigration in Europe has many friends in Germany. You should know that better than anyone. If the DAIE can get Eichmann out of Germany a few old files are not going to present much of a problem.'

'My compliments, Colonel. You seem to have thought of everything.'

'In Buenos Aires it is better to know everything than it is to know too much,' said the Colonel.

He crossed his legs and picked some fluff off his knee while he waited patiently for my answer. I felt certain I was about to trump him, but he looked so cool I couldn't help but think he still had something up his sleeve.

'Please don't think that I'm not flattered by your offer,' I said. 'But right now I have other things on my mind. You've thought of everything, it's true. Except the one reason why I'm not going to work for you. You see, Colonel, I'm not well. I had heart palpitations on the boat. I thought I was having a heart attack. Anyway, I've been to see Doctor Espejo, the one Perón recommended. And he says I don't have a heart condition at all, the heart palpitations are the result of thyro-toxicosis. I have cancer of the thyroid, Colonel Montalban. That's why I'm not going to work for you.'

FIVE

BUENOS AIRES. 1950.

Colonel Montalban took off his glasses and began to clean their tinted lenses with the end of his woollen tie. He was trying not to smile so as not to hurt my feelings but I could see that he really didn't care if he did. As if he was trying only a little not to give the game away.

I guessed what this was.

'But you knew that already, didn't you?'

The Colonel shrugged and went on polishing.

'What kind of a country is this? No banking secrecy. And no medical ethics. I suppose Doctor Espejo is a friend of yours.'

'Actually no. Quite the reverse. Espejo is what we call a *resentida*. It means he has a chip on his shoulder. Espejo is a man who dislikes Perón intensely.'

'I wondered why he seemed to be the only person I've met in this city who doesn't have a picture of the President on his wall.' I shook my head. 'Perón recommended a doctor who hates him? I don't get it.'

'Earlier on, you mentioned the *oyentes*.'

I smiled. 'You have a listening device planted in his surgery.'

'Several.'

'I guess that's one way of making sure you get an honest diagnosis.'

'Did you perhaps think you didn't?'

'It sure didn't feel like Espejo was keeping anything back. The man's got quite a left hook on him. It's been a while since anyone caught me one on the chin like that.' I paused. 'Don't tell me he was pulling his punches.'

'Not at all,' said the Colonel. 'Espejo's a good doctor. But there are better ones. If I were you, Herr Gunther, I should want to have someone treating me who's more of an expert in these matters than Espejo. A specialist.'

'Sounds expensive. Too expensive for my thousand dollars.'

'All the more reason to work for me. We have a saying here in Argentina. We say, "I can't trust you until I tell you a secret". So that's what I'm going to do. I'm going to trust you with one of the biggest secrets in the country. Then you will have to help me and I will have to help you. It will be a sign of good faith between us.'

'What if I prefer not to know what you know?'

'I can't tell you B if I don't also tell you A. I will tell you B first and then perhaps you will guess A. Doctor George Pack is one of the leading cancer specialists in the world. He is a consultant at the Memorial Sloan-Kettering Cancer Center in New York. He treats patients like the Rockefellers and the Astors. But quite often he also comes here, to Buenos Aires.'

'To treat someone equally important, no doubt,' I said. 'The General?'

The Colonel shook his head.

'The General's wife?'

He nodded. 'But even she does not know.'

'Is that possible?'

'It is if the General wishes it. Evita thinks she has a woman's problem. But it's something else. I have already spoken to Doctor Pack. And, as a favour to the General, he has agreed to treat you the next time he is in the country. At our expense, of course.' The Colonel threw up his hands. 'So you see, you have no choice, no excuse to refuse. There isn't one objection you can make that hasn't already been thought of.'

'All right,' I said. 'I can tell when I'm beaten. You seem to have a lot of faith in my abilities, Colonel.'

'Is it so hard to accept my admiration for your forensic abilities, Herr Gunther? It would be the same for you and Ernst Gennat, would it not? Or that other great Berlin detective, Bernard Weiss. These were your mentors. Your own heroes.'

'For a while, yes, they were,' I said. 'All the same, it does seem like you've been to a hell of a lot of trouble to have me investigate one murder and one missing girl.'

'It might seem that way to you, Herr Gunther. But to be brutal with you, it's really no trouble at all. We have some old papers sent from Berlin. We give you a job. We pay you some money. We employ a doctor to treat your illness. These are easy things to fix when you're a man in my position. What could be simpler?'

'When you put it like that,' I said.

'As it happens, though,' he added smoothly, 'the missing girl is no ordinary girl. Fabienne Von Bader is what we call a *paquete*. One of the elegant people. Her father, Kurt Von Bader, is a close friend of the Peróns, as well as being a director of the Banco Germanico here in B.A. Naturally the police are sparing no effort in looking for her. You will be merely a part of that effort. Perhaps she is already dead. Perhaps, as you suggested, she has only run away from home. Although, frankly, she is a little young to have a boyfriend, she's only fourteen years old. Grete Wohlauf you should leave to the regular police, but Fabienne is a different story. She should be your main focus. From what I hear missing persons were once something of a speciality for you after you left the Berlin police in 1933 – when you were a private detective.'

'You seem to know everything about me, Colonel,' I said. 'Too much for comfort.'

'Not too much. Just everything that is important. For the purpose of your inquiry you should assume that our potential murderer is a German and confine yourself to the community of recent immigrants, and those who are of German-Argentine origin. You are looking for a psychopath, yes, but always you

are looking for some clue as to the whereabouts of young
Fabienne Von Bader.'

'It won't be easy asking questions of my old comrades.'

'Which is why you must choose your questions carefully.
You must make your questions seem innocent.'

'You don't know them,' I said. 'There's no such thing as an
innocent question where they're concerned.'

'The Red Cross is an admirable institution,' said the
Colonel. 'But to go anywhere else outside of this country
again – Germany, for example – you will need an Argentine
passport. To get a passport you will have to prove that you
have been an Argentine resident of good conduct. Having
proved this, a good conduct pass will be issued. With a
conduct pass you can apply to a court of first instance for a
passport. I thought it would be a good cover story for your
inquiry if we said that you are carrying out background
checks for the Security and Intelligence Directorate to see
whether someone is a suitable candidate for this good conduct
pass. That way you can pry into the backgrounds of your old
comrades with impunity. I dare say most of them will be only
too willing to answer all your questions, Herr Gunther, no
matter how impertinent. Such a role allows you complete
licence. After all, who among your old comrades doesn't want
a passport in a new name?'

'It might work,' I said.

'Of course it will work. As I've said, a desk will be provided
for you at the Casa Rosada – that's where the SIDE is headquartered – and a car will be yours to use. You will receive
expenses. A salary. Full SIDE identification. And you will
report directly to me. Anything at all. No matter how small.
Doctor Pack will be here in a couple of weeks. You can see
him then. For obvious reasons, however, I'd like you to start
your inquiry immediately. A list of the names and addresses of
your old comrades will be given to you at the Casa Rosada.
Naturally, Fuldner and the DAIE have given us some idea of

who these people were back in Germany. What they did and when. But naturally I should like to know a lot more about them in order to assess what diplomatic and security risk they might pose for us in the future. You can update the files as you go. Clear?'

'Yes, I think so.'

'I assume you'll want to meet the parents of the missing girl as a matter of priority.'

'If I could.'

The Colonel nodded. He drew open a little drawer in the table from which he removed a leather briefcase. From one of the pockets in the briefcase he took out a pistol before emptying the rest of the contents onto the table.

'One Smith & Wesson semi-automatic pistol. One box of ammunition. One shoulder holster. One driver's licence in the name of Carlos Hausner. One SIDE identity warrant in the name of Carlos Hausner. One security pass for the Casa Rosada in the name of Carlos Hausner. One SIDE manual – make sure you read it carefully. One hundred thousand pesos in cash. There will be more when you need it. Naturally, receipts are required where possible. The manual will tell you exactly how to fill out an expense form. You'll find everything else – DAIE files on German immigrants, Kripo and Gestapo files from Alexanderplatz – in your filing cabinet at the Casa Rosada.'

I nodded silently. There didn't seem to be any point in mentioning the fact that all of this had been ready before I walked into the police station. He'd been so sure I'd agree that I almost told him to go and screw himself. I hated him taking me for granted like that. But I hated being ill even more. So how could I say no? We both knew I had no choice. Not if I wanted to receive the best medical treatment.

He fiddled in his pocket and handed over some car keys. 'It's the one outside. The lime-coloured Chevrolet we came in.'

'My favourite flavour,' I said.

He stood up. 'You can drive, can't you?'

'I can drive.'

'Good. Then you can drive us to Retiro.' He glanced at his watch. 'They're expecting us so we had better be getting along.'

'Before we go, I'd like to take another look at that dead body.'

The Colonel shrugged. 'If you like. Was there anything you noticed?'

'Nothing apart from the obvious.' I shook my head. 'I wasn't really paying attention before. That's all.'

SIX

BERLIN. 1932.

In a manual of forensic medicine that Ernst Gennat gave all the bulls that joined Department Four there was a photograph that always caused a certain amount of mirth the first time you saw it. In the photograph, a naked girl was lying on a bed with her hands tied behind her back; around her neck was a ligature pulled tight and half of her head had been blown off with a shotgun. Oh yes, and there was a dildo up her ass. Nothing funny about any of that, of course. It was the caption underneath the picture that was the funny part. It read, 'Circumstances Arousing Suspicion'. That used to kill us. Whenever any of us who were assigned to D4 saw an atrocious and obvious case of homicide we used to repeat the words of that caption. It helped lighten things up.

The body was found in Friedrichshain Park, close to the hospital, in the eastern part of Berlin. The area was popular with children because of the fairy tale fountain that was there. Water flowed down a series of shallow steps that were flanked by ten groups of characters from stories each of us had heard at his mother's knee. When the call came into the Police Praesidium on Alexanderplatz it was hoped that the dead girl might have drowned, accidentally. But one look at the body and I knew different. She looked like the victim of the wolf from one of those old fairy tales. The kind of big bad wolf who might have tried to eat any one of those little limestone heroes and heroines.

'Bloody hell, sir,' said my sergeant, KBS Heinrich Grund, as we shone our flashlights over the body. 'Circumstances arousing suspicion, or what?'

'Sure looks that way, doesn't it?'

'Only a bit, yeah. Shit. Wait till the boys at the Alex hear about this one.'

There was not a permanent staff of detectives for homicide investigations at the Alex. D4 was only supposed to be a supervisory body with three rotating teams of cops from other Berlin inspectorates, but in practice it didn't work like that. By 1932 there were three teams on active duty, with nothing left in reserve. That night I had already driven over to Wedding to take a look at the body of a fifteen-year-old boy who had been found stabbed to death in a bus shelter. The other two teams were still out on cases: KOK Muller was looking into the death of a man found hanging on a lamp-post in Lichtenrade; and KOK Lipik was in Neukolln investigating the fatal shooting of a woman. If this sounds like a crime wave, it wasn't. Most of the murders that took place in Berlin that spring and early summer were political. And but for the tit-for-tat violence carried out by Nazi storm troopers and Communist cadres, the city's crime figures would have shown a declining murder rate during the last months of the Weimar Republic.

Friedrichshain Park was a leafy mile north-west of the Alex. After the call came in we were there in less than twenty minutes. Me, District Secretary Grund, an ordinary Criminal Secretary, an Assistant Criminal Secretary and half a dozen uniformed polenta from the Protection Police – the Schutzpolizei.

'A lust murder, do you think?' asked Grund.

'Could be. There's not much blood around though. Whatever lust might have been involved must have happened elsewhere.' I looked up and around. The road junction at Konigs-Thor was only a few yards to the west of us. 'Whoever it was could have stopped his car on Friedenstrasse, or Am

Friedrichshain, lifted her out of the trunk, and carried her here just after it got dark tonight.'

'With the park on one side of the road and a couple of cemeteries on the other, it's a good spot,' said Grund. 'Lots of trees and bushes to keep him covered. Nice and quiet.'

Then, somewhere to the west of us, in the heart of Scheunvierte, we heard two shots fired.

'Although not so as you'd notice,' I said. Hearing a third shot, and then a fourth, I added, 'Sounds like your friends are busy tonight.'

'Nothing to do with me,' said Grund. 'More likely the Always True, I'd have thought. This is their patch.'

The Always True was one of Berlin's most powerful criminal gangs.

'But if it was a Red who just got shot then, presumably, that would be to your lot's advantage.'

Heinrich Grund was, or had been, just about my best friend on the force. We had been in the army together. There was a picture of him on the wall in my corner of the detective's room. In the picture no less a figure than Paul Von Hindenburg, the President of the Republic, was presenting Heinrich with the victor's plaque for winning the Prussian Police Boxing Championships. But the previous week I had discovered that my old friend had joined the NSBAG – the National Socialist Fellowship of Civil Servants. As a boxer, with a reputation for using the head, I had to admit that being a Nazi suited him. All the same, it felt like a betrayal.

'What makes you think it was a Nazi shooting a Red and not a Red shooting a Nazi?'

'I can tell the difference.'

'How?'

'It's a full moon, isn't it? That's usually the time when werewolves and Nazis creep out of their holes to commit murder.'

'Very funny.' Grund smiled patiently and lit a cigarette. He blew out the match and, careful not to contaminate the crime scene, he put it in his jacket pocket. He might have been a Nazi but he was still a good detective. 'And your lot. They're so different, are they?'

'My lot? What lot is that?'

'Come on, Bernie. Everyone knows the Official supports the Reds.'

The Official was the union of Prussian police officers to which I belonged. It wasn't the biggest union. That was the General. But the important names in the General's leadership – policemen like Dillenburger and Borck – were openly right-wing and anti-Semitic. Which was why I'd left the General and joined the Official.

'The Official isn't communist,' I said. 'We support the Social Democrats and the Republic.'

'Oh yeah? Then why the Iron Front against Fascism? Why not an Iron Front against Bolshevism, too?'

'Because, as you well know, Heinrich, most of the violence on the streets is committed or provoked by the Nazis.'

'How do you work that out, exactly?'

'That woman in Neukolln that Lipik's investigating. Even before he left the Alex he reckoned she had been shot dead by a storm trooper who was aiming at a commie.'

'So. It was an accident. I don't see how that proves the Nazis organise most of the violence.'

'No? Well you want to come round our way and take a look out of my apartment window on Dragonerstrasse. The Central Offices of the German Communist Party are just around the corner on Bulowplatz, and that's where the Nazis choose to exercise their democratic right to hold a parade. Does that seem reasonable? Does that sound law-abiding?'

'Proves my point, doesn't it? You living in a Red area like that.'

'All it proves is that the Nazis are always spoiling for a fight.'

I bent down and flicked my flashlight up and down the dead

girl's body. Her upper half looked more or less normal. She was aged about thirteen or fourteen, blonde with pale blue eyes and a small galaxy of freckles around her pixie's nose. It was a tomboyish sort of face and you could easily have mistaken her for a boy. The matter of her sex was only confirmed by her small, adolescent breasts, the rest of her sexual organs having been removed along with her lower intestines, her womb, and whatever else gets packed in down there when a girl gets born. But it wasn't her evisceration that caught my eye. In truth both Heinrich and I had seen this kind of thing many times in the trenches. There was also the calliper on her left leg. I hadn't noticed it before.

'No walking stick,' I said, tapping it with my pencil. 'You'd think she'd have had one.'

'Maybe she didn't need one. It's not every cripple that needs a stick.'

'You're right. Goebbels manages very well without one, doesn't he? For a cripple. Then again there's a big stick inside almost everything he says.' I lit a cigarette and let out a big smoky sigh. 'Why do people do this kind of thing?' I said to myself.

'You mean, kill children?'

'I meant why kill them like this? It's monstrous, isn't it? Depraved.'

'I should have thought it was obvious,' said Grund.

'Oh? How's that?'

'You're the one who said he must be depraved. I couldn't agree more, but is it any wonder? I say is it any wonder we have depraved people doing things like this when you consider the filth and depravity that's tolerated by this fag-end of a government? Look around you, Bernie. Berlin is like a big slimy rock. Lift it up and you can see everything that crawls. The oilers, stripe men, wall-sliders, boot girls, sugar-lickers, Munzis, T-girls. The women who are men and the men who are women. Sick. Venal. Corrupt. Depraved. And all of it tolerated by your beloved Weimar Republic.'

'I suppose everything will be different if Adolf Hitler gets into power.' I was laughing as I said it. The Nazis had done well in the most recent elections, but nobody sensible really believed they could run the country. Nobody thought for a minute that President Hindenburg was ever going to ask the man he detested most in the world – a guttersnipe NCO from Austria – to become the next Chancellor of Germany.

'Why not? We're going to need someone to restore order in this country.'

As he spoke we heard another shot travel through the warm night air.

'And who better than the man who causes all the trouble to put an end to it, eh? I can sort of see the logic behind that, yes.'

One of the uniforms came over. We stood up. It was Sergeant Gollner, better known as Tanker, because of his size and shape.

'While you two were arguing,' he said, 'I put a cordon around this part of the park so as to keep the pot watchers away. Last thing we want is any details of how she was killed getting into the newspapers. Giving stupid people stupid ideas. Confessing to things they haven't done. We'll have a closer look in the morning, eh? When it's light.'

'Thanks, Tanker,' I said. 'I should have—'

'Skip it.' He took a deep breath of night air made moist by water a light breeze had carried from the fountain. 'Nice here, isn't it? I always liked this place. Used to come here a lot, I did. On account of the fact that my brother is buried over there.' He nodded south, in the direction of the state hospital. 'With the revolutionaries of 1848.'

'I didn't know you were that old,' I said.

Tanker grinned. 'No, he got shot by the Freikorps, in December 1918. Proper lefty, so he was. A real troublemaker, but he didn't deserve that. Not after what he went through in the trenches. Reds or not, none of them deserved to be shot for what happened.'

'Don't tell me,' I said, nodding at Heinrich Grund. 'Tell him.'

'He knows what I think,' said Tanker. He looked down at the girl's body. 'What was wrong with her leg then?'

'Hardly matters now,' observed Grund.

'She might have had polio,' I said. 'Or else she was a spastic.'

'You wouldn't have thought they'd have let her out on her own, would you?' said Grund.

'She was disabled.' I bent down and went through the pockets of her coat. I came up with a roll of cash, wrapped in a rubber band. It was as thick as the handle of a tennis racquet. I tossed it to Grund. 'Plenty of disabled people manage perfectly well on their own. Even the kids.'

'Must be several hundred marks here,' he muttered. 'Where does a kid like this get money like that?'

'I don't know.'

'Had to manage,' Tanker was saying. 'The number of maimed and injured we had after the war. I used to have the beat next to the Charité Hospital. Got quite friendly with some of the lads who were there. A lot of them managed with no legs, or no arms.'

'It's one thing suffering a disability for something that happened fighting for the Fatherland,' said Grund, tossing the roll of cash in his hand. 'It's something else when you're born with it.'

'Meaning what exactly?' I asked.

'Meaning that life's difficult enough when you're a parent without having to look after a disabled child.'

'Maybe they didn't mind looking after her. Not if they loved her.'

'If you ask me, if she was a spastic she's better off out of it,' said Grund. 'Germany's better off in general with less cripples around.' He caught the look in my eye. 'No, really. It's a simple matter of racial purity. We have to protect our stock.'

'I can think of one cripple we'd all be better off without,' I said.

Tanker laughed and walked away.

'Anyway, it's only a calliper,' I said. Lots of kids have callipers.'

'Maybe,' said Grund. He threw the money back. 'But it's not every kid that's carrying several hundred marks.'

'Right. We'd better have a look around, before the site gets trampled over. See what we can find on our hands and knees with the flashlights.'

I dropped onto all fours and, slowly, crawled away from the body in the direction of Konigs-Thor. Heinrich Grund did the same, a yard or two to my left. The night was a warm one and the grass felt dry and smelt sweet under my hands. It was something we had done before. Something Ernst Gennat was keen on. Something that was in the manual he'd given us. How it was small things that solved murders: bullet casings, blood spots, collar buttons, cigarette ends, matchbooks, earrings, hanks of hair, party badges. Things that were large and easy to see were usually carried away from a crime scene. But the small stuff: that was different. It was the small stuff that could send a man to the guillotine. Nobody called them clues. Gennat hated that word.

'Clues are for the clueless,' was what the full Ernst would tell us. 'That's not what I want from my detectives. Give me little spots of colour on a canvas. Like that Frenchy who used to paint in little dots. Georges Seurat. Each dot means shit on its own. But when you take a few steps back and look at all of the dots together you see a picture. That's what I want you bastards to do. Learn how to paint me a picture like Georges Seurat.'

So there we were, me and Heinrich Grund, crawling along the grass in Friedrichshain Park, like a couple of dogs. The Berlin polenta trying to paint a picture.

If I had blinked I might have missed it. As spots of colour

go this one was as small as anything you might have seen on an Impressionist's canvas, but just as colourful. At first glance I mistook it for a cornflower because it was light blue, like the dead girl's eyes. It was a pill, lying on top of a few blades of grass. I picked it up and held it up to my eyes and saw that it was as immaculate as a diamond which meant it couldn't have been there that long. There had been a brief shower of rain just after lunch so it had to have fallen on the ground some time after that. A man hurrying back to the road from the fountains where he had dumped a body might easily have taken out a box of pills, fumbled it in his nervous state, and dropped one. Now all I had to do was find out what kind of pill it was.

'What have you got there, boss?'

'A pill,' I said, laying it on his palm.

'Kind of pill?'

'I'm not a chemist.'

'Want me to check it out at the hospital?'

'No. I'll get Hans Illmann to do it.'

Illmann was Professor of Forensic Medicine at the Institute for Police Science in Charlottenburg, and senior pathologist at the Alex. He was also a prominent member of the Social Democratic Party, the SPD. For this and other alleged character failings he had been frequently denounced by Goebbels in the pages of *Angriff*, Berlin's Nazi newspaper. Illmann wasn't Jewish but as far as the Nazis were concerned he was the next worst thing: a liberal-minded intellectual.

'Illmann?'

'Professor Illmann. Any objections?'

Grund looked up at the moon as if trying to learn patience. The white light had turned his pale blond head a steely shade of silver and his blue eyes became almost electric. He looked like some kind of machine man. Something hard, metallic and cruel. The head turned and he stared at me as he might have stared at some poor opponent in the ring – an inadequate subspecies of man who was not fit to enter a contest with one such as him.

'You're the boss,' he said and dropped the pill back in my hand.

But for how much longer? I asked myself.

We drove back to the Alex which, with its cupolas and arched entranceways, was as big as a railway station and, behind the four-storey brick facade, in the double-height entrance hall, very nearly as busy. All human life was in there. And quite a bit of pond life, too. There was a drunk with a black eye who was unsteadily awaiting being locked up for the night; a taxi driver making a complaint about a passenger who had run off without paying; an androgynous-looking young man wearing tight white shorts who was sitting quietly in a corner checking his make-up in a hand mirror; and a bespectacled man with a briefcase in his hands and a livid red mark across his mouth.

At the bunker-sized front desk we checked through a file containing a list of missing persons. The desk sergeant who was supposed to be assisting us had a big handlebar moustache and an eleven o'clock shadow that was so blue it made his face look like a house fly's. This effect was enhanced because his eyes were bulging out of his head at the sight of two tall boot girls a cop had shooed in off the street. They were wearing thigh-length, black leather boots and red leather coats which, thoughtfully, they had left undone, revealing to anyone who cared to look that they were wearing nothing underneath. One of them was carrying a riding crop that the arresting officer, a man with an eye patch – a man I knew, named Bruno Stahlecker – was having a hard job persuading her to give up. Clearly the girls had had a drink or two, and probably quite a bit else besides and while I flicked through the missing persons reports half of me was listening to what

Stahlecker and the girls were saying. It would have been hard not hear it.

'I like a man in uniform,' said the taller of the leather-booted Amazons. She snapped her riding crop against her boot and then fingered the hair at the base of her belly, provocatively. 'Which one of Berlin's bulls wants to be my slave tonight?'

Boot girls were the city's outdoor dominatrices. Mostly they worked west of Wittenberg Platz, near the Zoological Gardens, but Stahlecker had picked up this pair of whores in Freidrichstrasse after a man had complained of being beaten and robbed by two women in leather.

'Behave yourself, Birgit,' said Stahlecker. 'Or I'll throw the rules of the medical profession at you as well.' He turned to the man with the red mark on his face. 'Are these the two women who robbed you?'

'Yes,' said the man. 'One of them hit me across the face with a whip and demanded money or she'd hit me again.'

The girls loudly protested their innocence. Innocence never looked quite so venereal and corrupt.

Finally I found what I'd been looking for. 'Anita Schwarz,' I said, showing Heinrich Grund the missing persons report. 'Aged fifteen. Behrenstrasse 8, Flat 3. Report filed by her father, Otto. Disappeared yesterday. Five feet three inches tall, blonde hair, blue eyes, calliper on left leg, carries a walking stick. That's our girl all right.'

But Grund was hardly paying attention. I thought he was looking at the free nude show. And leaving him to it, I went to one of the other filing cabinets and found a more detailed report. There was a star on the file and, next to it, a letter W. 'It would seem that the Deputy Police President is taking an interest in our case,' I said. Inside the file was a photograph. Quite an old one, I thought. But there could be no doubt: it was the girl in the park. 'Perhaps he knows the girl's father.'

'I know that man,' murmured Grund.

'Who? Schwarz?'

'No. That man there.' Leaning back on the front desk he flicked his snout at the man with the whip mark on his face. 'He's an Alphonse.' An Alphonse was Berlin criminal under-world slang for a pimp. One of many slang words for a pimp, like Louie, Oiler, Stripe Man, Ludwig, and Garter Handler. 'Runs one of those bogus clinics off the Kudamm. I think his racket is that he poses as a physician and then "prescribes" an under-age girl for his so-called "patient".' Grund called out to Stahlecker. 'Hey, Bruno? What's the citizen's name? The one wearing the spectacles and the extra smile.'

'Him? Doctor Geise.'

'Doctor Geise, my eggs. His real name is Koch, Hans-Theodor Koch and he's no more a doctor than I am. He's an Alphonse. A medicine man who fixes old perverts up with little girls.'

The man stood up. 'That's a damn lie,' he said indignantly.

'Open his briefcase,' said Grund. 'See if I'm wrong.'

Stahlecker looked at the man who held the briefcase tightly to his chest as if he really did have something to hide. 'Well, sir? How about it?'

Reluctantly the man allowed Stahlecker to take the brief-case and then to open it. A few seconds later there was a pile of pornographic magazines lying on the desk sergeant's blotter. The magazine was called *Figaro* and on the cover of each copy was a picture of seven naked boys and girls, aged about ten or eleven, sitting in the branches of a dead tree, like a pride of small white lions.

'You old pervert,' snarled one of the boot girls.

'This puts rather a different complexion on things, sir,' Stahlecker told Koch.

'That is a naked culture magazine,' insisted Koch. 'Dedicated to the cause of free life reform. It doesn't prove anything of what this vile man has alleged.'

'It proves one thing,' said the boot girl with the whip. 'It proves you like looking at dirty pictures of little boys and girls.'

We left them all in heated argument.

'What did I tell you?' said Grund as we went back to the car. 'This city is a whore and your beloved Republic is her pimp. When are you going to wake up to that fact, Bernie?'

On Behrenstrasse I parked the car in front of a glass-covered arcade that led up to Unter den Linden. The arcade was nick-named the Back Passage because it was a popular pick-up spot for Berlin's male prostitutes. These were easily identifiable because of the short white trousers, sailor shirts and peaked caps many of them wore to appear younger to the tree stumps – their middle-aged clients who, until they had made their selection, would walk up and down the passage pretending to look in the windows of the arcade's antique shops.

It was a warm night. By my reckoning there were at least eighty or ninety of the city's sultriest boys milling around underneath the famous Reemtsma sign, one of the few left unbroken by the Nazi SA. Storm troopers were supposed to smoke a Trommler brand called Storm but, being Nazis and therefore very brand-loyal, they often took exception to other brands of tobacco, of which Reemtsma was perhaps the best known. If the SA did show up, all of the sultry boys would take to their heels or risk a beating – perhaps worse. The SA seemed to hate queers almost as much as they hated commu-nists and Jews.

We found the apartment above a café in a smart-looking Romanesque building. I pulled the polished brass bell and we waited. A minute later we heard a man's voice above our heads and we stepped back on the pavement to get a better look at him.

'Yes?'

'Herr Schwarz?'

'Yes.'

'Police, sir. May we come up?'

'Yes. Wait there. I'll come down and let you in.'

While we waited, Heinrich Grund fulminated against all the sultries we'd seen. 'Russian fairies,' he said.

Immediately after the Bolshevik Revolution many of Berlin's prostitutes, male and female, had been Russians. But this was no longer true and I did my best to ignore him. It wasn't that I liked queers. I just didn't dislike them as much as he did.

Otto Schwarz came to the door to let us in. We showed him our KRIPO warrant discs and introduced ourselves and he nodded as if he had been expecting us. He was a big man with a belly that looked as if a lot of money had been poured into it. His fair hair was cut very short at the sides and wavy on top. Underneath a swinish nose that was almost divided in two by a thick scar was a nearly invisible toothbrush moustache. That he reminded me strongly of Ernst Röhm, the SA leader, was a first impression reinforced by the uniform he was wearing, illegally. There had been a ban on Nazi uniforms since June 1930; and, as recently as April, in a campaign to reduce Nazi terrorism in Berlin, Reich President Hindenburg had dissolved the SA and the SS I wasn't much good at recognising the shoulder and collar insignia on their uniforms but Grund was. The two of them made polite conversation as we tramped upstairs. That was how I came to learn not only that Schwarz was an Oberführer in the SA but also that this was the equivalent of a Brigadier General. There was a small part of me that wanted to join in this polite conversation. I wanted to say I was surprised to find an SA Oberführer at home when there were communists to lynch and Jewish windows to smash. But since I was about to tell Schwarz that his daughter was dead, I had to make do with an observation about his wearing the uniform of a proscribed organisation. Half of the polenta in Berlin would have looked the other way, ignored it. But then half of the cops in Berlin were Nazis. And if many of my colleagues seemed quite happy to be sleep-walking their way to a dictatorship, I wasn't one of them.

'You know that since April fourteenth of this year, it's illegal to wear that uniform, don't you sir?' I said.

'Surely that hardly matters now. The ban on uniforms is about to be revoked.'

'Until then it's still illegal, sir. However, under the circumstances, I'll overlook it.'

Schwarz coloured a little and then squeezed his fists, one after the other. These made a noise like a noose tightening. I imagine he was wishing there was one around my neck. He bit his lip. It was easier to reach than my face. He pushed open the apartment door. Stiffly, he said, 'Please. Come in, gentlemen.'

The apartment was a shrine to Adolf Hitler. There was a portrait of him in an oval frame in the hall and another different portrait of him inside a square frame in the sitting room. A copy of *Mein Kampf* lay open on a bookstand that was on the sideboard, next to a family Bible and behind these was a framed photograph of Otto Schwarz and Adolf Hitler. They were wearing leather flying helmets and sitting in the front seat of an enormous open-top Mercedes with cheesy grins on their faces, as if they had just won the ADAC Eifelrennen, and in record time. By one of the armchairs on the floor lay a dozen or so copies of *Der Stürmer*, the vehemently anti-Semitic newspaper. I'd seen election posters for Adolf Hitler that were less obviously Nazi than the Schwarz family home.

In her own sweet, big-breasted, blonde and blue-eyed way, Frau Schwarz looked no less of a Nazi than her storm trooper of a husband. When she put her arm through her husband's arm I half expected them both to shout 'Germany Awake!' and 'Death to the Jews' before breaking up the furniture and then singing the 'Horst Wessel Song'. Sometimes it was only these daydreaming little fantasies that made the job at all bearable. It certainly wasn't two hundred and fifty marks a month. Frau Schwarz wore a full, gathered dirndl skirt with traditional embroidery, a tight-laced blouse, an apron, and an expression that was a combination of fear and hostility.

Schwarz put his hand on top of the hand his wife had threaded through his ham hock of an arm, and then she put her other hand on his. But for their grim and resolute faces they reminded me of a couple getting married.

At last they looked like they were ready to hear what they knew I was going to tell them. I'd like to say I admired their courage and that I felt sorry for them. The truth is I didn't, very much. The sight of Schwarz's illegal uniform and the battalion number on his collar patch made me almost indifferent to their feelings. Assuming they had any. A very good friend of mine, POWM Emil Kuhfeld, a first sergeant with the SCHUPO, had been shot dead at the head of the detachment of riot police trying to disperse a large group of communists in Frankfurter Allee. A Nazi commissar at Police Station 85 who had investigated the case had managed to pin the murder on a communist, but nearly everyone at the Alex knew he had suppressed the evidence of a witness who had seen Kuhfeld shot by an SA man with a rifle. The day after Kuhfeld's murder, this SA man, one Walter Grabsch, was discovered dead in his Kadinerstrasse flat, having conveniently committed suicide. Kuhfeld's funeral had been the biggest ever given to a Berlin policeman. I had helped to carry the coffin. Which was how I knew that the battalion number on Schwarz's blue collar patch was the same battalion to which Walter Grabsch had belonged.

I gave Herr and Frau Schwarz all of the hard words of grief straight from the holster. I didn't even try to rub them in the snow first.

'We think we've found the body of your daughter, Anita. We believe she was murdered. Obviously I'll have to ask you to come down to the station to identify her. Shall we say tomorrow morning, ten o'clock, at the Police Praesidium, on Alexanderplatz?'

Otto Schwarz nodded silently.

I had retailed bad news before, of course. Just the previous week I'd had to tell a mother in Moabit that her seventeen-year-old son, a schoolboy at the local gymnasium, had been murdered by communists who'd mistaken him for a brown-shirt. 'Are you sure it's him, Commissar?' she asked me more than once during the course of my lachrymose time with her. 'Are you sure there hasn't been a mistake? Couldn't it be someone else?'

Herr and Frau Schwarz seemed to be taking it on the chin, however.

I glanced around the apartment again. There was a little embroidery sampler in a frame above the door. It read 'Willingness for self-sacrifice' and was stitched in red, with an exclamation mark. I'd seen one before and knew it was a quotation from *Mein Kampf*. I wasn't surprised to see it, of course. But I was surprised that I could see no photographs of their daughter, Anita. Most people who are parents have one or two of their children around the place.

'We have the photograph you gave us, on file,' I said. 'So we're quite sure it's her, I'm afraid. But it would save time if you could spare us some others.'

'Save time?' Otto Schwarz frowned. 'I don't understand. She's dead, isn't she?'

'Save time, trying to catch her murderer,' I said coldly. 'Someone may have seen her with him.'

'I'll see what I can find,' said Frau Schwarz and left the room, quite composed and no more upset than if I'd told her that Hitler wouldn't be coming to tea.

'Your wife seems to be taking it very well,' I said.

'My wife is a nurse at the Charité,' he said. 'I suppose she's used to dealing with bad news. Besides, we were sort of expecting the worst.'

'Really, sir?' I glanced at Grund who stared balefully at me and then looked away.

'We're very sorry for your loss, sir,' he told Schwarz. 'Very sorry indeed. Incidentally, there's no need for both of you to come to the Praesidium, tomorrow. And if tomorrow's not convenient, we can always do it another time.'

'Thank you, Sergeant, but tomorrow will be fine.'

Grund nodded. 'Best to get it over with, sir,' he said, nodding. 'You're probably right. And then you can get on with your grieving.'

'Yes. Thank you, Sergeant.'

'What was the nature of your daughter's disability?' I asked.

'She was a spastic. It affected only the left side of her body. She had trouble walking of course. There were also occasional seizures, spasms, and other involuntary movements. She couldn't hear very well, either.'

Schwarz went over to the sideboard and, ignoring the Bible, laid his hand fondly on the open copy of Hitler's book, as if his Führer's warm words about the National Socialist move-ment might afford him some spiritual and philosophical solace.

'What about her capacity for understanding?' I asked.

He shook his head. 'There was nothing wrong with her mind, if that's what you mean?'

'It is.' I paused. 'And I just wondered if you might be able to explain how she came to have five hundred marks on her.'

'Five hundred marks?'

'In her coat pocket.'

He shook his head. 'There must be some mistake.'

'No sir, there's no mistake.'

'Where would Anita get five hundred marks? Someone must have put it there.'

I nodded. 'I suppose that's possible, sir.'

'No, really.'

'Do you have any other children, Herr Schwarz?'

He looked astonished even to be asked such a thing. 'Good God, no. Do you think we would have risked having another child like Anita?' He sighed loudly and suddenly there was a strong smell of something foul in the air. 'No, we had quite enough to do just looking after her. It wasn't easy I can tell you. It wasn't easy at all.'

Finally Frau Schwarz returned with several photographs. They were old and rather faded. One was folded down at the edge as if someone had handled it carelessly. 'These are all that I could find,' she announced, still quite dry-eyed.

'All of them, did you say?'

She nodded, carelessly. 'Yes. That's all of them.'

'Thank you, Frau Schwarz. Thank you very much.' I nodded, curtly. 'Well then, we had better be getting back to the Station. Until tomorrow.'

Schwarz started to move toward the door.

'It's all right, sir. We'll see ourselves out.'

We went out of the apartment and down the stairs to the street. The Café Kerkau, beneath the apartment, was still open but I was in the mood for something stronger than coffee. I cranked up the car's two cylinder engine and we drove east along Unter den Linden.

'I need a drink after that,' I said after a few minutes.

'I suppose it's lucky you didn't have a drink before,' observed Grund.

'Meaning?'

'Meaning, you were a bit hard on them, sir.' He shook his head. 'Christ, you didn't even rub it with snow. You just gave it to them, grit and all. Right between the eyes.'

'Let's go to the Resi,' I said. 'Somewhere with lots of people.'

'And we all know how good you are with people,' Grund

said bitterly. 'Was it because he was a storm trooper, that you treated him and his wife like they had no feelings?'

'Didn't you see that collar patch? Twenty-first battalion. That was the same SA battalion Walter Grabsch belonged to. You remember Walter Grabsch? He murdered Emil Kuhfeld.'

'That's not what the local police said. And what about all the polenta the commies have murdered? Those two police captains, Anlauf and Lenck. Not forgetting Paul Zankert. What about those fellows?'

'I didn't know them. But I did know Emil Kuhfeld. He was a good cop.'

'So were Anlauf and Lenck.'

'And I hate the bastards who murdered them every bit as much as I hate the man who killed Emil. The only difference between the reds and the Nazis as far as I'm concerned is that the reds don't wear uniforms. If they did it'd be lot easier for me to hate them on sight, too, the same way I hated Schwarz, back there.'

'Well, at least you admit it, you uncaring bastard.'

'All right. I admit it. I was a bit out of line. But it could have been a lot worse. It's only out of sympathy for that Nazi sod's feelings that I didn't pinch him for wearing the SA uniform.'

'That was big of you, sir.'

'Assuming either of them had any feelings. Which I very much doubt. Did you see her?'

'How do you work that out?'

'Come on, Heinrich. You know the play as well as I do. Your daughter's dead. Someone murdered her. Cue handkerchief. Are you sure? Yes, we're sure.'

'She's a nurse. They can take it.'

'My eggs. Did you see her? Her tits didn't even wobble when I told her that her daughter was dead. They were good tits. I liked looking at them. But they didn't so much as tremble when I gave it to them. Tell me I'm wrong, Heinrich.

And tell me I'm wrong that there weren't any photographs of Anita Schwarz on the sideboard. Tell me I'm wrong that she spent at least ten minutes trying to find one. And tell me I'm wrong that she said she'd given me all the photographs of her daughter.'

'What's wrong with that?'

'Wouldn't you want to keep at least one photograph to remember your dead daughter? Just in case some dumb cop like you lost them?'

'She knows she'll get them back. That's all.'

'No, no. People aren't like that, Heinrich. She'd have kept one back. At least one. But she gave me all of them. That's what she said. I asked her about it and she confirmed it. You heard her. Not only that, but these pictures aren't in the best of condition, like they've been kept in an old shoebox. A commie kills you tonight and someone asks me for a picture of you for the police newspaper, I can give them a nice one, in a frame, in twenty seconds. And I'm not even related to you. Thank God.'

'So what are you saying?'

I pulled up close to the Residenz Casino. It was well past midnight but there were still plenty of people going into the place. One or two of them cops, probably. The Resi was popular with KRIPO from the Alex and not just because of its proximity.

'I'm saying what you were saying back in the park.'

'What did I say back in the park?'

'That maybe they're both of them glad the kid's dead. That maybe they think she's better off. More importantly, that they're better off.'

'How do you work that out?'

'It's Nazi policy, isn't it? That cripples are a waste of all our tax marks. That's where I assumed you'd got all this racial purity shit from. Hell, Heinrich, you saw that photograph of Schwarz with Hitler.' I lit a cigarette. 'I'll bet you anything

Hitler would probably like Otto Schwarz a whole lot better if it wasn't for his gimp daughter.'

We went inside the Resi. The spanner on the door knew our faces and waved us past the ticket booth. None of the clubs made cops pay to get in. They needed us more than we needed them. Especially when, as with the Resi, there were more than a thousand people in the place. We found ourselves a little loge in the balcony and ordered a couple of beers. The club was full of alcoves and booths and private cellars, all of them equipped with telephones that encouraged patrons to flirt at a safe distance. These telephones were also one of the reasons the place was popular with detectives from the Alex. Informers liked them. The whores liked the telephones, too. Everyone liked the telephones at the Resi. The minute we sat down the phone on our table started to ring. I picked it up.

'Gunther?' said a man's voice. 'It's Bruno. Down here by the bar in front of the shooting gallery.' I glanced over the edge of the balcony and saw Stahlecker waving up at me. I waved back.

'For a man with one eye you do all right.'

'We booked that Alphonse. Say thanks to Heinrich.'

'Bruno says thanks Heinrich. They booked the Alphonse.'

'Good,' said Grund.

'On my way out of the Alex I saw Isidor,' Bruno said. 'If I saw you he told me to tell you he wants to see you first thing in the morning.'

Isidor was the name everyone called the DPP, Doctor Bernard Weiss. It was also the name *Der Angriff* called him. *Der Angriff* didn't mean the name to sound affectionate, just anti-Semitic. It didn't bother Izzy.

'Did he say what about?' I asked, although I was pretty sure I knew the answer.

'No.'

'What time is first thing for Izzy these days?'

'Eight o'clock.'

'I looked at my watch and groaned. 'There goes my evening.'

He was a small man with a small moustache, a longish nose and little round glasses. His hair was dark and combed back across a head full of brains. He wore a well-cut, three-piece suit, spats and, in winter, a coat with a fur collar. Easily caricatured, his Jewishness exaggerated by his enemies, Doctor Bernard Weiss cut an odd figure among the rest of Berlin's policemen. Heimannsberg, who towered over him, was everyone's idea of what a senior policeman should look like. Izzy's appearance was more that of a lawyer and indeed, he had once been a judge in the Berlin courts. But he was no stranger to uniform and had returned from the Great War with an Iron Cross, first class. Izzy did his best to seem like a hard-bitten detective, but it didn't work. For one thing he never carried a gun, not even after he was beaten up by a right-wing uniformed cop who claimed he'd mistaken the Deputy Police President for a communist. Izzy preferred to do his fighting with his tongue, which was a formidable weapon when deployed. His sarcasm was as caustic as battery acid and, surrounded by men of much lesser intellectual abilities than himself, it was frequently splashed around. This did not make him loved. That would hardly have mattered for most men in his elevated position but since there were no men in his elevated position who were also Jewish it ought to have mattered more to Izzy. His lack of popularity made him vulnerable. But I liked him and he liked me. More than any other man in Germany it was Izzy who had been responsible for the modernisation of the police force. But much of the impetus for this had come from the assassination of the Foreign Minister, Walther Rathenau.

It was said that everyone in Germany could say exactly

where they were on June 24th 1922 when they heard the news that Rathenau, a Jew, had been shot by right-wingers. I had been in the Romanisches Café, staring into a drink and still feeling sorry for myself after my wife's death three months before. Rathenau's murder had persuaded me to join the Berlin police. Izzy knew that. It was one of the reasons he liked me, I think.

His office at the Alex resembled that of a university professor's. He sat in front of a large bookcase that was full of legal and forensic tomes, one of which he himself had written. On the wall was a map of Berlin with red and brown pins indicating outbreaks of political violence. The map looked like it had the measles, there were so many pins. On his desk were two telephones, several piles of papers, and an ashtray where he tipped the ash from the Black Wisdom Havanas that were his one apparent luxury.

He was, I knew, under enormous pressure, because the Republic itself was under enormous pressure. In the March elections the Nazis had doubled their strength in the Reichstag and they were now the second largest party with eleven and a half million votes. The Chancellor, Heinrich Bruning, was trying to turn the economy around but with unemployment at almost six million and rising this was proving almost impossible. Bruning looked unlikely to survive now that the Reichstag had reconvened. Hindenburg remained President of the Weimar Republic and leader of the largest party, the SPD. But the aristocratic old man had little liking for Bruning. And if Bruning went, what then? Schleicher? Papen? Gröner? Hitler? Germany was running out of strong men who were fit to lead the country.

Izzy waved me to a chair without looking up from what he was writing with his black Pelikan. From time to time he put down the pen and lifted the cigar to his mouth, and I amused myself with the vague hope that he might put the pen in his mouth and try to write with the cigar.

'We must continue to do our duty as policemen even though others may make it difficult for us,' he said, in a voice that was deep and full-bodied like a lager darkened by coloured malts – a Dunkel or a Bock. He put down the pen and, sitting back on the creaking swivel chair, fixed me with an eye as pointed as the spike on a cuirassier's Pickelhaube. 'Don't you agree, Bernie?'

'Yes sir.'

'Berliners still haven't forgotten or forgiven their police force for what happened in 1918 when the Alex surrendered to anarchy and revolution without a shot.'

'No, sir. But what else could they do?'

'They could have upheld the law, Bernie. Instead they saved their own skins. Always we uphold the law.'

'And if the Nazis take over, what then? They'll use the law and the police for their own ends.'

'Which is exactly what the Independent Socialists did in 1918 under Emil Eichhorn. We survived that. We shall survive the Nazis, too.'

'Maybe.'

'We must have a little faith, Bernie,' he said. 'If the Nazis do get in we shall have to have faith that, eventually, the parliamentary process will restore Germany to its senses.'

'I hope you're right, sir.' Then, just as I was beginning to think Izzy had summoned me for a lesson in political science, he came to the point.

'An English philosopher called Jeremy Bentham once wrote that publicity is the very soul of justice. That's especially true in the case of Anita Schwarz. To bowdlerise a phrase from another English jurist, the investigation into her murder must not merely proceed, it must be seen to proceed vigorously. Now let me tell you why. Helga Schwarz, the murdered girl's mother, is Kurt Daluege's cousin. That makes this a high profile case, Bernie. And I just wanted to let you know that the last thing we want right now is Doctor Goebbels arguing

in the pages of his tawdry but nonetheless influential newspaper that the investigation is being handled incompetently, or
that we're dragging our feet because we have some anti-Nazi
axe to grind. All personal prejudices must be put aside. Do I
make myself clear, Bernie?'

'Very clear, sir.' I might not have had a doctorate in jurisprudence like Bernard Weiss but I didn't need to have it spelled
out with umlauts and ablauts. Kurt Daluege was a decorated
war hero. Currently in the SS, he was an ex-SA leader in
Berlin, not to mention Goebbels' deputy. More importantly
for us, he was an NSDAP member of the Prussian State parliament, to which the Berlin police owed its first loyalty. Daluege
could make political trouble for us. With friends like his he
could have made trouble in a hospice for retired Benedictine
monks. The smart money in Berlin said that if they ever got
into power the Nazis were planning to put Daluege in charge
of the Berlin police force. It wasn't that he had any experience
of policing. He wasn't even a lawyer. What he did have experience of was doing exactly what Hitler and Goebbels told
him to do. And I presumed the same was true of his relation
by marriage, Otto Schwarz.

'That's why I'm organising a press conference this afternoon,' said Izzy. 'So you can tell the newspapers just how
seriously we're taking this case. That we're pursuing all
possible leads. That we won't rest until the murderer is
caught. Well, you know the kind of thing. You've handled a
press conference many times before. On occasion you've even
handled them quite well.'

'Thank you, sir.'

'However, you have a natural wit that sometimes you would
do well to restrain. Especially in a political case like this one.'

'Is that what this is, sir?'

'Oh, I'd say so, wouldn't you?'

'Yes sir.'

'Ernst Gennat and I will attend the conference, of course.

But it's your investigation and your conference. If questioned, Ernst and I will confine ourselves to statements regarding your competence. Commissar Gunther's impressive reputation, his extraordinary perseverance, his keen psychological insights, his impressive clean-up record. The usual crap.'

'Thank you for your confidence, sir.'

Izzy's lips puckered as if savouring the taste of his own intelligence like a freshly made matzoh ball. 'Well, what have you come up with so far?'

'Not much. She wasn't killed in the park, that's for sure. We'll know more about the cause of death later on today. Hard to say if it was a lust murder or not. Maybe that was the point of removing all her sexual organs and everything that was attached to them. On the face of it you might say that's the most remarkable feature of the case. But you might just as easily point to the reaction of Herr and Frau Schwarz themselves. Last night, neither of them seemed particularly upset when I told them that their daughter was dead.'

'God, I hope you're not suggesting you think they did it?'

I thought for a moment. 'Maybe I'm misjudging them, sir. But the girl was disabled. Somehow I got the feeling that they were glad to be rid of her, that's all. Maybe.'

'I trust you won't be mentioning any of this at the press conference.'

'You know me better than that.'

'It's true, some Nazis do have a few ruthless ideas concerning the treatment of society's unfortunates. People who are physically and mentally handicapped. However, even the Nazis aren't stupid enough to think that's a vote winner. Nobody's going to vote for a political party that advocates the extermination of the sick and the infirm. Not after a war that left thousands of men disabled.'

'No, I suppose not, sir.' I lit a cigarette. 'There's one other thing. The murdered girl had five hundred marks on her.

That's a lot more pocket money than I used to get when I was her age.'

'Yes, you're right. Did you ask the parents about it?'

'They suggested there must have been some mistake.'

'I've heard of money disappearing from a dead man's pockets. But I've never heard of money being planted on one.'

'No sir.'

'Ask the neighbours, Bernie. Speak to her school friends. Find out what kind of girl Anita Schwarz was.'

'Yes sir.'

'And Bernie. Get yourself a new tie. That one looks like it's been in your soup.'

'Yes sir.'

Before the press conference I went and had my hair cut at the KaDeWe. Henry Ford himself couldn't have arranged the business of cutting German hair more efficiently. There were ten chairs and I was in and out in less than twenty minutes. The KaDeWe wasn't exactly round the corner from the Alex, but it was a good place to have a haircut and buy a new tie.

As always, the conference itself took place in the Police Museum at the Alex. This was Gennat's idea following the Police Exhibition of 1926, so that KRIPO might present itself to the world among the photographs, knives, test tubes, fingerprints, poison bottles, revolvers, rope and buttons that were the exhibits of our many proud investigative successes. The modern face of policing we were keen to display to the world might have looked a bit more efficient had the glass cases containing this assortment of forensic trash, and the heavy curtains that shrouded the tall windows of the exhibition hall, not been so dusty. Even the most recent photograph, of Ernst Gennat, looked like it had been there for a hundred years.

There were about twenty reporters and photographers who gathered among our previous triumphs. Behind a table that had been cleared of a selection of curious murder weapons, I sat between Weiss and Gennat as if we had been arranged in ascending order of size. The men of Berlin's press heard me appeal for any witnesses who might have seen a man behaving suspiciously in Friedrichshain Park on the night of the murder, and listened as I went on to assure the Berlin public that we were doing all in our power to catch the killer of Anita Schwarz – which, of course, was something I was determined to do. Things seemed to be going quite well until I uttered the usual bromides about interviewing known sex offenders. At this, Fritz Allgeier, the reporter for *Der Angriff*, a boss-eyed specimen with a grey beard and arms that seemed longer than his legs – hardly Master Race material – said that the German people demanded to be told why known sex offenders were allowed to walk our streets in the first place.

Later on, I agreed with Weiss that my next comments could have been a little more diplomatic:

'The last time I looked, Herr Allgeier, Germany still had a system of criminal justice in which people are brought before the courts, tried, and if found guilty, serve a prison sentence. After they've paid their debt to society, we let them go.'

'Maybe we shouldn't let them go at all,' he said. 'It might be best for the German people if these so-called "known offenders" were put back in prison as quickly as possible. Then this kind of lust murder might never happen.'

'Maybe. That's not for me to say. But where do you get off thinking that someone like you can speak for the German people, Allgeier? You used to be a Jack, in Moabit. A back-street Turk working the three-card trick. The German people might equally demand to know how you turned into a journalist.'

Several of the non-Nazi newspaper reporters thought this

was very funny. I might have got away with it, too, if I'd left it there. But I didn't. I was warming to my subject.

Germany had always had the death penalty for murder but, for several years, the newspapers – the non-Nazi newspapers – had waged a vigorous campaign against the guillotine. Lately, however, these same papers had bowed to Nazi influence and refrained from writing editorials urging the commutation of a murderer's sentence, with the result that the state executioner, Johann Reichhart, was working once again. His most recent victim had been the mass murderer and cannibal, Georg Haarmann. A lot of cops, myself included, didn't much like the guillotine. More so since the senior investigating officer was called upon to attend the executions of murderers he had arrested.

'The plain fact of the matter is that we've always relied on known offenders to give us information,' I said. 'There were even murderers serving sentences in prison who were once prepared to help us. Of course that was before we started executing them again. It's hard to persuade a man to talk to you when you've chopped his head off.'

Weiss stood up and, smiling patiently, announced that the conference was over. On our way out he said nothing. Just smiled sadly at me. Which was worse than a lashing from his tongue. Gennat said, 'Nice work, Bernie. They'll eat your eggs, son.'

'Just the fascist newspapers, surely.'

'All newspapers are fundamentally fascist, Bernie. In every country. All editors are dictators. All journalism is authoritarian. That's why people line bird cages with it.'

Gennat was right of course. He usually was. Only *Tempo*, Berlin's evening newspaper, gave me a good press. It used a picture of me that looked like Luis Trenker in *The Holy Mountain*. Manfred George, *Tempo*'s editor, wrote a piece in which he described me as one of Berlin's 'finest detectives'. Maybe they liked my new tie. The rest of the republican papers were like a cat creeping around the milk: they didn't dare say what they really thought for fear that their readers might not agree with them. I didn't read *Der Angriff*. What was the point? But Hans-Joachim Brandt in the Nazi *Volkischer Beobachter* referred to me as 'a liberal, left-wing stooge'. Probably the truth lay half way between the two.

SEVEN

BUENOS AIRES. 1950.

The Von Baders lived in the residential part of Barrio Norte, which is Castellano for 'people with money'. The Calle Florida, the commercial heart of the Barrio Norte, seemed to have come into being in order to make sure that people with money would not have to go too far out of their way to spend it. The house on Arenales was built in the best eighteenth-century French style. It looked more like a grand hotel than somewhere anyone could have called home. The façade was all relief Ionic columns and tall windows: even the air conditioning units seemed elegant and in keeping with the urban Bourbon look. Inside, things were no less formally French, with high ceilings and pilasters, marble fireplaces, gilt mirrors, lots of eighteenth-century furniture and expensive-looking art.

The Von Baders and their small dog received the Colonel and me from their seats on an over-stuffed red sofa. She was sitting in one corner of the sofa and he was sitting in the other. They were wearing their best clothes but in a way that left me thinking that they might wear the same clothes to do some gardening – always supposing they knew where the secateurs and trowels were kept. The way they sat there, I wanted to take hold of the Baroness's chin and move her head slightly toward her husband before picking up my brushes and getting started on their portrait. She was statuesque and beautiful, with good skin and perfect teeth and hair like spun gold and a neck like Queen Nefertiti's taller sister. He was just thin with

74

glasses but, unlike me, the dog seemed to prefer him to her. She was holding a handkerchief and looked as if she had been crying. The way anxious mothers are supposed to look, I suppose. He was holding a cigarillo and looked like he'd been making money. Rather a lot of it.

Colonel Montalban introduced me to them. We all spoke in German as if our meeting was taking place in some handsome villa in Dahlem. I uttered a few sympathetic noises. Fabienne had disappeared somewhere between Arenales and the cemetery at Recoleta, less than half a mile away. She often went there by herself to lay flowers on the steps of the Von Bader family vault. It was where they kept their bodies, not their money. It seemed that Fabienne had been very close to her grandfather who was buried there. They gave me some photographs to borrow. Fabienne looked like any other fourteen-year-old girl who was blonde, beautiful, and rich. In one of the photographs she was sitting on a white pony. The pony's bridle was held by a gaucho and behind this bucolic little trio was a ranch house against a backdrop of eucalyptus trees.

'That's our weekend house,' explained the Baron. 'In Pilar. To the north of Buenos Aires.'

'Nice,' I said, and wondered where they went when they wanted a proper holiday from the demands of being very rich.

'Yes. Fabienne loved it there,' said her mother.

'I take it you've already looked for her at this and any other homes you might own.'

'Yes,' he said. 'Of course we have.' He let out a sigh that was part patience and part anxiety. 'There's only the weekend house, Herr Gunther. I don't own any other houses in Argentina.' He shook his head and took a puff on the cigarillo. 'You make me sound like some stinking, plutocratic Jew. Isn't that right, Colonel?'

'There are no yids in this part of Buenos Aires,' said Montalban.

Von Bader's wife winced. She didn't seem to like that remark. Which was another reason why I liked her more than I liked her husband. She crossed her long legs and looked away for a moment. I liked her legs, too.

'It's really not like her at all,' she said. She blew her nose delicately on the small handkerchief, tucked it into the sleeve of her dress and smiled, bravely. I admired her for that. 'She's never done this kind of thing before.'

'What about her friends?' I asked.

'Fabienne isn't like most girls of her age, Herr Gunther,' said Von Bader. 'She is more mature than her peers, very much more sophisticated. I doubt that she would have shared a confidence with any of them.'

'But naturally we've questioned them,' added the Colonel. 'I don't think it would help to question them again. They said nothing that might help.'

'Did she know the other girl?' I asked. 'Grete Wohlauf?'

'No,' said Von Bader.

'I'd like to see her room if I may.' I was looking at the Baroness. She was easier on the eye than her husband. Easier on the ear, too.

'Of course,' she said. Then she looked at her husband. 'Would you mind showing him Fabienne's room, dear? It upsets me to go in there at the moment.'

Von Bader walked me to a little wooden elevator that was set in an open, wrought-iron shaft and surrounded by a steep, curving marble staircase. It's not every home that has its own elevator and, catching sight of my eloquently raised eyebrows, the Baron felt obliged to offer an explanation.

'During the last years of her life, my mother was in a wheel-chair,' he said, as if building an elevator was a solution available to everyone with an elderly parent.

It was just the two of us and the dog in the elevator car. I was close enough to smell the cologne on Von Bader's face and the oil in his grey hair, and yet he avoided my eye. Each time he spoke to me, he was looking somewhere else. I told myself he was preoccupied with his daughter's possible fate but, all the same, I'd handled enough cases involving missing persons to know when I wasn't getting the whole story.

'Montalban says that back in Berlin, before the war, you were a top detective with KRIPO, and in private practice.'

He made being a private detective sound like I'd been a top dentist. Maybe it was kind of similar to being a dentist at that. Sometimes getting a client to tell you everything relevant was like pulling teeth.

'I've had my Archimedes moments,' I said. 'With KRIPO and on my own.'

'Archimedes?'

'Eureka. I've found it.' I shrugged. 'These days I'm more the travelling salesman type.'

'Selling what, in particular?'

'Nothing. Nothing at all. Not even now. I'll do my best to find your daughter, sir, but I never was one for working miracles. Generally I do a lot better when people believe in me enough to give me all the facts.'

Von Bader coloured a little. Maybe that was because he was trying to wrestle the elevator car door open. Or maybe it wasn't, but he still wasn't looking at me. 'What makes you think you haven't had them?'

'Call it a hunch,' I replied.

He nodded as if considering some kind of offer, which was odd given that I hadn't actually made him one.

We stepped out of the car and into the thickly carpeted corridor. At the end of it he pushed a door open and ushered me into the bedroom of a neat and tidy girl. The wallpaper was red roses. The bed had little flowers painted on the enamelled iron frame. Above the bed were several Chinese fans in a picture frame. On a tall table was a large and empty Oriental bird cage. On a shorter table was a chess board set out in a game that still seemed to be in progress. I gave the pieces the once-over. Black or white, she was a clever little girl. There were some books and some teddy bears and a chest of drawers. I tugged one open.

'Do you mind?' I asked.

'Go right ahead,' he said. 'I suppose you're just doing your job.'

'Well I'm certainly not looking for her underwear.' I was hoping to goad something from him. After all, he hadn't exactly denied that he was keeping something back. I turned over some socks and looked underneath.

'What exactly *are* you looking for?'

'A diary. A commonplace book. Some letters. Some money you didn't know about. A photograph of someone you don't recognise. I'm not sure, exactly, but I'll know it when I see it.' I closed the drawer. 'Or maybe there's something you want to tell me now, while Colonel Montalban isn't here?'

He picked up one of the teddy bears and lifted it to his nose, like a hound trying to raise a scent. 'It's curious,' he said. 'The way you can smell them on their toys. It's so evocative of them. Kind of like Proust, really.'

I nodded. I'd heard a lot about Proust. One day I was going to have to find an excuse not to read him.

'I know what Montalban thinks,' he said. 'He thinks Fabienne is already dead.' Von Bader shook his head. 'I just don't believe that.'

'What makes you think not, Baron?'

'You would call it a hunch, I suppose. Easier to spell than intuition. But that's how it is. If she was dead I'm quite sure we would have heard something by now. Someone would have found her. I'm certain of it.' He shook his head. 'Since you were once a famous detective with the homicide police in Berlin, I assume Montalban's asking you to work on the assumption that she's dead. Well, I'm asking you to assume the opposite. To assume that perhaps, someone – someone German, yes, I think that must be true – is hiding her. Or keeping her against her will.'

I opened another drawer. 'Why would someone want to do that? Do you have enemies, Herr Baron?'

'I'm a banker, Herr Hausner. And as it happens, a damned important one. It might surprise you but bankers do make enemies, yes. Money or the getting of money always brings enemies. There's that. And then there's what I did during the war to consider. During the war, I worked for the Abwehr, German military intelligence. I and a group of other German-Argentine bankers, helped to bankroll the war effort on this side of the Atlantic. We funded a number of German agents in the United States. Without success, I'm sorry to say. Several of our most prominent agents were caught by the FBI and executed. They were betrayed, but I'm not sure by whom.'

'Could someone blame you for that?'

'I don't see how. I had no operational involvement, I was just a money man.'

Von Bader was making eye contact with me now. Plenty of it.

'I'm not sure how relevant any of this is to my daughter's disappearance, Herr Hausner, but there were five of us. Bankers funding the Nazis in Argentina. Ludwig Freude, Richard Staudt, Heinrich Dorge, Richard Von Leute, and me. And I only mention this because late last year Doctor Dorge was found dead on a street here in Buenos Aires. He'd been murdered. Heinrich was formerly an aide to Doctor Hjalmar Schacht. I take it you've heard of him.'

'I've heard of him,' I said. Schacht had been the Minister of Economics and then President of the Reichsbank. In 1946, he had been tried for war crimes at Nuremberg and acquitted.

'I'm telling you all this so you'll know two things in particular. One is that it's perfectly possible my previous life has caught up with me in some – some unfathomable way. I've received no threats. Nothing. The other thing is that I'm a very rich man, Herr Hausner. And I want you to take me seriously when I say that if you find my daughter alive, and bring about her safe return, I'll give you a reward of two million pesos, payable in whatever currency and whatever country you choose. That's about fifty thousand dollars, Herr Hausner.'

'That's a lot of money, Herr Baron.'

'My daughter's life is worth at least that much to me. More. Much more. But that's my business. Your business is to try to collect that two million pesos.'

I nodded thoughtfully. I guess it must have looked like I was weighing things up. That's the trouble with me, I'm coin-operated. I start thinking when people offer me money. I start thinking a lot more when it's a lot of money.

'Do you have any children, Herr Hausner?'

'No, sir.'

'If you did you would know that money's not that important next to the life of someone you love.'

'I'm obliged to take your word for that, sir.'

'You're not obliged to take my word for it at all. I'll have my lawyers draw up a letter of agreement regarding the reward.'

It wasn't what I'd meant, but I didn't contradict him. Instead I took a last look around the room.

'What happened to the bird in the cage?'

'The bird?'

'In the cage.' I pointed at the pagoda-sized cage on the tall table.

Von Bader looked at the cage almost as if he had never looked at it before. 'Oh that. It died.'

'Was she upset about it?'

'Yes, of course she was, but I don't see how her disappearance could have anything to do with a bird.'

'You'd be surprised what a fourteen-year-old girl can get upset about.'

He shook his head. 'I have a fourteen-year-old girl, Herr Hausner. You don't. As a result, and with all due respect, I think I can honestly say I know more about fourteen-year-old girls than you do.'

'Did she bury it in the garden?'

'I really don't know.'

'Perhaps your wife does.'

'I'd really rather you didn't ask her about it. She's upset enough about things as it is. My wife holds herself responsible for the death of the bird. And she's already looking around for reasons to blame herself for our daughter's disappearance. Any implied suggestion that these two events might be connected would only add to the sense of guilt she's feeling about Fabienne's disappearance. I'm sure you understand.'

That might just have been true. And maybe it wasn't. But out of respect for his two million pesos I was prepared to let the bird go. Sometimes, to take hold of the money, you have to let go of the bird. That's what they call politics.

We returned to the sitting room, where the Baroness had started crying again. I've made a close study of women crying. In my line of work it comes with the truncheon and the handcuffs. On the eastern front in 1941 I saw women who could have won Olympic gold medals for crying. Sherlock Holmes used to study cigar ash and wrote a monograph on the subject. I knew about crying. I knew that when a woman is crying it doesn't pay to let her get too close to your shoulder. It can cost you a clean shirt. Tears are, however, sacred, and you violate their sanctity at your peril. We left her to get on with it.

After we left the Von Bader house I insisted the Colonel and I go to Recoleta Cemetery. We were after all very close, and I wanted to see the place Fabienne had been visiting when she disappeared.

Like the Viennese, rich *porteños* take death very seriously. Enough to spend large sums of money on expensive tombs and mausolea. But Recoleta was the only cemetery I'd ever been where there weren't any graves. We went through a Greek-style entrance into what was a little city of marble.

Many of the mausolea were classically designed and looked almost habitable. Walking around the neat and parallel stone streets it was like touring some ancient Roman town swept clean of its human inhabitants by a cataclysmic natural disaster. Looking up at the bright blue sky, I half expected to see the smoking crater of a volcano. It was hard to imagine a fourteen-year-old girl coming to such a place. The few living people we saw were old and grey. I expect they had the same thought about me and the Colonel.

We got back in the car and headed for the Casa Rosada. It was a while since I'd driven a car. Not that anyone would have noticed. I had seen worse drivers than *porteños* but only in *Ben-Hur*. Ramon Novarro and Frances X. Bushman would have felt quite at home on the streets of Buenos Aires.

'Nice and handy for the President to have his secret police headquartered in the Casa Rosada,' I said, catching sight of the distinctive red building again.

'It has some advantages. Incidentally, you've already seen the boss. The youngish man in the pinstripe suit who was with us when you met Perón? That's him, Rodolfo Freude. He's never very far away from the President.'

'Freude? Von Bader mentioned a banker called Ludwig Freude. Any relation?'

'Rodolfo's father.'

'Is that how he got the job?'

'It's a long story, but yes, in effect.'

'Was he in the Abwehr, too?'

'Who? Rodolfo? No. But Rodolfo's deputy was. Werner Koennecke. Werner is married to Rodolfo's sister, Lily.'

'It all sounds very cosy.'

'That's Buenos Aires for you. It's just like the cemetery at Recoleta. You have to know someone to get in.'

'Who do you know, Colonel?'

'Rodolfo knows some important people, it's true. But I know people who are really important. I know an Italian woman who is the best whore in the city. I know a chef who makes the best pasta in South America. And I know a man who can kill someone and make it look like a suicide, with no questions asked. These are the important things to know in our strange profession, Herr Hausner. Don't you agree?'

'I don't often awake and feel the need to have someone murdered, Colonel. If I did I'd probably do it myself, but I guess I'm just a little bit strange that way. Besides, I'm too old to be impressed by anything very much. Except perhaps an Italian woman. I always did like Italian women. And I haven't even been to Italy.'

EIGHT

BERLIN. 1932.

Department 4, the ordinary criminal police, was supposed to stand apart from Department 1a, the political police. D1a was charged with the investigation of all political crime but it did not operate secretly. The political police were supposed to work, discreetly, to forestall political violence of whatever hue. Given the situation in Germany it was easy to understand why the Weimar government had thought it necessary to bring such a police force into being. In practice however, neither the regular police force nor the German public liked the politicals; and D1a had proved to be spectacularly unsuccessful at preventing political violence. What was more, the point of having two separate police departments became all but meaningless as the majority of the murders we investigated turned out to be political: a storm trooper murdering a communist, or vice versa. As a result, D1a struggled to establish its proper jurisdiction and to justify its continued existence. True republicans considered its functions as undemocratic and potentially ripe for exploitation by any unscrupulous government that might wish to establish a police state. It was for this reason that Professor Hans Illmann, the pathologist handling the Schwarz case, preferred to meet away from the Alex, in his laboratory and office at the Institute for Police Science in Charlottenburg. Department 4 and Department 1a might have existed on different floors of the Alex, but that was still too close for the politically sensitive nostrils of KRIPO's leading forensic scientist.

I found Illmann staring out of a deep bay window at a garden that had nothing to do with the police or pathology. It, and the villa it surrounded, came from a gentler time when scientists had more hair on their cheeks than a mandrill baboon. It was easy to see why he preferred being here instead of at the Alex. Even with a couple of bodies in the basement the place felt more like an expensive retirement home than a forensic science institute. The professor was as lean as a scalpel and wore rimless glasses and a little Dutch chin-beard that made him everyone's idea of what an artist ought to look like. Toulouse-Lautrec in his much taller period.

As we shook hands I jutted my chin at a copy of *Der Angriff* that was lying on his desk. 'What, are you turning Nazi on me? Reading shit like that.'

'If more people read this garbage then perhaps they wouldn't vote for these intellectual pygmies. Or at least they would know what Germany can expect if they ever come to power. No, no, Bernie, everyone should read this. You especially should read it. Your card has been well and truly stamped, my young Republican friend. And in public, too. Welcome to the club.'

He picked up the newspaper and started to read aloud:

' "The symbol of the Iron Front, which was designed by a Russian Jew, is three arrows pointing south-east inside a circle. The meaning of the arrows has been interpreted differently. Some say that the three arrows stand for the opponents of the Iron Front: communism, monarchism and National Socialism. Others say that these arrows stand for the three columns of the German worker's movement: party, trade union, and reichsbanner. But we say it stands for one thing only: the Iron Front is a political alliance that is full of pricks.

' "Chief among the Iron Front pricks that pollute the Berlin police force are Police President Grezinski, his yid deputy Bernhard Weiss and their KRIPO lackey Bernhard

Gunther. These are the policemen who are supposed to be investigating the murderer of Anita Schwarz. You would think that they would be sparing no effort to catch this monster. Far from it! Commissar Gunther astonished those attending yesterday's press conference when he informed this stunned reporter that he hopes the murderer will be spared the death penalty.

' "Let me tell Commissar Gunther this: that if he and his liberal-minded mates somehow scrape together the competence to apprehend the murderer of Anita Schwarz, there is only one sentence that will satisfy the German people. Death. The fact is, only brutality can now be respected in this country. The German people demand that criminals feel good wholesome fear. Why get so worked up about the execution and torture of a few law-breakers? The masses want it. They are shouting for something that will give criminals a proper respect for the law. That is why we need the strong governance of National Socialism as opposed to this bleeding-heart SPD government that is afraid of its own corrupt shadow. If Commissar Gunther spent more time worrying about catching killers and less time worrying about their rights, then, perhaps, this city would not be the sink of iniquity it is now." '

Illmann tossed the paper across the desk at me and started rolling a perfect cigarette with the fingers of one hand.

'To hell with those bastards,' I said. 'I'm not worried.'

'No? You should be. If this July election doesn't prove conclusive one way or the other, there might be another putsch. And you and I could find ourselves floating in the Landwehr Canal, just like poor Rosa Luxemburg. Be careful my young friend. Be careful.'

'It won't come to that,' I said. 'The army won't stand for it.'

'I'm afraid I don't share your touching faith in our armed forces. I think they're just as likely to fall in behind the Nazis as they are to stand up for the Republic.' He shook his head and grinned. 'No, if the Republic is to be saved, I'm afraid there's just one thing for it. You'll just have to solve this murder before July 31st.'

'Fair enough, Doc. So what have you got?'

'Death was from asphyxia, caused by chloroform. Anita Schwarz swallowed her tongue. I found traces of chloroform in her hair and in her mouth. It's a common enough death in hospitals. Heavy-handed anaesthetists have killed many a patient in this way.'

'That's a comforting thought. Any sign that she was interfered with sexually?'

'Impossible to tell, given her lack of plumbing. That could be why he did it of course. To conceal evidence of intercourse. He knew what he was about, too. A very sharp curette was used calmly and confidently. This was no frenzied attack, Bernie. The killer took his time. Perhaps that's why he used the chloroform. In which case her fear was not a factor in his motivation. She was probably unconscious and almost certainly dead when he butchered her. You remember the Haarmann case, of course. Well, this is something very different.'

'Someone with medical experience, perhaps,' I said, thinking aloud. 'In which case the proximity of the State hospital might be relevant.'

'Very likely it is,' said Illmann. 'But not for the reason we've just been discussing. No, I'd say it's the pill you found near the body that makes it relevant.'

'Oh? How? What is it?'

'It's nothing I've seen before. In chemical terms, it's a sulphone group connected to an amine group. But the synthesis is new. I don't even know what to call it, Bernie. Sulphanamine? I don't know. It certainly doesn't exist in the current pharmacopoeia. Not here. Not anywhere. Which means it's new and experimental.'

'Have you any idea what it might be for?'

'The active sulpha molecule was first synthesised in 1906 and has been widely used in the dye-making industry.'

'Dye-making?'

'My guess is that there's a smaller active compound that's contained inside the dye-making molecule. About fifteen years ago the Pasteur Institute in Paris was using the sulpha molecule as the basis for some kind of anti-bacterial agent. Sadly the work came to nothing. However, this pill would seem to indicate that someone, possibly here in Berlin, has successfully synthesised a sulpha-based drug.'

'Yes, but what could you use it for?'

'You could use it against any kind of bacterial infection. Any streptococci. However, you would have to test the drug on some volunteers before publishing any results, especially given the Pasteur's previous failures using dye-based drugs.'

'An experimental drug being tested at the State Hospital, perhaps?'

'Could be.' Illmann finished his cigarette, stubbing it out in a little porcelain ashtray made for the Police Exhibition of 1926. He seemed about to say something and then checked himself.

'No, go on,' I said.

'I was only trying to think what might make Berlin interesting to someone conducting a drug trial.' He shook his head. 'Because there are no drug companies based here in Berlin, and it's not like we suffer from anything more than anywhere else in Germany.'

'Ah, well now, that's where you're wrong, Doc,' I said. 'You want to read your Police Gazette instead of worrying about the shit that's in *Der Angriff*. There are more than one hundred thousand prostitutes working in Berlin today. More than anywhere else in Europe. And that's just the straight ones. God knows how many warm boys there are in this city. My sergeant, Heinrich Grund, is always going on about it.'

'Of course,' said Illmann. 'Venereal disease.'

'Since the war the figures have gone through the roof,' I said. 'Not that I'd know, never having had a dose of jelly myself. But the current treatment is Neosalvarsan, isn't it?'

'That's right. It contains organic arsenic, which makes its use somewhat hazardous. Even so, in its time it was such an important discovery and efficacious remedy – no proper remedy had existed before – that Neosalvarsan was called the Magic Bullet. That was a German discovery, too. Paul Ehrlich won the Nobel Prize for it in 1908. An exceptionally gifted man.'

'Could he—?'

'No, no, he's dead, alas. Interestingly, Salvarsan and Neosalvarsan are dye-based compounds, too. Which is where the problem with them lies. In the colour. And that must be where this new compound scores. Someone must have worked out how to remove the colour without compromising the anti-bacterial activity.' He nodded as if imagining the chemistry appearing on an invisible blackboard in front of his eyes. 'Ingenious.'

'So let's say we have a drug trial, here in Berlin,' I said. 'For patients suffering from big jelly and little jelly? Syphilis and gonorrhoea?'

'If it was effective against one, it might well be effective against the other, too.'

'How many patients would we be talking about for a trial?'

'In the beginning? A few dozen. A hundred at the most. And all highly confidential, mind you. No doctor's going to tell you which of his patients is suffering from a venereal disease. Not only that but, if it works, a drug like this could be worth millions. The clinical trials are very likely top secret.'

'How would you recruit your volunteers?'

Illmann shrugged. 'Neosalvarsan treatment is no ice-cream treat, Bernie. Its reputation goes ahead of it, and most of the horror stories you've heard are true. So I'd have thought there would be no shortage of volunteers for a new drug.'

'All right. Suppose some T-girl gives our man a dose of jelly. Which makes him hate women enough to want to kill one.

Meanwhile he volunteers for a drugs trial to get his meat and two veg sorted.'

'But if a T-girl gives him a dose,' said Illmann, 'then why not kill a T-girl? Why kill a child?'

'T-girls are too savvy. I saw one the other night. Built like a wrestler, she was. Some Fritz came in and wanted her charged with assault. She'd hit the bastard with her riding crop.'

'Some men would pay good money for that kind of thing.'

'My point is this. He kills Anita Schwarz because she's easier prey. She's crippled. Makes it hard for her to get away. Could be he didn't even notice it. After all, it was dark.'

'All right,' allowed Illmann. 'That's just about possible. Just.'

'Well then, here's another thing. Something I haven't told you yet. On account of the fact that I've only just remembered I can trust you. And this is hot stuff, mind, so keep it under your hat. Anita Schwarz may have been disabled. And she may have been just fifteen. But she wasn't above earning herself some pocket money on the side.'

'You're joking.'

'One of her neighbours told me the girl had a major morals problem. The parents won't talk about it. And I didn't dare mention it at the press conference after the lecture Izzy gave me about trying to keep the Nazis sweet. But we found quite a bankroll in her coat pocket. Five hundred marks. She didn't get that from running errands to the local shop.'

'But the girl was crippled. She wore a calliper.'

'And there's a market for that, too, believe me, Doc.'

'My God, there are some evil bastards in this city.'

'Now you sound like my sergeant, Grund.'

'Then maybe you are right. You know I never thought to test her for syphilis and gonorrhoea. I'll do it, immediately.'

'One more thing, Doc. What kind of dyes are we talking about here? Food dyes, cloth dyes, hair dyes, what?'

'Organic dyes. Direct or substantive dying. Direct dyes are

used on a whole host of materials. Cotton, paper, leather, wool, silk, nylon. Why do you ask?'

'I don't know.' But somewhere, at the bottom of the sock drawer I called my mind, there was something important. I rummaged around for a moment and then shook my head. 'No. It's probably nothing.'

My route back from Charlottenburg took me in a straight line all the way from Kaiserdamm to the Tiergarten. There were wild boar in the Tiergarten. You could hear them grunting as they wallowed in their enclosure or, sometimes, squealing like the brakes on my old DKW as they fought with each other. Whenever I heard that sound I thought of the Reichstag and German party politics. The Tiergarten was full of animal life – not just boar. There were buzzards and woodpeckers and pied wagtails and siskins and bats – there were lots of bats. The smell of cut grass and blossom that came through the open window of my car was wonderful. It was the clean, uncorrupted smell of early summer. At this time of year the Tiergarten was open until early dusk, which also made it popular with grasshoppers – the amateur prostitutes with no room-money who did it with their Fritzes lying down on the grass or in the shrubbery. Nature is wonderful.

I looked at my watch as I came through the Brandenburg Gate and onto Pariser Platz. There was time for lunch as long as lunch came in a brown bottle. I could have stopped almost anywhere south of Unter den Linden. There were lots of stand-ups around Gendarmen Market where I might easily have got myself a sausage and a beer, but anywhere wasn't where I wanted to go. Not when I was right outside the Adlon Hotel. It was true, I'd been there only a day or two before. And a day or two before that. The fact was, I liked the Adlon. Not for its ambience and its gardens and its whispering foun-tain and its palm court and its fabulous restaurant, which I couldn't have afforded anyway. I liked it because I liked one of the house detectives. She was called Frieda Bamberger. I liked Frieda a lot.

Frieda was tall and dark with a full mouth and an even fuller figure, and a voluptuous sort of fertility about her that I put down to the fact that she was Jewish but which was actually something rather more indefinable. She was glamorous, too. Had to be. Her job involved hanging around the hotel posing as a guest and keeping an eye out for prostitutes, con artists and thieves, who liked the Adlon for the rich pickings that were to be had from the even richer guests. I had got to know her in the summer of 1929 when I helped her to arrest a female jewel thief who was armed with a knife. I stopped Frieda getting stuck with it by the simple means of getting stuck myself. Clever Gunther. For that I got a nice letter from Hedda Adlon, the proprietor's daughter-in-law and, after I came out of hospital, a very personal kind of thank-you from Frieda herself. We weren't sharing an envelope, exactly. Frieda had a semi-detached husband who lived in Hamburg. But just now and then we'd search an empty bedroom for a lost Maharajah or a stolen movie-star. Sometimes it could take us a while.

As soon as I walked through the door Frieda was on my arm like a hawk. 'Am I glad to see you,' she said.

'And I thought you weren't the type who cares.'

'I'm serious, Bernie.'

'And so am I. I keep telling you, only you don't listen. I'd have brought flowers if I'd known you felt this way.'

'I want you to go into the bar,' she said, urgently.

'That's good. That's where I was going anyway.'

'I want you to take a look at the guy in the corner. And I mean the Fritz in the corner, not the redhead he's with. He's wearing a dove-grey suit with a double-breasted waistcoat and a flower in his lapel. I don't like the look of him.'

'If that's so then I hate him already.'

'No, I think he might be dangerous.'

I went into the bar, picked up a matchbook and lit a ciga-rette, and gave the Fritz the quick up and down. The girl he was with looked me up and down back. This was bad because the Fritz she was with was worse than bad. He was Ricci Kamm, the boss of the Always True, one of Berlin's most powerful criminal rings. Normally Ricci stayed put in Friedrichshain where his gang was based, which was fine since he tended not to give us any trouble there. But the girl he was with looked like she had an opinion of herself that was as high as the Zugspitze. Probably she figured she was too good for joints like the Zum Nussbaum, which was where the Always True boys usually went for their kicks. Very likely she was right, too. I've seen better-looking redheads but only on Rita Hayworth. She was wearing good curves, too. I doubt she could have cut a better figure if she'd been wearing Sonja Henie's favourite ice-skates.

Ricci's eyes were on mine. But my eyes were on her and there was a bottle of Bismarck in front of them both that said this might spell trouble. Ricci was a quiet sort with a small, softly-spoken voice and nice manners – until he had one drink too many and then it was like watching Doctor Jekyll turn into Mister Hyde. From the level in the bottle Ricci was about ready to grow an extra set of eyebrows.

I turned on my heel and went back into the lobby.

'You were right not to like him,' I told Frieda. 'He's a dangerous man and I think his timer's about to go off.'

'What are we going to do?'

I waved Max, the hall porter, toward me. I didn't do it lightly. Max paid Louis Adlon three thousand marks a month to have that job because he got a kickback on everything he did for the hotel's guests, which made him about thirty thou-sand marks a month. He was holding a dog lead, which was attached to a miniature dachshund. I figured Max was looking for a bellboy to walk the thing. 'Max,' I said. 'Call the

Alex and tell them to send the kiddy car. You'd better order up a couple of uniforms as well. There's going to be some trouble in the bar.'

Max hesitated as if he was expecting a tip.

'Unless you'd rather handle it yourself.'

Max turned and walked quickly to the house phones.

'And while you're at it, go and check the easy chairs in the library and see if you can't rustle up one of those overpaid ex-cops who call themselves house-bulls.'

Frieda had never been a cop so she didn't take offence at my remark about ex-cops, but I knew she could look after herself. Adlon had hired her on the strength of her having been in the German Women's Olympic fencing team in Paris in 1924, when she'd narrowly missed a medal.

I took her by the arm and walked her to the bar. 'When we sit down,' I said, 'I want you all over me like ivy. That way I'm not a threat to him.'

We sat down at the table right beside Ricci. The Bismarck had kicked in and he was sneering a series of swear words at a terrified bar waiter. The redhead looked like she'd seen it before. Most of the bar's other customers were wondering if they could make it as far as the door without crossing Ricci's eyeline, but one of them was made of sterner stuff: a businessman wearing a frock-coat and a meat-slicer of a collar, and a look of indignation at the kind of low German that was spilling out of Ricci's mouth, stood up and seemed inclined to take on the gangster. I caught his eye and shook my head, and for a moment he seemed to heed my warning. The moment he sat down Frieda let me have it. On the ears and the neck and the back of my head and on my cheek and finally on my mouth, which was where I liked it best of all.

'You're cute,' she said, with some understatement.

Ricci looked at her and then at the redhead beside him. 'Why can't you be more like that?' he asked her, jerking a thumb Frieda's way. 'Friendly, like.'

'Because you're drunk.' The redhead took out a powder compact and started to touch up her make-up. A futile effort in my estimation: like trying to touch up the Mona Lisa. 'And when you're drunk, you're a pig.'

She had a point but Ricci didn't care for it. He stood up, but the table stayed on his lap. The bottle and the glasses and the ashtray went on the floor. Ricci swore and the redhead started to laugh.

'A clumsy drunken pig,' she added, for good measure, and started to laugh again. I liked the effect it had on the redhead's mantrap of a mouth. I liked the way her sharp white teeth shucked off her red lips like cherry skins. But Ricci didn't like it at all and let her have it hard with the flat of his hand. In the Adlon's plush bar, the slap went off like New Year's Eve. This was too much for the man wearing the meat-slicer shirt collar. He looked like a real Prussian gentleman, the kind who cares what happens to a lady – even a lady who was probably a hundred-mark whore.

'Oh, oh,' Frieda murmured in my ear. 'The man from I.G. Farben is about to play Sir Lancelot.'

'Did you say I.G. Farben?'

I.G. Farben was Europe's largest dyestuff syndicate. The company's headquarters were in Frankfurt but they had an office in Berlin that was opposite the Adlon, on the other side of Unter den Linden. That was what I'd been trying to remember in Illmann's office.

'I'm sorry,' said the man from I.G. Farben. His tone was as stiff as a washboard, and just as square. 'But I really must protest at your loutish behaviour and your treatment of that lady.'

The redhead picked herself off the floor and uttered a few short words that were common enough in the engine rooms of German naval vessels. She was probably wondering if the Fritz with the high collar was referring to her. Collecting the now empty Bismarck bottle in her hand she swung it at

Ricci's head. The Always True leader caught it neatly in his palm, wrested it from her, tossed it in the air like a juggler's club, grabbed it by the neck and then swung it down hard against the edge of the upturned table, all in one easy, practiced, and delinquent gesture. The bottle came up again, glistening, meaningfully triangular, like a shard of razor-sharp ice. Ricci took hold of the IGF man's frock-coat, fisted him a foot closer, and seemed on the point of acquainting him with a more fundamental rebuttal when I interrupted their conversation.

The barman at the Adlon made the best cocktails in Berlin. He was fond of cucumbers, too. He put pickled cucumbers on the tables and slices of fresh cucumber in some of the drinks favoured by Americans. A large uncut cucumber lay on the bartop. Looking for a knife, I'd had my eye on it for a while. I don't care for anything in my drink except ice but I liked the look of that cucumber. Besides, my gun was in the glove box of my car.

I dislike hitting a man when his back is turned. Even with a cucumber. It goes against my inherent sense of fair play. But since Ricci Kamm didn't have a sense of fair play, I hit him hard, on the back of the hand that held the broken bottle. He yelped and dropped it. Then I struck him with the cucumber on the side of his head, twice. If I'd had some ice and a slice of lemon I'd probably have hit him with those as well. An exclamation tiptoed around the room, as if I'd made a rabbit disappear from inside a top hat. The only trouble was, the rabbit was still there. Ricci sat down heavily, holding his ear. Teeth bared, nose twitching, he reached inside his coat. I didn't think he was looking for his wallet. I saw a little black hippo's head peeking out from a holster and then a Colt automatic appeared in Ricci's hand.

It was a good firm cucumber, hardly ripe at all. Springy, with plenty of heft, like a good blackjack. I put a lot of weight into it. I had to. Ricci didn't move his head more than an inch.

He didn't try to block the cucumber. He was hoping to fire the gun before that happened. He took it across the nose, jerked back on the chair, dropped the gun and lifted both hands to the blood-spattered centre of his face. Figuring I might never get a better chance to do it, I cuffed both of his wrists before he even knew what was happening.

I let Ricci groan for a while before handing him a bar towel to press against his nose and hauling him by the cuffs to his feet. Acknowledging a round of applause from some of the other guests in the hotel bar, I pushed Ricci in the direction of two uniforms and then tossed the gun after him.

Frieda moved in on the redhead. 'Time to go, lovely,' she said, taking hold of a bony elbow.

'Take your hands off me,' said the redhead, trying to wrest her arm away, but the elbow stayed held in Frieda's strong fist. Then the redhead laughed and gave me a languorous north to south look. 'That was really something, what you did just now, comrade. Like a Christmas gift from the Kaiser. Wait until people hear about this. Ricci Kamm getting himself arrested by a Johann armed with just a cucumber? He's never going to live it down! Leastways, I hope he doesn't. That bastard's hit me once too often.'

Frieda steered her firmly towards the door, leaving me with the man from IGF. Tall, thin, and grey, he was as full of Prussian good manners as Berlin's Herrenklub and he bowed gravely.

'That was admirable,' he said. 'Quite admirable. I'm very grateful to you, sir. I don't doubt that thug would have seriously injured me. Perhaps worse.'

The IGF man had his wallet out and was pressing his business card on me. It was as thick and white as his shirt collar. His name was Doctor Carl Duisberg and he was one of the I.G. Farben directors, from Frankfurt.

'May I know your name, sir?'

I told him.

'I see the international reputation of Berlin's police force is well-deserved, sir.'

I shrugged. 'It's amazing what you can do with a cucumber,' I said.

'If there's anything I can do for you in return, to show my gratitude,' he said, 'name it, sir. Name it.'

'I could use some information, Doctor Duisberg.'

He frowned, slightly puzzled. He hadn't been expecting this. 'Of course. If it's in my power to give it.'

'Does the Dyestuff Syndicate have anything to do with drug companies?'

He smiled, and looked slightly reassured as if the information I was seeking was common knowledge. 'I can tell you that very easily. The Dyestuff Syndicate has owned Bayer since 1925.'

'You mean the company that makes aspirin?'

'No, sir,' he said proudly. 'I mean the company that invented it.'

'I see.' I did my best to look impressed. 'I guess I ought to be grateful, considering the number of hangovers your company has helped me cope with. So what's next in line, Doc? What's the new wonder drug your people are working on now?'

'It's not my field, sir, not my field at all. I'm a chemical engineer.'

'Whose field is it?'

'You mean one person?'

I nodded.

'My dear Commissar, we have dozens of research scientists working for us, all over Germany. But mainly in Leverkusen. Bayer is based in Leverkusen.'

'Leverkusen? Never heard of it.'

'That's because it's a new town, Commissar Gunther. It's made up of several small villages on the Rhine. And a number of chemical factories.'

'It sounds perfectly charming.'

'No, Commissar, Leverkusen is not at all charming. But it is making money. It is making money.' The doctor laughed. 'But why do you ask, sir?'

'Here in Berlin, we have an Institute for Police Science, in Charlottenburg,' I said. 'And we're always on the lookout for new experts we can call upon to help us with our enquiries. I'm sure you understand.'

'Of course, of course.'

'I met this doctor who's handling some very sensitive clinical trials at the State hospital in Friedrichshain here in Berlin. I think he said he was working for Bayer. And I was wondering if he might be the kind of discreet and reliable fellow who might help us out once in a while. From all accounts he's a very gifted man. I heard him described as the next Paul Ehrlich. You know? The Magic Bullet?'

'Oh, you must mean Gerhard Domagk,' said Duisberg.

'That's him,' I said. 'I just wondered if you might be able to vouch for him. As simple as that, really.'

'Well, I haven't actually met him myself, but from what I hear he's very brilliant. Very brilliant indeed. And very discreet. He has to be. Much of our work is highly confidential. I'm sure he would be delighted to help the Berlin police if it was within his power to do so. Was there something specific you wanted to ask him?'

'No. Not yet. Perhaps in the future.'

I pocketed the IGF man's card and let him get back to the rest of his lunch party. That let Frieda get back to me. She looked flushed and very grateful, which is the way I like my women.

'You handled that cucumber like a professional,' she said.

'Didn't you know? Before I joined the Berlin polenta I was a greengrocer, in Leverkusen.'

'Where the hell is Leverkusen?'

'Didn't you know? It's a new town, on the Rhine. The

centre of the German chemicals industry. What do you say we go there for the weekend and you can show me how grateful you are?'

Frieda smiled. 'We don't have to go that far to go that far,' she said. 'We only have to go upstairs. To Room 102. That's one of our VIP suites. Empty right now. Charlie Chaplin once slept in Room 102. So did Emil Jannings.' She smiled. 'But then neither of them had me around to help keep them awake.'

It was around four-thirty when I got back to the Alex. On my desk was a box of cucumbers. I waved one in the air as several of the KRIPO men in the Detective Room cheered and clapped. Otto Trettin, one of the best cops in the department and a specialist in criminal rings like the Always True, came over to my desk. There was a half cucumber in his shoulder-holster. He took it out, pointed it at me, and made a noise like a pistol shot.

'Very funny.' I grinned and removed my jacket, hanging it up on the back of my chair.

'Where's yours?' he asked. 'Your gun, I mean.'

'In the car.'

'Well, that explains the cucumber, I suppose.'

'Come on, Otto. You know how it is. When you wear a gun, you have to keep your jacket buttoned, and in this warm weather we've been having ...'

'You thought you could get away with it.'

'Something like that.'

'Seriously, Bernie. Now that you've gone up against Ricci Kamm, you're going to have to watch your back. Your front, too, most likely.'

'You think so?'

'A man who puts Ricci Kamm in the Charité with a broken nose and a concussion had better start carrying a firearm or he'll be wearing a knife between his shoulder blades. Even a cop.'

'Maybe you're right,' I admitted.

"Course I'm right. You live on Dragonerstrasse, don't you, Bernie? That's right on the doorstep of the Always True's territory. A gun's no good in the glove box, old man. Not unless you're planning to hold up a garage.' And still shooting the cucumber in my direction, Otto walked away.

'You should listen to him,' said a voice. 'He knows what he's talking about. When words fail, a gun can come in very handy.'

It was Arthur Nebe, one of the slipperiest detectives in KRIPO. A former right-wing Freikorps man, he had been made a commissar in D1a within just two years of joining the force and had a formidable record in solving crimes. Nebe was a founding member of the NSBAG – the National Socialist Fellowship of Civil Servants – and was rumoured to be a close friend of such leading Nazis as Goebbels, Count von Helldorf and Kurt Daluege. Strangely, Nebe was also a friend of Bernhard Weiss. There were other influential friends, in the SDP. And around the Alex it was generally held that Arthur Nebe had more options covered than the Berlin Stock Exchange.

'Hello, Arthur,' I said. 'What are you doing here? Is there not enough work in Political that you have to come and poach down here?'

Ignoring my remark, Nebe said, 'Since he arrested the Sass Brothers Otto's had to watch himself. Like he was painting his own portrait.'

'Well, we all know about Otto and the Sass Brothers,' I said. In 1928 Otto Trettin had almost been dismissed from the force after it became known that he had beaten a confession out of these two criminals. 'What I did was in no way similar to that. Pulling Ricci Kamm was a proper collar.'

'I hope he sees it that way,' said Nebe. 'For your sake. Look here, going without a barker is no good for a cop, see? Last April, after I put Franz Spernau in the cement, I got so many death threats they were offering even money at the Hoppegarten that someone would stall my motor before the end of the summer. It was a bet that was almost collected, too.' Nebe grinned his wolfish grin and swept back his jacket to reveal a big, broom-handle Mauser. 'Only I stalled them first, if you know what I mean.' He tapped the side of his not inconsiderable nose with clear meaning. 'By the way, how's the Schwarz case coming along?'

'What's it to you, Arthur?'

'I know Kurt Daluege a little. We were in the army together. He's sure to ask the next time I see him.'

'Actually, I think I'm beginning to make real progress. I'm more or less certain my suspect is a patient at the jelly clinic in the State hospital in Friedrichshain.'

'Is that so?'

'So you can tell your chum Daluege that it's nothing personal. I'd be working just as hard to catch this kid's murderer even if her father wasn't a lousy Nazi bastard.'

'I'm sure he'll be pleased to know it but, speaking personally, I can't see the point of bringing a kid like that into the world in the first place. As a society, I think we should follow the example of the Romans. You know? Romulus and Remus? We should leave them out on a hillside to die of exposure. Something like that, anyway.'

'Maybe. Only those two weren't left on a hillside because they were sick but because their mother was a Vestal Virgin who had violated her vow of celibacy.'

'Well I wouldn't even know how to spell that,' said Nebe.

'Besides, Romulus and Remus survived. Haven't you heard? That's how Rome was founded.'

'I'm talking about the general principle, that's all. I'm talking about wasting money on useless members of society. Did you realise that it costs the government sixty thousand marks more to keep a cripple alive in this country than an average healthy citizen?'

'Tell me, Arthur. When we talk about healthy citizens, are we including Joey Goebbels?'

Nebe smiled. 'You're a good cop, Bernie,' he said. 'Everyone says so. Be a shame to stall a promising career because of a few thoughtless remarks like that.'

'Who would say such a thing? That these are just thoughtless remarks?'

'Well, aren't they? You're no Red. I know that.'

'I put a lot of effort into my detestation of the Nazis, Arthur. You of all people should know that.'

'Nevertheless, the Nazis are going to win the next election. Then what will you do?'

'I shall do what everyone else will do, Arthur. I'll go home and stick my head in the gas oven and hope to wake up from a very bad dream.'

It was another fine, unusually warm evening. I threw Heinrich Grund's jacket at him. 'Come on,' I said. 'Let's go and do some detective work.'

We went downstairs and into the central courtyard of the Alex where I'd parked my car. I turned the key and pressed the button to operate the starter motor. The car rumbled into life.

'Where are we going?' he asked.

'Oranienburger Strasse.'

'Why?'

'We're looking for suspects, remember? That's the great thing about this city, Heinrich. You don't have to visit the nuthouse to seek out twisted, disordered minds. They're everywhere you look. In the Reichstag. In the Wilhelmstrasse. In the Prussian Parliament. I wouldn't be at all surprised if there were even one or two in Oranienburger Strasse. Makes the job a lot easier, don't you think?'

'If you say so, boss. But why Oranienburger Strasse?'

'Because it's popular with a certain kind of whore.'

'Gravel.'

'Precisely.'

It was a Friday night but I couldn't help that. Every night was a busy one on Oranienburger Strasse. Cars stopped outside the Central Telegraph Office which was open day and night. And, until the previous year, Oranienburger Strasse had been the location of one of Berlin's more notorious cabarets, the Stork's Nest, which was part of the reason the street had come to be popular with the city's prostitutes. It was rumoured that quite a few of the girls on Oranienburger had previously worked at the Stork before the club's manager had brought in some younger cheaper nude dancers from Poland.

On Friday nights there was even more traffic than usual because of all the Jews attending *shul* at the New Synagogue, which was Berlin's biggest. The New's size and magnificent onion dome was a reflection of the confidence the city's Jews had once felt about their presence in Berlin. But not any more. According to my friend Lasker, some of the city's Jews were already preparing to leave Germany should the unthinkable happen and the Nazis be elected. As we arrived, there were hundreds of them streaming through the synagogue's multi-coloured brickwork arches: men with large fur hats and long black coats, men with shawls and ringlets, boys with velvet skullcaps, women with silk headscarves – and all under the watchful, slightly contemptuous scrutiny of the several uniformed policemen who were positioned in twos at intervals along the length of the street, just in case a group of Nazi agitators decided to show up and cause trouble.

'Jesus Christ,' exclaimed Grund, as we got out of the car. 'Look at this. It's like the bloody Exodus. I've never seen so many damn Jews.'

'It's Friday night,' I said. 'It's when they go to pray.'

'Like rats, so they are,' he said, with obvious distaste. 'As for this ...' He stared up at the huge synagogue with its central dome and the two smaller pavilion-like domes flanking it, and shook his head, sadly. 'I mean, whose stupid idea was it to let them build this ugly thing here?'

'What's wrong with it?'

'It doesn't belong here, that's what's wrong with it. This is Germany. We're a Christian country. If they want this kind of thing they should go and live somewhere else.'

'Like where?'

'Palestine. Goshen. Somewhere with a hell of a lot of sand. I dunno and I don't care. Just not here in Germany, that's all. This is a Christian country.'

He stared malevolently at the many Jews entering the New. With their long beards and white shirts and black coats and big wide-brimmed hats and glasses, they looked more like short-sighted pioneers from America's nineteenth century.

We walked toward the Friedrichstrasse end of Oranienburger, where the more specialised whores I was looking for were given to waiting.

'You know what I think?' said Grund.

'Surprise me.'

'These Friedrichstrasse types should dress more like the rest of us. Like Germans. Not like freaks. They should try to blend in. That way people would be less inclined to pick on them. It's human nature, isn't it? Anyone who looks a bit different, who looks like they're setting themselves apart, well, they're just asking for trouble, aren't they?' He nodded. 'They should try to look like normal Germans.'

'You mean brown shirt, jackboots, shoulder belt, and swastika armband? Or how about leather shorts and flowery shirts?' I laughed. 'Yeah, I understand. Normal. Sure.'

'You know what I mean, boss. German.'

'I used to know what that meant. When I was in the trenches, for instance. Now, I'm not so sure.'

'That's just the point I'm making. Bastards like these have blurred things. Made it less obvious what being German is all about. I suppose that's why the Nazis are doing so well. Because they give us a clear idea of ourselves.'

I might have said that this was a clear idea of ourselves I didn't much like, but I wasn't in the mood to argue politics with him. Not again. Not now.

In Berlin all specialist tastes were catered for. The city was one big erotic – and sometimes not so erotic – menu. Provided you knew where to look and what to ask for, the chances were you could satisfy even the most peculiar taste. You wanted an old woman – and I mean an old woman, of the kind that lives in a shoe – you went to Mehnerstrasse, which, for obvious reasons, was also known as Old Maid Street. You wanted a fat woman – and I mean a fat woman, of the kind that has a twin brother who's a Sumo wrestler in Japan – you got yourself along to Landwehrstrasse, also known as Fat Street. If mothers and daughters were your thing, then you went to Gollnowstrasse. That was known as Incest Street. Racehorses, girls you could use the whip on, were most often found in the beauty shops and massage parlours that surrounded Hallesches Tor. Pregnant women – and I do mean pregnant women, not girls with cushions stuffed up the front of their dirndls – were found on Munzstrasse. Munzstrasse was also called Coin Street because there was a general sense that it was a place where people were prepared to sell absolutely anything.

Unlike Grund, I usually tried to avoid sounding righteous about Berlin's famous sex scene. What did we expect might happen to women in a country with almost two million German men dead in the war, and perhaps as many people dead again – my own wife included – from the influenza? What did we expect might happen with the country full of Russian immigrants after the Bolshevik Revolution, and inflation and the Depression and unemployment? What did convention and morality matter when everything else – money, work, life itself – turned out to be so utterly unreliable? But it was hard not to feel a little outraged at the trade going on around the north end of Oranienburger Strasse. It was difficult not to wish fire from the air to purge Berlin of this illicit trade in human flesh when you contemplated the life of the washed-up, stone-faced, outcast prostitutes collectively known as Gravel. You wanted a woman with one leg, one eye, a hunchback, or hideous scars, you went to the north end of Oranienburger Strasse and raked through the Gravel. You found them in the shadows, standing in the doorway of the defunct Stork's Nest, or in the old Kaufhaus arcade or, sometimes, inside a club called the Blue Stocking on the corner of Linenstrasse.

There were plenty of women we could have spoken to but I was looking for one woman in particular – a whore named Gerda and, not finding her on the street, I decided we should try the Blue Stocking.

The spanner on the door sat on a tall stool in front of the cash office. His name was Neumann and, occasionally, I used him as an informer. He'd once been a runner for the Dragonfly ring that operated out of Charlottenburg, only now he wouldn't go anywhere near the area, having double-crossed them somehow. For a spanner, Neumann wasn't all that tough but he had the kind of beaten, criminal face that made people think he might not care what happened to him, which, sometimes, amounts to a simulacrum of toughness. Plus (I happened to know) he kept an American baseball bat behind his stool and wasn't slow to use it.

'Commissar Gunther,' he said, nervously. 'What brings you to the Blue Stocking?'

'I'm looking for a garter snapper.'

Neumann grinned a grin so carious his teeth looked more like the discarded butts of twenty cigarettes. 'Aren't they all, sir?' he said. 'The Fritzes who waltz in here.'

'This one is gravel,' I said.

'I wouldn't have thought you was the type for that kind of trade.' His grin widened horribly, as he enjoyed what he hoped might be my embarrassment.

'Stop thinking I feel awkward asking about her because I don't,' I said. 'The only thing I feel awkward about is your dentist's feelings, Neumann. Her name is Gerda.'

The teeth disappeared behind thin, cracked lips that were all twitchy, like an angler had a hook in his mouth.

'You mean like the little girl what rescues her brother, Kay, in *The Snow Queen*?'

'That's right. Only this one's not so little. Not any more. Plus, she's short of an arm and a leg, not to mention a few teeth and half her liver. Now is she here or am I going to have to give the lads in E a call?'

E was Inspectorate E, that part of Department IV which dealt with all matters relating to morals or, more usually, the lack of them.

'No need to be like that, Herr Gunther. Just having a bit of fun, that's all.' He lifted a dog-trainer's clicker off a chain on his belt and clicked it loudly, three times. 'What happened to that sense of humour of yours, Commissar?'

'With each plebiscite it seems to get smaller.'

At the sound of the dog clicker, the door that led down into the club opened from the inside. At the top of a steep flight of stairs stood another spanner, only this one was wearing muscle.

Neumann chuckled. 'Bloody Nazis,' he said. 'I know just what you mean, Commissar. Everyone says they'll close us all down the minute they get in.'

'I sincerely hope so,' remarked Grund.

Neumann shot him a look of quiet distaste. 'Gerda's downstairs,' he said, stiffly.

'How does she get downstairs with one leg and one arm?' asked Grund.

Neumann looked at me and then at Grund, with a smile dancing on the cracked playground of his lips. 'Slowly,' he said and let out a roar of laughter that I enjoyed as much he did.

Grund wasn't laughing. 'Think you're a comedian, do you?' he said.

'Forget about it,' I told Grund, pushing him through the door and into the club. 'You walked right onto the end of that one.'

Gerda wasn't yet thirty although you wouldn't have known it. She could easily have passed for someone of about fifty. We found her, sitting in a wheelchair within spitting distance of a small stage where a zither player and a striptease dancer were having a competition to see which of them could look more bored. By my reckoning the striptease dancer had it won by a couple of droopy tits. On the table in front of Gerda stood a bottle of cheap schnapps, doubtless paid for by the man seated beside her who, on closer inspection, turned out to be a woman.

'Go and plaster it,' I told the Bubi.

'Yeah.' Grund flashed his warrant disc for good measure. 'Try the Eldorado.'

Gerda thought that was funny. The Eldorado was a club for transvestite men. The Bubi, sullen and predatory looking, like someone's outcast uncle, got up and went away. We sat down on chairs as wobbly as Gerda's remaining teeth.

'I know you,' she told me. 'You're that cop, aren't you?'

I put a ten under her bottle.

'What's the idea, putting a shine on my table? I don't know nothing.'

'Sure you do, Gerda,' I told her. 'Everyone knows something.'

'Maybe I do, and maybe I don't.' She nodded. 'I'm glad you're here, anyway, Commissar. I don't like that monbijou scene. You know? The ladies' club scorpions. I mean, beggars can't be choosers and I'd have done it with her if she'd asked me nicely, you know? But I take no pleasure in a woman touching me down there.'

I put a cigarette in Gerda's mouth and lit it. She was thin, with short red hair, bluish eyes, and a reddish face. She drank too much, although she could hold it well enough. Most of the time. The one time I knew she hadn't she'd fallen down in front of a number thirteen tram on Köpenicker Strasse. She might easily have been killed. Instead she lost her left arm and her left leg.

'I remember now,' she said. 'You put Ricci Kamm in hospital.' Smiling happily, she added, 'You deserve an Iron Cross for that, copper.'

'As usual, you're well informed, Gerda.'

I lit my own cigarette and tossed her the pack. Easily amused – I figured that was how he became a Nazi in the first place – Grund was already paying more attention to the show than to our conversation.

'Tell me, Gerda. Did you ever see a snapper with a calliper, aged about fifteen? Blonde, boyish, carried a stick. Name of Anita. She had cerebral palsy. A spastic. We know she was selling it because we found a bedroll in her pocket and because the neighbours said she was selling it.'

'Neet? Yeah, I heard she was dead, poor kid.' Gerda poured herself a drink from the bottle and swallowed it in one, like it was cold coffee. 'Came in here, sometimes. Nicely spoken girl, considering.'

'Considering what?' asked Grund. His eyes remained on the stripper's teats, which were altogether larger than would have seemed probable.

'Considering she couldn't speak very well.' Gerda made a noise that mostly came out of her nose. 'Talked like that, you know?'

'What else can you tell us about her?' I refilled Gerda's glass and poured one for myself, just to look sociable.

'From what I gathered, she didn't get on with her parents. They didn't like her being a gimp, you know? And of course they didn't like her being on the sledge. She didn't do it all the time, mind. Just when she wanted to irritate them, I think. Her dad was something in the Nazi party and it used to piss him off that she'd come out and sell it sometimes.'

'Hard to believe,' murmured Grund. 'That anyone would ... You know ... With a disabled kid.'

Gerda laughed. 'Oh no, darling. It's not hard to believe at all. Lots of men do it with disabled girls. In fact it's quite the thing these days. I expect it's something to do with the war. All those terrible injuries some of the men came home with. Left a lot of them feeling quite inadequate, in all sorts of ways. I think that doing it with gravel helps them find the confidence to get it up. Makes them feel superior to the gimp they're with. It's cheaper, too, of course. Cheaper than the regular. People don't have the money for that kind of thing. Not like they used to.' She shot Grund an amused, pitying look. 'Oh no, dearie. I've seen girls with half a face find a Fritz in here. 'Sides, most Fritzes aren't looking at you anyway. Won't meet your eye. So what a girl's shine looks like or whether she's got all her bits is not as important as the fact that she's got her mouse.' Gerda laughed. 'No, darling, you ask some of your mates at work and they'll tell you the same thing. You don't look at the whole house when you're putting a letter in the box.'

'Coming back to Anita,' I said. 'Was there ever anyone in particular you saw her with? A regular Fritz? Anything at all.'

Gerda grinned. 'How about a name?' She put some raw-looking fingers on the ten. 'Make it a gypsy and I'll give you his Otto Normal.'

I took out my wallet and put another ten on the table.

'As a matter of fact, there was a guy, one guy in particular. Licked his lollipop myself once or twice. But he preferred Anita. Name of Serkin. Rudi Serkin. She went to his apartment once or twice. It was in that big rent barracks on Malackstrasse. The one with all the entrances and exits.'

'The Ochsenhof?' said Grund.

'That's the one.'

'But that's in Always True territory,' he said.

'So take an armoured car.'

Gerda wasn't joking. The Ochsenhof was a big block of slum apartments in the epicentre of the toughest neighbour-hood in Berlin and a virtual no-go area for the police. The only way cops from the Alex were ever likely to visit the Ochsenhof was with a tank to back them up. They'd tried it before and failed, beaten back by snipers and petrol bombs. Not for nothing was it known as the Roast.

'What did he look like, this Rudi Serkin?' I asked.

'About thirty. Small, dark curly hair, glasses. Smoked a pipe. Bow tie. Oh, and Jewish.' She chuckled. 'At least, he didn't have a wrapper on his lollipop.'

'A Jew,' muttered Grund. 'I might have known.'

'Got something against Jews have you, darling?'

'He's a Nazi,' I said. 'He's got something against every-one.'

For a moment or two we were all silent. Then a voice said, loudly: 'Finished your talking, have you?'

We looked around and saw the striptease dancer staring drill holes through us. Gerda laughed. 'Yeah, we've finished.'

'Good,' said the dancer and dropped her drawers in one quick and unerotic movement. She bent over and paused just to make sure everyone got a good view of everything. Then, collecting her underwear off the floor, she straightened up again and stalked crossly off the stage.

I decided it was time we followed her example.

Leaving Gerda to finish her bottle alone, we went upstairs and took a deep breath of clean Berlin air. After the venereal atmosphere of The Blue Stocking, I felt like going home and washing my feet in disinfectant. And planning my next trip to the dentist. The sight of Neumann's hideous smile as we were leaving was a dreadful warning.

Grund nodded with enthusiasm. 'At least now we've got a name,' he said.

'You think so?'

'You heard her.'

I smiled. 'Rudolf Serkin is the name of a famous concert pianist,' I said.

'All the better. Make a nice splash in *Tempo*.'

'Better still, in *Der Angriff*,' I said and shook my head. 'My dear Heinrich, the real Rudolf Serkin would no more get involved with a crippled whore than he'd play "My Parrot Doesn't Like Hard Boiled Eggs" at the Bechstein Hall. Whoever it was Gerda met, and whoever it was she saw Anita with, they just gave a false name. That's all.'

'Maybe there are two Rudolf Serkins.'

'Maybe. But I doubt it. Would you give your real name to a bit of gravel you picked up in The Blue Stocking?'

'No, I suppose not.'

'You suppose right. Gerda knew it, too. Only she had nothing else to give.'

'What about the address?'

'She gave out the one address in Berlin she knows the polenta doesn't dare set foot in. She was playing us a tune, chum.'

'Then why did you let her keep the gypsy?'

'Why?' I looked up at the sky. 'I dunno. Maybe because she's only got one leg and one arm. Maybe that's why. Anyway, the next time I see her, she'll know she owes me.'

Grund grimaced. 'You're too soft to be a cop, do you know that?'

'From a Nazi like you I'll take that as a compliment.'

The next morning I left my Peek & Cloppenburg suit in the closet and put on my father's tail coat and stiff collar. Until his untimely death, he had worked as a clerk for Bleichroder's Bank, on Behren Strasse. I don't think I ever saw him wearing a lounge suit. Lounging was not something he did much of. My father was a pretty typical Prussian: deferential, loyal to his Emperor, respectful, punctilious. I got all those qualities from him. While he was alive, we never got on as well as we might have done. But things were different now.

I took a good look at myself in the mirror and smiled. I was just like him. Apart from the smile and the cigarette and the extra hair on top of my head. All men come to resemble their fathers. That isn't a tragedy, but you need a hell of a sense of humour to handle it.

I walked to the Adlon. The hotel car service was run by a Pole called Carl Mirow. Carl had once been Hindenburg's chauffeur but left the Weimar President's service when he discovered he could make more money driving for someone important. Like the Adlons. Carl was a member of the German Automobile Club and was very proud of the fact that in all his many years on the roads he had kept a clean licence. Very proud and very grateful, too. In 1922 a raw young Berlin policeman named Bernhard Gunther had stopped Carl for going through a red light. He smelt like he'd gone through quite a bit of schnapps as well but I decided to let him off. It wasn't very Prussian of me. Maybe Grund was right. Maybe I was too soft to be a cop. Anyway, Carl and I had been friends ever since.

The Adlons had a huge black Mercedes-Benz 770 Pullman convertible. With headlamps the size of tennis rackets and fenders and running boards as big as the ski jump at Holmenkollen, it was a real plutocrat's car. The kind of plutocrat who might be a director on the board of the Dyestuffs Syndicate. Impersonating Doctor Duisberg wasn't much of a plan but I couldn't figure out another way of getting anything out of Doctor Gerhard Domagk at the State Hospital's jelly clinic. Illmann wasn't usually wrong about such things. It did seem highly unlikely that any doctor would ever give out the kind of sensitive information that I was after. Unless he thought that, effectively, he was giving out that information to his employer.

Carl Mirow had agreed to drive me to the State. The big Mercedes-Benz made quite an impact as we drove through the hospital's grounds, especially when I wound down the window and asked a nurse for directions to the Urological Clinic. Carl got a little cross about that. He said, 'Suppose someone sees the licence plate and thinks that Mister Adlon has got a dose of jelly.'

Mister Adlon was Louis Adlon, the hotel's owner. He was a man in his sixties, with thinning white hair and a rather neat white moustache. 'Do I look anything like Mister Adlon?'

'No.'

'Besides, if you had a dose of jelly, would you come to the clinic in a car like this? Or with your collar up and your hat pulled down?'

We pulled up outside the redbrick outbuilding that housed the Urological Clinic. Carl sprang out and opened the door for me. In his driver's livery he looked like my old company commander. Which was probably the real reason I hadn't pinched him for running a red light back in 1922. I was always a bit sentimental like that.

I went into the clinic. The entrance doors were double and had frosted glass windows. The hall inside was bright and cool and the linoleum floor was wearing so much polish that your shoes squeaked loudly as you tried to tiptoe up to the front desk. Once there, under the vaulted ceiling your muttered plea for medical care would have sounded like a stage whisper in an opera. A strong smell of ether wasn't just in the air. The strawberry blonde behind the welcome desk looked like she gargled with the stuff. I placed Doctor Duisberg's business card on her desk and told her I wanted to see Doctor Domagk.

'He's not here,' she said.

'I suppose he's in Leverkusen.'

'No, he's in Wuppertal.'

That was somewhere else I hadn't ever heard of. There were times when I hardly recognised the country in which I was living.

'I suppose that's another new town.'

'I wouldn't know,' she said.

'Who's in charge while he's away?'

'Doctor Kassner.'

'Then he's the person I want to see.'

'Have you an appointment?'

I smiled, affecting a show of self-important patience. 'I think you'll find I don't need one if you give Doctor Kassner that business card. You see, nurse, I fund all of the research in this clinic. So unless you want to join the ranks of the six million unemployed, I suggest you hurry along and tell him I'm here.'

The nurse coloured a little, stood up, took Duisberg's card and, her feet squeaking like a series of squashed mice, disappeared through a set of swing doors.

A minute passed and a pale, awkward man came through the main entrance of the clinic. He was walking slowly, like someone with a bad leg. He kept his eyes on the linoleum as if expecting to find a better explanation than an overdose of floor polish for the noise under his shoes. At the desk, he stopped and gave me a sideways sort of look, probably wondering if I was some kind of doctor. I smiled at him.

'Lovely day,' I said, breezily.

Then a man in a white coat appeared in the hall, striding powerfully towards me like a founder member of the Wandervögel, one hand outstretched and the other holding Duisberg's business card. He was big and bald-headed, which made him seem more military than medical. Underneath the white coat he was dressed much as I was, a professional man, with a position in the community.

'Doctor Duisberg, sir,' he said unctuously, with a slight speech impediment that might have been referable to some ill-fitting false teeth. 'What an honour, sir. What an honour. I'm Doctor Kassner. Doctor Domagk will be so very disappointed to have missed you. He's in Wuppertal.'

'Yes, so I've just been informed.'

The doctor looked pained. 'I trust there hasn't been some kind of mix-up and that he wasn't expecting you,' he said.

'No, no,' I said. 'I'm only in Berlin for a brief visit. I had a short time to kill between appointments so I thought I might just drop by and see how the clinical trial is coming along. The Dyestuff Syndicate is very excited by your work, here.' I paused. 'Of course, if it's inconvenient ...'

'No, no sir.' He bowed. 'If you're happy to make do with my own inadequate explanations.'

'I'm sure they will be quite sufficient for a layman like me.'

'Then, do, please, come this way, sir.'

We went through the swing doors and into a corridor where a dozen or more rather miserable-looking men were seated along the wall, each of them holding what was either a urine sample or a very poor example of Berlin's notoriously unpleasant tap water. Kassner ushered me into his office which was suitably clinical. There was an examination couch, some shelves stuffed with medical textbooks, a couple of chairs, some filing cabinets and a small desk. On the desk was a portable Bing with a sheet of paper rolled into the carriage, and a telephone. On the walls were some graphic illustrations that had me shrinking into my bladder and almost enough to persuade me to take a vow of celibacy. I reflected I was probably the first man in a long while who'd walked into that little office and not been asked to drop his trousers.

'How much do you know about our work here?' he asked.

'Only that you're working on a new magic bullet,' I said. 'I'm not a medical doctor. I'm a chemical engineer. Dyestuffs are my forte. Just assume you're explaining things to an educated layman.'

'Well, as you probably know, sulpha drugs are synthetic anti-microbial agents that contain sulphonamides. One of those drugs – a drug called Protonsil – was synthesised by Josef Klarer at Bayer and tested on animals by Doctor Domagk. Successfully, of course. Since then, we've been testing it on a small group of outpatients who are suffering from syphilis and gonorrhoea. But, in the course of time, we hope to find that Protonsil will be effective in treating a whole range of bacterial infections inside the body. Oddly, it has no effect in the test-tube. Its anti-bacterial action only seems to work inside living organisms, which leads us to suspect, and to hope, that the drug is successfully metabolised inside the body.'

'How big is your trial group?' I asked.

'Really we've only just started. So far we've given Protonsil to approximately fifty men and about half as many women – there's a separate clinic for them, of course, at the Charité. Some of our test cases have only just caught a venereal disease and others have had one for a while. It's intended that over the next two or three years we shall test the drug on as many as fifteen hundred to two thousand volunteers.'

I nodded, almost wishing I had thought to bring Illmann with me. At least he might have asked some pertinent questions; even a few impertinent ones.

'So far,' continued Kassner, 'the results have been very encouraging.'

'Might I see what the drug looks like?'

He opened his desk drawer and took out a bottle and then emptied some little blue pills onto my gloved palm. These looked exactly the same as the little pill I'd found near Anita Schwarz's dead body.

'Of course it won't look like that when the trial is over. The German medical establishment is rather conservative and prefers its pills white. But they're blue for the moment to help distinguish them from anything else we're using.'

'And your study group notes? Might I see one case file?'

'Yes, indeed.' Kassner turned to face one of the wooden filing cabinets. There was no key. He drew up the tambour front and then pulled open the top drawer. 'This is a summary file containing brief notes on all of the patients who've been treated with Protonsil to date.' He opened the file and handed it over.

I took out my father's pince-nez. A nice touch, I told myself, and pinced them on the bridge of my nez. This was my list of suspects, I told myself. With these names I might very well have solved the case in less time than it took to cure a dose of jelly. But how was I going to get hold of this list of names? I could hardly memorise it. Nor could I ask to borrow it. One name caught my eye, however. Or rather not the name – Behrend – so much as the address. Reichskanzlerplatz, in the west end of the city, near the Grunewald, was undoubtedly one of the most exclusive addresses in the city. And for some reason it appeared familiar to me.

'As you probably know,' Kassner was saying, 'the problem with Salvarsan is that it is slightly more toxic for the microbe than the host. No such problems have presented themselves with Protonsil Rubrum. The human liver deals with it quite effectively.'

'Excellent,' I murmured, glancing further down the list. But when I saw two Johann Mullers, a Fritz Schmidt, an Otto Schneider, a Johann Meyer, and a Paul Fischer I began to suspect that the list might not be all I'd hoped it was. These were five of the commonest surnames in Germany. 'Tell me something, Doctor. Are these real names?'

'To be honest, I don't know,' admitted Kassner. 'We don't insist on seeing identity cards here, otherwise they might never volunteer for the clinical trial. Patient confidentiality is an important issue with moral diseases.'

'I suppose that's especially true since the National Socialists started talking about a clean-up of morals in this city,' I said.

'But all of those addresses are real enough. We do insist on that so that we might correspond with our patients over a period of time. Just to keep a check on how they're all doing.'

I handed back the file and watched as he placed it back in the top drawer of the cabinet.

'Well, thank you for your time,' I said, standing up. 'I'll certainly be making a favourable interim report to the Dyestuff Syndicate on your work here.'

'I'll walk you to your car, Herr Doctor.'

We went outside. Carl Mirow threw away his cigarette, and opened the heavy car door. If Doctor Kassner had harboured any doubts about who I was they were banished by the sight of a uniformed chauffeur and a limousine as big as a Heinkell.

Carl drove to Dragonerstrasse and dropped me in front of my building. He was glad to see the back of me and especially glad to see the back of Dragonerstrasse, which wasn't anywhere to bring a chauffeur and a Mercedes-Benz 770. I went up to my apartment, put on some normal clothes and went out again. I got into my car and headed toward the west end. I had an itch I suddenly wanted to scratch.

Number Three Reichskanzlerplatz was an expensive, modern-looking apartment building in just about the richest, leafiest suburb in Berlin. A little further away to the west lay Grunewald Racecourse and the athletics stadium where some Berliners hoped that the Olympics might be staged in 1936. My late wife had been especially fond of this area. To the south of the racecourse was the Seeschloss restaurant where I had asked her to marry me. I parked the car and went over to a kiosk to get some cigarettes and, perhaps, some information.

'Give me some Reemtsmas, a *New Berliner, Tempo*, and *The Week*,' I said. I flashed my warrant disc. 'We had a report of some shots fired in this area. Anything in it?'

The vendor, who wore a suit, an Austrian hat, and a little moustache like Hitler's, shook his head. 'Car backfire probably. But I've been here since seven this morning and I haven't heard a thing.'

'I figured as much just looking around,' I said. 'Still, you have to check these things out.'

'There's never any trouble round here,' he said. 'Although there could be.'

'How do you mean?'

He pointed across Reichskanzlerplatz to where it intersected with Kaiserdamm. 'See that car?' He was pointing at a dark green Mercedes-Benz parked right in front of number three.

'Yes.'

'There are four SA men sitting in that car,' he said. Pointing north, up Ahorn Allee, he added: 'And another truckload of them over there.'

'How do you know they're SA?'

'Haven't you heard? The ban on uniforms has been lifted.'

'Of course, it's today, isn't it? Some cop I am. I didn't even notice. So who lives around here? Ernst Röhm?' Ernst Röhm was the leader of the SA.

'Nope. Although he does visit on occasion. I've seen him going in there. To the ground floor apartment on the corner of number three. Owned by Mrs Magda Quandt.'

'Who?'

The vendor grinned. 'For a bull who takes as many newspapers as you do, you don't know much.'

'Me? I just look at the pictures. So go ahead and educate me.' I handed over a five. 'And while you're at it, keep the change.'

'Magda Quandt. She got married last December to Josef Goebbels. I see him every morning. Comes out and buys all the papers.'

'It gives the club foot some exercise, I suppose.'

'He's not so bad.'

'I'll take your word for it.' I shrugged. 'Well, I can see why he married her. Nice building like that. Wouldn't mind living here myself.' I shook my head. 'Thing is. I can't for the life of me see why she married a little Fritz like him.'

I tossed the papers in the car, crossed over to the other side of the square and glanced in the window of the car parked out front of number three. The vendor was right. It was full of Nazi brownshirts who eyed me suspiciously as I went by. Apart from some clowns I'd seen fooling around in an old Model T at the circus one Christmas it would have been hard to have seen more obvious stupidity in one car. It was all coming back to me now: why the address had jogged my memory in Kassner's office. One of the other homicide teams at the Alex had been obliged to check an SA man's alibi with Goebbels a month or two before.

The building had its own doorman, of course. All the nice apartment buildings in the west end had a doorman. Probably there was an armed SA man somewhere inside the lobby keeping him company. Just to make sure Goebbels was well protected. He probably needed it, too. The communists had already made several attempts on Hitler's life. I didn't doubt they wanted to assassinate Goebbels. I wouldn't have minded taking a poke at the little satyr myself.

Naturally I'd heard the rumours. That despite his cloven hoof and his diminished size he was really quite a ladies' man. The word around the Alex was that it wasn't just Goebbels's foot that looked like a club; that while he may have been short of stature he was outsized on the butcher's counter; that Goebbels was what Berlin's line-boys would have called a Breslauer, after a large sausage of the same name. Much as I disliked him, however, I was still finding it hard to imagine Joey the Crip taking the risk of an open trip to the jelly clinic in Friedrichshain. Unless of course he'd gone in as a private patient, after hours, when no one else was about.

I rounded the rusticated corner of the building and stopped below what must have been Joey's bathroom window. It was slightly open. I looked back over my shoulder. The car containing the storm troopers was out of sight. The truck was nowhere to be seen. I glanced back up at the frosted glass window. If I put my foot on the horizontal joint of the ground floor's rusticated brickwork, it looked as though it would be just possible to push myself up the side of the building and reach the bottom of the window. I tried it once, just long enough to check that the bathroom was empty, before dropping back down onto the deserted pavement. I waited for a moment. No storm troopers came to beat me up. So much for security.

The next time I did it, I pulled myself up the side and slid quickly through the open bathroom window. Breathing heavily, I sat on the toilet and, while I waited to see if my entry would be detected, I took a closer look at the window and saw that the rat's tail casement was broken on the sill. Even when the window looked like it was closed it would have been a relatively simple matter to open it from the outside.

It was a big bathroom, with pink tiles all over and a round pedestal basin. There was a liberal dusting of talcum powder on the bathroom mat. The boxed-in bath was as deep as a car door, with a hand shower in case Magda wanted to wash her hair. By the wall-mounted soap dish was a small framed picture of Hitler, as if even here the devoted Joey could keep his beloved leader in mind. At right angles to the bath was a stool on which sat a pile of fluffy towels, and next to this a matching table on which stood a loofah and an antiquarian statue of a naked lady. Above the table was a large, mirrored bathroom cabinet which, naturally, I opened. Most of the shelves were Magda's. She used Joy perfume, Kotex, Nivea, Wella shampoo, Wellapon, Kolestral, and Blondor. I remembered her now. I remembered the pictures of the wedding in the magazines. A winter wedding. The happy smiling couple arm-in-arm in the snow accompanied by several SA men – probably the same careless louts who were sitting outside in the car – and, of course, Hitler himself. I wonder what Hitler would have said if he'd known that Magda's beautiful perfectly Aryan blonde hair was dyed?

Joey had only one shelf in the cabinet, and it seemed we had something in common after all. Joey shaved with a Schick Injector Razor and Mennen shaving cream and cleaned his teeth with Colgate toothpaste. A bottle of Anzora hair cream explained Joey's perfectly brushed head of dark hair. Then, between a packet of Beechams laxative pills and some Acqua di Parma cologne, was a bottle containing some blue pills. I opened it and emptied one out in my hand. It was the same pill I had seen in Kassner's office earlier that morning. Protonsil. I decided that was my cue to leave. But not before using Joey's toilet. And not flushing it was my way of thanking him for what he'd written about me in his newspaper.

I went out the window, returned to my car and drove quickly away. In Germany, there were things that it didn't seem healthy to know about. I didn't doubt for a minute that Joey's jelly was one of these.

There were nine technical inspectorates at the Alex. Inspectorate A dealt with murder, and C dealt with thefts. Gunther Braschwitz was the boss of C and specialised in burglaries. He had a younger brother, Rudolf, who was in the political police but we didn't hold that against him. Braschwitz was as elegant as your little finger, and a real champagne pisser. He wore a bowler hat, carried a stick with a sword in it, which he would sometimes use and, in winter at least, wore gaiters above his boots. He knew all the screens – the city's professional burglars – and, it was said, could look at a break-in and tell which of them had probably done it.

'Jewface Klein,' I said. 'Seen him lately?'

'Jewface? He claims he's going straight,' said Braschwitz. 'Managed to get himself a job at Heilbronner's on Mohrenstrasse.'

'The antique shop?'

'That's right. He always had a very good eye that Jewface. Why? Has he been up to his old tricks?'

'No. But he knows someone I'm looking for. A friend of that widow he used to partner. Eva Zimmer.' Only half of this was true, but I didn't want Braschwitz asking too many questions.

'Poor Eva,' he said. 'She was a good widow, that girl.'

A widow was someone a screen used to get rid of his ill-gotten goods. Not a real widow, just someone pretending to be one. Some of them, like Eva Zimmer, were professional actresses. They would dress up in black and, with a well-rehearsed hard-luck story, try to sell stolen gold, silver, or jewellery to the high street goldsmiths. Until I'd arrested Jewface he and Eva had had one of the best partnerships in Berlin. I knew he was six months out of Tegel Prison but there was nothing on file of what he'd been doing since.

After Braschwitz had told me all he knew about Jewface, I telephoned the Adlon and asked Frieda what she could tell me about Josef Goebbels. Goebbels was a regular patron of the Adlon and Frieda was able to give me some information which I thought I might use to help bait Klein.

I walked to Heilbronner's, but the manager told me Klein wasn't there. 'It's his lunch hour,' he said. 'You'll probably find him across the street at Gsellius, the bookshop. He usually goes in there at lunchtime.'

I crossed the street and peered in the bookshop window. Jewface was in there all right. I saw him straight away. A little older than I remembered, but a year in the cement can put five on your shine. His face wasn't particularly Jewish, to be honest. He had the nickname from the jeweller's eyeglass he used to wear when he was appraising something he'd stolen. But he did have a nose – for cops. I hadn't been there for more than a few seconds when he looked up from the book he held and met my eye. I nodded at him to come outside and, reluctantly, he did. We weren't friends exactly. But I was counting on his not having forgotten that it was me who found the pimp who'd stabbed Eva Zimmer the previous year. A man named Horst Wessel. And the pity of it was that Wessel, who was also a member of the SA, had then been murdered by another pimp called Ali Hohler in an argument over some whore before I could make the arrest. Because Hohler happened also to be a communist, Goebbels had managed to turn these tawdry events into a political melodrama, which was how Horst Wessel had achieved his unlikely immortalisation in a song that was now heard all over Berlin when the SA went on one of its provocative marches through a communist neighbourhood. Naturally, Goebbels had left out of the story the underworld connections of these plankton protagonists. Meanwhile Hohler had been arrested by one of my colleagues and sentenced to life imprisonment. Which left Jewface very much aggrieved with Goebbels for having waxed Eva Zimmer's sordid murder from the Nazis' *canta storia* of Horst Wessel's heroic past.

We went around the corner to Siechen's on Friedrichstrasse where I bought us a couple of Nurembergs and took a closer look at him. His face was all sharp angles, thin and pointed, like something Pythagoras had doodled on the corner of his scroll before getting on with his theorem.

'So what can I do for you, Herr Gunther?'

'I need a favour, Jewface. I want someone to break into a doctor's office at the State Hospital. Someone intelligent who can read and write and not get greedy. I don't want anything stolen.'

'That's good, because I'm retired. I don't steal. And I don't go breaking and entering. Not since Eva got stabbed.'

'Look, all I want you to do is open a file and do a bit of copying out. A secretary with a key could do it, but I don't have a key. For a man of your experience, it couldn't be simpler.' I sipped my beer and let him blow me off like the froth on top of his own untouched glass.

'You're not listening, Commissar. I'm retired. Prison worked for me. Give yourself a medal.'

'Medals is it? I can't give you a medal, Jewface. But you do what I ask, copy out some names from some files at the hospital and I can give you something else.'

'I don't want your money, copper.'

'I wouldn't insult you. No, this is something better than money. It's even patriotic – that is, if you believe in the Republic.'

'I don't, as it happens. It was the Republic that put me in the cement.'

'All right. Call it revenge then. Revenge for Eva.' I sipped some more of my beer and let him wait.

'Keep talking.'

'How would you like to shove one up Joey Goebbels?'

'I'm listening.'

'Joey the Crip lives at number three Reichskanzlerplatz. Corner apartment, ground floor, eastern end. A bunch of SA men sits out front so you'll have to be careful. But they can't see around the corner to where Joey's bathroom faces the side street. There's a rat's tail casement stay on the bathroom window that's broken. You can be in and out in no time. Bread and butter to a man like you, Jewface. I did it myself just an hour or two ago. The man is a fanatic, Jewface. Do you know he's got a photograph of Hitler on the side of the bath? Anyway, the apartment is owned by his wife, Magda. She used to be married to a rich industrialist called Gunther Quandt who was very generous with the divorce settlement. He let her keep all her mints. You know? The ones you like. The ones you can sell at Margraf's? Of course, with an election

127

coming Goebbels is out a lot. Making speeches, that kind of thing. In fact, I happen to know that Joey's making a speech tomorrow night at Nazi Party headquarters on Hedemannstrasse. It will be an important speech. They're all important between now and the end of the July, but maybe this one is more important than most. Hitler will be there. Afterwards, Magda's throwing a little soirée for him at the Adlon Hotel. Which would give a man plenty of time.' I sipped some more beer and thought about ordering some sausage. It had been a busy morning. 'So. What do you say? Do we have a deal? Will you copy out these names for me, like I asked?'

'Like I told you already Gunther, I'm a reformed character. I'm trying to lead an honest life.' Jewface smiled and offered me his hand. 'But that's the thing about the Nazis. They bring out the worst in people.'

The next morning I had a handwritten list of names and addresses from all over the city and beyond. Not as good as a list of suspects, but perhaps the next best thing. Now all I had to do was check them out.

The Resident's Registrations Office was on the railway station side of the Alex, in room 359. From this third floor office the address of any resident of Berlin might be obtained, quite legally, by any other resident of the city. The Prussian authorities had meant well: the knowledge that information in the State was freely available was supposed to help buttress faith in our fragile democracy. In practice, however, it just meant that Nazi storm troopers and communists alike were able to find out where their opponents lived and take appropriately belligerent action. Democracy has its disadvantages, too.

Not available to the general public at the Registration Office, but available to police, was what we called the

Devil's Directory, so-called because it worked backwards. All you had to do was look up a street name and a house number and the Devil's Directory told you the name of the person or people living there. So it was the work of a morning to put a real name alongside each of the addresses and bogus patient names that Jewface Klein had copied from the summary file in Doctor Kassner's office. This was a mundane task I might normally have ordered one of my sergeants to attend to. But I never was very good at giving orders – any more than I was any good at taking them. Besides, if I'd given the job to a sergeant, I might have ended up having to explain where and how I'd got hold of the list in the first place. KRIPO could be very unforgiving of bent coppers. Even coppers who bent not for themselves, but for the job.

For the same reason, another mundane task I was going to have to do myself was check out every name on that list. There was however nothing mundane about one name in particular I had found, using the Devil's Directory. This was Doctor Kassner's own name. And I was looking forward to finding out why his home address should have been on a list of patients involved in Bayer's clinical trial of Protonsil.

When I got back to my desk Grund was typing something on my ancient Carmen, one ponderous finger at a time, as if he was killing ants or playing the opening notes of some tuneless Russian piano concerto.

'Where the hell have you been?' he asked.

'Where the hell have you been, *sir*?' I said.

'Illmann called. The Schwarz girl tested negative for jelly. And Gennat wants us to go and check out some girl found dead in the Municipal Cattle Market. Looks like she was shot but we're to give it a quick sketch anyway, just in case.'

'Makes sense, I suppose.' The cattle market was only a few hundred yards from where we found the Schwarz girl, in Friedrichshain Park.

We were there in a matter of minutes. Market days were Wednesdays and Saturdays so the place was closed and deserted. But the restaurant was open and some of the patrons – wholesale butchers mostly, from Pankow, Weissensee and Petershagen – reported seeing three men chasing the girl into the yards. But the descriptions were vague. Too vague to be worth writing down. The body itself was in the slaughter-house. She looked about twenty. She'd been shot in the head at fairly close range. There was a brown mark around the bullet hole. All the clothing below her waist was gone and, from the smell of her, it seemed probable she'd been raped. But that was it. There had been no amateur surgery on this poor creature.

'Circumstances arousing suspicion, right enough,' said Grund, after quite a while.

I would have been surprised if he hadn't said it.

'Nice looking box on her,' he added.

'Go ahead and give her one, why don't you? I'll look the other way.'

'I was just saying,' he said. 'I mean, look at it. Her box. It's been shaved, mostly. Not something you often see, that's all. Bare like that. Like a little girl.'

I rifled through her handbag, which one of the uniformed SCHUPOs had found a short distance away from the body, and found a communist party card. Her name was Sabine Färber. She'd worked at KPD headquarters close to where I lived. Her home was in Pettenkofer Strasse, on the edge of Lichterfelde, just a hundred yards east of where she'd been murdered. Already it seemed abundantly clear to me what had probably happened.

'Fucking Nazis,' I said with loud disgust.

'Christ, I'm fed up with this,' he said, frowning. 'How do you work that out? That they were Nazis who did this. You heard the descriptions given by those butchers. No one mentioned seeing any brownshirts or swastikas. Not even a toothbrush moustache. So how do you figure that they're Nazis?'

'Oh it's nothing personal, Heinrich.' I tossed him Sabine Färber's party card. 'But they weren't Jehovah's Witnesses trying to find a convert.'

He looked at the card and shrugged, as if allowing only the possibility that I was right.

'Come on. It's got their fingerprints all over it. My guess is that the three men the butchers reported seeing were storm troopers wearing plain clothes so as not to draw attention to themselves. They must have been waiting for her when she came out of the KPD headquarters on Bülow Platz. It's a nice day, so she decided to walk home and didn't notice that they were following. Waiting for a good opportunity to attack her. When she spotted them she ran in here, hoping to escape. Only they cornered her and then did what brave storm troopers do when they're fighting a terrible menace like International Bolshevism. Heinrich?'

'I suppose some of that might be right,' he said. 'More or less.'

'Which part do you agree with less?' I asked.

Grund didn't answer. He put Sabine Färber's card back in her bag and stared down at the dead girl.

'What is it that Hitler says?' I asked. 'Strength lies not in defence but in attack?' I lit a cigarette. 'I always wondered what that meant.' I let the smoke char my lungs for a moment and then said, 'Is this the kind of attack that he means, do you think? Your great leader?'

'Of course not,' muttered Grund. 'You know it isn't.'

'What then? You tell me. I'd like to know.'

'Give it a rest, why don't you?'

'Me?' I laughed. 'It's not me who needs to give it a rest, Heinrich. It's the people who did this. They're your friends. The National Socialists.'

'You don't know any of that for a fact.'

'No, you're right, I don't. For real vision you need a man like Adolf Hitler. Perhaps he should be the detective here. Not a bad idea – I'm sure I prefer the idea of him as a cop to the idea of him becoming the next Chancellor of Germany.' I smiled. 'And it's an even bet he'd have a superior clean-up rate to me. Who better to solve a city's crimes than the man who instigates most of them?'

'Christ, I wish I didn't have to listen to you, Gunther.'

Grund spoke through gritted teeth. There was colour in his face that ought to have warned me to be careful. He was a boxer, after all.

'You don't,' I told him. 'I'm going back to the Alex to tell the political boys that this is one for them. You stay here and see if you can't get some better witnesses than those sausage makers. I dunno, perhaps you'll get lucky. Perhaps they're Nazis themselves. They're certainly ugly enough. Who knows? Perhaps they'll even give you descriptions of three orthodox Jews.'

I suppose it was the sarcastic grin that did it for him. I hardly saw the punch. I hardly even felt it. One second I was standing there, grinning like Torquemada, and the next I was lying on the cobbled ground, felled like a heifer and feeling as if I'd been struck by a bolt of electricity. In the half light available to my eyes, Grund was standing over me with fists clenched, like Firpo staring down at Dempsey, and shouting something at me. His words were quite silent to my ears. All I could hear was a loud high-pitched noise. Finally Grund was hustled away by a couple of uniformed bulls while their sergeant bent down and helped me to my feet.

My head cleared and I shifted my jaw against my hand.

'The bastard hit me,' I said.

'He did that,' said the cop, searching my eyes like a referee wondering if he should allow the fight to proceed or not. 'We all saw it, sir.'

From his tone I assumed he meant that he took it for

granted I was going to press disciplinary charges against Grund. Hitting a superior officer was a serious offence in KRIPO. Almost as bad as hitting a suspect.

I shook my head. 'No you didn't,' I said.

The cop was older than me. Nearing retirement probably. His short hair was the colour of polished steel. He had a scar in the centre of his forehead: it looked as if a bullet had struck him there.

'What's that you say, sir?'

'You didn't see anything, sergeant. Any of you. Got that?'

The sergeant thought about this for a moment and then nodded. 'If you say so, sir.'

There was blood in my mouth but I was uncut.

'No harm done,' I said, and spat onto the ground.

'What was it all about?' he asked.

'Politics,' I said. 'That's what everything's always about in Germany these days. Politics.'

I didn't go straight back to the Alex. Instead I drove to Kassner's apartment on Donhoff Platz, which wasn't exactly on the way, being at the eastern end of Leipziger Strasse. I stopped on the north side of some ornamental gardens. The bronze statues of two Prussian statesmen stared at me across a low privet hedge. A small boy out for a walk with his mother was looking at the statues and probably wondering who they were. I was thinking about how Doctor Kassner's home address had come to be on a list of names I had got from Jewface Klein. I knew Kassner would still be at the hospital, so I really hadn't a clue what I was expecting to find out. But I am an optimist like that. When you're a detective, you have to be. And sometimes, you just have to do what your instincts tell you to do.

I walked up to the shiny black front door and took a closer look. There were three bells. One of them was clearly labelled

Kassner. Beside the door were two cast-iron planters filled with geraniums. The whole area oozed respectability. I pulled the bell and waited. After a while I heard the key being turned and the door opened to reveal a man in his early twenties. I lifted my hat, innocently.

'Doctor Kassner?'

'No,' said the man. 'He's not here.'

'My name is Hoffmann,' I said, raising my hat once again. 'From Isar life Insurance.'

The young man nodded politely but said nothing.

I glanced quickly at the other two names by the bell pulls. 'Herr Körtig?'

'No.'

'Herr Peters is it?'

'No. I'm a friend of Doctor Kassner's. And as I said, he's not here right now.'

'When will the doctor be back do you think, Herr—?'

'You can probably find him at the State Hospital. At the Urological Clinic.' The man grinned as if somehow he hoped that this piece of information might embarrass me. There was a large gap between his front teeth. 'I'm sorry, but I really do have to go. I'm late for an appointment. Would you excuse me?'

'Certainly.'

I stepped aside and watched him descend the front steps onto the square. He was of medium height, good-looking and dark in a gypsy kind of way, but neat with it. He was wearing a light-coloured, summerweight suit, a white shirt, but no tie. At the bottom of the steps he climbed over the door of a little open-topped Opel. It was white with a blue stripe. I hadn't paid any attention to it before – maybe I was still a little bit punchy but as he started the engine and drove off, I suddenly realised I needed to take down the licence plate. All I got was a letter M before the car disappeared around the corner of Jerusalemstrasse. At least I knew that the slippery young man was from Munich.

An hour later I was back at my desk. I saw Heinrich Grund on the other side of the detectives' room and was just about to go over and tell him there were no hard feelings on my part when the full Ernst arrived beside me like a bus reaching its depot. He was wearing a blue pinstripe, three-piece suit in a size Huge and had a Senior going full blast in the corner of his mouth. He removed the cigar and I heard what sounded like the bellows on a church organ. An invisible choir of smoke and sweet coffee, and something stronger perhaps, descended on me as from Mount Sinai and a lung ailment of a voice commanded my attention.

'Anything in that murder over at the cattle yard?' he asked.

'It looks like an aggravated political killing,' I said.

'Aggravated?'

'They raped her as well.'

Gennat grimaced.

'The DPP wants to see us.' Gennat never called Weiss Izzy. He didn't even call him Bernhard. He called him Weiss or the DPP. 'Now.'

'What's it about?' I asked, wondering if Grund had been stupid enough to report himself for striking a senior officer.

'The Schwarz case,' he said.

'What about it?'

But Gennat had already waddled off, expecting me to follow. As I went after him I reflected that Gennat had the flattest feet of any cop I'd ever seen, which was hardly surprising given the bulk they had to carry. He must have weighed almost three hundred pounds. He walked with his arms behind him which was hardly surprising either, given how much of him was in front.

We went upstairs and along a quieter corridor, lined with the pictures of previous Prussian police presidents and their deputies. Gennat knocked on Izzy's door and opened it without waiting. We went inside. Bright sunshine was streaming through grimy, double-height windows. As usual

Izzy was writing. On the window seat, like a warm looking cat and smelling lightly of cologne sat Arthur Nebe.

'What's he doing here?' I growled, sitting down on one of the hard wooden chairs. Gennat sat on the chair next to it and hoped for the best.

'Now, now, Bernie,' said Izzy. 'Arthur's just here to help.'

'I just came back from the cattle market. There's a dead girl in one of the pens. Murdered by Nazis, most probably, given that she was a card-carrying Red. He could apply his formidable skills to that case, if he wants. But there's nothing political about the murder of Anita Schwarz.'

Izzy put down his pen and leaned back. 'I thought I made it clear that there is,' he said.

'Whoever killed Anita Schwarz was a nutcase not a Nazi,' I said. 'Although I will concede that it's not at all uncommon for these two particulars to be coterminous.'

'I believe Commissar Gunther makes the point for me,' said Nebe. 'Quite eloquently, as usual.'

'And what point might that be, Commissar Nebe?'

'Look here, Bernie,' said Izzy. 'There are certain officials in the General—'

'I'm not in the General,' I said. 'I'm in the Official.'

'—Have queried your ability to remain impartial,' he continued. 'They think your open hostility to the National Socialist party and its adherents might actually get in the way of solving this murder.'

'Who said I was hostile to Nazism?'

'Oh come on, Bernie,' said Nebe. 'After that press conference? Everyone knows you're Iron Front.'

'Let's not talk about that press conference,' said Gennat. 'It was a disaster.'

'All right,' I said. 'Let's not. After all, what's any of it got to do with me finding the killer?'

'The dead girl's parents, Herr and Frau Schwarz have alleged that you have behaved aggressively and unsympathetically toward them because of their politics,' said Izzy. 'Since then, they've alleged that you have been acting on some malicious gossip concerning her moral character.'

'Who told you that? Heinrich Grund, I suppose.'

'Actually, they spoke to me,' said Nebe.

'She was a prostitute,' I told Izzy. 'An amateur, it's true, but a prostitute nevertheless. Call me old-fashioned but I thought that it might just have a bearing on why she was murdered. As well as how. After all, it's not like prostitutes haven't been murdered before in this city. And genital mutilation is something we've come across in cases of lust murder. Even Arthur would admit that much, surely.' I lit a cigarette. I didn't ask permission to do it. I wasn't in that kind of mood. 'But if we are talking politics can I remind everyone – especially you Arthur – that it's not against police regulations to be part of the Iron Front. It is against police regulations to be a member of the Nazi Party or the KPD.'

'I'm not a member of the Nazi party,' said Nebe. 'If Bernie's referring to my belonging to the National Socialist Fellowship of Civil Servants, then that's something different. You don't have to be a member of one to be a member of the other.'

'I feel we're getting off the subject here, a little,' said Izzy. 'What I really wanted to talk about was Herr Schwarz's position as a member of Kurt Daluege's family. Daluege has been mentioned as a possible future police president. For that reason we're keen to avoid any possible embarrassment to him.'

'I thought an election had to happen before that was even a possibility, sir,' I said. 'As a matter of fact, I was counting on it. I believe lots of people are. You included, if I'm not wrong. But maybe that's just me being old-fashioned again. I was under the strong impression that our job was to protect the Republic, not the reputations of thugs like Daluege and Schwarz.'

'Not old-fashioned, Bernie,' said Gennat, 'but perhaps a little naïve. Regardless of what happens in the July election, this country will have to reach some sort of accommodation with the National Socialists. I don't see how else anarchy and chaos are to be avoided in Germany.'

'We just want what's best for the Berlin Police,' added Izzy. 'I think we all do. And it's in the best interests of the Berlin police that this matter is dealt with more sensitively.' Izzy shook his head. 'But you. You are not sensitive, Bernie. You are not diplomatic. You tread heavily.'

'You want me off the case, is that it?' I asked him.

'No one wants you off the case, Bernie,' said Gennat. 'You're one of the best detectives we've got. I should know, I trained you myself.'

'But we think it might be useful to have Arthur on board,' said Izzy. 'To take care of the finer points of community relations.'

'You mean when it comes to speaking to bastards like Otto Schwarz and his wife,' I said.

'Precisely,' said Izzy. 'I couldn't have put it better myself.'

'Well I'd certainly be grateful for any help in that department,' I said, and smiled at Nebe. 'I suppose I'll just have to try my best to conceal my prejudices when I'm speaking to you, Arthur.'

Nebe smiled his crafty smile. He seemed impossible to provoke. 'Since we're all of us on the same side ...'

'Yes, indeed,' I murmured.

'Perhaps you would care to share with us what you have discovered so far.'

I didn't tell them everything, but I told them a lot. I told them about the autopsy and the Protonsil pill and the five hundred marks and how Anita Schwarz had been on the sledge and that I had started to suspect that her probable killer was most likely a Fritz who'd caught a dose of jelly and wanted to get even with a snapper and that he had probably picked Anita Schwarz because her disability made her an easy victim, and that as soon as I spoke to Doctor Kassner at the State Hospital's Urological Clinic I could have a list of possible suspects. I didn't mention I already had one. And I certainly didn't mention what I'd discovered about Joey the Crip.

'You won't get anything out of a doctor,' said Gennat. 'Not even with a court order. He'll sit on his big fat doctor–patient privilege and tell you to go and screw yourself.'

This sounded good coming from a man whose own fat bottom would have been the envy of a pocket battleship.

'And he'll be entitled to do so. As I'm sure you know.'

I stood up and bowed. 'Ordinarily, I'd agree with you, sir. But I think you're forgetting something.'

'Oh? What's that?'

'I think you're forgetting that Arthur's not the only cop in the Alex who can play Prince bloody Charming. I can do that, too. At least, I can when the cause seems even vaguely worthwhile.'

I rang the urological clinic to find out what time it closed and was told five p.m. At four-thirty I filled a Thermos and drove back to Kassner's house in Donhoff Platz. Once there I switched off the engine, poured myself some coffee and started on the papers I'd bought in Reichskanzlerplatz. They were a day old but that didn't seem to matter very much. In Berlin the news was always the same. German Chancellors made. German Chancellors overthrown. And all the while the number of unemployed kept on rising. Meanwhile Hitler raced around the country in his Mercedes-Benz telling people that he was the solution to everyone's problems. I didn't blame those who believed him. Not really. Most Germans just wanted to have something to hope for in the future. A job. A bank that stayed solvent. A government that could govern.

Good schools. Streets that were safe to walk on. Good hospitals. A few honest cops.

At about six-thirty, Doctor Kassner showed up in a new black Horch. I got out and followed him up the steps to his front door. Recognising my face, he started to smile but it quickly faded when he saw my cheap suit and the KRIPO disc in my hand.

'Commissar Gunther,' I said. 'From the Alex.'

'So, you're not Doctor Duisberg, from the Dyestuffs Syndicate.'

'No, sir. I'm a homicide detective. I'm investigating the murder of Anita Schwarz.'

'I thought you looked rather young to be on the board of a company of that size and importance. Well, you'd better come in, I suppose.'

We went up to his apartment. The place was modern. A lot of bleach burr walnut and cream leather and bronzes of naked ladies standing on tiptoe. He opened a cocktail cabinet the size of a sarcophagus and helped himself to a drink. He didn't offer me one. We both knew that I didn't deserve to have a drink. He sat down and put his drink on a scallop-edged wooden coaster that was on a scallop-edged coffee-table. He crossed his legs and silently invited me to sit down.

'Nice place,' I lied. 'Live here alone?'

'Yes. Now what's this all about, Commissar?'

'There was a girl found dead in Friedrichshain Park several nights ago. She'd been murdered.'

'Yes, I read about it in *Tempo*. Terrible. But I don't see—'

'I found one of your Protonsil pills near the body.'

'Ah. I see. And you think one of my patients might be the culprit.'

'It's a possibility I'd like to explore, sir.'

'Of course, it might just be a coincidence. One of my patients walking home from the clinic could have dropped his pills several hours before the body was found.'

'I don't buy that. The pill hadn't been there that long. There was a shower of rain that afternoon. The pill we found was in pristine condition. Then there's the girl herself. She was a juvenile prostitute.'

'Lord, how very shocking.'

'One theory I'm exploring is that the killer may have contracted venereal disease from a prostitute.'

'Thus giving him a motive to kill one. Is that it?'

'It's a possibility I'd like to explore.'

Kassner sipped his drink and nodded thoughtfully.

'So why that stupid pantomime in the clinic?'

'I wanted to see a list of patients you were treating.'

'Couldn't you have asked to see it legitimately?'

'Yes. But you wouldn't have shown it to me.'

'That's quite right, I wouldn't. I couldn't. It would have been unethical.' He smiled. 'So what are you? A memory man? Did you hope to remember every name on the list?'

'Something like that.' I shrugged.

'But there were rather more names than you had bargained for. Which is why you're back here now. And at my home rather than the clinic because you hoped that this might make it easier for me to forget my doctor–patient duty of confidentiality.'

'Something like that, yes.'

'My first duty, Commissar, is to my patients. Some of whom are very dangerously ill. Suppose for a moment that I did share information regarding their true identities with you. And suppose you chose to interview some of them. All of them. I don't know. They might very well feel I'd betrayed their confidence. They might never again return to the clinic to complete their treatment. In which case they might very easily go and infect someone else. And so on, and so on.' He shrugged. 'You do see what I mean? I regret the murder of anyone. However I do have to be mindful of the bigger picture.'

'Here's my bigger picture, Doctor Kassner. The person who killed Anita Schwarz is a psychopath. She was horribly mutilated. The kind of person who kills like that usually does it again. I want to find this maniac before that happens. Are you prepared to have another murder on your conscience?'

'You make a very fair point, Commissar. It's quite a dilemma, isn't it? Perhaps the best thing would be to put the matter before the Prussian Medical Ethics Committee and let them decide.'

'How long would that take?'

Kassner looked vague. 'A week or two? Perhaps a month.'

'And what do you think they would decide?'

He sighed. 'I would never like to second-guess a medical ethics committee. I'm sure it's the same in the police. There are always proper procedures to be observed. Although they don't really seem to have been observed here. I wonder what your superiors would make of your conduct towards me?' He shook his head. 'But, let us suppose that the committee turns down your request. That's a realistic possibility, I think. What could you do then? I suppose you could try to interview everyone coming in and out of the clinic. Of course, it's only a small percentage who are in the clinical trial. The vast majority of my patients – and I do mean a vast majority, Commissar – is still using Neosalvarsan. And what would happen then? Why you would frighten people away, of course, and we would have an epidemic of venereal disease in Berlin. As things stand now, we are barely controlling the disease. There are tens of thousands of people in this city suffering from jelly, as you call it. No, Commissar, my own suggestion to you would be to try to find a separate line of inquiry. Yes sir, I do believe that would be the best thing for all concerned.'

'You make some good points, Doctor,' I said.

'I'm so glad you think so.'

'However, when I was in your office I couldn't help noticing that one of the addresses on your list of patients using Protonsil is this address. Perhaps you'd care to comment on that.'

'I see. That was very sharp of you, Commissar. I suppose you think that might make me a suspect.'

'It's a possibility I can't afford to ignore, sir.'

'No, of course not.' Kassner finished his drink and got up to pour himself another, but I still wasn't on his list of people he wanted to have a drink with. 'Well then, it's like this. It's not uncommon for doctors to infect themselves with a disease they're trying to cure.' He sat down again, burped discreetly behind his glass and then toasted me silently.

'Is that what you're saying, Doctor? That you deliberately infected yourself with a venereal disease to test Protonsil on yourself?'

'That's exactly what I'm saying. Sometimes it's not enough to test the side effects of a drug on other people. They are less able to describe the full effects of a drug on the human body. As I believe I stated when first we met, it's rather difficult to keep tabs on patients in these cases. Sometimes the only patient one can really trust is oneself. I'm sorry if you think that makes me a suspect, but I can assure you that I've never murdered anyone. As it happens though, I believe I can supply an alibi for the day and night of that poor girl's death.'

'I'm delighted to hear it.'

'I was attending a urologist's conference, in Hanover.'

I nodded and took out my cigarettes. 'Do you mind?'

He shook his head and sipped some of his drink. The alcohol hit his stomach and made it start rumbling.

'Here's what I'd like to suggest, Doctor. Something that might help this inquiry. Something you might like to do voluntarily that wouldn't offend your sense of ethics.'

'If it's within my power.'

I lit my cigarette and leaned forward so I was in range of the scallop-edged ashtray.

'Have you ever had any psychiatric training, sir?'

'Some. As a matter of fact I did my medical training in Vienna and went to several lectures on psychiatry. Once I even considered working in the field of psychotherapy.'

'If you are agreeable, I'd like you to look over all your own patient notes. See if there's any one of them who perhaps stands out as a possible murderer.'

'And supposing there was? One patient who stood out. What then?'

'Why, then we could discuss the matter. And perhaps discover some mutually acceptable way forward.'

'Very well. I can assure you I've no desire to see this man kill again. I have a daughter myself.'

I glanced around the apartment.

'Oh, she lives with her mother, in Bavaria. We're divorced.'

'I'm sorry.'

'Don't be.'

'And the man who was here when I called earlier on today?'

'Ah, you must mean Beppo. He's a friend of my wife's and came to collect some of her things in his car. He's a student, in Munich.' Kassner yawned. 'I'm sorry, Commissar, but it's been a very long day. Is there anything else? Only I'd like to take a bath. You can't imagine how much I look forward to taking a bath after a day in the clinic. Well, perhaps you *can* imagine.'

'Yes sir, I can imagine it quite well enough.'

We parted, more or less cordially, but I wondered just how cordial Kassner would have been if I'd mentioned Josef Goebbels. There was nothing around the apartment to indicate Kassner was a Nazi. On the other hand I couldn't imagine Goebbels taking the risk of being treated by anyone other than a trusted Nazi party member. Joey wasn't the type to put much faith in things like ethics and professional confidence.

Sadly, there was nothing to suggest that the Nazi party leader in Berlin might actually be a psychopathic murderer, either. A dose of jelly was one thing. The murder and mutilation of a fifteen-year-old girl was quite another.

NINE

BUENOS AIRES. 1950.

I did not open the old KRIPO files that Colonel Montalban had somehow obtained from Berlin. In spite of what I had told him, the details of the case were still quite familiar to me. I knew perfectly well why it was I had been unable to apprehend Anita Schwarz's murderer. But I started work all the same.

I was looking for a missing girl who might just be dead. And I was looking out for one of my old comrades who might just be a psychopath.

Neither of the investigative questions I had been set by the hero-worshipping Argentine policeman seemed likely to get the answer he was looking for. Mostly, I was just looking out for myself. But I went along with his idea, of course. What other choice did I have?

At first I was nervous about playing the part the Colonel had written for me. For one thing, I wanted as little to do with other ex-SS men as possible; and, for another, I was convinced that, in spite of Montalban's assurances, they would be hostile to someone asking a lot of questions concerning events most of them probably wanted to forget. But, more often than not, the Colonel turned out to be right. As soon as I mentioned the word 'passport' it seemed there was nothing that Europe's most wanted war criminals were not prepared to talk to me about. Indeed, sometimes it seemed that many of these creatures actually welcomed the chance to unburden themselves – to talk about their crimes and even to justify them, as if they were meeting a psychiatrist or a priest.

In the beginning, I went to their places of work. Most of the Nazis in Buenos Aires had good, well-paid jobs. They worked for a variety of companies such as the Capri Construction Company, the Fuldner Bank, Vianord Travel, the local Mercedes-Benz plant, the Osram Lightbulb company, Caffetti, Orbis Gas Appliances, the Wander Laboratory, and Sedalana Textiles. A few worked in slightly humbler occupations at the Dürer Haus bookshop in the city centre, the Adam restaurant, and the ABC café. One or two worked for the secret police although these remained – for the moment at least – something of a mystery to me.

A man at work, however, is often a very different person to the man he is at home. It was important that I encountered these men relaxed and off-guard. And, after a short while, I started turning up at their houses and their apartments in true Gestapo fashion, which is to say late at night, or early in the morning. I kept my eyes and ears open and, always, I kept my true opinion of these men a secret. It would hardly have done to give my honest impression of any of them. There were times, of course, when I wanted to unholster the Smith & Wesson given to me by Montalban and put a bullet in an old comrade's head. More commonly, I went away from their homes wondering what kind of country I was in that would give sanctuary to beasts like these. Of course, I already knew, only too well, what kind of country had produced them.

Some were happy, or at least content with their new lives. Some had attractive new wives or mistresses, and sometimes both. One or two were rich. Only a few were filled with quiet regret. But mostly they were ruthlessly unrepentant.

The only sorrow displayed by Doctor Carl Vaernet related to his no longer being able to experiment freely on homosexual prisoners at Buchenwald Concentration Camp. He was quite open about this, his life's 'most important work'.

Vaernet was from Denmark but living with his wife and children at 2251 Uriarte Street, close to the Plaza Italia in the Palermo District of Buenos Aires. Dark, thick-set, with shadowy eyes and a mouth full of pessimism and bad breath, he was operating an endocrinology clinic offering expensive 'cures' to the better-off parents of Argentine homosexuals. A very masculine country, Argentina regarded being *joto* or *pajaro* as a danger to the health of the nation.

'When your Red Cross passport runs out,' I told Vaernet, 'that is, if it hasn't run out already, you will have to apply to the federal police for a special passport. To get this passport you will have to prove that while you have been resident in Argentina you've been a person of good conduct. Friends – if you have any – will have to oblige with testimonials as to your character and integrity. If this proves to be the case, as I'm sure it will, I myself will issue you with the good conduct pass that you can then use to apply to a court of first instance for an Argentine passport. Naturally, the passport can be in a different name. The important thing is that you will be able to travel freely again in Europe like any normal Argentine citizen, without fear of arrest.'

'Well, of course, we'd like to visit our eldest son, Kjeld, in Denmark,' confessed Vaernet. He smiled at the thought of it. 'Much as we love it here in Buenos Aires, home is always home, eh, Herr Hausner?'

We were sitting in the drawing room. There was a baby grand piano with a number of framed photographs on the lid. One of the photographs was of the Peróns and their poodles – Eva holding the black one, Juan holding the white – together looking like an advertisement for Scotch whisky.

Vaernet's wife served tea and *facturas*, little sweet pastries that were very popular with the sweet-toothed *porteños*. She was tall, thin and nervous. I took out a pad of paper and a pen and tried to appear properly bureaucratic.

'Date and place of birth?' I asked.

'April 28th, 1893. Copenhagen.'

'My own birthday is April 20th,' I said. When he looked blank, I added, 'The Führer's birthday.' It wasn't true of course, but it was always a good way of making men like him think that I was some kind of die-hard Nazi and, therefore, someone to be trusted.

'Of course. How silly of me not to remember.'

'That's all right. I'm from Munich.' Another lie. 'Ever been to Munich?'

'No.'

'Lovely city. At least it was.'

After a short series of anodyne questions, I said, 'Many Germans have come to Argentina believing that the government is not interested in their backgrounds, that it doesn't care what a man did in Europe before he arrived in this country. I'm afraid that just isn't true. At least not any more. The government doesn't judge a man for what he did during the war. The past is past. And whatever you've done it certainly won't affect your being able to stay in this country. But I'm sure you'll agree it does have some bearing on who you are now and what kind of citizen you might become. What I'm saying is this: the government doesn't want to issue a passport to anyone who might do something to make themselves an embarrassment to the government. So. You may speak to me in total confidence. Remember, I was an SS officer, like yourself. My Honour is Loyalty. But I do urge you to be candid, Doctor.'

Doctor Vaernet nodded. 'I'm certainly not ashamed of what I did,' he said.

At this his wife got up and left the room, as if the prospect of her husband speaking frankly about his work might be too much for her. The way the conversation turned out, I can't say I blamed her.

'Reichsfuhrer Himmler regarded my attempts to surgically cure homosexuals as work of the greatest national importance to the ideal of German racial purity,' he said, earnestly. 'At

Buchenwald I implanted hormone briquettes into the groins of a number of the pink triangles. All of these men were cured of their homosexuality and released back into normal life.'

There was a lot, lot more of this and while Vaernet struck me as being a thoroughgoing bastard – I never yet met a queer who didn't strike me as someone quite comfortable being that way – I wasn't convinced he was a psychopath of the kind that could have eviscerated a fifteen-year-old, just for the hell of it.

On the piano, next to the picture of the Peróns, was a photograph of a girl who was about the same age as Fabienne von Bader. I picked it up. 'Your daughter?'

'Yes.'

'She goes to the same school as Fabienne von Bader, doesn't she?'

Vaernet nodded.

'Naturally you'd be aware she's disappeared.'

'Yes, of course.'

'Were they friends?'

'No, not really.'

'Has she spoken about it?'

'Yes, but nothing important, you understand. If it had been of any relevance I'd have called the police.'

'Of course.'

He shrugged. 'They asked a lot of questions about Fabienne.'

'They were here?'

'Yes. My wife and I formed the impression that they thought Fabienne had run away.'

'It's what children do, sometimes. Well.' I turned toward the door. 'I had better be going. Thank you for your time. Oh, one more thing. We were talking about proving oneself to be a person of good character.'

'Yes.'

'You're a respectable man, Herr Doctor. Anyone can see that. I shouldn't think that there will be any problems about issuing you with a good conduct pass. No problems at all. However ...'

'Yes?'

'I hesitate to mention it. But you being a doctor ... I'm sure you'll understand why I have to ask this kind of thing. Is there anyone among our old comrades here in Argentina who you think might not be worthy of a good conduct pass? Someone who might potentially bring real disrepute to Argentina?'

'It's an interesting question,' said the doctor.

'I know, and I hate asking it. We're all of us in the same boat after all. But sometimes, these questions have to be asked. How else are we to judge a man if we don't listen to what other people say about him?' I shrugged. 'It might be something that's happened here, or something that happened back in Europe. During the war, perhaps.'

'No, no, you're quite right to ask, Herr Hausner, and I appreciate your confidence. Well then, let me see.' He sipped some tea and thought for a moment. 'Yes. There's a fellow called Eisenstedt, Wilhelm von Eisenstedt, who was an SS captain at Buchenwald. He lives in a house on Monasterio Street and calls himself Fernando Eifler. He's let himself go a bit. Drinks too much. But at Buchenwald he was notoriously and sadistically homosexual.'

I tried to suppress a smile. Eifler had been the man in the dressing gown with whom I'd shared the safe house in Monasterio Street when first I had arrived in Argentina. So that was who and what he was.

'Also, yes, also a man called Pedro Olmos. His real name is Walther Kutschmann and he's another ex-SS captain. Kutschmann was a murderer by anyone's definition of the world. Someone who enjoyed killing for killing's sake.'

Vaernet described Kutchsmann's wartime activities in detail.

'I believe he now works for Osram, the lightbulb company. I can't answer for what kind of man he is today. But his wife, Geralda's, conduct is less than proper in my opinion. She gasses stray dogs for a living. Can you imagine such a thing? What kind of a person could do that? What kind of a woman is it who gasses poor dumb animals for a living?'

I could easily have answered him, only he wouldn't have understood. But I went to see Pedro Olmos anyway.

He and his wife lived on the outskirts of the city near the electrical factory were Pedro Olmos worked. He was younger than I'd imagined, no more than thirty-five, which meant he was in his mid-twenties when he'd been a Gestapo captain in Paris; and little more than a boy when he'd been a lieutenant murdering Jews in Poland as part of a Special Action Group. He had been just eighteen when Anita Schwarz was murdered in 1932, and I thought he was probably too young to be the man I was looking for. But you never can tell.

Pedro Olmos was from Dresden. He had met and married Geralda in Buenos Aires. They had several dogs and cats but no children. They were a good-looking couple. Geralda didn't speak German, which was probably why Pedro felt able to confess that he'd been a lot more than just friendly with Coco Chanel while he was stationed in Paris. He was certainly smooth enough. He spoke excellent Spanish, French, and some Polish, which, he said, was why he was working in Osram's travel department. Both he and Geralda were much exercised about the city's stray-dog population, which was considerable, and they had a grant from the city authorities to round them up and gas them. It did seem an unusual occupation for a woman who described herself as an animal lover. She even took me to their basement and showed me the humane killing facility she used. This was a simple metal hut with a rubber-sealed door that was attached to a petrol generator. Geralda carefully explained that when the dogs were dead she burnt the bodies in their household incinerator. She seemed very proud of her 'humane service' and described it in a way that made me think she'd never heard of such a thing as a gas van. Given Olmos' SS background it wasn't too difficult to imagine that perhaps she had got the idea from her husband.

I asked him the same question I had asked Vaernet. Was there anyone among our old comrades in Argentina who he considered to be beyond the pale.

'Oh yes.' Olmos spoke with alacrity, and I was beginning to realise that among the old comrades there was not much loyalty. 'I can give you the name of just such a man. Probably the most dangerous man I've ever met, anywhere. His name is Otto Skorzeny.'

I tried not to look surprised. Naturally I knew of Otto Skorzeny. Few Germans had not heard of the daring author of Mussolini's mountain-top rescue in 1943. I even remembered seeing photographs of his heavily scarred face in all the magazines when Hitler had awarded him the Knight's Cross. He certainly looked like a dangerous man. The trouble was, Skorzeny did not appear on the list of names that the Colonel had given me and, until Olmos mentioned him, I'd had no idea that he was still alive, let alone living in Argentina. A ruthless killer, yes. But a psychopath? I decided to ask Montalban about him when next I saw him.

Meanwhile, Pedro Olmos had thought of someone else he considered a person undeserving of a good-conduct pass. The ratline, as the Americans called organisations like the Odessa and the Old Comrades, which existed to help Nazis escape from Europe, was beginning to look as though it was well-named. The man Olmos thought of was called Kurt Christmann.

Christmann was interesting to me because he was from Munich and born in 1907, which made him twenty-five at the time of Anita Schwarz's murder. He was forty-three years old, once a lawyer who now worked for the Fuldner Bank on Cordoba Avenue. Christmann lived in a comfortable apartment on Esmeralda and, within five minutes of meeting him, I had marked him down as a definite suspect. He had commanded a killing detail in the Ukraine. For a while I'd been in the Ukraine myself, of course. It gave us something to talk about. Something I could use to help gain his confidence and get him talking.

Fair-haired, with rimless glasses and a musician's slender hands, Christmann wasn't exactly the kind of blond beast you'd have seen striding across the screen in a Leni Riefenstahl movie. He was more the sort you'd have seen walking quietly through a law library with a couple of books under his arm. Until he'd joined the SS in 1942, he'd worked for the Gestapo in Vienna, Innsbruck and Salzburg, and I marked him down as the kind of promotion-hungry, medal-seeking Nazi I'd often met before. Not so much blood and iron as bleach and Bakelite.

'So you were out in Ukraine, too,' he said, going all comradely on me. 'Which part?'

'White Ruthenia. Minsk. Lvov. Lutsk. All over.'

'We were in the southern part,' he said. 'Krasnodar and Stavropol. And in the Northern Caucasus. The action group was headed by Otto Ohlendorf, and Beerkamp. My unit was commanded by an officer named Seetzen. Nice fellow. We had three gas vans at our disposal, two big Saurers and a little Diamond. Mostly it was clearing out hospitals and asylums. The children's homes were the worst. But don't think these were normal healthy kids, mind. They weren't. They were gimps, you know? Feeble-minded, retarded kids. Bedridden, disabled. Better off out of it if you asked me. Especially given the way the Popovs looked after them, which was to say hardly at all. The conditions in some of these places were appalling. In a way, gassing them like we did was a bloody kindness. Putting them out of their misery, we were. You'd have done the same for an injured horse. Anyway, that's the way we looked at it.'

He paused, as if recalling some of the terrible scenes he had witnessed. I almost pitied him. I wouldn't have had his thoughts for anything.

'Mind you, it was still hard work. Not everyone could stick it. Some of the kids would catch on what was happening and we'd have to throw them in the vans. That could be pretty rough. We had to shoot a few who tried to escape. But once they were inside the van and the doors were shut it was pretty quick, I think. They'd hammer on the sides of the truck for a few minutes and that would be it. Over. The more of them we managed to squeeze into the truck, the quicker it would be. I was in charge of that detail between August 1942 and July 1943, by which time we were in general retreat, of course.

'Then I went to Klagenfurt, where I was chief of the Gestapo. Then Koblenz, where I was also head of the Gestapo. After the war I was interned in Dachau, by the Amis, only I managed to escape. Hopeless, they were, the Amis. Couldn't guard a fire. Then it was Rome, and the Vatican, before I ended up here. Right now, I'm working for Fuldner but I'm planning to try the real estate business. There's plenty of money to be made in this city, but I do miss Austria. Most of all I miss the skiing. I was the German police ski-champion, you know.'

'Really?' Clearly I had misjudged him completely. He might have been a murdering bastard but he was a sporting murdering bastard.

'You are right to look surprised, Herr Hausner.' He laughed. 'I've been ill, you see. I was in Brazil before coming here to Argentina and managed to pick up a case of malaria. Really, I've still not recovered full health.' He went into the kitchen and opened the door of a new-looking DiTella refrigerator. 'Beer?'

'No, thanks.' I was particular about who I drank with. 'Not while I'm on duty.'

Kurt Christmann laughed. 'I used to be like you,' he said, opening a beer bottle. 'But now I try to be more like the Argentines. I even take a siesta in the afternoon. People like me and you, Hausner, we're lucky to be alive.' He nodded. 'A passport would be good. But I don't think I'll be going back to Germany. Germany's finished I think, now that the Popovs are there. There's nothing there for me, except perhaps a hangman's noose.'

'We did what we had to do,' I said. 'What we were told to do.' I knew this speech well enough by now. I'd heard it often during the last five years. 'We were just carrying out orders. If we'd refused to obey we would have been shot ourselves.'

'That's right,' agreed Christmann. 'That's right. We were only obeying orders.'

Now that I'd let him run a bit I decided to try to reel the line in.

'Mind you,' I said. 'There were some. A few. A few rotten apples who enjoyed the killing. Who went beyond the normal course of duty.'

Christmann pressed the beer bottle to his cheek and thought for a moment; then he shook his head. 'You know something? I really don't think that's true. Not that I saw, anyway. Maybe it was different in your outfit, but the men I was with in the Ukraine? All of them handled themselves with great courage and fortitude. That's what I miss most. The comradeship. The brothers in arms. That's what I miss the most.'

I nodded, in seeming sympathy. 'I miss Berlin, most of all,' I said. 'Munich, too. But Berlin most of all.'

'You know something? I never went to Berlin.'

'What? Never?'

'No.' He chuckled and drank some more beer. 'I don't suppose I shall ever see it now, eh?'

I went away, full of satisfaction at having done an excellent day's work. It's the people you meet that make being a detective so rewarding. Once in a while you meet a real sweetie, like Kurt Christmann, who restores your faith in medieval justice and vigilantism and other, thoroughly sensible Latin-American practices like strappado and the garrotte. Sometimes it's hard to walk away from people like that without shaking your head and wondering how it ever got to be that bad.

How did it ever get to be that bad?

I think something happened to Germany after the Great War. You could see it on the streets of Berlin. A callous indifference to human suffering. And, perhaps, after all those demented, sometimes cannibalistic killers we had during the Weimar Years, we ought to have seen it coming: the murder squads and the death factories. Killers who were demented but also quite ordinary. Krantz, the schoolboy. Denke, the shopkeeper. Grossmann, the door-to-door salesman. Gormann, the bank clerk. Ordinary people who committed crimes of unparalleled savagery. Looking back at them now they seemed like a sign of that which was to follow. The camp commanders and the Gestapo types. The desk murderers and the sadistic doctors. The ordinary Fritzes who were capable of such dreadful atrocities. The quiet, respectable Mozart-loving Germans whom I was now cast away to live among.

What did it take to murder thousands of children, week in week out? An ordinary person? Or someone who might have done it before?

Kurt Christmann had spent a whole year of his life gassing Ukrainian children. The feeble-minded, the retarded, the bedridden, and the disabled. Children like Anita Schwarz. Perhaps, with him, there had been more to it than just obeying orders. Perhaps he had actually disliked disabled children. Maybe even enough to have murdered one in Berlin. I certainly hadn't forgotten that he was from Munich. I'd always had a strong suspicion that the man I'd been looking for, in 1932, had come from Munich.

TEN

BERLIN. 1932.

There were two men waiting by my car. They were wearing hats and double-breasted suits that were all buttoned up the way you do when you've got more than just a fountain pen in your breast pocket. I told myself they were a little far south to be Ricci Kamm's. A little too smooth, too. Ring members tended to wear broken noses and cauliflower ears the way some men wear watch chains and carry canes. There was all that and the fact that they looked pleased to see me. When you've been in the zoo as long as I have you kind of get to know when an animal is going to attack. It gets all nervous and agitated because, for most people, it's upsetting to kill someone. But these two were calm and self-assured.

'Are you Gunther?'

'That all depends.'

'On what?'

'On what you say next.'

'Someone wants to talk to you.'

'So why isn't someone here?'

'Because he's in the Eldorado. Buying you a drink.'

'Does this someone have a name?'

'Herr Diels. Rudolf Diels.'

'Maybe I'm the shy type. Maybe I don't like the Eldorado. Besides it's a little early for a nightclub.'

'Exactly. Makes it nice and quiet. Somewhere private you can hear yourself think.'

'I get all sorts of strange ideas when I hear myself think,' I said. 'Like maybe there's some point to my existence. But since there isn't, we'd better get along to the Eldorado.'

The Eldorado on Motzstrasse was on the ground floor of a modern building that was in the High Concrete style. Like the old Eldorado, which still existed on Lutherstrasse, the new was a he/she club popular with Berlin high society, expensive prostitutes, and adventurous tourists eager to get a taste of real Berlin decadence. Inside, the club was a facsimile of a Chinese opium den. Only it wasn't just a facsimile. If sex was one reason to visit the Eldorado, then the ready supply of drugs was another. But at that hour of the day the place was more or less deserted. The Bernd Robert Rhythmics had just finished rehearsing and, in the corner beside a copper gong as big as a truck tyre, a youngish man with a largish scar on his face was sharing a bottle of champagne with two girls. I knew they were girls not because of their womanly hands and mani-cured fingernails but because of their private parts, which were easy to see since both girls were naked.

Seeing me arrive in the club with his two double-breasted scouts, the scar-faced man stood up and waved me toward him. He was dark, with a weak chin. I guessed his age was about thirty. His suit looked handmade and he was smoking a Gildemann cigar. He had a woman's lips and his eyebrows were so neat and fine that they almost looked plucked and then drawn in with a pencil. His eyes were brown with long lashes. His hands were womanish, too, and but for the scar and the company he was keeping, I might have wondered if he was a bit warm. But he was polite and welcoming, which made me wonder how he'd come by his scar.

'Herr Gunther,' he said. 'I'm glad you came. This is Fraulein Oloffson, and Fraulein Larsson. They are both on holiday from Sweden. Aren't you, ladies?' He looked quickly around. 'There's another one somewhere. Fraulein Liljeroth. But I think she must have gone to powder her nose, if you know what I mean.'

I bowed politely. 'Ladies.'

'They're trying to behave like true Berliners,' said Diels. 'Isn't that right, ladies?'

'Nakedness is normal,' said one of the Swedes. 'Desire is healthy. Don't you agree?'

'Here, sit down and have a drink,' said Diels and pushed a glass of champagne toward me.

It was a little early for me but, noting the label and the year on the bottle, I drank it anyway.

'What can I do for you, Herr Diels?'

'Please. Call me Rudi. And by the way, you can speak quite freely in front of our two lady friends. They don't speak very good German.'

'Neither do I,' I said. 'Only that might have something to do with the fact that my tongue is hanging out of my mouth.'

'Ever been here before?'

'Once or twice. But I don't get any kick out of guessing whether someone's a man or a woman.' I nodded at Fraulein Oloffson. 'It makes a pleasant change to have any doubts on that score removed so unequivocally.'

'You'd better enjoy it while you can. In just a month or two a lot of these clubs are going to be closed down by the new government. This one is already earmarked to be the Nazi Party headquarters in Berlin South.'

'You're taking a lot for granted. There's the small matter of an election to be fought first.'

'You're right. It is a small matter. The National Socialists may not manage to win an outright majority in the Reichstag but it seems more than probable that they will be the largest party.'

'They?'

'I'm not a party member, Herr Gunther, but I am broadly sympathetic to the cause of National Socialism.'

'Is that how you got those scars on your face? By being broadly sympathetic to the Nazis?'

Diels touched his cheek without any trace of self-consciousness. 'This?' He shook his head. 'No. I'm afraid there wasn't much honour in the way they were earned. I used to drink a lot. More than was good for me. Sometimes, when I wanted to amuse or intimidate someone, I would chew a beer glass.'

There was a bowl of fruit on the table. I nodded at it. 'Me, I prefer a nice apple,' I said, and lit a cigarette. Leaning back in my chair, I took a good look at our two naked companions. I didn't mind looking at them any more than they minded being looked at.

'Help yourself.'

'No, thanks. Some of my concentration is still caught up with the fate of the Republic.'

'That's too bad, because the Republic's days are numbered. We're going to win.'

'So it's "we" now. A minute ago you weren't even in the party. I guess you must be what's called a floating voter.'

'You mean like Rosa Luxemburg?' Diels smiled at his own little joke. 'Oh, I'm not much of a Hitlerite,' he said, 'but I do believe in Hermann Goering. He's a much more impressive figure than Hitler.'

'He's certainly a larger one.' It was my turn to smile at my little joke.

'Hitler cares nothing for human life,' continued Diels, 'but Goering is different. I work for him, in the Reichstag. After the Nazis come to power Goering is going to be in overall charge of the police in Germany. Kurt Daluege is going to be in charge of the uniformed police. And I'm going to be in charge of a much expanded political police.'

'The number of people wanting to join the police these days. And we haven't even had a recruiting drive.'

'We're going to need men we can trust. Good men who are prepared to devote body and soul to the fight against Jewry and Bolshevism. But not just against Jewry and Bolshevism.

It's imperative that the power of the SA be curtailed, too. Which is where you come in.'

'Me? I don't see how I can be of any use to you. I don't even like the political police we've got now.'

'You're well known in KRIPO as someone who dislikes the SA.'

'Everyone in KRIPO dislikes the SA. Everyone who's worth a damn.'

'That is what I'm looking for. To get rid of the SA we'll need men who aren't afraid. Men like you.'

'I can see your dilemma. You need the SA to strong-arm the election. But once you're elected you need someone else to strong-arm it back into line.' I grinned. 'I have to hand it to you. There's sophism and then there's Nazism. Hitler adds a whole new section to that part of the dictionary that deals with specious argument and dirty dealing.' I shook my head. 'I'm not your man, Herr Diels. Never will be.'

'It would be a real shame if the force was to lose a man of your forensic capabilities, Herr Gunther.'

'Wouldn't it just? But there it is.'

The third Swede came back from powdering her nose. Like her two friends, she was as naked as a hatpin without a hat. Obviously bored, the other two got up from the table and went over to her. They put their arms around her and, slowly, they began to dance to some silent music. They looked like the Three Graces.

'They really are tourists, you know,' he said. 'Not demi-castors, or half-silks, or whatever you cops call them. Just three girls on holiday from Stockholm, who felt like being true Berliners and taking off their clothes for the sheer hell of it.' He sighed. 'I think it will be a real shame when this kind of thing is gone. But things have to change. It can't be allowed to go on like this. The vice, the prostitution, the drugs. It's corrupting us.'

I shrugged.

'You're a cop,' he said. 'I thought you would surely agree with me about that, at least.'

Two of the band came back and started to play gently, for the benefit of the impromptu floor show.

'You're not from Berlin, are you Herr Diels? In Berlin we say that you should leave another man's moustache alone, even if it droops into his coffee cup. That's why the Nazis will never do well in this city. Because you people can't leave another man's moustache alone.'

'That's an unusual attitude for a policeman. Don't you want to make councillor, or director? You could, you know, the minute this election is over. Everyone is going to want to help us then, but you're in a position to help us now. When it really counts.'

'I told you. I'm not interested in being a part of your expanded political police.'

'I'm not talking about that. I mean that you could stay on, in Department IV. That you could keep doing what you're doing now. It's not like you're a communist or anything. We can easily overlook something like the Iron Front.' He shrugged innocently. 'No, all you would have to do is a favour for us.'

'What kind of favour?' I asked, intrigued.

'We want you to drop the Schwarz case.'

'I'm a police officer, Herr Diels. I can't do that. I've been ordered to investigate a murder and it's my duty to carry out that investigation to the best of my abilities.'

'You were ordered to do it by people who won't be around for much longer. Besides, we both know that in this city there are lots of cases that remain unsolved.'

'I go slow, is that it? So Goebbels can accuse Grezinski and Weiss of sparing the horses because the victim's old man is a big noise in the SA?'

'No, it's nothing like that. The Schwarz girl was disabled. She had a bad leg. Like Goebbels. It's a little embarrassing for him to have this kind of issue in the public eye. It magnifies it, somewhat. Anita Schwarz had a bad leg. That reminds people that Goebbels has one, too. Doctor Goebbels would be greatly in your debt if the Schwarz case could be driven into a sand dune, so to speak.'

'Is Joey's foot the only reason he'd like this case to go nowhere?'

Diels looked puzzled. 'Yes. What other reason could there be?'

It seemed imprudent to mention just how much I knew about the true extent of Joey's current disabilities. 'And what if another girl gets murdered in similar circumstances. What then?'

'So you investigate it. Just lay off the Schwarz case. That's all I'm asking. Just until after the election.'

'To spare Joey's feelings.'

'To spare Joey's feelings.'

'You make me think that maybe there's a lot more to this case than I realised before.'

'It might be unhealthy to think that. For you – and your career.'

'My career?' I laughed. 'That really keeps me awake at night.'

'At least you are still awake at night, Herr Gunther.' He grinned and blew on the end of his cigar. 'That's something, isn't it?'

I'd heard all I wanted to hear. I reached for the fruit bowl, picked out a nice golden apple and stood up.

The three naked women were now too caught up in themselves to pay me any regard and it was looking like a proper floorshow that Berliners would have paid good money to sit and watch.

'Hey you,' I said. 'Aphrodite.'

I tossed the apple and one of them caught it. Naturally she was the best looking of the three Swedes. 'My name is not Aphrodite,' she said, dully. 'It is Gunila.'

I didn't say anything back. I just walked away with my clothes and my sense of humour and my classical education. It was a lot more than she had.

Outside I crossed the road and bought some cigarettes. In front of the tobacconist's there were six men wearing placards for the forthcoming election. One was for Bruner and the SPD, two of them were for Thalmann and the communists, and three of them were for Hitler. All in all, the prospects for the Republic were looking no better than my own.

In 1932 I didn't go to the cinema theatre very much. Maybe if I had I might not have been tricked so easily. I'd heard about Fritz Lang's film *M* because there was a detective in it who was supposedly based on Ernst Gennat. Certainly Gennat thought that was the case. But with one thing and another I'd missed the film when it came out. It was still showing at my local Union Theatre but, in summer there always seemed to be something more important to do than to spend an evening watching a movie. Like investigate a murder. The night before it happened I'd been up all night checking out political killings in Wedding and Neukölln. The descriptions given by witnesses were predictably vague. But then all murderers look the same when they're wearing brown shirts. That's my excuse. One thing was for sure. The people who ambushed me must have seen the movie.

As I walked out of my apartment building a small boy ran up to my car. I wasn't sure if I'd seen the boy before but even if I had I'm not sure I'd have recognised him. All boys in the Scheunvierte looked much the same. This one was shoeless with short blond hair and bright blue eyes. He wore grey shorts, a grey shirt, and sported a number eleven of snot on his upper lip. I guessed him to be about eight years old.

'A girl I know just went off with a strange man,' he said. 'Her name is Lotte Friedrich and she's twelve years old and the Fritz isn't from around here. Creepy-looking dad he was, with a funny look on his shine. He's the same schlepper who tried to give my sister some sweets yesterday if she'd go for a walk with him.' The boy tugged my sleeve urgently and pointed west along Schendelgasse until I agreed to look. 'See them? She's wearing a green dress and he's wearing a coat. See?'

Sure enough, crossing Alte Schonhauserstrasse were a man and a girl. The man had his hand on the girl's neck, like he was steering her somewhere. Wearing a coat seemed just a little suspicious as the day was already a warm one.

Ordinarily I might have been more suspicious of the boy. But then it wasn't every month that an adolescent girl turned up dead with half of her insides removed. Nobody wanted that to happen again.

'What's your name, sonny?'

'Emil.'

I gave him ten pfennigs and pointed in the direction of Bulow Platz.

'You know that armoured car outside the Red HQ?'

Emil nodded and wiped the snot onto the back of his shirt-sleeve.

'I want you to go and tell the SCHUPO in the armoured car that Commissar Gunther from the Alex is following a suspect onto Mulackstrasse and requests them to come and give him support. Got that?'

Emil nodded again and ran off in the direction of Bülow Platz.

I walked quickly west, unholstering my Parabellum as I went because as soon as I had crossed onto Mulackstrasse I would be in the heart of Always True's territory. I might have lacked caution but I wasn't stupid.

The man and the girl ahead of me were walking briskly, too. I quickened my pace and came onto Mulackstrasse just in time to hear a scream and see the man pick the girl up under his arm before ducking into the Ochsenhof. At this point I should probably have waited for the Twenty-First Brigade and its armoured car. Only I was still thinking about Anita Schwarz and the girl in the green dress. Besides when I looked back at where I had come from there was still no sign of the cavalry. I took out my whistle, blew it several times, and waited for some sign that they were coming. But nothing happened. Either the Twenty-First didn't care for the idea of chasing a suspect into the most lawless part of Berlin, or they just didn't believe the story Emil had told them. Probably it was a combination of the two.

I worked the slide on the Parabellum and went in a narrow door and up a darkened stair.

The Ochsenhof, also known as the Roast, or the Cattle Shed, was home to some of the worst animals in Berlin. A so-called rent barracks that occupied three acres, it was a slum tenement from the last century with more entrances and exits than a lump of Swiss cheese. Rats ran along the balconies at night and were hunted for sport by dogs and feral children with air rifles. Cellar dives housed illegal stills while, on the granite back courts that were laughingly called 'greens', packing-case colonies of huts housing some of the city's many homeless and unemployed squatted under lines of grey washing. On a dark, foul-smelling gas-lit stairwell I found a group of young men already playing cards and sharing stumps of cigarette ends.

I looked at the card players and they looked at the nine-millimetre ace I was holding in my hand.

'Did any of you see a man come in here just now?' I asked. 'He was wearing a light-coloured coat and a hat. With him was a girl of about twelve wearing a green dress. He might have been abducting her.'

Nobody said anything. But they were still listening. It pays to listen when it's a man with a gun who's doing the talking.

'Maybe she's got a brother, like you,' I said.

'Nobody's got a brother like him,' quipped a voice.

'Maybe he'll be upset if his little sister gets sliced up and eaten by some rent barracks cannibal,' I said. 'Think about that.'

'Cops,' said another voice in the half-darkness. 'They're the last people in Berlin who still care about anything.'

The dealer jabbed a thumb over his shoulder. 'They went across the green.'

I ran up some steps and out onto the back court. It looked like a heavy, grey stone frame for the brilliantly blue sky. Something zipped past my left ear and I heard a bang as loud as a truck backfiring an eight-millimetre rifle bullet. Half a second later my brain registered the subliminal image of a flash from the third floor balcony and impelled my body to take cover behind some bed sheets that were flapping on a clothesline. I didn't stay put. As soon as I had crawled several metres on my hands and knees I heard another gunshot and something flicked through the sheet I'd been kneeling behind. I scrambled to the end of the line of washing and then sprinted like Georg Lammers into the relative safety of another stairwell. Several ragged-looking men cowering in the shadows stared at me fearfully. Ignoring them, I hared up to the third floor. Of a gunman there was no sign unless you counted the sound of a pair of stout shoes descending another set of stairs three or four steps at a time. Angry, I went after the sound of the shoes. Some people had come out onto the Roast balconies to see what all the fuss was about, but the sensible ones stayed quietly in their sties.

Reaching the bottom of the stairwell I paused briefly, and then pushed a couple of planks that were leaning against the wall out onto the court to draw the rifleman's fire. By now I had a good idea that it was a German rifle. The 7.97 Mauser Gewehr 98. During the war I'd heard its voice often enough to know its middle name. The 98 was an accurate enough weapon but it was unsuited to rapid fire on account of its peculiar bolt arrangement. And, in the several seconds it took for him to put another one up the spout I was out of the stair-well and shooting. There's nothing slow about a nine-millimetre Parabellum.

The first shot missed him. The second, too. By the time the Parabellum was ready for a fourth I was close enough to see the pattern on his bow tie. This matched the pattern on his shirt, and the pattern on his coat. Red spots aren't normally a favourite of mine but on him they looked just fine. Especially as their source was the hole I'd made in his face. He was dead before he hit the concrete.

This was unfortunate, for two reasons. One was that I hadn't killed anyone since August 23rd 1918 when I shot an Australian at the Battle of Amiens. Possibly more than one. When the war was over I promised myself I'd never kill anyone again. The second reason it was unfortunate was that I'd wanted to question the dead man and find out who had put him up to killing me. Instead, I had to go through his pockets and all under the curious eyes of a gathering crowd of rent-barrack vultures.

He was tall, thin and losing his hair. He had already lost his teeth. At the moment of his death his tongue must have forced one of the plates from his mouth and now it sat on his upper lip like a pink, plastic moustache.

I found his wallet. The dead man's name was Erich Hoppner and he was a member of the Nazi Party since 1930. His membership card stated that his number was 510,934. None of that meant he wasn't also a member of the Always True gang. It wasn't unusual for gangsters from Berlin's underworld to be contracted and paid to carry out political murders. The question was, who had ordered my murder? The Always True for what I had done to Ricci Kamm, or the Nazis for what I hadn't done for Josef Goebbels?

I took Hoppner's wallet – and his rifle and his watch and his ring – and left him there. The vultures were already taking his false teeth as I walked out of the Ochsenhof. False teeth were an expensive luxury for the kind of folk who lived in the Roast.

On Bülow Platz the PHWM in charge of the SCHUPO troop stationed there denied ever having received a message from a small boy to come to my aid. I told him to take some of his men and go and mount a guard on Hoppner's body before it was eaten. Reluctantly, he agreed.

I went back to the Alex. First I visited the Record Department of Inspectorate J, where the criminal secretary on duty helped me discover that Erich Hoppner didn't have a criminal record. This was surprising. Then I went upstairs and handed over Hoppner's party card to the political boys in D1a. Naturally they'd never heard of him either. Then I sat down and typed out a statement and gave it to Gennat. After I'd handed in my report I was asked into an interview room and questioned by Gennat and two police councillors, Gnade and Fischmann. My statement was then filed for later comparison with the findings of an independent homicide team. More paperwork followed. Then I was interviewed again, by KOK Muller who was leading the investigating homicide team.

'Sounds like they led you on a nice little trot,' observed Muller. 'And you never saw the girl in the green dress again?'

'No. And after the shooting, I didn't see any point in looking for her.'

'And the boy? Emil? The one who fed you the sugar lump?'

I shook my head.

Muller was a tall man with lots of hair, only it was all on the sides of his head with none of it on top, as if he had grown through it like a rubber plant.

'They had you measured pretty well,' he said. 'They did everything but chalk a letter M on the dead man's coat for you. Like in that movie with Peter Lorre. It's the kid in the movie who tips off the cop about Lorre.'

'Haven't seen it.'

'You should get out more.'

'Sure. Maybe I'll buy a horse.'

'See the sights.'

'I've seen them already. Besides, maybe I see too much as it is. Soon it's going to be unhealthy to be a cop with good eyesight in this country. That's what people keep telling me, anyway.'

'You talk like the Nazis were going to win the election, Bernie.'

'I keep hoping they won't. And I keep worrying that they might. But I've got seven loaves and five fishes telling me the Republic needs more than just a lucky break this time. If I wasn't a cop I might believe in miracles. But I am and I don't. In this job you meet the lazy, the stupid, the cruel, and the indifferent. Unfortunately that's what's called an electorate.'

Muller nodded. He was an SDP man like me. 'Hey, did you hear the good news? About Joey Clovenhoof? His new wife Magda's apartment got screened. Her jewels were lifted.' Muller was grinning. 'Can you credit it?'

'Credit it? They should give whoever did it the Blue Max.'

I needed a drink, I needed some female company, and I probably needed a new job. As things turned out, I went to the best place for all three. I went to the Adlon Hotel. Inside the sumptuous lobby I looked around for Frieda. Instead I found Louis Adlon. He was wearing a white tie and tails and, in his lapel, a white carnation that matched his moustache. He wasn't a tall man but he was every inch a gentleman.

'Commissar Gunther,' he said. 'How nice to see you. And you must think me rude for not writing to thank you for the way you dealt with that thug. But I was hoping to run into you and thank you in person.' He pointed to the bar. 'Do you have a minute?'

'Several.'

In the bar Adlon waved for service but it was already on its way, like a small express train. 'Schnapps for Commissar Gunther,' he said. 'The best.'

We sat down. The bar was quiet. The old man poured two glasses to the brim and then toasted me silently.

'There's an old Confucian curse that says "May you live in interesting times". I'd say these were very interesting times, wouldn't you?'

I grinned. 'Yes, sir, I would.'

'Given that, I just wanted you to know that there is always a job for you here.'

'Thank you, sir. It might just be that I take you up on that offer.'

'No, sir. Thank *you*. It may interest you to know that your superior, Doctor Weiss, speaks very highly of you.'

'I didn't know you two knew each other, Herr Adlon.'

'We're old friends. It was he who led me to suppose that the police service may soon change in ways we do not yet care to imagine. For that reason I felt able to make you an offer like this. Most of the house detectives here are, as you know, retired policemen. The incident in the bar proved to me that one or two of them are no longer equal to the task.'

We sipped the excellent schnapps for a while and after that he went to have dinner with his wife and some rich Americans, while I went to find Frieda. I found her on the second floor, on a corridor leading to the hotel's Wilhelmstrasse extension. She was wearing an elegant black evening gown. But not for long. The smaller, less expensive rooms were on that floor. These had views of the Brandenburg Gate and, beyond it, the Victory Column on Konigsplatz. But I had the best view of all. And I wasn't even looking out of the window.

I was trying to avoid Arthur Nebe. This had been easy while I was checking through the list of suspects I had compiled using the Devil's Directory, but it was always more difficult when I was in the Alex. Still, Nebe wasn't the kind of cop who liked leaving his desk very much. He did most of his detective work on the telephone and, for a while, by not answering mine, I managed not to speak to him at all. But I knew it couldn't last, and a couple of days after the shooting I finally ran into him on the stairwell outside the washrooms.

'What's this?' said Nebe. 'Has someone else been shooting at you?' He put his fingers in some old bullet holes in the walls of the stairwell. We both knew they'd been there since 1919, when the Freikorps had taken the Alex back by force from the left-wing Spartakists. It was a very German occasion. 'If you're not careful you're going to spend the rest of your life dead.' He smiled. 'So, what's the story?'

'No story. Not in this town anyway. A Nazi thug took a pot-shot at me, that's all.'

'Any idea why?'

'I figured it was because I'm not a Nazi,' I said. 'But maybe you can tell me.'

'Erich Hoppner. Yes. I checked him out. It doesn't look particularly political, since you mention it.'

'How can you tell?'

'You're not KPD. He wasn't SA.'

'But he was a Nazi party member.'

'Lots of people are party members, Bernie. In case you hadn't noticed. At the last count, there were eleven and a half million people who voted for the party. No, I'd say this has more to do with what happened to Ricci Kamm. The Roast is in the heart of Always True territory. You were asking for trouble going in there.'

'At the time I had the quaint idea I might be preventing it. Trouble, I mean. That's what we cops call it when a real person gets murdered. Not some thug with an ideology.'

'For the record,' said Nebe. 'And between you and me? I don't like the Nazis. It's just that I like the communists a little less. The way I see it, it's going to come down to a choice between them and the Reds.'

'Whatever you say, Arthur. All I know is that it's not the Reds who have been threatening me. Telling me to lay off the Schwarz case so we can spare the feelings of Josef Goebbels's crummy foot. It's the Nazis.'

'Oh? Who, in particular?'

'Rudolf Diels.'

'He's Fat Hermann's man, not Joey's.'

'They're all the same bastard to me, Arthur.'

'Anything else you want to tell me? About the Schwarz case, I mean. How's that coming along?'

I smiled bitterly. 'A murder investigation works like this, Arthur. Sometimes the worst has to happen first before you can hope for the best.'

'Like another murder, you mean?'

I nodded.

Nebe was silent for a moment. Then he said, 'I can understand that. Anyone can. Even you.'

'Me? What do you mean, Arthur?'

'Sometimes the worst has to happen before you can hope for the best? That's the only reason anyone is going to vote for the Nazis.'

Looking up from his typewriter, Heinrich Grund could hardly conceal his disgust. 'There's some Jew looking for you,' he said, as I returned to my desk.

'Really? Did this Jew have a name?'

'Commissar Paul Herzefelde. From Munich.' He uttered the name Paul Herzefelde with sneering lip and wrinkled nose as if he was describing something on the sole of his shoe.

'And where is the Commissar now?'

Grund pointed into the air above our heads. 'The Excelsior,' he said.

The Alex had once been a barracks for the Prussian police and the Excelsior was what cops called that part of the building that still existed to accommodate policemen who were working late or who were visiting Berlin from outside the city.

'They won't like it,' said Grund.

'Who won't like what?'

'The other lads. In the Excelsior. They won't like having to share their quarters with a Jew.'

I shook my head wearily. 'Doesn't your mouth hurt sometimes? On account of the nasty things that come out of it? The man's a brother police officer, for Christ's sake.'

'For Christ's sake?' Grund looked sceptical. 'For Christ's sake, his kind did nothing. That's the point, isn't it? The Jews wouldn't be in the spot they're in now, if they'd recognised our Lord for what he was.'

'Heinrich? You're the kind of rotten cop that gives rotten cops a bad name.' I thought of something Nebe had said, and borrowed it. 'And it's not that I love Jews. It's that I love anti-Semites just that little bit less.'

I went upstairs to find Herzefelde. After Heinrich Grund's bigotry I don't know what sort of man I expected to meet. It wasn't that I was expecting to see a cop with a phylactery strapped to his forehead and a prayer shawl wrapped around his shoulders. Just that Paul Herzefelde wasn't what I was expecting. I suppose I thought he might look a bit more like Izzy Weiss. Instead he looked more like a film star. Well over six feet tall, he was a handsome man with grey, wiry hair and thick dark eyebrows. His hard, shiny suntanned face looked as if it had been made by a diamond cutter. Paul Herzefelde had as much in common with the kind of swarthy fat Jew wearing a top hat and coat tails beloved of Nazi caricaturists as Hitler had in common with Paul von Hindenburg.

'Are you Commissar Herzefelde?'

The man nodded. 'And you are?'

'Commissar Gunther. Welcome to Berlin.'

'Not so as I noticed.'

'I'm sorry about that.'

'Skip it. To be honest with you, Munich is a hell of a lot worse.'

'Then I'm glad I don't live in Munich.'

'It has its moments. Especially if you like a beer.'

'The beer's pretty good in Berlin, too, you know.'

'I wouldn't know.'

'Then how about we go have one and you can find out?'

'I thought you'd never ask, copper.'

We went to the Zum Pralaten, in the arches of the S-Bahn station. It was a good place to drink beer and popular with cops from the Alex. About every ten minutes a train passed overhead and, since there was no point in saying anything while this was happening, you could give your mouth a rest and concentrate on the beer.

'So what brings you to Berlin?'

'Bernhard Weiss. We kike cops have to stick together. We were thinking of starting our own yid union. Trouble is, with so many Jewish cops, it's knowing where to begin.'

'I can imagine. Actually, Berlin's not so bad. The reds do better here than the Nazis. Thalmann got twenty-nine percent in the last election compared to Hitler's twenty-three.'

Herzefelde shook his head. 'Unfortunately Berlin is not Germany. I don't know how things are for Jews in this town but in the south they can be pretty rough. Back home in Munich there's hardly a day passes when I don't get some kind of death threat.' He swallowed some beer and nodded his appreciation. 'As a matter of fact, that's why I was speaking to Weiss. I've been thinking of moving here, with my family.'

'You mean, be a cop? Here in Berlin?'

Herzefelde smiled. 'Weiss was similarly appalled. It looks like I'm going to have to consider my plan B. Something that's got nothing to do with government.'

'I've been sort of looking around myself.'

'You? But you're not a Jew, are you?'

'No. I'm SDP. Iron Front. A Weimar die-hard who dislikes the Nazis.'

Herzefelde raised his glass and toasted me. 'Then here's to you, comrade.'

'So, do you have a plan B yet?'

'Thought I might go private.'

'Here in Berlin?'

'Sure. Why not? If the Nazis get in, I've a feeling there's going to be a lot of missing persons work.'

'Me, I've been offered a job at the Adlon Hotel. House detective.'

'Sounds nice.' He lit a cigarette. 'Going to take it?'

'I thought I'd wait and see what happens in the election.'

'You want my advice?'

'Sure.'

'If you can, stay in the force. Jews, liberals, communists are going to have need of friendly policemen like you.'

'I'll bear it in mind.'

'You'll be doing everyone a favour. God only knows what the police will be like if everyone in it is a lousy Nazi.'

'So. Why did you want to see me?'

'Weiss told me about this case you've been working on. The murder of Anita Schwarz. We had a similar case in Munich. You know Munich?'

'A little.'

'About three months ago, a fifteen-year-old girl turned up dead at the Schloss Park. Just about everything in her pants had been sliced out. The whole bag of love and life. A real neat job, too. Like a surgeon had done it. The dead girl's name was Elizabeth Bremer and she went to the gymnasium in Schwabing. Nice family, too. Her father works at the Customs House, in Landsberger Strasse. Mother's a librarian at some kind of Latin library on Maximilianeum. Weiss told me about your girl. That she was an amateur whore.' Herzefelde shook his head. 'Elizabeth Bremer wasn't anything like that. She was a good student with good prospects. Wanted to be a doctor. About the only thing you could hold against her was an older boyfriend. He was a skating teacher at the Prinzregenten Stadium. That's how they met. Anyway we hauled him over the coals for it but got nothing. He didn't do it. He had a cast-iron alibi for the day of her death and that was that. According to him, they'd stopped seeing each other before she wound up dead. He'd been pretty broken up about it. The way he told it, she'd thrown him over for no good reason other than she caught him reading her diary. So he'd gone back home to Gunzberg, to see his family and get over it.'

Herzefelde waited as an S-Bahn train passed overhead.

'We had a list of possible suspects,' he continued, after the train had gone. 'Naturally we checked them out, but with no luck. I thought the case had gone cold until Weiss told me about your murder victim.'

'I'd like to see that list,' I said. 'That and the rest of the case file.'

'State law forbids me from sending my papers on the case in the mail,' said Herzefelde. 'However, there's nothing to stop you coming to Munich to look them over. You could stay in my house.'

'That would be quite impossible,' I said. 'I couldn't stay in a Jew's house.' I paused, long enough to change the expression on Herzefelde's handsome face. 'Not unless he'd stayed in my house first.' I smiled. 'Come on. Let's go and get your bag from the Alex. You're staying with me tonight.'

ELEVEN

BUENOS AIRES. 1950.

It was lunchtime and the café at the Richmond Hotel was busy with hungry *porteños*. I went down to the basement, found an empty table, and set out a chessboard. I wasn't looking for a game with anyone other than myself. That way I figured I stood a better chance of winning. Also I needed to clear my head of old Nazis and their war crimes for a while. They were starting to get me down.

I tried not to stare at her but this was almost impossible. She was a stunningly beautiful girl. Eyes just naturally followed her around the room like cows trotting after a milk-maid. But mostly it was hard not to stare at her because she seemed to be staring at me. I didn't flatter myself she actually wanted to meet me. I guessed I was old enough to be her father. There had to be some mistake. She was tall and slim with a spectacular waterfall of black curly hair. Her eyes were the shape and colour of chocolate-covered almonds. She wore a tailored tweed jacket buttoned tight at the waist, and a matching long pencil skirt that made me wish I had a couple of sheets of paper. Her figure was all right if you liked them built like expensive thoroughbreds. I happened to like them built that way just fine.

She walked toward me, her high heels perforating the polished wooden air of the Richmond's quiet basement like the slow beat of a tall clock. Expensive perfume tugged an edge of the air I was breathing. It made a very pleasant change from the smell of coffee and cigarettes and my own dyspeptic middle age.

As soon as she spoke to me it was obvious she hadn't mistaken me for someone else. She spoke in Castellano. I was pleased about that. It meant I had to pay extra attention to her lips and the way her small pink tongue rested on her gypsum white teeth.

'Forgive me for interrupting your game, señor,' she said. 'But are you Carlos Hausner, perhaps?'

'I am.'

'Might I sit down and talk to you for a moment?'

I looked around. Three tables away the little Scotsman, Melville, was playing chess with a man whose leathery brown face belonged on the back of a horse. Two younger *porteños* with Cuban heels and silver-buckled belts were engaged in a rather vigorous game of billiards. They put as much vitality into their noisy cue shots as Furtwangler conducting the Kaim Orchestra. All of their eyes were on their respective games but their ears and their attention to the Richmond's resolutely masculine traditions were on us.

I shook my head. 'My opponent, the Invisible Man, gets a little irritated when people sit on his knees. We'd better go upstairs.'

I let her walk ahead of me. It was the polite thing to do and it gave me a chance to study the seams of her stockings. These were straight, as if someone had fixed them using a theodolite. Fortunately her legs were anything but. They had better curves than the Mille Miglia and were probably just as challenging to negotiate. We found a quiet table near the window. I waved a waiter over. She ordered a coffee and I ordered something I had no interest in drinking so long as she was around. When you're having a cup of coffee with the best-looking woman who's spoken to you in months, there are better things to do than drink it. She took one of my cigarettes and let me light her. It was yet another excuse to pay close attention to her big sensuous mouth. Sometimes I think that's why men invented smoking.

'My name is Anna Yagubsky,' she said. 'I live with my parents in Belgrano. My father used to be a musician in the orchestra at the Teatro Colón. My mother sells English ceramics from a shop on Bartolemé Mitre. Both of them are Russian immigrants. They came here before the Revolution, to escape the Tsar and his pogroms.'

'Do you speak Russian, Anna?'

'Yes. Fluently. Why?'

'Because my Russian is better than my Spanish.'

She smiled a little smile and we spoke in Russian.

'I am a legal officer,' she explained. 'I work in an office next to the law courts on Calle Talcahuano. Someone – a friend of mine in the police, it doesn't matter who – told me about you, Señor Hausner. He told me that before the war you were a famous detective, in Berlin.'

'That's right.' I saw no advantage to myself in disagreeing with her. No advantage at all. I was keen to be someone who looked good in her eyes, not least because every time I saw myself in a mirror my own eyes were telling me something different. And I'm not just talking about my appearance. I still had all my hair. There was even quite a bit of colour left in it. But my face was hardly what it was while my stomach was more than it had ever been. I was stiff when I awoke in the morning, in all the wrong places and for all the wrong reasons. And I had thyroid cancer. Apart from all that I was just fine and dandy.

'You were a famous detective and now you're working for the secret police.'

'It wouldn't be much of a secret police if I admitted that was true, now would it?'

'No, I suppose not,' she said. 'Nevertheless, you are working for them, aren't you?'

I smiled my best enigmatic smile – the one that didn't show my teeth. 'What can I do for you, Señorita Yagubsky?'

'Please. Call me Anna. In case you hadn't already guessed, I'm a Jew. That's an important part of my story.'

'I rather supposed you were when you mentioned pogroms.'

'My aunt and uncle went to Germany from Russia. Somehow they survived the war and came to South America in 1945. But Jews were not welcome in Argentina, in spite of the fact there were a lot of Jews living here already. You see this is a fascist, anti-Semitic country. And until recently there existed a secret government directive called Directive Eleven that denied entry visas to all Jews, even those who had family here already, such as my aunt and uncle. But like many other Jews who wanted to live here, they managed to get into Paraguay. And from there, eventually, they were successful in coming across the land border and entering the country illegally. For a while they lived very quietly in a small town called Colón, in the province of Entre Rios, north of Buenos Aires. From time to time my father would go and see them with money, clothes, food, whatever we could spare. And they waited for an opportunity to come and live here in Buenos Aires.

'But then one day, about three years ago, they disappeared. My father went to Colón and found them gone. The neighbours knew nothing about where they had gone or if they did they weren't saying. And because they were illegal, my father couldn't very well go to the police and ask them. Since then, we've heard nothing from them. Nothing at all. For obvious reasons my parents are reluctant to make enquiries about them in case they get into trouble. The Directive may have ended but this is still a military dictatorship and people – opposition people – are sometimes arrested and thrown into prison and never seen again. So we still have no idea if they are alive or dead. What we do know is that they weren't the only illegal Jews who have disappeared. We've heard of other Jewish families who have lost relatives in Argentina but nobody knows anything for sure.' She shrugged. 'Then I heard about you. I heard that you used to look for missing persons in Germany, before the war. And well, it seemed more than likely that some of those missing persons must also have been Jewish. And I thought – no, that's not true, I *hoped* – that you might help. I'm not asking that you do anything very much. In your position you might hear something. Something that might shed a little light on what happened to them.'

'Couldn't you hire yourselves a private detective?' I suggested. 'Or a retired policeman, perhaps.'

'We already tried that,' she said. 'Policemen here are not very honest, Señor Hausner. He robbed us of all our savings and told us nothing.'

'I'd like to help you, Señorita.' I shook my head. 'But I don't know what I could do. Really I don't. I wouldn't know where to start. I don't really know my way around, and I'm still learning the language. Trying to settle in. To make myself feel a little bit at home. You'd be wasting your money. Really.'

'Perhaps I didn't make myself clear. I wasn't offering to pay you, Señor. All my extra money goes to supporting my parents. My father doesn't play much any more. He used to give music lessons but he doesn't have the necessary patience. My mother works in someone else's shop. The pay is not good. The fact is, I hoped you might help me out of the kindness of your heart.'

'I see.'

This was one I hadn't heard before. A request to work *for nothing*. In the ordinary course of things I might have shown her the door. But she was hardly ordinary. Among the many things I had to admire about her already I was now obliged to add her *chutzpah*. But it seemed she hadn't finished telling me what she was prepared to offer in lieu of money. She coloured a little as she told me what this was.

'I can imagine how difficult it might be to settle in to a new life in a new country,' she said. 'It takes time to adjust. To make new friends. You might say that as the daughter of immigrants I have a greater understanding of the challenges that lie ahead of you.' She took a deep breath. 'Anyway. I was thinking that, since I can't afford to pay you, perhaps ... perhaps I might become your friend.'

'Well, that's a new one,' I said.

'Don't get me wrong. I'm not suggesting anything else. No, I was thinking that we might go and see a play, perhaps. I could show you around the city, introduce you to some people. From time to time I might even cook you dinner. Really, I'm very good company.'

'I don't doubt it.'

'In a way, we'd be helping each other.'

'Yes, I can see how you might think that.'

Maybe, if she hadn't been quite so good-looking I might have turned her down. There was also her Jewishness to take into account. I hadn't forgotten the Ukraine in 1941. And the guilt I felt toward all Jewish people. I didn't want to help Anna Yagubsky, but somehow I felt I had to.

'All right, I'll help you.' Stammering a little, I added, 'That is to say, I'll do what I can. I'm not promising anything, you understand. But I will try to help you. I could use a home-cooked dinner now and then.'

'Friends,' she said, and we shook hands.

'Actually, you're the first friend I've made since I got here. Besides, I'd like to do something noble, for once.'

'Oh? Why? I'm curious.'

'Don't be. It doesn't help either of us.'

'What you say makes me think that you think you have to do something noble to atone for something else you did. Something not so noble, perhaps.'

'That's my business. I will tell you this, though, don't ever ask me about it. That's part of my price, Anna. You don't ever ask me about it. All right? Are we agreed?'

She nodded, finally.

'Promise?'

'I promise.'

'All right then. Now, tell me. How did you find me?'

'I told you. I have a friend in the police. As a matter of fact he's the same bastard cop who robbed us of our savings, but he feels guilty about it now and wants to help in any way he can. Unfortunately he has spent all the money. Gambled it away. It was him who told me where you were staying. It wasn't so very difficult I think. It's on your *cedula*. All he had to do was to look it up. I went to your hotel and followed you here.'

'The less this cop knows about what I'm doing the better, as far as I'm concerned.'

She nodded and sipped her coffee.

'Your uncle and aunt. What were their names?'

'Yagubsky, same as mine.' She picked up her bag, found her wallet and handed me a business card. 'Here,' she said. 'That's how you spell it. Their names were Esther and Roman Yagubsky. Roman is my father's twin brother.'

I pocketed the card. 'Three years you say?'

She nodded.

I lit a cigarette and sighed pessimistically.

'Three years is a long time with a missing persons case. Three months, maybe we could find a lead. But three years … And not a word? Not even a postcard?'

'Nothing. We went to the Israeli Embassy to find out if maybe they had emigrated to Israel, but there was no trace of them there, either.'

'Shall I tell you what I think? Honestly?'

'If it's that you think they're probably dead then I agree with you. I'm not an idiot, Señor Hausner. I can read the runes with something like this. But my father is an old man. And a twin. Let me tell you, twins are strange about things like this. My father says he feels Roman is still in Argentina. And he'd like to know for sure, that's all. Is it so much to ask?'

'Maybe. And nothing is ever for sure in this business. You'd better take that on board now. Nothing is ever for sure.'

'Except death,' she said. 'That's about as sure as anything can get, isn't it?'

I nodded. 'You might certainly think that. What I meant was that truth is rarely the truth and the things you thought weren't true often turn out not to be false. I realise that sounds confusing and it was meant to be, because that's the business I'm in. Although I don't want to be in it particularly. Not again. I thought I was finished with the whole dirty process of asking questions I don't get straight answers to. That, and putting myself in harm's way just because someone asks me to look for his lost dog when really they'd lost their neighbour's cat. I thought I was through with it and I'm not, and when I say nothing's for sure in this business I mean it because, generally, I say exactly what I mean. And I'm right, too, because it'll turn out that there was something you didn't tell me that you should have told me, which would have made things clearer right from the start. So, nothing's for sure, Anna. Not when there are people involved. Not when they bring you their problems and ask for your help. Especially then. I've seen it a hundred times, angel. Nothing's for sure. No, not even death when the dead turn out to be alive and well and living in Buenos Aires. Believe me, I know what I'm talking about. If the dead people walking around this city all of a sudden really were dead, the undertakers wouldn't be able to cope with the sudden rush of business.'

Her face had coloured again. Her nostrils had flared. The isosceles of muscles between her chin and her collar-bone had stiffened, like something metallic. If I'd had a little wand I could have used it to tap out the part for triangle in the Bridal Chorus from *Lohengrin*.

'You think I'm lying?' She started gathering her gloves and her handbag as if she was about to climb up to the highest hills of Dudgeon. 'You mean you think I'm a liar.'

'Are you?'

'And I thought we were going to be friends,' she said, her thighs pushing back at the chair underneath her bottom.

I grabbed her wrist.

'Easy on the floor polish,' I said. 'I was just giving you my client speech. The one I use when there's nothing in it for me. It takes a lot longer than a hard slap on the ear and a palm pressed on top of a Holy Bible but, in the end, it saves a lot of time. That way if it does turn out that you're lying you won't hold it against me when I have to warm your cheeks.'

'Are you always this cynical? Or is it just me?' Her bottom stayed on the chair, for now.

'I'm never cynical, Anna, except when I'm questioning the sincerity of human motives.'

'I wonder. What was it that happened to you, Señor Hausner? Something, I don't know, in your own personal history that made you this way.'

'My history?' I grinned. 'You make it sound like it's something that's over. Well it's not. In fact it's not even history. Not yet. And didn't I tell you? Don't ever ask me about it, angel.'

Being sort of a spy myself I swiftly came to the conclusion that what I needed most was the help of another spy. And there was only one person I could trust, almost, in the whole of Argentina, and that was Pedro Geller who had come across on the boat from Genoa with Eichmann and me. He was working for Capri Construction in Tucumán and, since half of the ex-SS men in the country were also working for Capri, enlisting his help seemed like a way of swatting two flies with one newspaper. The only trouble was that Tucumán was more than seven hundred miles to the north of Buenos Aires. So, a couple of days after my meeting with Anna Yagubsky, I took the Mitre Line from the city's Retiro Railway Station. The train, which went via Córdoba and terminated in La Paz, Bolivia, was comfortable enough in first class. But the journey lasted twenty-three hours, so I took the advice of Colonel Montalban and equipped myself with books and newspapers and plenty to eat and drink and smoke. Since the weather in

Tucumán was likely to be warmer than in Buenos Aires and much of the journey there took place at altitude, the doctor had also given me some tranquillisers in case my thyroid problem caused me difficulty in breathing. So far I had been lucky. The only time I'd had difficulty breathing was when Anna Yagubsky had introduced herself to me.

The heating on the train failed soon after we left Retiro and, for most of the journey, I was cold. Too cold to sleep. By the time we reached Tucumán, I was exhausted. I checked into the Coventry Hotel and went straight to bed. I slept for the next twelve hours, which was something I hadn't done since before the war.

Tucumán was the most populous city in the north, with about two hundred thousand people. It sat on a plain in front of some spectacular mountains called the Sierra de Aconquija. There were lots of colonial-style buildings, a couple of nice parks, a government palace, a cathedral, and a statue of liberty. But New York it wasn't. There was a prevailing smell of horse shit in the air of Tucumán. Tucumán wasn't a one-horse town so much as a horse-shit town. Even the soap in my hotel bathroom seemed to smell of it.

Pedro Geller worked at Capri's technical office in Cadillal, a small town about twenty miles outside Tucumán, but we met up in the city at the company's main office on Rio Portero. Given the nature of my mission we didn't stay there for very long. I asked him to let me take him to the best restaurant he could think of and so we went to the Plaza Hotel, close to the cathedral. I made a mental note to stay there instead of the Coventry if ever I was unlucky enough to come to Tucumán again.

Geller, whom I knew better as Herbert Kuhlmann, had been, at twenty-six years old, a captain with an SS Panzer division. During the battle for France in 1944, his unit had executed thirty-six captured Canadians. Geller's commanding officer was now serving a life sentence in a Canadian jail and, fearing an arrest and a similar sentence, he had wisely fled to South America. He looked tanned and fit and seemed to be enjoying his new life.

'Actually the work is rather interesting,' he explained, over a glass of German beer. 'The Dulce River runs for about three hundred miles through Córdoba Province and we're building a dam on it. The Los Quiroga dam. It'll be quite a sight when it's finished, Bernie. Three hundred yards long, fifty metres high, with thirty-two floodgates. Of course it's not exactly popular with everyone. These things rarely are. A lot of local farms and villages will disappear forever under millions of gallons of flood water, but the dam is going to provide water and hydro-electric power for the whole province.'

'How's our more famous friend?'

'Ricardo? He hates it here. He lives with some peasant girl in a small mountain village called La Cocha, about seventy miles south of here. He doesn't come into Tucumán any more than he has to. Scared to show his face I shouldn't wonder. We're both of us working for an old comrade, of course. They're everywhere in Tucumán. He's an Austrian professor by the name of Pelkhofer, Armin Pelkhofer. He's a water engineer. He and Ricardo seem to know each other from the war when he was called Armin Schoklitsch, but I have no idea what he did then that brought him here now.'

'Nothing good,' I said, 'if he knew Ricardo.'

'Quite so. Anyway, we carry out river survey reports for the Prof. Hydrological analysis, that kind of thing. Not much to it really, but I'm out in the fresh air a lot which suits after all those months of hiding out in lofts and basements. I shall miss this. Did I tell you? After another six months here I shall transfer to Capri's personnel department in Buenos Aires.'

We ate some lunch. The steaks were good. The food was always good in Argentina. Just as long as you ordered steak.

'What about you, Bernie? What brings you this far north?'

'I'm working for the police. I'm supposed to be checking

out old comrades. Deciding whether or not they're worthy of the good conduct pass they will need to get an Argie passport. Yours is already in the file.'

'Thanks. Thanks a lot.'

'Don't mention it. To be honest, it's mostly just a cover story so that I can ask some of our old comrades a lot of awkward questions. Like, what did you do in the war, Fritz? The Argies are a bit jumpy that they'll unwittingly hand out a passport to some mass-murdering psycho and that the Amis will find out about it and kick up an international fuss.'

'I see. Tricky stuff.'

'I was hoping you might help, Herbert. After all, it goes without saying that Capri – the *Compañía Alemana Para Recién Immigrados* – is the largest employer of ex-SS in the country.'

'Of course I'll help,' said Geller. 'You're just about my only friend in this country, Bernie. Well, there's you, and a girl I met back in Buenos Aires.'

'Good for you, kid. Apart from Ricardo, who else have you come across who might be worse than the worst?'

'I get the picture. A bastard who gives the rest of us bastards a bad name, eh?'

'That's the idea.'

'Let's see now. There's Erwin Fleiss. He's a nasty piece of work. From Innsbruck. He made a rather tasteless joke about organising some Jewish pogrom there, in 1938. We've got a couple of gauleiters, one from Brunswick and one from Styria. Some Luftwaffe general called Kramer, and another fellow who was part of Hitler's bodyguard. Of course there's a lot more of them back at head office in Buenos Aires. I could probably find out quite a lot about them for you when I'm working there but, like I say, that won't be for a while.' He frowned. 'Who else? There's Wolf Probst. Yes, he's a ruthless character, I think. Might be a good idea to check him out.'

'I'm particularly looking for someone who might just have murdered again, since arriving here in Argentina.'

'Now I see. Set a thief to catch a thief, is that it?'

'Something like that,' I said. 'The kind of man I'm looking for is someone who probably enjoys cruelty and killing for its own sake.'

Geller shook his head. 'No one springs to mind, I'm afraid. I mean, Ricardo's a bastard but he's not a psychopathic bastard, if you follow me. Look here, why don't you ask him? I mean, he must have been to murder camps and seen some horrible things. Met some horrible people. Probably the very types you're looking for.'

'I wonder,' I said.

'What?'

'If he'd cooperate.'

'Passport's a passport. We both know what that's worth when you're sweating it out in someone's basement in Genoa. Ricardo, too.'

'This village where he lives—'

'La Cocha.'

'How long would it take me to get there?'

'At least two hours, depending on the river. We've had a lot of rain in these parts of late. I could drive you there if you wanted. If we left now we could be there and back before dark.' Geller chuckled.

'What is it?' I asked.

'Just that it might be amusing to see Ricardo's face when you tell him that you're working for the police. That's really going to make his day.'

'Worth a two-hour drive?'

'I wouldn't miss it.'

Geller's car was a Jeep the colour of an apricot: just four heavy-duty wheels, a tall steering column, two uncomfortable seats, and a tailgate. We hadn't driven very far before I realised why Geller was driving it. The roads south of Tucumán were little better than dirt tracks through sprawling fields of sugar cane with only the *ingenios* – the industrial mills – of the large sugar companies to remind us that we weren't about to fall off the edge of the earth. By the time we reached La Cocha it was impossible to imagine being anywhere further from Germany and the long arm of Allied military justice.

If Tucumán was a horse-shit town then La Cocha was its poor pig-shit cousin. A Gadarene number of swine seemed to be wandering about the muddy streets as our Jeep bounced into the place, scattering a flock of chickens like an exploding mortar bomb of clucks and feathers, and attracting the attention of a number of dogs whose prominent rib-cages didn't seem to interfere with their propensity to bark. From a tall chimney poured a cloud of black smoke and, at its base, was an open oven. For Eichmann it looked like a home from home. Using a long-handled wooden peel a man was moving bread in and out of the oven. In his excellent Castellano Geller asked the baker for directions to the house of Ricardo Klement.

'You mean the Nazi?' asked the baker.

Geller looked at me and grinned. 'That's him,' he said.

With a finger that was all knuckle and dirty fingernail, as if it belonged to an orang-utan that was studying witchcraft, the baker pointed down the track, past a small auto-repair shop, to a two-storey blockhouse with no visible windows.

'He lives at the villa,' said the baker.

We drove on a short distance and pulled up between a line of washing and an outhouse from which Eichmann hurriedly emerged, carrying a newspaper and buttoning his trousers. He was followed by a strong, cloacal smell. It was evident he had been alarmed by the sound of the Jeep and the obvious relief he felt that we were not the Argentine military come to arrest and hand him over to a war-crimes tribunal, quickly gave way to irritation.

'What the hell are you doing here?' he said, his lip curling in a way I now regarded as quite characteristic. It was strange, I thought, how one side of his face appeared to be quite normal, even pleasant, while the other side looked twisted and malevolent. It was like meeting Doctor Jekyll and Mister Hyde at the same moment.

'I was in Tucumán, so I thought I'd come and see how you are,' I said affably. I opened my bag and took out a carton of Senior Service. 'I brought you some cigarettes. They're English but I figured you wouldn't mind.'

Eichmann grunted a thank you and took the carton. 'You'd better come into the villa,' he said grudgingly.

He pushed open a very tall wooden door that was in need of several licks of green paint and we stepped inside. From the outside things did not augur well. Calling that blockhouse a villa was a bit like calling a child's sandcastle the Schloss Neuschwanstein. Inside though, things were a little better. There was some plasterwork on top of the brickwork and the floors were level, covered with flagstones and some cheap Indian rugs. But a couple of small, barred windows gave the place a suitably penal atmosphere. Eichmann might have evaded Allied justice but he was hardly living a life of luxury. A half-naked woman peered out from behind a door. Angrily, Eichmann jerked his head at her and she disappeared again.

I walked over to one of the windows and looked out at a small, well-planted garden. There were some hutches containing several rabbits he must have kept for meat, and beyond, an old black De Soto with three wheels. A quick getaway did not seem to be on Eichmann's mind.

He collected a large kettle off a cast-iron range and poured hot water into a couple of little hollow gourds. 'Maté?' he asked us.

'Please,' I said. Since coming to Argentina I hadn't tasted the stuff, but everyone in the country drank it.

He put a couple of little metal straws in the gourds and then handed them to us.

There was sugar in it but it still tasted bitter, like green tea with a froth on it. Akin to drinking water with a cigarette in it, I thought, but Geller seemed to like the stuff. And so did Eichmann. As soon as Geller had finished his gourd he handed it over to our host who added some more hot water and, without changing the straw, drank some himself.

'So what brings you all the way out here?' he said. 'It can't just be a social call.'

'I'm working for the SIDE,' I said. 'The Perónist Intelligence Service?'

His eyelid flickered like an almost spent lightbulb. He tried not to let it show, but we all knew what he was thinking. Adolf Eichmann, the SS colonel and close confidant of Reinhard Heydrich, reduced to performing hydrological surveys in the other side of nowhere, while I enjoyed a position of some power and influence in a field Eichmann might have considered his own. Gunther, the reluctant SS man and political adversary, possessing the very job that he, Eichmann, should have had. He said nothing. He even took a shot at a smile. It looked more like something had got stuck under his bridge.

'I'm supposed to decide which of our old comrades is worthy of a good conduct pass,' I said. 'You need one to be able to apply for a passport in this country.'

'I should have expected that loyalty to your blood and your oath as an SS man would oblige you to treat the issue of any such documentation as a mere formality.' He spoke stiffly. Softening just a little, he added, 'After all, we're all sitting on the same inkblot, are we not?' He finished the maté noisily, like a child sucking up the very last drop of a fizzy drink.

'On the face of it, that's true,' I said. 'However, the Perónist government is already under considerable pressure from the Americans—'

'From the Jews more like.'

'—To clean up its backyard. While there's no question that any of us are about to be shown the door, nevertheless there are a few people in government who worry that some of us may be guilty of greater crimes than was originally suspected.' I shrugged and looked at Geller. 'I mean, it's one thing to kill men in the heat of battle. And it's another to take pleasure in the murders of innocent women and children. Wouldn't you agree?'

Eichmann shrugged. 'I don't know about innocent,' he said. 'We were exterminating an enemy. Speaking for myself, I didn't hate the Jews so much, but I don't regret anything I did. I never committed any crimes. And I never killed anyone. Not even in the heat of battle, as you put it. I was little more than a civil servant. A bureaucrat who only obeyed orders. That was the code we all lived by in the SS. Obedience. Discipline. Blood and Honour. If I have any regrets at all it is that there wasn't time to finish the job. To kill every Jew in Europe.'

This was the first time I had ever heard Eichmann speak about the Jewish extermination. And wanting to hear more I tried to lead him on.

'I'm glad you mentioned blood and honour,' I said. 'Because it seems to me that there were a few who dragged the reputation of the SS down into the dirt.'

'Quite,' said Geller.

'A few who exceeded their orders. Who killed for sport and pleasure. Who carried out inhumane medical experiments.'

'A lot of that has been exaggerated by the Russians,' insisted Eichmann. 'Lies told by the communists to justify their own crimes in Germany. To stop the rest of the world from feeling sorry for Germany. To give the Soviets *carte blanche* to do whatever they like with the German people.'

'It wasn't all lies,' I said. 'I'm afraid a lot of it was true, Ricardo. And even if you don't believe it, the possibility that some of it might be true is what worries the government, now. Which is why I've been charged to conduct this investigation. Look, Ricardo, I'm not after you. But I'm afraid I can't regard some SS as old comrades.'

'We were at war,' said Eichmann. 'We were killing an enemy who wanted to kill us. That can get pretty brutal. At a certain level the human costs are immaterial. What mattered most was making sure that the job got done. Trouble-free deportations. That was my speciality and, believe me, I tried to make things as humane as I could. Gas was seen as the humane alternative to mass shootings. Yes, there were some, perhaps, who went too far but, look here, there's always some bad barley in the beer. That's inevitable in any organisation. Especially one that achieved what was achieved. And during a war, too. Five million. Can you credit the scale of it? No, I don't think you can, either of you. Five million Jews. Liquidated, in less than two years. And you're quibbling about the morality of a few bad apples.'

'Not me,' I said. 'The Argentine government.'

'What? You want a name, is that it? In return for my good conduct pass? You want me to play Judas for you?'

'That's about the size of it, yes.'

'I never liked you Gunther,' said Eichmann, his nose wrinkled with distaste. He tore open the carton of cigarettes and lit one with the air of a man who hadn't had a decent smoke in a long while. Then he sat down at a plain wooden table and studied the smoke from the tip as if trying to divine guidance from the gods about what to say next.

'But perhaps there is such a man as you describe,' he said carefully. 'Only I want your word that you won't ever tell him that it was I who informed on him.'

'You have my word on it.'

'This man, he and I met by chance at a café in the centre of Buenos Aires. Not long after we arrived. The ABC café. He told me he's done very well for himself since he came here. Very well indeed.' Eichmann smiled thinly. 'He offered me money. Me. A colonel in the SS and him, a mere captain. Can you imagine it? Patronising bastard. Him, with all his connections and his family money. Living in the lap of luxury. And me, buried here, in this godforsaken hole.' Eichmann took a near mortal drag at his cigarette, swallowed, and then shook his head. 'He was a cruel man. Still is. I don't know how he sleeps. I couldn't. Not in his skin. I saw what he did. Once. A long time ago. It seems so long ago that I must have been a child when it happened. Well, perhaps I was, in a way. But I've never forgotten it, no one could. No one human. I first met him in 1942, in Berlin. How I miss Berlin. And then again in 1943. At Oswiecim.' He grinned bitterly. 'I don't miss that place at all.'

'This captain,' I said. 'What's his name?'

'He calls himself Gregor. Helmut Gregor.'

TWELVE

BERLIN. 1932.

I got off the train from Berlin, walked to the end of the platform, handed over my ticket, and then looked around for Paul Herzefelde. There was no sign of him. So I bought some cigarettes and a newspaper and parked myself on a seat near my arrival platform to wait for him. I didn't spend long with the paper. The election was only two weeks away and this being Munich, the paper was full of stuff about how the Nazis were going to win. So was the station. Hitler's stern disapproving face was everywhere. After thirty minutes I couldn't take it any longer. I put the paper in the bin and went out into the fresh air.

The station was in the west end of the central part of Munich. The Police Praesidium was a ten minute walk to the east, on Ettstrasse, between St Michael's Church and the Cathedral of Our Lady. It was a newish, handsome building on the site of a former monastery. Outside the main entrance were several stone lions. Inside I found only rats.

The desk sergeant was as big as a wrecking ball and just as helpful. He had a bald head and a waxed moustache like a small German eagle. Every time he moved his leather belt creaked against his belly like a ship straining on its hawsers. From time to time he lifted his hand to his mouth and burped. You could smell his breakfast from the front door.

I tipped my hat politely and showed him my warrant disc.

'Good morning,' I said.

'Good morning.'

'I'm Commissar Gunther, from Berlin Alexanderplatz. To see Commissar Herzefelde. I just arrived at the station. I thought he'd be there to meet me.'

'Did you now?' He said it in a way that made me want to punch him on the nose. You get a lot of that in Munich.

'Yes,' I said patiently. 'But since he wasn't I assumed he'd been delayed and that I'd better come and find him here.'

'Spoken like a Berlin detective,' he said, without a trace of a smile.

I nodded patiently and waited for some good manners to kick in. They didn't.

'Spare me the sweet talk and tell him I'm here.'

The sergeant nodded at a polished wooden bench by the front door. 'Have a seat,' he said coolly. 'Sir. I'll deal with you in a minute.'

I went over to the bench and sat down. 'I'll be sure to mention your red-carpet treatment when I see your commissar,' I said.

'You do that, sir,' he said. 'I'll look forward to it.'

He wrote something on a piece of paper, rubbed his ham hock of a nose, scratched his arse with his pencil, and then used it to pick his ear. Then he got up, slowly, and put something in a filing cabinet. The telephone rang. He let it ring a couple of times before answering it, listened, took down some details and then put a sheet of paper into a tray. When the call finished he looked at the clock above the door. Then he yawned.

'If this is how you look after the polenta in this town, I'd hate to be a criminal.' I lit a cigarette.

He didn't like that. He pointed at a No Smoking sign with his pencil. I stubbed it out. I didn't want to wait there all morning. After a while he picked up the phone and spoke, in a lowered voice. Once or twice he flicked his eyes my way so that I got the idea he was probably talking about me. So when he finished the call I lit another cigarette. He tapped the pencil on the desk in front of his belly and, having received my attention, pointed at the No Smoking sign again. This time I ignored him. He didn't like that either.

'No smoking,' he growled.

'No kidding.'

'You know what the trouble is with you Berlin cops?'

'If you could point to Berlin on a map I might be interested, fat boy.'

'You're all Jew lovers.'

'Ah, now we're getting to it.' I blew some smoke his way and grinned. 'We're not all Jew lovers in the Berlin police. As a matter of fact, some of us are a bit like you, sergeant. Ignorant. Bigoted. And a disgrace to the uniform.'

He tried to stare me out for minute or two. Then he said, 'The Jews are our misfortune. It's time the polenta in Berlin woke up to that fact.'

'Well, that's an interesting sentiment. Did you just think of it yourself, or was it written on the skin of the banana you ate for breakfast?'

A detective arrived. I knew he must be a detective because he wasn't dragging his knuckles on the floor. He glanced at the ape on the desk who jerked his head my way. The detective came over and stood in front of me, with a sheepish expression. It might have worked, too, if his face hadn't looked so peculiarly wolf-like.

'Commissar Gunther?'

'Yes. Is something wrong?'

'I'm Criminal Secretary Christian Schramma.' We shook hands. 'I'm afraid I have some bad news. Commissar Herzefelde is dead. He was murdered last night. Shot three times in the back as he left a bar in Sendling.'

'Do you know who did it?'

'No. As you may know, he'd had several death threats.'

'Because he was Jewish. Of course.' I glanced the desk sergeant's way. 'There's hatred and stupidity everywhere. Even in the police force.'

Schramma remained silent.

'I'm very sorry,' I said. 'I didn't know him for very long but Paul was a good man.'

We went up to the detectives' room. It was a warm day and through the open windows you could hear the sound of children playing in the yard of the nearby gymnasium school. Human life never sounded so lively.

'I saw your name in his police diary,' said Schramma. 'But he didn't think to write down a telephone number or where you were from, otherwise I would have called you.'

'That's all right. He was about to share some information on a murder he'd been working on. Elisabeth Bremer?'

Schramma nodded.

'We had a similar case in Berlin,' I explained. 'I came down here to read the files and find out just how similar they were.'

He bit his lip uncomfortably, which did little to alter my first impression of him. He looked like a werewolf.

'Look, I'm really sorry to tell you this after you've come all the way from Berlin. But all Paul's case files have been sent upstairs. To the Government Councillor's office. When a police officer gets killed it's standard procedure to assume it might have something to do with a case he was working on. I seriously doubt that you're going to be able to see those files for a while. Maybe as long as a couple of weeks.'

It was my turn to bite my lip. 'I see. Tell me, did you work with Paul?'

'A while ago. I'm not up to date with his current cases. Of late, he mostly worked on his own. He preferred it that way.'

'He preferred it or other detectives preferred it?'

'I think that's a little unfair, sir.'

'Is it?'

Schramma didn't answer. He lit a cigarette, flicked the match out of the open window and sat on the corner of a desk that I assumed must be his own. On the opposite side of the big room a detective with a face like Schmeling's was questioning a suspect. Every time he got an answer he looked pained, as if Jack Sharkey had hit him below the belt. It was a nice technique. I felt the cop was going to win on a disqualification, the same way Schmeling did. Other detectives came and went. A few of them had loud laughs and louder suits. You get a lot of that in Munich. In Berlin we all wore black armbands when a cop got killed. But not in Munich. A different kind of armband – a red Nazi one with a black swastika – looked a lot more probable. It didn't look like anyone was about to shed any tears over the death of Paul Herzefelde.

'Could I see his desk?'

Schramma got up slowly and we walked over to a grey steel desk in a far-flung corner of the office that was surrounded with a wall of files and bookcases, like a one-man ghetto. The desk top was clear but his photographs were still on the wall. I bent over to take a closer look at them. Herzefelde's wife and family in one. Him wearing a military uniform and decoration in the other. On the wall, next to this photograph, was the faint outline of a graffito that had been rubbed out: the Star of David and the words 'Jews Out'. I traced the outline with my finger just to make sure Schramma knew I'd seen it.

'That's a hell of a way to honour a man who got himself a Knight's Cross with oak leaves,' I said loudly, and glanced around the detectives' room. 'Three bullets and some cave art.'

Silence descended on the room. Typing stopped. Voices quietened. Even the children playing outside seemed to cease their noise for a moment. Everyone was now looking at me like I was the ghost of Walther Rathenau.

'So who did it? Who murdered Paul Herzefelde? Does anyone know?' I paused. 'Can anyone guess? After all, you're supposed to be detectives.' More silence. 'Doesn't anyone care who killed Paul Herzefelde?' I walked over to the centre of the room and, facing down Munich's KRIPO waited for someone to say something. I looked at my watch. 'Hell, I've been here for less than half an hour and I could tell you who killed him. It was the Nazis killed him, that's who. It was the bloody Nazis who shot him in the back. Maybe even the same Nazis who wrote "Jews Out" on the wall beside his desk.'

'Go home you Prussian pig,' someone shouted.

'Yes, clear off back to Berlin you stupid Pifke.'

They were right, of course. It was time to go home. After a short time among Munich's Neanderthals the men of Berlin were already looking like a real advance in human evolution. By all accounts Munich was Hitler's favourite town. It was easy to see why.

I went out of the Police Praesidium by a different set of stairs, which led into the central courtyard where several police cars and vans were parked. As I was making my way under the arches to the street, I encountered the burly desk sergeant who was now coming off duty. I knew this because he wasn't wearing his leather belt or his duty epaulettes. Also he was carrying a Thermos flask. Moving to block my way out he said:

'Sure it's always a shame when a cop goes down in the line of duty.' He chuckled. 'Except when it's a Jew, of course. The fellows who shot that yid bastard, Herzefelde. They deserve a medal, so they do.' He spat onto the ground ahead of me for good measure. 'Have a nice trip back to Berlin you Jew-loving prick.'

'One more word from you, you worthless Nazi gorilla, and I'm going to pull the tongue out of your thick Bavarian head and scrape the shit off it with the heel of my shoe.'

The sergeant put his Thermos on a window sill and bent his ugly mug toward me. 'Who the hell do you think you are, coming to my city and threatening me? You're lucky I don't run you in just for the fun of it. One more word out of you, sonny, and I'll have your eggs hanging from our flagpole in the morning.'

'If I threaten you you'll stay threatened and write me a thank-you letter on nice notepaper in your best writing.'

'This is a man with a broken jaw who's talking to me,' said the sergeant and threw a punch at my head.'

He was tall and strong with shoulders like the yoke on a Fresian milkmaid and a fist as big as a fire-bucket. But his first mistake was to miss. His tunic was still buttoned and this slowed him down, so that I was already ducking the blow by the time it arrived. His second mistake was to miss again. And to lead with his chin. By now I was ready to take a swing myself, as if I'd been taking a swing at the very man who had shot Paul Herzefelde. And I let him have it hard, very hard, right under the chin. This, as Von Clausewitz would probably have agreed, is the best part of the chin with which to make decisive contact. I saw his legs go the minute I struck him. But I punched him again, this time in the belly and when he doubled up I hammered him in each kidney with a heavy-weight contender's high ambition and strength of will. He fell back against the wall of the archway. And I was still hitting him when three SCHUPO men pulled me off and pinned me against the wrought iron gate.

Slowly the sergeant picked himself off the cobbles. It took him a while to straighten up but eventually he managed it. I'll say one thing for him: he could take a punch. He wiped his mouth and, panting hard, came towards me with a look in his eyes that told me he wasn't about to invite me to stay for the Oktoberfest.

'Hold him up,' he told the other cops, taking his time about it. And then he hit me. A short right hook that went up to his elbow in my stomach. Then another, and another until his knuckles were tickling my backbone. Except it wasn't funny. And I wasn't laughing. They let me go when I started throwing up. But they hadn't finished. In fact, they'd only just started.

They dragged me back into the building and down into the cells, where they went at me again – good, expert blows from cops who knew what they were doing and who, clearly, enjoyed their work. After a while I heard a voice from a long way off reminding them that I was a cop which was when they left me alone. I had an idea it was Schramma who got them to lay off but I never found out for sure. I lay on the floor of that cell for a while. As long as no one was kicking me it felt like the most comfortable place in the world. All I wanted to do was to stay there and sleep for twenty years. Then the floor slid to one side and I fell into a deep dark place where a group of dwarves were playing a game of ninepins. For a while I joined the game, but then one of the dwarves gave me a magic drink and I slept the sleep of Jacob and Mount Moriah. Something Jewish anyway.

The cells in the prison below the Munich Police Praesidium were once occupied by Augustine monks. They must have been tough men, those Augustine monks. My cell had a hard bunk and a straw pallet on top that was about as thick as a blanket. The blanket was made of thin air. Job or Saint Jerome would have been very comfortable down there. There was an open toilet without a seat and no window in the smooth, porcelain brick wall. The cell was hot and smelly and so was I. 'Love the sinner and hate the sin,' said Saint Augustine. That was easy for him to say. He never had to spend the night in a cell beneath the Munich Police Praesidium.

They left the lights on all the time and it wasn't in case you were scared of the dark. After a while I had no idea what time of the day or night it was. A few days of that and you're ready to do more or less whatever they tell you just to see the sky again. That's the theory anyway. And after what seemed like a week but was probably only two or three days a doctor came to look at me – a real Schweitzer type with a moustache as big as an octopus and more white hair than Liszt's grandmother. He examined the bruises on my ribs and asked me how I'd come by them. I told him I'd fallen off my bunk when I'd been asleep.

'Do they hurt?'

'Only when I laugh, which is not so much since I've been here, oddly enough.'

'You may have a couple of broken ribs,' he said. 'Really, you need an X-ray.'

'Thanks but what I really need is a cigarette.'

He went away. But I was still smoking the cigarette when a short, pale blond-haired man showed up and asked me for my clothes.

'I don't think they'll fit you,' I said, but I took them off all the same. I just wanted to go home.

'We'll get these things cleaned,' he said, handing my clothes to the custody officer. 'You, too, if you're up to it. There's a shower at the end of the corridor. Soap and a razor.'

'Kind of late to be handing out hospitality, isn't it?' But I had the shower and the shave all the same.

When I was clean the short man handed me a blanket and took me into an interview room to await the return of my clothes. We sat down at opposite ends of a table. He opened a leather cigarette case and put it in front of me. Then someone brought me a cup of hot sweet coffee. It tasted like ambrosia.

'My name is Commissar Wowereit,' he said. 'I've been instructed to inform you that no charges are to be made and that you are free to go.'

'Well, that's very generous of you,' I said, and took one of his cigarettes. He lit me with a match and then sat back on his chair. He had slim, delicate hands. They didn't look like they'd ever thrown a tomato let alone a punch. I couldn't imagine how he fitted in with the rest of the Munich polenta with hands like his. 'Very generous,' I repeated. 'Considering I was the one who got rough-housed.'

'A report of the incident that occurred has already been sent to your new police president and his deputy.'

'What do you mean, my new police president and his deputy? What the hell are you talking about, Wowereit?'

'Of course. I'm sorry. How could you know?'

'Know what?'

'Ever heard of Altona?'

'Yeah. It's a dump outside Hamburg that's notionally part of Prussia.'

'Much more important than that, it's a communist town. The day you arrived in Munich a group of uniformed Nazis staged a parade there. There was a brawl. Actually it was more of a riot. And seventeen people were killed, and several hundred people wounded.'

'Hamburg's a long way from Berlin,' I said. 'I don't see how—'

'The new Chancellor, Von Papen, with the support of General Von Schleicher and Adolf Hitler, drafted a presidential decree, signed by Von Hindenburg, to seize control of the Prussian Government.'

'A putsch.'

'In effect, yes.'

'I assume the army did nothing to stop any of this.'

'You assume correctly. General Rundstedt has imposed martial law on Greater Berlin and the province of Brandenburg, and taken control of the city's police force. Grezinski has been removed. Weiss and Heimannsberg have been placed under arrest. Doctor Kurt Melcher is the new police president of Berlin.'

'Never heard of him.'

'I believe he was formerly the police president of Essen.'

'Where's the new deputy come from? Toytown?'

'I believe the new deputy is someone called Doctor Mosle.'

'Mosle,' I exclaimed. 'What does he know about policing? He's the head of Berlin's traffic police.'

'Colonel Poten is the new head of the uniformed police in Berlin. I believe he was director of the police academy in

Eichen. All Prussian law enforcement officers are now directly
subordinate to the army.' Wowereit allowed himself a thin
hint of a smile. 'I suppose that also includes you. For the
moment.'

'The Berlin police won't stand for it,' I said. 'Weiss wasn't
popular, it's true. But Magnus Heimannsberg's a different
story. He's hugely popular with the rank and file.'

'What can they do? To believe that the army won't use force
to put down any resistance is wishful thinking.' He shrugged.
'But none of this is of any immediate concern to us here in
Munich, and has little relevance to the case in hand. Namely
yours. The report we sent to your superiors describes in detail
what we believe happened here. Doubtless you will put your
own side of the story to your superiors when you get back to
Berlin.'

'You can bet on it.'

'A storm in a water glass, wouldn't you agree? Compared
with what has happened. Politically speaking.'

'That's easy for you to say. You didn't get beaten up and
tossed in the hole for several days. And perhaps you've
forgotten the reason for the fight. A murdered police officer
was defamed by one of your colleagues. I wonder if that'll be
in your damn report.'

'Germany is for the Germans now,' said Wowereit. 'Not a
bunch of immigrants who are only here for what they can get.
And this stupid putsch in Berlin will solve nothing. It's the last
desperate act of a Republic trying to forestall what is
inevitable: the election of a National Socialist government on
July 31st. Von Papen hopes to prove he is strong enough to
stop Germany from sinking into the mess the Jews and the
communists have made for us. But everyone knows there's
only one man who is equal to that historical task.'

I said I hoped he was wrong. I said it quietly and I said it
politely. Saint Augustine would probably have approved of
that. There's a lot to be said for turning the other cheek when

you've been in receipt of a severe beating. You stay alive longer. You get to go back to Berlin. I just hoped that when I did get back there I would still recognise the place.

I found the Third Army all over Berlin. Armoured cars outside all public buildings, and platoons of soldiers enjoying the July sunshine in all of the main parks. It was as if the clock had been turned back to 1920. But there seemed little chance of Berlin's workers organising a general strike to defeat this particular putsch, as had happened then. Only inside the Alex did there appear to be any appetite for resistance. Police Major Walter Encke, who lived in the same apartment building as Commander Heimannsberg and was his close friend, was the focus for a counter-putsch. The Alex was full of Nazi spies, however, and Encke's plan to use uniformed SCHUPO riot brigades to arrest all of the Nazis in the Berlin police came to nothing when a rumour began to go around that he and Heimannsberg were lovers. Later on, the rumour proved to be entirely without foundation but by then it was too late. Fearing for the loss of his reputation as a policeman and as a man, Encke quickly wrote and circulated a letter in which he condemned all talk of a counter-putsch using riot brigades and assured the army of his loyalty 'as a former officer of the Imperial army'. Meanwhile, no fewer than sixteen KRIPO officials, among them four commissars, denounced Bernhard Weiss for alleged improprieties in office. And I was summoned to the office of the new Berlin Police President, Doctor Kurt Melcher.

Melcher was a close associate of Doctor Franz Bracht, the former Mayor of Essen and now Deputy Reichskommissar of the Prussian Government. Melcher was originally a lawyer from Dortmund and the author of a well-known but turgidly written history of the Prussian Police, which only made what happened next all the more remarkable. Ernst Gennat was present at my meeting with the new Police President. So was the new Deputy Police President, Johann Mosle. But it was the fifty-four-year-old Melcher who did most of the talking. An obviously irascible man, he lost little time in coming to the point, with the assistance of an accusatory and nicotine-stained forefinger.

'I will not have officers of the Berlin police force brawling with other policemen. Is that clear?'

'Yes sir.'

'I'm sure you think you had a good reason but I don't want to hear it. The political differences that have existed between various officers are now over. All disciplinary proceedings against officers with Nazi affiliations are to be dropped, and the ban on membership of the Nazi party for officials in the service of the Prussian State is to be lifted. If you can't live with these changes then there's no place for you in this force, Gunther.'

I was about to say that I'd been living and working with men who were openly Nazi for a while. But then I caught sight of Gennat, who closed his eyes and, almost imperceptibly, shook his head as if counselling silence.

'Yes sir.'

'There's a greater enemy than Nazism abroad in this country. And this city in particular. Bolshevism and immorality. We're going to go after the communists. And we're going to crack down on vice of all kinds. The meat market shows are going to close. And the whores are going to be kicked off our streets.'

'Yes sir.'

'And that's not all. KRIPO is going to operate more like a team. There will be no more star detectives giving press conferences and getting their names in the newspapers.'

'What about police officers writing books, sir?' I asked. 'Will that be permitted? I've always wanted to write a book.'

Melcher smiled a toad-like smile and leaned forward as if taking a closer look at some kind of grubby schoolboy.

'You know, it's plain to see how you got those bruises on your face, Gunther. You've got a smart mouth. And I don't like detectives who think they're smart.'

'Surely there would be no point in employing stupid detectives, sir.'

'There's smart and there's smart, Gunther. And then there's clever. The clever cop knows the difference. He knows when to shut his strudel hole and listen. He knows how to put his personal politics aside and get on with the job in hand. I'm not sure that you know how to do any of that, Gunther. I can't see how else you ended up spending three days and nights in a Munich police cell. What the hell were you doing there anyway?'

'I went there at the invitation of a brother police officer. To look at the case notes on a murder I've been investigating. The Anita Schwarz case. There were some striking similarities between that case and a murder they'd been investigating. I had hoped to find a new lead. But when I arrived in Munich I discovered that this police officer, Commissar Herzefelde, a Jew, had been murdered.'

I used the word 'brother' with emphasis in an attempt to provoke Melcher into some sort of anti-Semitic outburst. I hadn't forgotten Izzy Weiss and the lies that were now being spread about my old boss and friend.

'All right. What did you find out?'

'Nothing. Commissar Herzefelde's case notes were placed under an interdiction by those detectives now investigating his murder. As a result I wasn't able to do what I set out to do, sir.'

'And so, you took out your frustration at being forbidden to look at Herzefelde's case notes on a fellow officer.'

'It wasn't like that at all, sir. The sergeant in question—'

Melcher was shaking his head. 'I told you I don't want to hear your reasons, Gunther. There's no excuse for hitting another officer.' He glanced Mosle's way for a moment.

'No excuse,' echoed the DPP.

'So where are you with this case?'

'Well sir, I think our murderer might be from Munich. Something brought him to Berlin. Something medical perhaps. I think he's been having treatment for venereal disease. A new treatment that's being pioneered here in the city. Anyway, when he got here, he met Anita Schwarz. Possibly he was a client of hers. It seems that she was an occasional prostitute.'

'Nonsense,' said Melcher. 'A man with a venereal disease does not usually go and have sex with a prostitute. It just doesn't make sense.'

'With all due respect sir, that's how venereal disease is spread.'

'And this notion that Anita Schwarz was a whore. That's nonsense, too. I tell you frankly Gunther, it's my belief, and the belief of several senior detectives around the Alex, that you've cooked up this whole line of inquiry just to embarrass the Schwarz family. For political reasons.'

'That's just not true, sir.'

'Do you deny that you eluded the oversight of the political officer who was assigned to this case?'

'Arthur Nebe? No, I don't deny it. I just didn't think it was necessary. I was satisfied in my own mind that I wasn't remotely biased against the Schwarz family. All I've ever wanted to do was catch the lunatic who killed their daughter.'

'Well, I'm not satisfied. And you're not going to catch her murderer. I'm taking you off the case, Gunther.'

'If you'll permit me to say so, sir, you're making a big mistake. Only I can catch this man. If you could arrange for me to see Herzefelde's files, sir, I'm sure I can wrap this case up in less than a week.'

'You've had all the time you're going to get on this one, Gunther. I'm sorry but that's how it is. I'm also reassigning you. I'm taking you out of the A Inspectorate.'

'Off Homicide? Why? I'm good at my job, sir.' I looked at

Gennat. 'Tell him, Ernst. Don't just sit there looking like a meat pie. You know I'm good. It was you who trained me.'

Gennat shifted awkwardly on his enormous bottom. He looked pained, as if his haemorrhoids were giving him trouble. 'It's out of my hands, Bernie,' he said. 'I'm sorry. Really I am. But the decision has been made.'

'Sure, I get it. You want a quiet life, Ernst. No trouble. No politics. And by the way, is it true that you were one of the detectives who turned up in Izzy's office with a bottle of wine to toast Doctor Mosle here? When he got Izzy's job?'

'It wasn't like that, Bernie,' insisted Gennat. 'I've known Mosle for longer than I've known you. He's a good man.'

'So was Izzy.'

'That remains to be seen, I think,' said Melcher. 'Not that your opinion really matters here. I'm transferring you from the A Inspectorate to J. With immediate effect.'

'J? That's the criminal records department. It's not even a proper inspectorate, damn it. It's an auxiliary inspectorate.'

'The move is a temporary one,' said Melcher. 'While I decide which of the other seven inspectorates can best use a man of your investigative experience. Until that happens I want you to use that experience to suggest some ways in which the records department might be improved. By all accounts the trouble with records is that it has no real appreciation of how a proper investigation works. It'll be your job to put that right, Gunther. Is that clear?'

Normally I would have put up more of an argument. I might even have offered my resignation. But I was tired after the rail journey from Munich and very sore from the beating I had received. All I wanted to do was go home, have a bath and a drink and sleep in a proper bed. Besides, there was still the small matter of a general election in a few days time, on July 31st. I still held out some hope that the German people would come to its senses and make the Social Democrats the largest party in the Reichstag. After which the army would have little choice but to restore the Prussian government and throw the likes of Papen and Bracht and Melcher and Mosle out of their illegally held offices.

'Yes sir,' I said.

'That's all Gunther.'

'Permission to take a week's leave of absence, sir.'

'Granted.'

I walked slowly out, with Ernst Gennat bringing up the rear. Mosle remained behind in what was, for a while, Melcher's office.

'I'm sorry, Bernie,' said Gennat. 'But there was really nothing I could do.'

'So you can talk after all.'

Gennat smiled a small weary smile. 'I've been in the force for more than thirty years, Bernie. I was a commissar in 1906. One thing I've learned in that time is to know which battles to fight and which ones to concede. There's no point in arguing with these bastards any more than there was a point in going up against the army. To my mind Papen's government is doomed one way or the other. We just have to hope and pray that the election turns out right. After which you can go back to being a homicide detective. Maybe Izzy and the rest of them as well. Although after what happened to your friend Herzefelde in Munich, I rather think that he's well out of it. Martial law will be lifted in days, I suspect. They won't dare try to hold the elections with the army still on the streets. And the charges against Weiss and Heimannsberg will be dropped for lack of evidence. Grezinski's already planning a series of speeches around the city to defend his policy of non-violence. So. Go home. Get well. Put your faith in German democracy. And pray that Hindenburg stays alive.'

THIRTEEN

BUENOS AIRES. 1950.

I was working late in my office at the Casa Rosada. It wasn't much more than a desk and a filing cabinet and a coat-stand in the corner of the larger SIDE office over looking Irigoyen and facing the Ministry of Finance. My so-called colleagues left me quite alone which reminded me a little of Paul Herzefelde's desk in the detectives' room at police head-quarters in Munich. It wasn't that they thought I was Jewish, merely that they didn't trust me, and I can't say I blamed them. I had no idea what Colonel Montalban had told people about me. Perhaps nothing at all. Perhaps everything. Perhaps something quite misleading. But that's the thing about being a spy. It's easy to get the idea you're being spied on.

The KRIPO case files from Berlin were open on the desk in front of me. The box that had contained them was the nearest thing to a time machine I was ever likely to encounter. It all seemed so long ago. And it seemed like yesterday. What was it that Hedda Adlon used to say? The Confucian Curse. May you live in interesting times. Yes, that was it. I'd certainly done that all right. As lives went mine had been more interesting than most.

By now I had a clear recollection of everything that had happened during the last months of the Weimar Republic, and it was plain to me that the only reason I hadn't managed to solve the Anita Schwarz murder was that following my meeting with Kurt Melcher I never worked Homicide again. After I came back from a week's leave I took up my new post in the records department, hoping against hope that somehow the SDP would turn its fortunes around and that the Republic might be restored to full health. It didn't happen.

The elections of July 31st, 1932 found the Nazis gaining more seats in the Reichstag but still without the overall majority that would have enabled Hitler to form a government. Incredibly, the Communists then sided with the Nazis in parliament to force a vote of no-confidence in Papen's hapless government. After that, I disliked the Communists even more than I disliked the Nazis.

Once again the Reichstag was dissolved. And once again an election was called, this time for November 6th. And, once again, the Republic clung on by its fingernails as the Nazis failed to achieve an overall majority. It was now Schleicher's turn to take a shot at being Chancellor of Germany. He lasted two months. Another putsch was forecast. And, desperate for someone who could govern Germany with any authority whatsoever, Hindenburg sacked the incompetent Schleicher and asked Adolf Hitler, the only party leader who hadn't had a turn at being Chancellor, to form a government.

Less than thirty days later Hitler made certain that there could be no more inconclusive elections. On February 27th, 1933, he burnt down the Reichstag. The Nazi revolution had begun. Not long after that I left the police and went to work at the Hotel Adlon. I forgot all about Anita Schwarz. And I never again spoke to Ernst Gennat. Not even when, five years later, I went back to the Alex at the request of General Heydrich.

It was all there in the box file. My notes, my reports, my police diary, my memoranda, Illmann's forensic report, my original list of suspects. And more. Much more. Because it was only now I realised it wasn't just the Anita Schwarz notes the box contained, it was the case notes on the murder of Elizabeth Bremer as well. After I left Homicide the Schwarz case had been handed over to my sergeant, Heinrich Grund, and he had managed to have Herzefelde's notes sent to him from Munich. Much to my surprise I was now looking at the very case file I had travelled from Berlin to see during that fateful July of 1932.

Most of Herzefelde's inquiry had been focused on Walter Pieck, a twenty-two-year-old man from Gunzburg. Pieck was Elizabeth Bremer's skating teacher at the Prinzregenten Stadium in Munich. In summer he was a tennis coach at the Ausstellungspark. He was also a member of the right-wing Stahlhelm and a Nazi party member since 1930. It was hard to understand what a twenty-two-year-old man could have seen in a fifteen-year-old girl. At least it was until you looked at Elizabeth Bremer's photograph. She looked just like Lana Turner and, just like Lana, filled every inch of the sweater she was wearing in the picture. The happiest moments of my life have been the few I passed at home in the bosom of my family. They would have been even happier if my family had been possessed of a bosom like Elizabeth Bremer's. I'd seen a bigger chest but only on a pirate ship.

Reading Herzefelde's case notes, I was reminded that Pieck had maintained that Elizabeth had binned him the week before her murder because she had caught him reading her diary. In Elizabeth's eyes this was an unpardonable sin, and to me her upset was easy to understand: over the years I've read a few private diaries myself and not always for the best. Hardly satisfied with this explanation, Grund had got hold of the diary and noticed that Elizabeth was in the habit of noting her menstrual period with the Greek letter omega. In the weeks leading up to her murder a sigma had replaced omega in Elizabeth Bremer's diary, leading Grund to suppose that she may have been pregnant. Grund had interviewed Pieck and suggested that this had been the real reason why he had been in the habit of reading his young girlfriend's diary; and that he had helped to procure her an illegal abortion. But, despite several days of questioning,

Pieck had steadfastly denied this. What was more, Pieck had a cast-iron alibi in the shape of his father who just happened to be the police chief of Gunzburg, which is several hundred miles from Berlin.

Neither Elizabeth's own doctor nor any of her school friends knew about a pregnancy. But Grund noted Elizabeth had inherited some money in her grandfather's will that she had used to open a savings account; and that the day before her death she had withdrawn almost half of this money and none of it had been found on her body. And he had concluded that even if Pieck had not helped her to procure an abortion, Elizabeth – by all accounts a resourceful and capable girl – must have managed to do so by herself. And that Anita Schwarz might have done the same. And that these abortions had been botched. And that the illegal abortionist had sought to cover his tracks by making their accidental deaths look like lust murders.

I couldn't disagree with much of Grund's conclusions. And yet no one was ever arrested for the murders. The leads seemed to dry up, and after 1933 there were only two more notes on the file. One was that in 1934, Walter Pieck joined the SS and became a guard at Dachau Concentration Camp. The other concerned Anita Schwarz's father, Otto.

Having joined the Berlin police in 1933, as Kurt Daluege's deputy assistant, Otto Schwarz was subsequently appointed as a judge.

I got up from my desk and went to the window. The lights were on in the Ministry of Finance. Probably they were trying to work out what to do about Argentina's rampant inflation. Either that, or they were having to work late to decide how they were going to raise the money to pay for Evita's jewellery. The street below was busy with people. For some reason there was a long line of people outside the Ministry of Labour. And traffic. Buenos Aires was always full of traffic: taxis, trolley-buses, micros, American cars, and trucks, like so many unconnected thoughts in a detective's brain. Outside my window all the traffic was going in the same direction. So were my thoughts. I told myself that just maybe I had it all figured out, more or less.

Anita Schwarz must have got pregnant and, fearing the scandal that might result from the discovery of their disabled daughter's amateur prostitution, Herr and Frau Schwarz must have paid the medicine man from Munich to carry out an abortion on her. Probably that was why she had been carrying so much money in her pocket. Only the abortion procedure had gone wrong and, anxious to cover up his crime the medicine man had tried to make her death look like a lust murder. The same way he had done in Munich. After all, it was better for him that the police should be looking for some kind of crazed sex-killer than an incompetent doctor. Lots of women had died at the hands of illegal abortionists. They weren't called back-street angel-makers for nothing. I recalled the case of one man, a dentist in the Bavarian city of Ulm, who, during the 1920s, had actually strangled several pregnant women for sex while he was supposed to have been giving them abortions.

The more I thought about it the more I liked my solution. The man I had been looking for was a doctor, or some sort of medicine man, most probably from Munich. My first idea was the jelly doctor, Kassner, until I remembered checking out his alibi: on the day of Anita Schwarz's murder he'd been at a urologist's conference in Hanover. And then I remembered his estranged wife's young friend, the gypsy-looking type with a little open-topped Opel, from Munich. Beppo. That was his name. A strange name for a German. Kassner had said he was a student at Munich University. A medical student perhaps. But how many students could have afforded a new Opel? Unless of course he'd been supplementing his income by carrying out illegal abortions. Possibly in Kassner's own apartment when he wasn't there. And if, like many students who came to sample Berlin's world famous night life, this Beppo had contracted a venereal disease, who better than Kassner to help him out with a course of Protonsil, the new magic bullet cure? It would certainly have explained why Kassner's own address had appeared on the suspect list I'd made using KRIPO's Devil's Directory and the patient list copied in Kassner's office. Beppo then. The man I'd met outside Kassner's own front door. Why not? In which case if somehow he was here, in Argentina, I might easily recognise him again. Of course, if he was in Argentina that would have to mean that he'd done something criminal to have left Germany in the first place. Something in the SS perhaps. Not that he'd seemed like the ideal SS type. Not in 1932. Back then they liked them to look Aryan, blond and blue-eyed, like Heydrich. Like me. Beppo had certainly not been that.

I tried to picture him again in my mind's eye. Medium height, good-looking, but swarthy with it. Yes, like a gypsy. The Nazis had hated gypsies almost as much as they hated Jews. Of course, he wouldn't have been the first person to have joined the SS who wasn't the perfect Aryan type. Himmler for one. Eichmann for another. But if Beppo had been possessed of a medical qualification, and had been able to prove that his family had been free of non-Aryan blood for four generations, he might easily have got himself into the medical corps of a Waffen SS unit. I decided to ask Doctor Vaernet if he could remember such a man.

'Working late, I see.' It was Colonel Montalban.

'Yes. I do my best thinking at night. When it's quiet.'

'Me, I'm more of a morning person.'

'You surprise me. I thought you lot liked to arrest people in the middle of the night.'

He smiled. 'Actually no. We prefer to arrest people first thing in the morning.'

'I'll try to remember that.'

He came over to the window and pointed at the line of people outside the Ministry of Labour. 'You see those people? On the other side of Irigoyen? They're there to see Evita.'

'I thought it was a little late to be looking for a job.'

'She spends every evening and half the night in there,' he said. 'Handing out money and favours to the country's poor and sick and homeless.'

'Very noble. And, during an election year, pragmatic, too.'

'That's not why she does it. You're a German. I wouldn't expect you to understand. Was it the Nazis who made you so cynical?'

'No. I've been cynical since March 1915.'

'What happened then?'

'The Second Battle of Ypres.'

'Of course.'

'I sometimes think if we'd won that, we'd have won the war, which would have been better for everyone in the long run. The British and the Germans would have agreed on a peace, and Hitler would have remained in well-deserved obscurity.'

'Luis Irigoyen, who was our president and, later on, our ambassador in Germany – he's the one this street is named after – he met Hitler many times and admired him enormously. He told me once that Hitler was the most fascinating man he ever met.'

This mention of Hitler prompted me to recall Anna Yagubsky and her missing relatives. And, choosing my words carefully, I tried to bring up the subject of Argentine Jews with Montalban.

'Is that why Argentina resisted Jewish emigration?'

He shrugged. 'It was a very difficult time. There were so many who wanted to come here. It just wasn't possible to accommodate them all. We're not a big country like America, or Canada.'

I resisted the temptation to remind the Colonel that,

according to my travel guide, Argentina was the eighth largest country in the world.

'And was that how Directive Eleven came into existence?'

Montalban's eyes narrowed. 'Directive Eleven is not a healthy thing to know about in Argentina. Who told you about it?'

'One hears things.'

'Yes, but from whom?'

'This is the Central State Intelligence Department,' I said. 'Not Radio El Mundo. It would be surprising if one didn't hear the odd secret in a place like this. Besides, my ability to speak Castellano is improving all the time.'

'So I noticed.'

'I even heard that Martin Bormann is living in Argentina.'

'That's certainly what the Americans believe. Which is the best reason of all to know that it's not. Only do try to remember what I told you. In Argentina it is better to know everything than to know too much.'

'Tell me, Colonel. Have there been any other murders?'

'Murders?'

'You know. When one person kills another on purpose. In this case, a schoolgirl. Like the one you showed me at police headquarters. The one missing her wedding trousseau.'

He shook his head.

'And the missing girl? Fabienne von Bader?'

'She is still missing.' He smiled sadly. 'I had hoped you would have found her by now.'

'No. Not yet. But I may be close to discovering the true identity of the man who killed Anita Schwarz.'

For a moment he looked puzzled.

'She was the girl who was murdered in Berlin, back in 1932. You know? The one you remembered reading about in the German newspapers when I was still your idea of a hero.'

'Yes, of course. Do you think he might be here after all?'

'It's a little early to say if he is. Especially as I'm still waiting to see that doctor you told me about. The one from New York? The specialist?'

'Doctor Pack? That's exactly why I came to see you. To tell you. He's here, in Buenos Aires. He arrived today. He can see you tomorrow, or perhaps the day after, depending on—'

'His other more important patient. I know, I know. But not too much. Just everything. I won't forget.'

'See that you don't. For your own sake.' He nodded. 'You're an interesting man, señor. No doubt about it.'

'Yes. I know that, too. I've had an interesting life.'

I ought to have paid more attention to the warning the Colonel had given me, but I always was a sucker for a pretty face. Especially a pretty face as beautiful as Anna Yagubsky's.

My desk was on the second floor. On the floor below was the *archivo* where SIDE's files were stored. I decided to look in on my way out. I was already in the habit of going in there. For each old comrade I interviewed I added a detailed record to his file of who he was and what crimes he had committed. I didn't think I would be risking very much by looking in some other, unrelated files. The only question was how this was to be achieved.

In Berlin all known and suspected enemies of the Third Reich had been registered in the A Index, located in Gestapo headquarters on Prinz Albrechtstrasse. The A Index, also known as the Office Index, was the most modern criminal records system in the world. Or so Heydrich had once told me. The Index comprised half a million cards on people the Gestapo considered to be worthy of attention. It was set on a huge, horizontally-mounted circular card carousel with an electric motor, and a dedicated operator who could locate any one of those half millions cards in less than a minute. Heydrich, a firm believer in the old axiom that knowledge is power, called it his wheel of fortune. More than anyone it was

Heydrich who helped to revolutionise the old Prussian political police and made the SD one of the largest employers in Germany. By 1935 more than six hundred officials worked in the Gestapo's Berlin records division alone.

Nothing so sophisticated or large existed in Buenos Aires, although the system worked well enough at the Casa Rosada. A staff of twenty worked around the clock in five shifts of four. Files were kept on opposition politicians, trades union officials, communists, left-wing intellectuals, members of parliament, disaffected army officers, homosexuals, and religious leaders. These files were stored in mobile shelving that was operated by a system of locking hand-wheels and referenced according to name and subject by a series of leather bound ledgers called *los libros marrónes*. Access to the files was controlled via a simple signature system, unless the file was deemed sensitive, in which case the entry in *los libros marrónes* was written up in red.

The senior officer on duty in the *archivo* was known as the OR – the *oficial registro* – and he was supposed to supervise and authorise the acquisition and use of all written material. I knew at least two of these ORs reasonably well. To them I had confessed my former trade as a Berlin policeman and, in an effort to ingratiate myself, I had even regaled them with descriptions of the apparent omniscience of the Gestapo filing system. Most of what I told them, however, was based on the few months I had spent in KRIPO's records division following my exit from Homicide, but sometimes I just made it up. Not that the ORs knew the difference. One of them, who I knew only as Marcello, was keen to use the Gestapo filing system as a model for updating its SIDE counterpart and I had promised to help him write a detailed memo for submission to the head of SIDE, Rodolfo Freude.

I knew that Marcello would be on duty in the *archivo*, and as I came through the swing doors I saw him in his usual position behind the main desk. This was completely circular and, with its Argentine flag and side-armed military officers, it looked more like a defensive redoubt than a records division. Except that Marcello hardly resembled anything military in a uniform that fitted him only where it gripped him. Whenever I saw him, he reminded me of one of those baby-faced boy soldiers drafted to defend Hitler's bunker against the Red Army during the fall of Berlin.

I returned the updated files on Carl Vaernet and Pedro Olmos and asked for the file on Helmut Gregor. Marcello took the returned files, checked *los libros marrónes* for Helmut Gregor and then dispatched one of the junior officers to go and retrieve it from the shelves. I watched as the officer started to wind the hand-wheel, like a man opening a lock gate, until the relevant shelf had moved far along an invisible track to permit his ingress.

'Tell me more about your A Index,' said Marcello, who was of Italian-Argentine origin.

'All right,' I said, hoping that I might waltz him in the direction I wanted. 'There were three kinds of cards. In Group One, all cards had a red mark indicating an enemy of the state. In Group Two, a blue mark indicating someone to be arrested in time of national emergency. And in Group Three, a green mark indicating people who were subject to surveillance at all times. All these marks were on the left side of the card. On the right side of the card a second colour mark indicated a communist, someone suspected of being in the resistance, a Jew, a Jehovah's Witness, a homosexual, a Freemason, and so on. The whole index was updated twice a year. At the beginning and at the end of the summer – our busiest time. Himmler insisted on it.'

'Fascinating,' said Marcello.

'Informers had special files. And so did agents. But all of these files were completely separate from those held by the Abwehr – German military intelligence.'

'You mean they didn't share intelligence?'

'Absolutely not. They hated each other.'

Now that I'd danced with him I figured it was time to make my move.

'Do you have a file on a Jewish couple called the Yagubskys?' I asked innocently.

Marcello removed the heavy brown leather ledger from the curving shelf behind him and consulted it with a frequently licked forefinger. He must have licked it a thousand times every day and I was surprised it wasn't worn away, like a stick of salt. A minute or so later he was shaking his head. 'Nothing, I'm afraid.'

I told him some more. Made up stuff about how Heydrich had planned to build a huge, switch-programmed electronic machine to deliver the same information as the wheel of fortune by teleprinter paper tape, and in a tenth of the time. I let Marcello 'ooh' and 'aah' about that for a while before I asked him if I could see the files relating to Directive Eleven.

Marcello didn't consult his brown books before answering; and he flinched a little as if it bothered him that he was about to fail me again.

'No, we've got nothing about that either,' he explained. 'Files like that aren't kept here. Not any more. All files relating to the Argentine Immigration Service were removed by the Ministry of Foreign Affairs about a year ago. And I believe they were put in storage.'

'Oh? Where?'

'At the old Hotel de Inmigrantes. It's on the north dock, on the other side of the Avenue Eduardo Madero. It was constructed at the beginning of the century to deal with the huge number of immigrants coming here to Argentina. Rather like Ellis Island, in New York. The place is more or less derelict now. Even the rats stay clear of it. I believe there's just a skeleton staff that works there. I haven't been there myself but one of the other ORs helped to move some cabinets there and said it was all a bit primitive. If you were looking for something there it would probably be best to go through the Ministry of Foreign Affairs.'

I shook my head. 'It's really not that important,' I said.

I drove to President Perón Station, parked my car, and found a telephone. I called the number Anna Yagubsky had given me. An old man answered, his voice full of suspicion. I guessed it was her father. When I gave him my name he started to ask a lot of questions, none of which I could have answered even if I'd wanted to.

'Listen, Señor Yagubsky, I'd love to talk a while with you, only I'm a little pressed for time right now. So would you mind just putting your questions on hold and fetching your daughter to the phone?'

'There's no need to be rude about it,' he said.

'As a matter of fact I was trying very hard not to be rude about it.'

'I'm amazed that you have any clients at all, Señor Hausner, if this is how you treat them.'

'Clients? Uh-huh. Exactly what did your daughter tell you about me, Señor Yagubsky?'

'That you're a private detective. And that she hired you to find my brother.'

I smiled. 'What about your sister-in-law?'

'To be really honest with you, my sister-in-law I can live without. I never understood why Roman married her, and we never got along that well. Are you married, Señor?'

'Have been. Not any more.'

'Well, at least you know what you're doing without.'

I pushed another coin into the telephone. 'Right now, I'm in danger of going without speaking to your daughter. That was my last five centavos.'

'All right, all right. That's the trouble with you Germans. You've always got a reason to be in a hurry.' He laid the receiver down with a clunk and, a long minute later, Anna came on the line.

'What did you say to my father?'

'There's really no time to explain. I want you to meet me at President Perón Station in half an hour.'

'Couldn't it be tomorrow night?'

'Tomorrow's no good. I might have a hospital appointment tomorrow. Maybe the day after as well.' I quickly lit a cigarette. 'Look, just be here as soon as you can. I'll wait by the Belgrano platform.'

'Can't you tell me anything?'

'Wear some old clothes. And bring a torch. Two if you have them. And a flask of coffee. We're liable to be a while.'

'But where are we going?'

'To do a little digging.'

'You're scaring me. Maybe I should bring a pick and shovel, too.'

'No, angel, not with those lovely hands of yours. Take it easy, we're not looking to dig anyone up. We're just going to dig around in some old immigration files and it's liable to get a little dusty, that's all.'

'I'm very relieved to hear it. For a minute I thought – I mean, I'm a little bit squeamish about digging up dead bodies. Especially at night.'

'I hear that normally that's the best time to do that kind of thing. Even the dead aren't paying much attention.'

'This is Buenos Aires, Señor Hausner. The dead are always paying attention in Buenos Aires. That's why we built La Recoleta. So we wouldn't forget it. Death is a way of life for us.'

'You're talking to a German, angel. When we invented the SS we had the last word in death cults, believe me.' The phone began to demand more money. 'And that was my last five centavos, so get your beautiful behind over here, like I told you.'

'Yes, sir.'

I put down the receiver. I regretted involving Anna. There was some risk in what I was planning. But I couldn't think of anyone else who might have helped me to understand whatever documents were being stored in the Hotel de Inmigrantes. Then again, she *was* involved. It was her aunt and uncle we were looking for. She wasn't paying me enough to take all of the risks on my own. And since she wasn't paying me anything at all she could damn well come along for the ride and like it. I was in two minds about her calling me sir like that. It made me feel like someone worthy of respect by virtue of my age. Which was something I told myself I was going to have to get used to. As long as I was getting older. That was OK. You had to remain alive to get older.

I bought some more cigarettes, a *Prensa*, and a copy of the *Argentisches Tageblatt* – the only German-language newspaper it was safe to read in the sense that it didn't mark you out as a Nazi. But the main reason for going into the station was the knife shop. Mostly the blades were for tourists: bone-handled cutlery for chartered surveyors and accountants who fancied themselves as gauchos or street-fighting tango dancers. A few of the less spectacular knives looked about right for what I had in mind. I bought two: a long, thin stiletto for pushing right through a keyway and tripping the catch within a lock-housing; and something bigger for jemmying a window. I tucked the big one under my belt, in the small of my back, gaucho-style, and slipped the little stiletto inside my breast pocket. When the shop clerk shot me a look I smiled benignly and said, 'I like to be well-armed when my sister comes to dinner.'

He'd have looked a lot more surprised if he'd seen my shoulder holster.

Half an hour passed. Forty-five minutes turned into an hour. I'd just started to curse Anna when, finally, she showed up wearing an ensemble of old clothes supplied by Edith Head. A nice plaid shirt, neatly-pressed jeans, a tailored tweed jacket, a pair of flat heels, and a large leather handbag. And, too late, I realised my mistake. Telling a woman like Anna to come out wearing old clothes was like telling Berenson to frame a great painting with firewood. I guessed she had probably changed her clothes several times just to make sure that the old clothes she had on were the best old clothes she could have chosen to wear. Not that it mattered what she wore. Anna Yagubsky would have looked wonderful wearing half a pantomime horse.

She eyed the Belgrano train uncertainly.

'Are we taking the train somewhere?'

'The thought had crossed my mind. But not this one. I hear the slow train to paradise is more comfortable. No, I wanted to meet you here so I wouldn't miss you in the dark outside. But now that I've seen you again I realise I wouldn't miss you in an exodus.'

She blushed a little. I led her out of the station. With that huge, echoing cathedral of a building behind us, we walked east, through a double row of parked trolley buses and into a big open square dominated by a red-brick clock tower that was now striking the hour. Under acacia trees people played music and lovers trysted on benches. Anna took my arm and it would have seemed romantic if we hadn't been planning trespass and the illegal entry of a public building.

'What do you know about the Immigrants Hotel?' I asked her as we crossed Eduardo Manero.

'Is that where we're going? I wondered if it might be.' She shrugged. 'There's been an Immigrants Hotel here since the middle of the last century. My parents could probably tell you more about it. They stayed there when they first came to Argentina. In the beginning, any poor immigrant arriving in the country could get free board and lodging there for five days. Then, in the thirties, it was any poor immigrant who wasn't Jewish. I'm not sure when they closed it. There was something in the paper about it last year, I think.'

We approached a honey-coloured, four-storey building that was almost as big as the railway station. Surrounded by a fence, it looked more like a prison than a hotel and I reflected that this had probably been closer to its real purpose. The fence wasn't more than six feet high but the top wire was barbed and it did the job. We kept walking until we found a gate. There was a sign that read PROHIBIDA LA ENTRADA and, underneath it a large Eagle padlock that must have been there since the hotel was built.

Seeing the big gaucho knife in my hand, Anna's eyes widened.

'This is what happens when you ask questions people don't want you to ask,' I said. 'They lock up the answers.' I flicked open the padlock.

'Aiee,' said Anna, wincing.

'Fortunately for me, they use crummy locks that wouldn't keep out a rat with a toothpick.' I pushed open the gate and walked into an arrivals yard overgrown with tufts of grass and jacaranda trees. A gust of wind blew a sheet of newsprint to my feet. I picked it up. It was a two-month-old page from *El Laborista*, a pro-Perónist rag. I hoped it was the last time anyone had been there. It certainly looked that way. There were no lights in any of the hundred or so windows, and only the sound of distant traffic driving along Eduardo Manero and a train moving in the rail yards disturbed the quiet of the abandoned hotel.

'I don't like this,' admitted Anna.

'I'm sorry about that,' I said. 'But my Castellano isn't up to the kind of legalese and bureaucratic language you usually find in official documents. If we do find something we'll probably need those beautiful eyes of yours to read it.'

'And here was me thinking you just wanted some company.' She glanced around nervously. 'I just hope there aren't any rats. I get enough of those at work.'

'Just take it easy, OK? From the look of this place, nobody's been here in a while.'

The main doorway smelt strongly of cat piss. The frosted windows were covered with cobwebs, and salt from the estuary river. A largish spider scrambled away as my shoes disturbed its gossamer repose. I forced another padlock with the big knife and then raked the Yale on the door with the stiletto.

'Do you always carry a complete cutlery drawer in your pockets?' she asked.

'It's that or a set of keys,' I said, gouging at the lock's mechanism.

'Where were you during choir practice? You do that like you've done it before.'

'I used to be a cop, remember? We do all of the things criminals do, but for much less money. Or in this case no money at all.'

'Money's a big thing with you, I can tell.'

'Maybe that's because I don't have very much.'

'Well then. We have something in common.'

'Maybe when this is all over you can show me your gratitude.'

'Sure. I'll write you a nice letter on my best notepaper. How does that sound?'

'If we find your miracle you can write to the local archbishop with evidence of my heroic virtue. And maybe, in a hundred years, they'll make me a saint. Saint Bernhard. They did it before, they can do it again. Hell, they even did it for a lousy dog. By the way, that's my real name. Bernhard Gunther.'

'I suppose there is a dog-like quality about you,' she said.

I finished raking the lock.

'Sure. I'm fond of children and I'm loyal to my family, when I have one. Just don't hang a little barrel of brandy around my neck unless you expect me to drink it.'

My voice was full of bravado. I was trying to stop her from being scared. In truth I was just as nervous as she was. More so, probably. When you'd seen as many people killed as I had you know how easy it is to get killed.

'Did you bring those torches?'

She opened her bag to reveal a bicycle lamp and a little hand dynamo you had to keep squeezed to make it light. I took the bicycle lamp.

'Don't switch on until we're inside,' I told her. I opened the door and poked my muzzle inside the hotel. It wasn't the one on my face. It was the one on my gun.

We went inside, our footsteps echoing on the cheap marble floor like two ghosts uncertain about which part of the building to go and haunt. There was a strong smell of mildew and damp. I switched on the bicycle lamp, illuminating a double-height hallway. There was no one about. I put away my gun.

'What are we looking for?' she whispered.

'Boxes. Packing cases. Filing cabinets. Anything that might contain records of immigration. The Ministry of Foreign Affairs decided to dump them here when this place closed down.'

I offered Anna my hand but she brushed it off and laughed.

'I stopped being afraid of the dark when I was seven,' she said. 'These days I even manage to put myself to bed.'

'Maybe you shouldn't,' I said.

'It's odd of me, I know, but somehow I feel safer that way.'

We walked the length of the building and found four large dormitories on the ground floor. One of these still had beds and I counted two hundred and fifty which meant that as many as five thousand people had once lived in the building.

'My poor parents,' said Anna. 'I had no idea that it was like this.'

'It's not so bad. Believe me, the German idea of resettlement was a lot worse than this.'

In the communal washrooms between the dormitories were sixteen square sinks, each as big as a car door. And beyond the furthest washroom was a locked door. The padlock, which was a new one, told me we were probably in the right place. Someone had felt obliged to secure what was on the other side of the door with a lock superior to those on the gate and on the front door. But, new or not, this padlock yielded just as easily to my gaucho's knife. I pushed the door open with the sole of my shoe and shone the light inside.

'I think we've found what we're looking for,' I said, although it was evident that the real work was only just beginning. There were dozens of filing cabinets – as many as a hundred – in five ranks, one in front of the other, like tightly dressed lines of soldiers, so that it was impossible to open one without moving the one in front of it.

'This is going to take hours,' said Anna.

'It looks as though we are going to spend the night together after all.'

'Then you'd better make the most of it,' she said. She put the lamp down on the floor, faced the cabinet at the head of the first rank and pointed at the cabinet heading the second. 'Here, you look in that one and I'll look in this one.'

I blew some dust off. A mistake. There was too much dust. It filled the air and made us cough. I pulled open the top drawer of the filing cabinet and started to riffle through a lot of names beginning with the letter Z. 'Zhabotinsky, Zhukov, Zinoviev. These are all Zs. You don't suppose the one behind this one could be the Y cabinet, do you? Like Y for Yrigoyen, Youngblood and Yagubsky?'

I slammed the drawer shut and we moved that cabinet out of the way of the one behind. Even before I had wrestled it completely clear Anna had hauled the top drawer of the next cabinet open. There was more strength in her arm than she realised. Or possibly she was suddenly too excited to know her own strength. Either way she managed to pull the entire drawer completely out of the cabinet and, narrowly missing her toes and mine, it thudded on the marble floor with the sound of a door closing in some deep pit of hell.

'Do you want to try that again?' I asked. 'Only I don't think they heard it in the Casa Rosada.'

'Sorry,' she whispered.

'Let's hope not.'

Anna was already kneeling in front of the fallen drawer and, with the light from the little hand dynamo she was holding, was examining the contents. 'You were right,' she cried excitedly. 'These are the Ys.'

I picked the bicycle lamp off the floor and trained the beam on her hands.

Then she said, 'I don't believe it,' and removed one thin file from the pack. 'Yagubsky.'

Even in the semi-darkness I could see the tears in her eyes. Her voice was choked, too.

'It seems that you can work miracles after all. Saint Bernhard.'

Then she opened the file.

It was empty.

Anna stared at the empty file for a long moment. Then she flung it aside angrily and, sinking back on her haunches, let out an enormous sigh. 'So much for your miracle,' she said.

'I'm sorry.'

'It's not your fault.'

'I didn't want to be a saint anyway.'

After a while I went to find the empty file. I picked it up and looked at it more closely. It was empty all right. But the file wasn't without information. There was a date on the plain manila cover.

'When did you say they disappeared?'

'January 1947.'

'This file is dated March 1947. And look. Underneath their names are written the words "Judio" and "Judia". Jew and Jewess. And there's the small matter of a rubber stamp in red ink.'

Anna looked at it. 'D12,' she said. 'What's D12?'

'There's another date and a signature inside the stamp. The signature is illegible. But the date is clear enough. April 1947.'

'Yes, but what is D12?'

'I have no idea.'

I went back to the cabinet and removed another file. This one belonged to a John Yorath. From Wales. And it was full of information. Details of entry visas, details of John Yorath's medical history, a record of his stay at the Hotel de Inmigrantes, a copy of a *cedula*, everything. But not Jewish. And no D12 stamp on the cover.

'They were here,' said Anna, excitedly. 'This proves that they were here.'

'I think it also proves that they're not here any longer.'

'What do you mean?'

I shrugged. 'I don't know. Clearly, however, they were arrested. And then deported, perhaps.'

'I told you. We've never heard from them. Not since January 1947.'

'Then perhaps they were imprisoned.' Warming to my theme, I said, 'You're a lawyer, Anna. Tell me about the prisons in this country.'

'Let's see. There's the prison at Parque Ameghino, here in the city. And the Villa Devoto, of course, where Perón imprisons his political enemies. Then there's San Miguel where regular criminals are sent. Where else? Yes, a military jail on Marin Garcia Island, in the River Plate. That's where Perón himself was imprisoned when he was originally deposed, in October 1945. Yes, yes, you might imprison a great many people on Marin Garcia.' She thought for a moment. 'But wait a minute. There's nowhere more remote than Neuquen prison in the Andean foothills. You hear stories about Neuquen, but almost nothing is known about it except that the people who are sent there never return. Do you really think it's possible? That they could be in jail? All this time?'

'I don't know, Anna.' I waved at the regiment of filing cabinets ranked in front of us. 'But it's just possible we'll find the answers in one of these.'

'You really know how to show a girl a good time, Gunther.' She stood up and went over to the next cabinet and drew the drawer open.

An hour or so before dawn, exhausted, grimy with dust, and having found nothing else of any interest, we decided to call it a night.

We had stayed too long. I knew that because as we came back into the front hall someone switched on the electric lights. Anna uttered a little stifled scream. I wasn't exactly happy about this turn of events myself. Especially as the person who had switched on the lights was pointing a gun at us. Not that he was much of a person. It was easy to see why Marcello had talked about a skeleton staff. I've seen healthier looking men in coffins. He was about five feet six inches tall with lank, greasy grey hair, eyebrows that looked like two halves of a moustache that had been separated for its own good, and a rat's narrow, recreant features. He wore a cheap suit, a vest that looked like a rag in a mechanic's greasy hands, no socks and no shoes. There was a bottle in his coat pocket that was probably his breakfast and, in the corner of his mouth, a length of drooping tobacco ash that had once been a cigarette. As he spoke it fell onto the floor.

'What are you doing here?' he said, in a voice made indistinct with phlegm and alcohol and a lack of teeth. In fact there was just one tooth on his prominent upper jaw: a front tooth that looked like the last pin standing in a game of skittles.

'I'm a policeman,' I said. 'I needed to look at an old file urgently. I'm afraid there was no time to go through proper procedures.'

'Is that right?' He nodded at Anna. 'And what's her story?'

'None of your goddamn business,' I said. 'Look, take a look at my ID, will you? It's just like I told you.'

'You're no cop. Not with that accent.'

'I'm secret police. SIDE. I'm one of Colonel Montalban's people.'

'Never heard of him.'

'We both report to Rodolfo Freude. You've heard of him, haven't you?'

'Matter of fact I have. It was him who gave me my orders. Explicit orders. He says, *no one*. And I mean *no one*. *No one* gets in this place without the express authority, in writing, of the President himself.' He grinned. 'Have you got a letter from the President?'

He crept forward and patted me down, his fingers quickly turning my pockets inside out. He grinned. 'Thought not.'

Up close I wasn't inclined to change my impression of him. He looked inferior and second-rate. But there was nothing second-rate about the gun in his hand. That was special. A thirty-eight Police Special, with a two-inch barrel and a nice bright blue finish. It was the only thing about him that looked like it was in perfect working order. It had crossed my mind to tackle him while he was searching my pockets. But the Police Special quickly changed it for me. He found my gun and tossed it away. He even found the little stiletto in my breast pocket. But he didn't find the gaucho knife hidden under my belt in the small of my back.

He backed away and patted Anna down, mostly on her breasts, which seemed to give him an idea.

'You,' he told her. 'Pretty lady. Take off your jacket and your shirt.'

She stared at him with dumb insolence and, when nothing

happened, he got handy with the gun, pressing it under her chin. 'You'd better do it pretty lady or I'll blow your head off.'

'Do as he says, Anna. He means it.'

The man grinned his one-toothed grin and stood back to enjoy the sight of her undressing. 'The brassiere, too. Take it off. Let's see those titties.'

Anna looked at me, hopelessly. I nodded back at her. She unhooked her bra and let it fall onto the ground.

The man licked his lips, staring at her bared breasts. 'Now those are nice,' he said. 'Real nice titties. Nicest titties I've seen in a while.'

I pressed my spine back a little against my belt, feeling the big sheath knife that was there and wondering if I even knew how to throw a knife – especially one that looked as if it belonged on a butcher's chopping block.

The man with one tooth reached forward and tried to take one of Anna's nipples between his forefinger and thumb; but she shrank away from his touch behind the shield of her fore-arms.

'Stand still,' he said, twitching nervously. 'Stand still or I'll shoot you pretty lady.'

Anna closed her eyes and let him take hold of her nipple. At first he just kneaded it with his fingers like a man rolling tobacco. But then he started to squeeze, hard. Her face told me that much. So did his. He was smiling with sadistic pleasure, enjoying the pain he was inflicting on her. Anna bore it silently for a while but that only seemed to make him do it harder until, whimpering, she begged him to stop. He did. But only to squeeze her other nipple.

By now I had the knife in my hand. I slid it up inside the forearm of my sleeve. There was too much distance between the two of us to risk attacking him with the blade in my hand. Most likely he would have shot me, and then raped and killed her. It was too much gun to take a chance with. But throwing the knife was risky, too.

I let the knife slide into the palm of my hand and gripped the blade like a hammer.

Anna sank onto her knees, whimpering with pain, only he kept hold of her, his face contorted with ghastly pleasure, enjoying every second of the agony that was written in her face.

'You bastard,' she said.

That was my cue and, taking a small step forward and pointing both arms straight at the target I threw the knife, putting my whole hip into it to add to the power of my throw. I aimed at his side, just below his outstretched hand that was still twisting her nipple.

He cried out. The knife appeared to hit him in the ribs but then it was in his hand. He let it go and it fell onto the ground. At the same time he shot at me and missed. I felt the bullet zip over my head. I rolled quickly forward expecting to find myself facing the two-inch barrel, or worse. Instead I found myself staring at a man who was now on all fours, coughing blood onto the ground between his hands and then curling up into a ball, holding his side. I glanced at the knife and, seeing the blood on the blade, guessed that it must have pierced his side to a depth of several inches before he had plucked it out of his torso.

My close proximity seemed to deflect him from the pain and distress of his wound. Twisting his whole body to one side, he tried to shoot again only this time without lifting his forearm from the stab wound in his side.

'Look out,' yelled Anna.

But I was already over him, wrestling the gun from the grip of his bloody hand even as it fired harmlessly into the ceiling. Anna screamed. I punched him hard on the side of the head but the fight had already gone out of him. I tiptoed away from him, trying to avoid the pool of his blood that was spreading on the floor like an expanding red balloon. He wasn't dead yet, but I could tell there was no saving him. The blade had gone through a major artery. Just like a bayonet. From the amount of blood on the floor it was clear he would be dead in minutes.

'Are you all right?' I picked up Anna's brassiere and handed it to her.

'Yes,' she whispered. Her hands were cupping her breasts and her eyes were full of tears. She was looking at him, almost as if she pitied him.

'Put your clothes on,' I said. 'We have to leave. Now. Someone might have heard those shots.'

I put his gun under my belt, holstered my own, put the flashlights in Anna's bag and picked up the two knives. Then I glanced around for anything the cops might get their teeth into. A button. A hank of hair. An earring. The little spots of colour on a canvas, like Georges Seurat, that Ernst Gennat had been fond of. But there was nothing. Just him, wheezing his last breaths away. A dead body that didn't know it yet.

'What about him?' asked Anna, buttoning her shirt. 'We can't just leave him here.'

'He's finished,' I said. 'By the time an ambulance gets here he'll be dead.' I took hold of her arm and moved her smartly towards the door then switched out the light. 'With any luck, by the time anyone finds him the rats will have spoiled the evidence.'

Anna took my hand off her arm and switched the light on again. 'I told you. I don't like rats.'

'Maybe you can flash a message in Morse code while you're at it,' I said. 'Just to make sure people know that there's someone here.' But I left the light on.

'He's still a human being,' she said going back to the body on the floor. Trying to keep her shoes out of the blood she dropped down on her haunches and, shaking her head helplessly, she looked back at me as if begging for a clue about what to do next.

The man twitched, several times and then lay still.

241

'I had a rather different impression,' I said.

Crouching down beside her I pressed my fingers hard under his ear and paused for the sake of verisimilitude.

'Well?'

'He's dead,' I said.

'Are you sure?'

'What do you want me to do, write out a death certificate?'

'The poor man,' she whispered. Then she did something that struck me as an odd thing to do if you were a Jew: she crossed herself.

'Speaking for myself, I'm glad the poor man's dead. The poor man was going to rape and kill you. But not before the poor man killed me, probably. The poor man had it coming, if you ask me. Now if you're quite through grieving for the poor man I'd like to get out of here before the cops or any of the poor man's friends show up and wonder if this murder weapon I'm holding in my hand makes me a suspect. In case you've forgotten, they have the death penalty for murder in Argentina.'

Anna glanced at the gaucho knife and nodded.

I went to the door and switched out the light. She followed me outside. At the gate in the fence I told her to wait a minute. I ran to the edge of the North Dock and hurled the knife as far as I could into the River Plate. As soon as I heard the evidence hit the water I felt better. I've seen what lawyers can do with evidence.

Together we walked back to where I had left my car, in front of the railway station. The sun was coming up. Another day was dawning for everyone except the man with one tooth who was now lying dead on the floor of the Immigrants Hotel. I felt very tired. In every way it had been a long night.

'Tell me something,' she said. 'Does this sort of thing often happen to you, Herr – what did you say your real name was again?'

'Gunther, Bernhard Gunther. And you make it sound like you weren't there, Anna.'

'I can assure you, I'm not likely to forget this evening in a hurry.' She stopped walking for a moment and then threw up.

I gave her my handkerchief. She wiped her mouth and took a deep breath.

'All right now?' I asked.

She nodded. We reached my car and got in.

'That was quite a date,' she said. 'Next time let's just go to the theatre.'

'I'll take you home,' I said.

Anna shook her head and wound down the window. 'No. I can't go home. Not yet. Not feeling the way I do now. And after what happened I don't want to be alone, either. Let's stay here for a moment. I just need to be still for a while.'

I poured some of the coffee she'd brought. She drank it and then watched me smoke a cigarette.

'What?'

'No trembling hands. No unsteady lips on that cigarette. No deep drags. You smoke that cigarette like nothing happened. Just how ruthless are you, Herr Gunther?'

'I'm still here, Anna. I guess that speaks for itself.'

I leaned across the seat and kissed her. She seemed to enjoy it. Then I said, 'Tell me your address and I'll drive you home. You've been out all night. Your father will be worried about you.'

'I guess you're not as ruthless as I thought.'

'Don't bet on it.'

I started the engine.

'So,' she said. 'You really are going to drive me home. That's a first. Maybe you do want to be a saint after all.'

She was right, of course. The fact is I wanted to prove to her how polished and shiny my armour really was. I drove quickly. I wanted to get her home before I changed my mind. Nobility only swims so far in my gut before it hits its head on something hard and unyielding. Especially where she was concerned.

FOURTEEN

BERLIN, 1932 AND BUENOS AIRES, 1950.

The first we knew about it was a strong smell of burning. Then we heard the fire engines and the ambulances from Artilleriestrasse. Frieda went outside the hotel entrance to take a look and saw an excited crowd of people heading north-west across Pariser Platz. Above the rooftops of the French Embassy something lit up the night sky like an open-furnace door.

'It's the Reichstag,' said Frieda. 'The Reichstag is on fire.'

We ran back into the hotel intending to get a better view from the roof. But in the lobby I met Herr Adlon. I told him the Reichstag was on fire. It was just after ten p.m.

'Yes, I know.' He drew me to one side, thought better of what he had been about to say, and then took me into the manager's office. He closed the door. 'There's something I want you to do. And it might well be dangerous.'

I shrugged it off.

'Do you know where the Chinese Embassy is?'

'Yes, it's on Kurfurstendamm. Next to the Nelson Theatre.'

'I want you to go there, to the Chinese Embassy, in the hotel laundry van,' said Louis Adlon, handing me some keys. 'I want you to pick up some passengers and bring them straight back here. But on no account let them alight at the front door of the hotel. Drive them through the gate to the tradesman's entrance. I'll be waiting for you there.'

'Might I ask who it is, sir?'

'You may. It's Bernhard Weiss and his family. Someone

tipped him off that the Nazis were coming to his house tonight to lynch him. Fortunately Chiang Kai-shek is a friend of Izzy's and agreed to let him and his family take refuge there. He just called me a few minutes ago and asked if I could help. Naturally I agreed to let him stay here. And I assumed you would want to help, too.'

'Of course. But wouldn't he be safer remaining in the embassy?'

'Perhaps, but he'd be more comfortable here, wouldn't you agree? Besides, we are used to having people stay here in our VIP suites in conditions of almost total secrecy. No, we shall look after him very well, and for as long as is necessary.'

'This has something to do with the Reichstag fire, I'm certain of it,' I said. 'The Nazis must be planning a complete overthrow of the Republic. And to declare martial law.'

'I think you must be right. Are you carrying a gun?'

'No sir. But I can fetch one.'

'There's no time. You can take mine.' He took out a key chain and unlocked the safe. 'The last time I took this gun out of the safe was during the Spartakist uprising of 1920. But it's been well-oiled.' He handed me a broom-handle Mauser and a box of ammunition. Then he upended a leather briefcase, emptying the contents onto his desk. 'Put the Mauser in this. And be careful, Bernie. I don't think it's going to be the kind of night that makes one feel proud to be a German.'

Louis Adlon was right. The streets of Berlin were full of marauding gangs of storm troopers. They sang their songs and waved their flags as if the fire was a cause for celebration. I saw some smashing the windows of a Jewish-owned store near the zoo. It was all too easy to imagine what would have happened if they'd met up with an old rabbi or some luckless idiot wearing a Lenin-style peaked cap and a red flag on his lapel. There were police vans and armoured cars everywhere but I didn't suppose they were intent on protecting communists and Jews. And seeing the SCHUPO men doing very little to stop disorder in the city I was very glad I was no longer a policeman. On the other hand it was an excellent night to be Chinese. When I arrived I saw that no one was paying any attention to the Chinese Embassy or its occupants.

Leaving the engine running and the doors open, I got out of the van and rang the embassy's doorbell. A Chinese answered the door and asked who I was. I told him Louis Adlon had sent me at which point the double-doors to a ground floor ante-room were flung open and I saw Izzy and his family waiting there with their luggage. They looked at me anxiously. Izzy shook my hand and nodded silently. We didn't say anything much. There wasn't time. I grabbed their suitcases, threw them in the van and, when I was satisfied that it was quite safe, I waved my passengers out of the embassy, slamming the doors of the van shut behind them.

When I reached the Adlon I drove through to the tradesman's entrance as instructed and found Louis Adlon waiting. Max, the hall porter, loaded the Weiss family belongings onto a baggage trolley and disappeared into a service elevator. He didn't even look for a tip. Everything was strange about that night. Meanwhile we hurried the refugees into another service elevator and along to the best suite in the hotel. That was typical of Louis Adlon and I knew the significance would not be lost on Izzy.

Inside the magnificent suite the heavy silk curtains were already drawn and a fire was burning brightly in the grate. Izzy's wife disappeared into the bathroom with her children, and Adlon poured drinks for us all. Max appeared and began putting the luggage away. While you couldn't see anything of what was happening outside, you could hear a lot. Some storm troopers had come along Wilhelmstrasse and were chanting 'Death to the Marxists'. Izzy's eyes were full of tears, but he tried to smile.

'It sounds as though they have already found the people to blame for the fire,' he said.

'People will never believe that,' I said.

'They'll believe what they want to believe,' said Izzy. 'And right now they certainly don't want to believe in the communists.'

He took the glass offered by Louis and the three of us toasted each other.

'To better days,' said Louis.

'Yes,' said Izzy. 'But I fear this is just the beginning. This is more than just a fire. Mark my words, this is the funeral pyre of German democracy.' He placed an avuncular hand on my shoulder. 'You're going to have to watch yourself, my young friend.'

'Me?' I grinned. 'I'm not the one who was hiding out in the Chinese embassy.'

'Oh, it's been over for me for a while. We've been prepared for something like this. Our suitcases have been packed for weeks.'

'Where will you go, sir?'

'Holland. We'll be safe there.'

I could see he was tired. Exhausted. So we shook hands and I left him. I never saw him again.

I went up to the roof and found Frieda, watching the fire with some of the guests and hotel staff. One of the waiters from the cocktail bar had brought up a bottle of schnapps to help ward off the cold night air but no one was drinking very much. Everyone knew what the fire meant. It looked like a beacon from hell.

'I'm glad you're back,' she said. 'I'm scared.'

I put my arm around her. 'Why? There's nothing to be scared of. You're perfectly safe up here.'

'I didn't mean that. Bernie, I'm Jewish, remember?'

'I'd forgotten. I'm sorry.' I drew her closer to me and kissed her on the forehead. Her hair and overcoat smelled strongly of smoke almost as if she herself had caught fire.

I coughed a little. 'So much for Berlin's famous air,' I said.

'I was worried about you. Where have you been?'

A strong gust of bitterly cold wind filled our faces with smoke. Where had I been? I didn't know. I was dull, without thoughts. I swallowed with some difficulty and tried to answer. The smoke was bothering me a lot now. There was so much of it that I couldn't see the fire anymore. Nor the Adlon's rooftop. Or even Frieda. After a minute I took a deep breath that hurt my throat. Then I called out to her. 'Where are you?'

A man peered at me out of the smoke. He was wearing a white coat and a gold wristwatch. His eyes were on my collar bone and then his fingers, too, like he expected to find something he was looking for under my Adam's apple.

I turned my head on the pillow and yawned.

'How does that feel?' asked the man wearing the white coat.

'Hurts a bit when I swallow,' I heard myself say. 'Otherwise it feels fine.'

He was tanned and fit-looking with a smile as neat as the teeth on a comb. His Castellano wasn't up to much. He sounded English, or American perhaps. His breath was cold and perfumed, like his fingers.

'Where am I?'

'You're in the British Hospital in Buenos Aires, Señor Hausner. You had an operation on your thyroid. Remember? I'm your doctor. Doctor Pack.'

I frowned, trying to remember who Hausner was.

'As it happens, you're a very lucky man. You see, the thyroid sits either side of your Adam's apple like two small plums. One of them was cancerous. We took that part of your thyroid out. But the other part was fine. So we left it there. All of which means you won't have to spend the rest of your life having to take thyroxin pills. Just a little calcium, until we're satisfied with your blood analysis. You'll be out of here and back at work in just a few days.'

There was something attached to my throat. I tried to touch it, to feel what it was, but the doctor stopped me.

'Those are some little clips to keep the skin over the wound together,' he explained. 'We won't stitch you up finally until we're quite satisfied that everything in there is all right.'

'And if it's not?' I croaked.

'Ninety-nine times out of a hundred, it is all right. If the cancer hasn't already spread from one side of your thyroid to the other it probably won't now. No, the reason we don't sew you up yet is because we like to keep an eye on your windpipe. Sometimes, after removing a thyroid or part of a thyroid there's a small danger of asphyxiation.' He brandished a pair of surgical pliers. 'If that happens we unlock those clips with these, and open you up again. But I can assure you, sir, there's really very little chance of that happening.'

I closed my eyes. I didn't mean to be rude. But there was too much dope inside me to mind my manners. And I was having a hard job just trying to remember my real name. My name wasn't Hausner, I was certain of that much.

'I hope you operated on the right patient, Doc,' I heard myself whisper. 'I'm someone else, you know. Someone I used to be, a long time ago.'

The next time I woke up she was there, stroking the hair back from my forehead. I'd forgotten her name but I certainly hadn't forgotten how lovely she was. She was wearing a figure-hugging, cigar-brown dress with short, tight sleeves. It made her look like she'd been rolled on a Cuban girl's thigh. If I'd had the strength I'd have put her in my mouth and sucked at her toes.

'Here,' she said, putting a little necklace around my neck. 'It's a l'chaim necklace. For life. To help you get well.'

'Thanks, angel. By the way, how did you find out I was here?'

'They told me at your hotel.' She glanced around my room. 'It's a nice room. You've done all right for yourself.'

I had a private room at the British Hospital because they didn't have a private room at the American Hospital and because Colonel Montalban didn't want Doctor George Pack from Memorial Sloan-Kettering Hospital in New York seen anywhere near the President Juan Perón Hospital, and especially nowhere near the Evita Perón Hospital. But I couldn't tell Anna any of that. It was a very British room. There was a nice picture of the King on the wall.

'But why here instead of the German Hospital?' asked Anna. 'I suppose you're scared someone will recognise you, is that it?'

'It's because my doctor is an American and doesn't speak German,' I said. 'And because his Castellano isn't much either.'

'Anyway, I'm cross with you. You didn't tell me you were ill.'

'I'm not, angel. Not any more. As soon as I get out of here I'll prove it.'

'All the same, I think I would have mentioned something if it had been me who had cancer,' she said. 'I thought we were friends. And that's what friends are for.'

'Maybe I thought you'd think it was contagious.'

'I'm not an idiot, Gunther. I know cancer's not contagious.'

'Maybe I didn't want to take that risk.'

I could tell the King agreed with me. He didn't look too well himself. He was wearing a naval uniform and enough gold braid to supply a shipful of ambitious officers. There was pain in his eyes and in the sinews of his thin hands but he seemed the type to stick it out in silence. I could tell we had a lot in common.

'And talking of risk,' I told her sternly. 'I meant what I said, angel. You're to say nothing about what happened. Or to ask questions concerning what we found out about Directive Eleven.'

'I don't know that we found out very much,' she said. 'I'm not convinced you're the great detective my friend said you are.'

'Well, that makes two of us. But either way this is not something people in this country want anyone asking about, Anna. I've been in this business a long time and I know a big secret when I smell one. I didn't tell you this before but when I mentioned Directive Eleven to someone in SIDE he started twitching like a divining rod. Promise me you won't talk about it. Not even to your father and your mother and your rabbi confessor.'

'All right,' she said sulkily. 'I promise. I won't say anything about any of it. Not even in my prayers.'

'As soon as I'm out of here we'll put the wheels in motion again. See what we can find out. In the meantime you can answer me this question. What are you? A Jewish Catholic? Or a Catholic Jew? I'm not sure I can tell the difference. Not without chucking you in the village pond, anyway.'

'My parents converted when they left Russia,' she said. 'Because they wanted to fit in when they got here. My father said that being a Jew made you too noticeable, that it was best to keep a low profile and seem like everyone else.' She shook her head. 'Why? Have you got something against Jewish Catholics?'

'On the contrary. If you go back far enough you'll find that all Catholics are Jewish. That's the great thing about history. If you go back far enough even Hitler's Jewish.'

'I guess that explains everything,' she said, and kissed me tenderly.

'What was that for?'

'That was in lieu of some grapes. To help you get well soon.'

'It might just help, at that.'

'Then so should this. I've fallen for you. Don't ask me why, because you're too old for me, but I have.'

I had other visitors but none of them as lovely as Anna Yagubsky, and none who made me feel as good. The Colonel looked in on me. So did Pedro Geller. And Melville from the Richmond Café. He was kind enough to beat me at chess. It all felt very civilian and commonplace, as if I was part of a community instead of a man in exile from his own country. With one very tall and scar-faced exception.

He was about six feet four and two hundred and fifty pounds. His hair was thick and dark and, brushed back from a broad, lumpy forehead, looked like a Frenchman's beret. His ears were enormous, like an Indian elephant's and his left cheek was covered with the *schmisses* beloved of German students for whom a duelling sabre had been a more attractive diversion than a slim volume of poetry. He was wearing a light-brown sports jacket, a pair of very baggy flannel trousers, a white shirt and a green silk tie. His shoes were very polished and stout and probably contained a tape-recording of a military parade ground. In his left hand was a cigarette. I guessed he was in his early forties and when he spoke German it was with a strong Viennese accent. 'So, you're awake,' he said.

I sat up in bed and nodded. 'Who are you?'

He picked up the surgical pliers in his huge mitts – the ones that were supposed to open the clips on my neck in case anything went wrong with my windpipe – and started to play crab with them.

'Otto Skorzeny,' he said. His voice sounded almost as rough as my own, as if he gargled with battery-acid.

'That's a relief,' I said. 'Most of the nurses have been quite pretty up until now.'

He chuckled. 'So I noticed. Maybe I should check in here myself. I'm still plagued with an old war wound I got in forty-one. I was blown up with a Katyusha rocket and buried alive for a while.'

'I hear that's the best way, in the long run.'

He chuckled again. It sounded like a drain emptying.

'What can I do for you, Otto?' I called him Otto because all three buttons were done up on his jacket and there was something bulging under his right arm-pit. I didn't think it was his thyroid.

'I heard you were asking questions about me.' He smiled, but it was more like a way of stretching his face than anything pleasant.

'Oh?'

'At the Casa Rosada.'

'Maybe one or two.'

'That might not be a healthy thing to do, my friend. Especially for a man in your position.' He tapped the jaws of the pliers together meaningfully. 'What are these things for anyway?'

I thought it better not to tell him in any detail. 'They're surgical pliers.'

'You mean for pulling out in-grown toenails and things like that?'

'I imagine so.'

'I saw a man have all his fingernails pulled out by the Gestapo once. That was in Russia.'

'I've heard it's a fascinating country.'

'Those bloody Russians can take pain like no one else,' he said with real admiration in his voice. 'Once, I saw a Russian soldier, both of whose arms had been taken off at the elbow just an hour or two earlier, get up from his mattress and take himself to the latrine.'

'Must have been some pair of pliers.'

'Anyway, I'm here now. So what did you want to know?

And don't give me that phoney passport story. A good conduct pass, or whatever it is. What do you really want to know.'

'I'm looking for a killer.'

'Is that all?' Skorzeny shrugged. 'We're all of us that, I imagine.' He put out his cigarette in the ashtray on my bedside cabinet. 'Otherwise we'd hardly be here, in Argentina.'

'True. But this man has killed children. Young girls, anyway. Gutted them like pigs. In the beginning I thought one of our old comrades might have developed a taste for psychopathic murder. Now I know it's something else altogether. Also there's a missing girl who may or may not be connected with any of this. She might be dead. Or abducted.'

'And you thought I might have had something to do with all this?'

'Abduction used to be your main claim to fame, as I recall.'

'You mean Mussolini?' Skorzeny grinned. 'That was a rescue mission. There's a hell of a difference between pulling the Duce's eggs out of the fire and kidnapping a bloody schoolgirl.'

'I know that. All the same I felt obliged to look under every stone. Those are my orders anyway.'

'Who's giving them?'

'I can't tell you that.'

'I like you Hausner. You've got guts. Unlike most of our old comrades. Here I am, quietly intimidating you—'

'Is that what you're doing?'

'—And you refuse to be intimidated, damn you.'

'So far.'

'I could go to work on those clips with these pliers,' he said. 'I bet that's what they're for, as a matter of fact. But it occurs to me that I'd rather have a man like you on my side. Allies, men you can rely on, are rather thin on the ground in this country.'

He nodded, as if agreeing with himself. From the look of him, and the reputation he had, it was probably the safest thing to do.

'Yes, I could use a good man on my side, in Argentina.'

'Sounds like you're offering me a job, Otto.'

'Maybe I am at that.'

'Everyone wants me to work for them. At this rate I'll make employee of the year.'

'So long as you stay alive you might.'

'Meaning?'

'I wouldn't want you shooting off your mouth about my business,' he said. 'If you did I'd have to shoot off your mouth.'

He said it in a way that made me think he thought it sounded cute. Only I didn't doubt that he was serious about it. From what I knew about Otto Skorzeny – Waffen SS Colonel, Knight's Cross, hero of the Eastern Front, the man who rescued Mussolini from British custody – it would have been a grave mistake not to have taken him seriously. An unmarked grave mistake.

'I can keep my mouth shut,' I said.

'Everyone can keep their mouths shut,' Skorzeny said. 'The trick is to do it and stay alive at the same time.'

That was cute, too. The scars, the Knight's Cross, the reputation for ruthlessness, all of it was starting to make a lot of sense. The man who put Otto Skorzeny's nose out of joint wasn't about to get the loan of his collection of pressed wild flowers. He was a killer. Maybe not the kind of killer who enjoyed killing for killing's sake, but certainly the kind who killed without even the least idea of how anyone could lose any sleep over it.

'All right. I'll help you out if I can, Otto. I'm not awful busy right now, so go ahead. Pretend I'm your priest or your doctor. Tell me something confidential.'

'I'm looking for some money.'

I tried to stifle a yawn. 'Small world,' I said.

'Not that sort of money,' he snarled.

'There's a kind I don't know about?'

'Yeah. The kind you can't count because there's so bloody much of it. Serious money.'

'Oh. That kind of money.'

'Here in Argentina, about two hundred million US dollars.'

'Well, I can understand why you would be looking for that kind of money, Otto.'

'Maybe twice that. I don't know for sure.'

This time I stayed silent. Four hundred million dollars is the kind of figure that commands a lot of respectful silence.

'During the war, two, maybe three or four U-Boats came to Argentina with gold, diamonds and foreign currency. Jew money mostly. From the camps. On arrival the Monte Cristo was handled by five German bankers. German-Argentines who were supposed to be financing the war effort on this side of the Atlantic.' He shrugged. 'I don't have to tell you how successful they were at that. And most of the money remained unspent. Safely tucked up in vaults at the Banco Germanico and the Banco Tourquist.'

'That's a nice little legacy for someone,' I said.

'Now you're getting it,' said Skorzeny. 'After the war, the Peróns had the same thought as you. The greasy general and his bitch blonde started putting a little pressure on these five bankers, suggesting that they might like to make a generous campaign contribution in return for all the traditional Argentine hospitality that was being shown to our old comrades. So the bankers ante'd up and hoped that was the end of it. Of course it wasn't. It's expensive being a dictator. Especially one without the same line of Jewish credit that Hitler enjoyed. So the Peróns, bless their black shirts, asked for another contribution. And this time the bankers demurred. As bankers do. Big mistake. The President started to apply a little pressure. One of the bankers, the eldest, Ludwig Freude, was charged with espionage and fraud. Freude made a deal with Perón, and in return for turning over the control of a nice chunk of change his son, Rodolfo Freude, was made the head of security police.'

'That's a nice quid pro quo,' I said.

'Isn't it? Heinrich Dorge, who was formerly aide to Hjalmar Schacht, was less cooperative. He didn't have a son like Rodolfo. Which was too bad for him. The Peróns had him murdered. To encourage the other three bankers – Von Leute, Von Bader, and Staudt. And they were encouraged. They handed over the lot. The whole Monte Cristo. Since when they have remained effectively under house arrest.'

'Why? If the Peróns have the loot, then what's the point of that?'

'Because there's a lot more to it than the money that walked down the gangplank of a couple of U-Boats. A lot more money anyway. You see, the Peróns have got this foundation going. For the last five years Eva's been giving Reichsbank money away to just about every Argie bastard who can spin her a hard luck story. They've been buying the loyalty of the people. The trouble is, at the rate they're spending the U-Boat cash they're going to run out. And so, to stay in power for another ten, maybe twenty years, they would dearly like to get their hands on the real prize. The big prize. The motherlode.'

'You mean your four hundred million dollars isn't it?'

'We didn't lose the war for lack of money, my friend. At the end of the war, there was so much money held in the Reichsbank's Swiss accounts it made what was in German banks here look like small change. There are billions of Nazi dollars in Zurich. And it's all of it, every last cent, under the control of those three remaining bankers here in Buenos Aires. At least, it is so long as they remain alive.'

'I see.'

'For the Peróns, the question is this: how to get their hands on it. To exercise control of the Zurich accounts requires the physical presence in Switzerland of at least one of those bankers, accompanied by the signed letters of the other two. But which one of them can be trusted to go? Trusted by the Peróns. Trusted by the other bankers. Naturally there's no guarantee that the one who goes to Zurich is ever going to come back again. Nor any guarantee that he will do what the Peróns want him to do when he's there. Which is, of course, to sign control of the money over to them. It leaves these three in a bit of a tight spot. And that's where I come in.'

'Oh? Are you a banker now, Otto?'

I tried to look and sound like all this was news to me. But my meeting with the Von Baders and the disappearance of their daughter, Fabienne, left me in no doubt that the money and her disappearance were somehow connected.

'More of a banking regulator, you might say,' said Skorzeny. 'You see, I'm here to make sure the Peróns never see a pfennig of that money. To this end I've managed to become quite close to Eva. Largely on account of how I managed to foil an attempt on her life. Well, it was easy enough.' He chuckled. 'Especially since it was me who set her up. Anyway she's come to rely on me, rather.'

'Otto,' I said, grinning. 'You don't mean…?'

'We're not lovers exactly,' he admitted. 'But, like I said, she's come to rely on me. So who knows what might happen? Especially as the President is off fucking young girls.'

'Oh? How young?'

'Thirteen. Fourteen. Sometimes younger, according to Eva.'

'And how is this trust in you going to manifest itself in a way that's relevant to the money in Switzerland?' I asked carefully.

'By making sure I can be in a position to find out if ever she manages to send one of these bankers to Zurich. Because then I should have to act to prevent that from happening.'

'You mean kill someone. One of the bankers. Maybe all three of them.'

'Probably. As I said, the trust won't be under their control for ever. Eventually the money will be dispersed to certain organisations throughout Germany. You see, it's our plan to use the money to rebuild the cause of European fascism.'

'Our plan? You mean the Old Comrades plan, don't you, Otto? The Nazi plan.'

'Of course.'

'And double-crossing the Peróns? It sounds dangerous, Otto.'

'It is.' He grinned. 'Which is why I need someone in the secret police watching my back. Someone like you.'

'Suppose I'm the nervous type. Suppose I don't want to be involved.'

'That would be a shame. For one thing, it would mean you'd have no one watching *your* back. Besides, Eva trusts me. You, she hardly knows. If you denounce me you'll be the one who disappears, not me. Think it over.'

'How long have I got?'

'Time's up.'

'I can hardly say no, can I?'

'That's the way I see it, too. You and me. We're two of a kind. You see it was Eva that told me about you. About that little speech you made to her and the greaseball. How you used to be a cop. Stuff like that. That took a boxful of eggs. Perón appreciated that. So do I. We're both mavericks, you and I. Loners. Outsiders. We can help each other out. A phone call here, a phone call there. And, depend on it, we never forget our friends.' He produced a business card and placed it carefully on my bedside table. 'On the other hand ...'

'On the other hand?'

He glanced at the picture of the British King that was hanging on the wall beside my bed. For a moment, he just stared at it with something like malevolence, then he punched it hard. Hard enough to smash the glass and knock the picture off the wall. The picture fell on the floor. Small pieces of glass showered my chest and legs. Skorzeny ignored them, preferring to concentrate on allowing a small trickle of blood to run off his lacerated knuckles and onto my head. He smiled but his meaning was less than companionable.

'On the other hand, the next time we meet this could be your blood we're looking at, not mine.'

'That's a nasty cut you've got there, Otto. You should get it seen to. I believe there's a good veterinary hospital over on Viamonte. Maybe they'll even give you a rabies shot while they're fixing your paw.'

'This?' Skorzeny lifted his hand and let the blood drip onto my face. For a moment he seemed fascinated by the sight of it. Maybe he was at that. There were plenty of people in the SS who'd been fascinated by bloodshed. Most of them seemed to be living in Argentina. 'This is just a scratch.'

'You know, it might be a good idea if you were to leave now, Otto. After what you did to their King. This is the British Hospital, after all.'

Otto spat onto the fallen picture. 'I always hated that bastard,' he said.

'No need to explain. No need at all.' I was humouring him now. Anxious for him to be gone. 'Not from a man who once met Adolf Hitler.'

'More than once,' he said quietly.

'Really?' I said, feigning interest. 'The next time we see each other you must tell me all about it. In fact, I'll look forward to it.'

'Then we're partners.'

'Sure, Otto, sure.'

He held out his bloody hand for me to shake. I took it and

felt the strength in his forearm and, closer to him now, I saw the dirty ice in his blue eyes and breathed the rank odour of his decaying breath. There was a little gold star in his lapel. I didn't know what it was but I wondered whether, if I had removed it, he would have ground to a halt, like the murderous creature in Gustav Meyrink's book *The Golem*.

If only life was that simple.

FIFTEEN

BUENOS AIRES. 1950.

It was a short convalescence. But not so short that I wasn't able to lie in bed and do nothing but think. And, after a while, I managed to put some of the bits together in my mind. Unfortunately it was the kind of puzzle where the jigsaw was still moving and, if I wasn't very careful, the narrow vertical blade might slice off my fingers while I was trying to arrange the interlocking pieces. Or worse than that. Living long enough to see the whole picture might prove to be difficult. Yet I could hardly just put it all down and walk away. I don't care for a word like 'retirement' but that was what I wanted. I was tired of doing puzzles. Argentina was a beautiful country. I wanted to sit on the beach at Mar del Plata, to see the regattas at Tigre, or visit the lakes at Nahuel Huapi. Unfortunately, nobody wanted me to do what I wanted. What they wanted was for me to do what they wanted. And much as I wished things to be different I couldn't see a way around any of this. I did, however, decide to attend to things according to my own idea of precedence.

Contrary to what I'd told Colonel Montalban I did hate loose ends. It had always bothered me that I'd never arrested Anita Schwarz's killer. Not just for the sake of my professional pride but for Paul Herzefelde's professional pride, too. So the first thing I did when I got out of hospital was drive to the house of Helmut Gregor. By now I had a pretty shrewd idea of who and what he was but I wanted to make sure before I threw it back in the Colonel's face.

Helmut Gregor lived in the nicest part of Florida. The house, at Calle Arenales 2460, was a handsome, spacious, colonial-type white stucco mansion that was owned by a wealthy Argentine businessman called Gerard Malbranc. There was a nice pillared veranda out front and, chained to the balustrade, was a medium-sized dog, which was doing its best to ignore the tantalising proximity of a long-haired cat that seemed to have the run of the place.

I staked the house out. I had a flask of coffee, some cognac, one or two newspapers, and several books in German from the Durer Haus bookshop. I had even borrowed a small telescope. It was a nice quiet street and, despite my best intentions, I left the books and the papers alone and slept, with one eye half-open. One time I sat up and saw a rather handsome couple ride by on even more handsome horses. They wore normal clothes and used English saddles. Florida wasn't the kind of neighbourhood to see anything more picturesque. On Calle Arenales a gaucho would have looked about as inconspicuous as a football on a cathedral altar. Another time I looked up to see a van from Gath & Chaves delivering a bed to a woman wearing a pink silk dressing gown. From the way she was dressed, I had the idea she was probably planning to sleep on it the minute the two apes lifting it into her home were back in their van. I wouldn't have minded joining her.

In the late afternoon, after I'd been there several hours, a police car showed up. A policeman and a girl of about fourteen got out of the car. The policeman looked old enough to be her grandfather. He might have been her *caballero blanco*, which was what *porteños* called a sugar daddy, but uniformed cops don't usually make enough to spend it on anyone other than their fat wives and their ugly children. Of course, he might actually have been a father taking his stunningly attractive young daughter to an appointment with the family doctor – but for the fact that most fathers don't usually put their daughters in handcuffs. Not unless they've been very bad indeed. The dog started to bark as they mounted the steps to the front door. The cop patted the dog's head. It stopped barking.

Through the telescope I watched the polished black front door. It was opened by a man wearing a light-coloured tweed suit. His hair was dark and he had a short, Errol Flynn-style moustache. He and the policeman seemed to know each other. The man from the house smiled to reveal a noticeable gap between the two front teeth on his upper jaw. Then he placed an avuncular hand on the girl's shoulder and spoke kindly to her. The girl, who had seemed nervous until now, was reassured. The man pointed at the handcuffs and the cop took them off. The girl rubbed her wrists and then put her thumbnail between her teeth. She had long brown hair and skin that was the colour of honey. She was wearing a red corduroy dress and red and black stockings. Her knees touched together when she talked and when she smiled it was like the sun came out from behind a cloud. The man from the house ushered the girl inside, looked at the cop and pointed after her, as if inviting him in, too. The cop shook his head. The man went inside, the door closed and the cop went to sit in the car, where he smoked a cigarette, tipped his cap forward, folded his arms, and went to sleep.

I glanced at my wristwatch. It was two o'clock.

Ninety minutes passed before the door opened again. The man from the house followed the girl onto the veranda. He picked up the cat and showed it off to her. The girl stroked the cat's head and put some candy in her mouth. The man put down the cat and they went down the steps. The girl was moving more slowly than before, coming down the steps as if each one had been several feet high. I looked through the telescope again. Her head hung heavy on her shoulders but not as heavy as her eyelids. She looked like she'd been drugged. Several paces ahead of her the man tapped the window of the police car and the cop sat bolt upright as if something sharp had come through the bottom of his seat. The man opened the rear passenger door of the car and turned to see where the girl was and saw that she had stopped walking altogether, although she was hardly standing still. She resembled a tree that was about to topple. Her face was pale and her eyes were closed and she was breathing deeply through her nose in an effort not to faint. The man went back to her and put his arm around her waist. The next thing she bent forward and vomited into the gutter. The man looked around for the cop and said something sharply. The cop came over, collected the girl up in his arms and laid her on the back seat of the car. He closed the door, took off his cap, wiped his brow with a hand-kerchief and said something to the man who bent forward, waved at the prostrate girl through the car window and then stood back and waited. He looked around. He looked in my direction. I was about thirty yards up the street. I didn't think he could see me. He didn't. The police car started, the man waved again as it drove off and then he turned and went back up to the house.

I folded away the telescope and returned it to the glove box. I swallowed a mouthful of cognac from the flask in my pocket and got out of the car. I collected a file and notepad off the passenger seat, shifted my shoulder-holster a few inches, rubbed the still tender scar on my collarbone, and walked up the steps. The dog started barking again. The cat, which was the size and shape of a feather duster, sat on the white balustrade and viewed me with vertical-eyed scrutiny. It was a minor demon, the familiar to its diabolic owner.

I hauled on the doorbell, heard a chime that sounded like something from a clock tower, and gazed back across the street. The woman with the pink dressing gown was getting dressed now. I was still watching when the door opened behind me.

'You certainly couldn't miss the postman,' I said, speaking

German. 'Not with a bell like that. It lasts as long as a heavenly choir.' I showed him my ID. 'I wonder if I might come in and ask you a few questions.'

A strong smell of ether hung in the air, underscoring the obvious inconvenience of my visit. But Helmut Gregor was a German and a German knew better than to argue with credentials like mine. The Gestapo no longer existed but the idea and influence of the Gestapo lived on in the minds of all Germans old enough to know the difference between wedding rings and a set of brass knuckles. Especially in Argentina.

'You'd better come in,' he said, standing politely to one side. 'Herr—?'

'Hausner,' I said. 'Carlos Hausner.'

'A German working for Central State Intelligence. That's rather unusual, isn't it?'

'Oh, I don't know. There was a time when we were quite good at this sort of thing.'

He smiled thinly and closed the door.

We were standing in a high-ceilinged hallway with a marble floor. I had a brief glimpse of what looked like a surgery at the far end of that hallway, before Gregor closed the frosted door in front of it.

He paused as if half-inclined to force me to ask my questions in the hallway, then he seemed to change his mind and led the way into an elegant sitting room. Beneath an ornate gilt mirror was a graceful stone fireplace, in front of which stood a hardwood Chinese tea table and a couple of handsome leather armchairs. He waved me to one of them.

I sat down and glanced around. On a sideboard was a collection of silver maté gourds and, on the table in front us, a copy of the *Free Press*, which was the Nazi-leaning German language daily. On another table was a photograph of a man wearing plus-fours and riding a bicycle. Another photograph showed a man wearing white tie and tails on his wedding day.

In neither of these two photographs did the man have a moustache and this made it easier for me to remember him as the man whom I'd met on the steps of Doctor Kassner's Berlin house, back in the summer of 1932. The man he'd called Beppo. The man who was now calling himself Helmut Gregor. Apart from the moustache he didn't look so very different. He was not quite forty and his hair was still thick and dark brown, and without a hint of grey. He wasn't smiling but his mouth remained slightly open, his lip curled like a dog that was getting ready to growl, or to bite. His eyes were different to how I remembered them. They were like the cat's eyes: wary and watchful and full of nine lives' worth of dark secrets.

'I'm sorry for disturbing your lunch.' I pointed at a glass of milk and a sandwich that lay uneaten on a silver tray on the floor, next to the leg of his chair. At the same time I wondered if the milk and the sandwich might have been meant for his young female visitor.

'That's all right. What can I do for you?'

I rattled off the usual spiel about the Argentine passport and the good conduct pass and how everything was nothing more than a formality because I was ex-SS myself and knew the score. Hearing this, he asked me about my war service and, after I'd supplied the edited version that left out my time with the German War Crimes Bureau, he seemed to relax a little, like a fishing-line slackening after several minutes in the water.

'I was also in Russia,' he said. 'With the medical corps of the Viking Division. And, in particular, at the Battle of Rostow.'

'I heard it was tough there,' I offered.

'It was tough everywhere.'

I opened the file I had brought with me. Helmut Gregor's file. 'If I could just check a few basic details.'

'Certainly.'

'You were born on—?'

'March 16th, 1911.'

'In—?'

'Gunzburg.'

I shook my head. 'It's somewhere on the Danube. That's as much as I know about it. I'm from Berlin, myself. No. Wait a minute. There was someone I knew who was from Gunzburg. A fellow named Pieck. Walter Pieck. He was in the SS, too. At Dachau concentration camp, I think it was. Perhaps you knew him.'

'Yes. His father was the local police chief. We knew each other slightly, before the war. But I was never at Dachau. I was never at any concentration camp. As I said, I was in the Viking Division of the Waffen SS.'

'And what did your own father do? In Gunzburg?'

'He sold – still sells – farm machinery. Threshing machines, that kind of thing. All very ordinary, but I believe he's still the town's largest employer.'

'I'm sorry,' I said, pen poised. 'I've missed out a question. Name of father and mother, please.'

'Is this really necessary?'

'It's normal on most passport applications.'

He nodded. 'Karl and Walburga Mengele.'

'Walburga. That's an unusual name.'

'Yes. Isn't it? Walburga was an English saint who lived and died in Germany. I assume you've heard of Walpurgis night? On the first of May? That's when her relics were transferred to some church or other.'

'I thought that was some kind of witch's Sabbath.'

'I believe it's also that,' he said.

'And you are Josef. Any brothers or sisters?'

'Two brothers. Alois and Karl Junior.'

'I won't keep you much longer, Doctor Mengele.' I smiled.

'I prefer Doctor Gregor.'

'Yes, of course. I'm sorry. Now then, where was it that you qualified?'

'Why is this relevant?'

'You're still practising as a doctor, aren't you? I should say it was highly relevant.'

'Yes. Yes, of course. I'm sorry. It's just that I'm not used to answering so many questions truthfully. I've spent the last five years being someone else. I'm sure you know what that's like.'

'I certainly do. Now perhaps you understand why it is that the Argentine government asked me to carry out this task. Because I'm a German and an SS man, just like you. In order that you and our other old comrades could be put at ease about the whole process. You can see that, can't you?'

'Yes. It makes quite a lot of sense, when you think about it.'

I shrugged. 'On the other hand, if you don't want to have an Argentine passport, we can stop this right now.' I shook my head. 'I mean, it certainly won't make me itch, as the saying goes.'

'Please, do carry on.'

I frowned as if thinking of something else.

'I insist,' he added.

'No, it's just that I've got a feeling we've met before.'

'I don't think so. I'm sure I would have remembered.'

'In Berlin, wasn't it? The summer of 1932.'

'In the summer of 1932, I was in Munich.'

'Yes, surely you remember. It was at the home of another doctor. Doctor Richard Kassner. On Donhoff Platz?'

'I don't recall knowing a Doctor Kassner.'

I unbuttoned my coat so that I could treat his eyes to a little taste of the gun I was wearing. Just in case he thought to try something surgical on me. Like trepanning a little hole in my head with a pistol. Because by now I had no doubt he was armed. There was something heavier than a packet of cigarettes in one of his coat pockets. I didn't know exactly what Mengele had done during the war. The only thing I knew was what Eichmann had told me. That Mengele had done something bestial at Auschwitz. And that for this reason, he was one of the most wanted men in Europe.

'Come now. Surely you remember. What was it he used to call you? Biffo, wasn't it? No wait a minute. It was Beppo. Whatever happened to Kassner?'

'I really think you're mistaking me for someone else. If you don't mind me saying so, this was eighteen years ago.'

'No, it's all coming back to me now, you see, Herr Doctor Mengele. Beppo. I was a policeman in 1932. Working for the Homicide Division in Berlin KRIPO. A detective investigating the murder of Anita Schwarz. Do you remember *her*, perhaps?'

He crossed his legs, coolly. 'No. Look, this is all very confusing. I think I need a cigarette.'

His hand went into the pocket. But I was quicker.

'Uh-uh,' I said, and holding the Smith & Wesson just a few inches above his belly, I smacked his hand out of his coat pocket and then took out a walnut-handled PPK. I glanced at it briefly. It was a thirty-eight with a Nazi eagle on the grip.

'Not very clever of you,' I said. 'Keeping something like this.'

'You're the one who's not being very clever,' he said.

I pocketed the pistol and sat down again. 'Oh? How's that?'

'Because I'm a friend of the President.'

'Is that so?'

'I advise you to put that gun away and leave now.'

'Not before we've had a little talk, Mengele. About old times.' I thumbed back the hammer on the Smith. 'And if I don't like the answers then I'm going to have to offer you a prompt. In the foot. And then in the leg. I'm sure you know how it works, Doctor. A Socratic dialogue?'

'Socratic?'

'Yes. I encourage you to reflect and to think and, together—' I waved the gun at him. '—Together we search for the truth to some important questions. No philosophical training is needed but, if I think you're not trying to help us reach a consensus – well, you remember what happened to Socrates, don't you? His fellow Athenians forced him to put a gun to his head and blow his own brains out. Something like that anyway.'

'Why on earth do you care what happened to Anita Schwarz?' Mengele asked angrily. 'It was almost twenty years ago.'

'Not just Anita Schwarz. Elizabeth Bremer, too. The girl in Munich?'

'It wasn't what you think,' he insisted.

'No? What was it then? Dadaism? I seem to remember that was quite popular before the Nazis. Let's see now. You eviscerated those two girls because you were an artist who believed in meaning through chaos. You used their insides for a collage. Or perhaps a nice photograph. There were you and Max Ernst and Kurt Schwitters. No? How about this then: you were a medical student who decided to make a bit of extra money by offering back-street abortions to underage girls. It's the details I'm not clear about. The when and the how.'

'If I tell you, will you leave me alone?'

'If you don't tell me I'm going to shoot you.' I took aim at his foot. 'Then I'll leave you alone. To bleed to death.'

'All right, all right.'

'Let's start in Munich. With Elizabeth Bremer.'

Mengele shook his head until, seeing me take aim at his foot again, he waved his hands. 'No, no, I'm just trying to cast my mind back. But it's difficult. So much has happened since then. You've no idea how irrelevant all this seems to a man like me. You're talking about two accidental deaths that happened almost twenty years ago.' He laughed bitterly. 'I was at Auschwitz, you know. And what happened there was, of course, quite extraordinary. Perhaps the most extraordinary thing that has ever happened. Three million died at

Auschwitz. Three million. And you just want to talk about two children.'

'I'm not here to judge you. I'm here to finish an investigation.'

'Listen to yourself. You sound like one of those stupid Canadian cowboys. What is it that they call them? The Mounties? They always get their man. Is that really all this is? Professional pride? Or is there something else I'm missing?'

'I'm asking the questions, doctor. But as it happens there is some professional pride here, yes. I'm sure you know what that's like, you being a professional man yourself. I got taken off this case, for political reasons. Because I wasn't a Nazi. I didn't like that then and I don't like it now. So. Let's start with Walter Pieck. You knew him quite well, didn't you? From Gunzburg.'

'Of course. Everyone knows everyone else in Gunzburg. It's a very Catholic little town. Walter and I were at school together. At least until he failed his Abitur. He was always more interested in sport, especially winter sports. He was a fantastic skater and skier. And I should know, I'm a good skier myself. Anyway, he quarrelled with his father and went to work in Munich. I passed my Abitur and went to study in Munich. We lived very separate lives but occasionally we would meet up for a beer. I even lent him a bit of money now and then.

'My family was quite wealthy by the standards of Gunzburg. Even today, Gunzburg *is* the Mengele family. But my father, Karl, was a cold figure and somewhat jealous of me, I think. For this reason, perhaps, he kept me short of money when I was at medical school and I resolved to earn some extra myself. It so happened that another old friend's girl was pregnant and, having already read quite a bit on the subject of obstetrics and gynaecology as a student, I offered to help them get rid of it. Actually, it's quite a simple procedure. Before long I'd carried out several abortions. I made quite a bit of money. I bought a small car with the proceeds.

'Then Walther's girlfriend got pregnant. Elizabeth was a lovely girl. Too good for Walther. Anyway she was adamant that she didn't want to keep the child. She wanted to go to university and study medicine herself.' Mengele frowned and shook his head. 'I thought I was helping her, but there were complications. A haemorrhage. Even in a hospital bed she would probably have died, you understand, but this was in my apartment in Munich. And I had no way of helping her. She bled to death on my kitchen table.' He paused for a moment and almost looked troubled at the memory of it. 'You must remember I was still a young man, with my whole future ahead of me. I wanted to help people. As a doctor, you understand. Anyway, I panicked. I had a dead body on my hands, and it would have been quite obvious to any pathologist that she had had an abortion. I was desperate to cover my tracks.

'It was Walther's idea really, that I should remove all her sexual organs. There had been some lurid details of an old lust murder in some magazine he'd been reading and he said that by making Elizabeth's death look like one of those it would at least ensure the police did not come looking for an illegal abortionist. I agreed. So, I cut her up, like something out of an anatomy lesson and Walther disposed of her body. His father in Gunzburg gave him an alibi, said he'd been at home at the time of Elizabeth's death. He was used to doing that for Walther. But after that Walther had to toe the line, do what his father told him. Which is how he ended up joining the SS. To keep him out of trouble.' Mengele laughed. 'Ironic really, when you think about. The Americans shot him at Dachau.' He shook his head. 'But I certainly didn't mean to kill that poor girl. She was lovely. A real Aryan beauty. I was trying to help her. And why not? She made a mistake that's all. It happens all the time. And to the most respectable people.'

'Tell me about Kassner,' I said. 'How did you know him?'

'From Munich. His estranged wife lived there. He was trying to persuade her to come back to him. Unsuccessfully, as it turned out. Someone introduced us at a party. And it turned out we shared a number of interests. In anthropology, in human genetics, in medical research, and in National Socialism. He was a friend of Goebbels, you know. Anyway, I used to go and visit him in Berlin. To spend some of what I'd been making from carrying out abortions in the fleshpots. They were the best times of my life. I'm sure I don't have to tell you what Berlin was like in those days. There was complete sexual licence.'

'Which is how you caught a dose of jelly.'

'Yes, that's right. How did you know about that?'

'And Kassner treated you with the new "magic bullet" he was testing for I.G. Farben. Protonsil.'

Mengele looked impressed. 'Yes. That's right, too. I can see that the reputation of the Berlin police force was well-deserved.'

'He was also treating Goebbels for venereal disease. Did you know that? I suspect it's one of the reasons I was taken off the case. Because someone thought that I might find out about it. Which I did, of course.'

'I knew he was treating someone famous, but I didn't know it was Goebbels. Actually, I thought it might be Hitler. There was some talk, you know. That the Führer was syphilitic. So, it was Goebbels all along.' Mengele shrugged. 'Anyway, Protonsil was highly effective. Until the advent of penicillin I think it was the most successful drug that the Dyestuff Syndicate ever had. I got to know them quite well myself when Kassner went to work for them. I tested a number of drugs for them at Auschwitz. It was important work. Not that anyone remembers that now, all they're interested in are the medical mishaps that I'm afraid were an inevitable consequence, given the exigencies of wartime scientific and medical life.'

'That's a nice clinical way of describing mass murder,' I said.

'And I suppose you're here in Argentina for the beef,' he said.

'Never mind that. Just tell me about Anita Schwarz.'

'I can't believe that you're wasting my time with this shit.'

'If you can't believe me, then believe this.' I brandished the gun for a second. 'How did you come to meet her?'

'I met her father when I started coming to Berlin. He was in the SA. Later on, when he became a judge, we became much better acquainted. Anyway, someone introduced us. Kurt Daluege, I think. I had performed an abortion on his mistress, without complications. Actually, it was her second and I asked Daluege if he'd ever considered the advantages of having her sterilised. He hadn't, of course. But he talked her into it, eventually.'

'You're joking.'

'Not at all. It's simply a question of tying off the fallopian tubes. Anyway, Daluege mentioned this to his brother-in-law, Otto Schwarz. As a possibility for his daughter.'

I shook my head, horrified at what Mengele was telling me although, given what I remembered about Otto Schwarz's general demeanour upon being told that his disabled daughter was dead, the doctor's explanation also seemed to make perverted sense. 'Are you telling me that you sterilised a fifteen-year-old girl?'

'Look here, this girl was hardly the same type as Elizabeth Bremer. Not at all. Anita Schwarz was disabled and, despite her young age, an occasional prostitute. It made a lot of sense to have her sterilised. Not just for the benefit of her poor parents but also for the genetic health of the country. She was quite unfit to reproduce. Later on, of course, Otto and I were colleagues. He became a judge in one of the Genetic Health Courts that came into being under the 1933 Law for the Prevention of Genetically Diseased Offspring, to decide upon matters of "racial hygiene". Certain people were forbidden to marry while others were the victims of forcible sterilisations.' He paused.

'So the sterilisation of Anita Schwarz was cooked up by the two of you, for the genetic health of the country,' I said. 'Did Anita have any say in the matter?'

Mengele shook his head, irritably. 'Her consent was irrelevant. She was spastic, you understand. Hers was an unworthy life. Any genetic health court would have agreed with our decision.'

'Where did the operation take place?'

'In a private clinic in Dahlem, where the girl's mother worked as a night nurse. It was quite suitable, I can assure you.'

'But something went wrong.'

He nodded. 'Unlike carrying out an abortion, a general anaesthetic is required in sterilisation procedures. And so the services of an anaesthetist were required. Naturally I called on the services of the same person I'd used in the procedure on Kurt Daluege's mistress. Someone Daluege knew. Someone less than competent as it turned out. I was unaware of the fact that he himself was a drug addict. And he made a mistake. It was not the procedure that killed her, you understand. It was the anaesthetic. Quite simply, we were unable to revive her. And, left with a similar dilemma to Elizabeth Bremer's death in Munich, I decided to mutilate her dead body in the same sensational fashion. With, I may add, the full complicity of the girl's mother. She was a strict Roman Catholic and believed that God had not meant her daughter to have lived in the first place, which was a great relief to my colleague and myself. He and I disposed of the body at the opposite end of the city, in Friedrichshain Park. And the rest you know.'

'And after that?'

'I went home.'

'I meant in the years after that. Up to your joining the SS.'

'I carried on doing abortions and sterilisations until 1937. Legally, I might add. Then I joined the Reich Institute for Heredity, Biology and Racial Purity at the University of Frankfurt, where I was a Research Assistant.'

'And now?'

'Now? I live a very quiet life. I am a humble doctor, as you can see.'

'Not so humble, I think. Tell me about the girl who was here half an hour ago. I suppose you just polished her toenails and combed her hair.'

'You are way out of your depth, Hausner.'

'That's all right. I'm a good swimmer.'

'You'll have to be. You know what they do with the people they don't like, in Argentina? They take them for a plane ride, and push them out over the River Plate at ten thousand feet. Listen to me, man. Forget you ever saw that girl.'

I put the gun down and sprang forward, gathering his cashmere coat lapels in one hand and then slapping him hard on each side of his astonished, swarthy face – forehand and backhand, like a ping-pong champion.

'When I want to listen to you, I'll slap you first,' I said. 'Now let's have the rest of it. Every rotten detail of your filthy work in this city. You got that? I want it all or I'll show you the real meaning of an unworthy life.'

I pushed him back down on the chair and let go of his lapels. Mengele's eyes were cold and narrow now, his face pale except where the palm and back of my hand had crimsoned his cheeks. He put his hand on his jaw and snarled an answer back at me like a cowed dog.

'Perón has a taste for young girls,' he said. 'Twelve, thirteen, fourteen. Virgins. And none who are using contraception any more than he does. He likes the tightness of a young girl because his penis is so small. I'm telling you that because just knowing that in a country like this will get you killed, Hausner. He told me this when we first met, and since July of last year when I came to Argentina, I've carried out as many as thirty abortions for him.'

'And Grete Wohlauf?'

'Who's she?'

'A fifteen-year-old girl in the police morgue.'

'I don't know their names,' he said. 'But I can tell you this. None of these girls has died. I'm good at what I do now.'

I didn't doubt it. Everyone has a skill in life. Destroying life was his.

'Fabienne Von Bader? What about her?'

'As I said, I don't know their names.'

For some reason, I believed him.

'You know, I'm not the only one,' he said. 'The only German doctor doing this, I mean. Being an SS doctor is an attractive combination for the General. It means that, unlike the local Catholic doctors, who have scruples about carrying out abortions, we have to do what we're told or risk being sent back to face Allied justice.'

'So that's why he likes to meet doctors from Germany.'

'Yes. And that means I'm important to him. That I'm serving his needs. Can you say the same?' Mengele smiled. 'No, I thought not. You're just a stupid policeman with a taste for the sentimental. You won't last long here. These people are just as ruthless as we Germans. Perhaps more so. You see, they're easier to understand. It's money and power that moti-vates them. Not ideology. Not hatred. Not history. Just money and power.'

I showed him the Smith in my fist. 'Don't be so sure I'm not as ruthless as they are. I'm liable to shoot you in the stomach and then sit back to watch you die. Just for the hell of it. You would probably call that an experiment. Maybe I will shoot you, at that. They'd probably give me the Nobel Prize for Medicine. Right now, however, you're going to find a pen and paper and then you're going to write out everything you just told me. Including the part about the President's taste in young girls and the useful cleaning-up service you provide for him afterwards. And then you're going to sign it.'

'With pleasure,' said Mengele. 'I'll be signing your death warrant. Before you die, I think I'm going to visit you in your cell. I'll make sure to bring my medical bag. Perhaps I'll remove one of your organs while you're still alive.'

'Until then,' I said, 'you'll do what I tell you and smile while you're doing it, or I'll want to know why.'

I slapped him again just for the pleasure of it. I could have slapped him all afternoon. He was that kind of guy. Some people just bring out the worst in me.

He wrote out the confession. I read it and put it in my pocket.

'Since you're in a confessional mood,' I said. 'I have one more question for you.' I brought the gun nearer his face. 'And remember. I'm in the mood to use this. So you'd better answer carefully. What do you know about Directive Eleven?'

'All I know is that it was something to do with preventing displaced Jews from coming here.' He shrugged. 'That's it.'

I reached into my pocket and took out the little l'chaim necklace Anna Yagubsky had given to me. I let it spin in the light for a moment. I could see that he recognised what it was.

'That was a neat trick, ripping their guts out like that so as to put us off the scent,' I said. 'But you're not the only one who can do that kind of thing. If I have to shoot you I'll leave this little l'chaim near your body. l'chaim is a Hebrew word that means life. The police will find it and assume that one of those Israeli murder squads caught up with you. They won't look for me, Mengele. So I'm going to ask you just one more time. What do you know about Directive Eleven?'

Mengele had gripped the underside of his chair. Still holding it tightly he leaned forward and yelled at me. 'I don't know anything else about it! I don't know anything else! I don't know anything else!' Then his head fell onto his chest and he started to weep. 'I don't know anything else,' he sobbed. 'I've told you all I know.'

I stood up, slightly horrified at this outburst and the way I'd suddenly reduced him to the level of a schoolboy. It was odd. I felt only disgust for him. But what was odder still was the disgust I now felt for myself. At the darkness that dwelt within me. At the darkness that dwells within us all.

SIXTEEN

BUENOS AIRES. 1950.

I got up at six, just like always, had a bath and then ate some breakfast. The Lloyds served something called a 'fried breakfast': two fried eggs, two strips of bacon, a sausage, a tomato, some mushrooms, and toast. I certainly felt full by the time I'd finished. Every time I ate one I came away with the same thought: that it was hard to believe anyone could have fought a war on a breakfast like that.

I went outside to buy some cigarettes. I paid no attention to the car that overtook me until it stopped and two doors opened. It was a black Ford sedan with nothing to indicate that it was a police car, unless you counted the two men with dark glasses and matching moustaches who sprang out and walked swiftly toward me. I'd seen them before. In Berlin. In Munich. In Vienna. All over the world, they were always the same thick-set men with thick-set brains and thick-set knuckles. And they had the same practical and dynamic manner, regarding me as if I were an embarrassing piece of furniture to be moved as quickly as possible to the back seat of a black car. I'd been removed before. Many times. As a private detective in Berlin it had been a kind of occupational hazard. The Gestapo never much liked private bulls, even though Himmler had once used a Munich firm to find out if his brother-in-law was cheating on his sister.

Instinctively I turned to avoid them and came up against thick-set number three. I was searched and inside the car before I drew my next nervous breath. Nobody said anything.

Except me. It kept my mind off the road ahead and the speed at which we were now moving.

'You boys are good,' I said. 'Look here, I don't suppose it would do any good to mention that my SIDE credentials are in my breast pocket. No? I guess not.'

We headed south, toward San Telmo. I made a few more cracks in Castellano, which got ignored and, after a while, I gave in to their thick-set silence. The car turned west near the Ministry of War. At sixteen storeys with two separate wings, it was the thickest-set building in Buenos Aires and it dominated the surrounding area like the Great Pyramid of Cheops. From the look of it, things hardly augured well for neighbouring countries like Chile and Uruguay. After a while we came to a pleasant little park and, behind this, a castellated fortress that looked as if it had been there since Francisco Pizarro had come to South America. As we drove through the main wooden gate I almost expected the car to be hit with boulders and boiling oil poured on us from the battlements. We parked, and I was hustled out of the car and down some steps in the courtyard. At the end of a long, damp corridor, I was placed in a short damp cell, searched by a man who was almost as big as the thick-set Ministry of War, and then left alone with a chair, a wooden bunk, and a pot for company. The pot was half-full or half-empty, depending on the way you look at these things.

I sat on the floor, which looked more comfortable than the chair or the bunk, and waited. In some faraway, rat-infested tower, a man was laughing hysterically. Nearer to where I was being held, water was trickling noisily onto a floor and, not being particularly thirsty, I hardly minded the sound. But after several hours had elapsed, I started to feel differently about it.

It was dusk when the door finally opened again. Two men came into my cell. They had their sleeves rolled up as if they meant business. One was small and muscular and the other was large and muscular. The smaller one held what looked like a walking stick made of metal, with a two-pin electric plug on the end. The larger one held me. I struggled against him but he didn't seem to notice. I didn't see his face. It was somewhere above the cloud-line. The smaller one had tiny blue eyes like semi-precious stones.

'Welcome to Caseros,' he said with mock politeness. 'Outside there is a little monument to the victims of the 1871 yellow fever outbreak. In the deepest dungeon of this fortress is a pit where the bodies were thrown. Every year there are more and more victims of the 1871 yellow fever outbreak. Understand?'

'I think so.'

'You've been asking questions about Directive Eleven.'

'Have I?'

'I should like to know why that is. And what you think you know.'

'So far I know very little. Possibly it precedes Directive Twelve. And I wouldn't be at all surprised if someone one day discovers that it followed Directive Ten. How am I doing so far?'

'Not very well. You're German, yes?'

I nodded.

'The country of Beethoven and Goethe. Printing and X-rays. Aspirin and the rocket engine.'

'Don't forget the Hindenburg,' I said.

'You must feel very proud. In Argentina we have given the modern world only one invention.' He lifted his metal stick. 'The electric cattle prod. It speaks for itself, does it not? The device emits a strong bolt of electricity, sufficient to move a cow wherever one wants it to go. On average a cow weighs about two thousand pounds. Ten times as much as you, perhaps. But this is still a highly effective means of shocking the animal into submission. So, you can imagine the effect it will have on a human being. At least I hope you can imagine it while I'm asking my next question.'

'I'll certainly try my best,' I said.

He rolled up one sleeve to reveal an arm covered in a shocking amount of hair. Somewhere in Argentina there was a freak show missing its missing link. The frayed cuff of the sleeve went all the way up the arm to the crescent of sweat underneath his armpit before he stopped rolling. Probably he didn't want to get anything on his shirt. At the very least he looked like a man who took his work seriously.

'I should like to know the name of the person who told you about Directive Eleven.'

'It was someone at the Casa Rosada. One of my colleagues, I suppose. I don't remember who, exactly. Look, one hears all kinds of talk in a place like that.'

The small hairy man tore open the body of my shirt to reveal the scar on my collarbone. He tapped it with his filthiest fingernail. 'Aiee. You've had an operation. Forgive me, I didn't know. What was the matter with you?'

'I had half of my thyroid removed.'

'Why?'

'It was cancerous.'

He nodded, almost sympathetic, 'It's healing nicely.' Then he touched the scar with the end of the cattle-prod. Fortunately for me it was not yet switched on. 'Normally, we concentrate on the genitals. But in your case I think we might make an exception.' He jerked his head at the big man holding me. A moment or two later I was tied securely to the chair in my cell.

'The name of the person who told you about Directive Eleven, please,' he said.

I tried to put Anna Yagubsky's name to the furthermost corner of my mind. I wasn't worried that I'd reveal that she was the person who'd told me about Directive Eleven, but I'd seen the way pain can jolt words out of a man. I hated to think what a pair like this would do to a woman like her. So I started telling myself that the person who'd told me about

Directive Eleven was Marcello, the duty officer in the record department at the Casa Rosada. Just in case I had to say something. I shook my head. 'Look. Honestly. I don't remember. It was weeks ago. There were several of us talking in the records department. It could have been anyone.'

But he wasn't listening. 'Here,' he said. 'Let me help jog your memory.' He touched my knee with the cattle prod and this time it was switched on. Even through the material of my trousers the pain shifted me and the chair several feet along the floor and left my leg jerking uncontrollably for several minutes.

'Feels nice, doesn't it?' he said. 'And you're going to think that was just a tickle when I put it on your bare flesh.'

'I'm laughing already.'

'Then the joke is on you, I'm afraid.' He came at me again with the cattle prod, aiming it squarely at the scar on my collarbone. For a split second I had a vision of the remains of my thyroid sizzling inside my throat like a piece of fried liver. Then a voice I recognised said, 'That's enough, I think.' It was Colonel Montalban. 'Untie him.'

There were no words of protest. Certainly none from me. My two would-be tormentors obeyed instantly, almost as if they had expected to be stopped. Montalban himself lit a cigarette and put it in my grateful, trembling mouth.

'Am I glad to see you,' I said.

'Come on,' he said quietly. 'Let's get out of this place.'

Resisting the temptation to say something to the man with the cattle-prod I followed the Colonel outside into the fortress courtyard where a nice white Jaguar was parked. I drew a deep breath that was a mixture of relief and exhilaration. He opened the trunk and took out a neatly folded shirt and a tie that I half-recognised.

'Here,' he said. 'I brought you these from your hotel room.'

'That was very thoughtful of you, Colonel,' I said, unbuttoning the ragged remains of the shirt I was almost wearing.

'Don't mention it,' he said climbing into the driver's seat.

'Always a nice car, Colonel,' I said, getting in beside him.

'This car belonged to an admiral who was plotting a coup d'état,' he said. 'Can you imagine an admiral owning such a car?' He lit a cigarette for himself and drove out of the gate.

'Where is he now? The admiral?'

'He disappeared. Perhaps he is in Paraguay. Perhaps he is in Chile. Then again perhaps he is nowhere in particular. But then again sometimes it is best not to ask such a question. You understand?'

'I think so. But who's minding the navy?'

'Truly the only safe questions to ask in Argentina are the questions one asks of oneself. That is why there are so many psychoanalysts in this country.'

We drove east, towards the River Plate.

'Are there? Many psychoanalysts in this country?'

'Oh yes. A great many. There is more psychoanalysis done here in Buenos Aires than almost anywhere else in the world. No one in Argentina thinks himself so perfect that he can't be improved. Take you, for instance. A little psychoanalysis might help you to stay out of trouble. That's what I thought, anyway. That's why I arranged for you to see two of the best men in the city. So that you might understand yourself and your relation to society. And to appreciate what I told you before: that in Argentina it is better to know everything than to know too much. Of course, my men are better than most at helping a man to understand himself. Fewer sessions are required. Sometimes only one. And of course they work much more cheaply than the kind of Freudian analysts that most people go to see. But the results, I'm sure you'll agree, are much more spectacular. It's rare anyone comes out of a session at Caseros without a profound sense of what is needed to survive in a city like this. Yes. Yes, I do believe that. This city will kill you unless, psychologically, you are equipped to deal with it. I hope I'm not being too cryptic here.'

'Not at all, Colonel. I understand you perfectly.'

'You'll find a hip-flask in the glove-box,' he said. 'Sometimes therapy gives a man a keen thirst for more than just self-knowledge.'

There was cognac in the flask. It tasted just fine. It gave me more breathing space as if someone had opened a window. I offered him the flask. He shook his head and grinned.

'You're a nice guy, Gunther. I wouldn't want anything to happen to you. I've told you before, you used to be a real hero of mine. In life a man should have a hero, don't you think so?'

'That's sweet of you, Colonel.'

'Rodolfo – that's Rodolfo Freude, the head of SIDE – he thinks my belief in your abilities is irrational, and perhaps it is. But he's not a real policeman, like us, Gunther. He doesn't understand what it takes to be a great detective.'

'I'm not so sure I understand that myself, Colonel.'

'Then I shall tell you. To be a great detective one must also be a protagonist. A dynamic sort of character who makes things happen just by being himself. I think you are this kind of a person, Gunther.'

'In chess, we'd call that a gambit. Usually it involves the sacrifice of a pawn or a knight.'

'Yes. That is quite possible, also.'

I laughed. 'You're an interesting man, Colonel. A trifle eccentric, but interesting. And don't think I don't appreciate your confidence in me, because I do appreciate it. Almost as much as your booze and your cigarettes.' I took his packet and lit another.

'Good. Because I should hate to think you needed a second session of therapy in Caseros.'

It was evening. The shops were closing and the clubs were opening. All over the city people were getting depressed that they were so far away from the rest of the civilised world. I knew how they felt. On one side was the ocean and on the other, the vast emptiness of the pampas. We were all of us surrounded by nothing, with nowhere else to go. Perhaps most people just resigned themselves to that. Just as they had in Nazi Germany. I was different. Saying one thing and thinking another were second nature to me.

'I get the picture, Colonel,' I told him. 'I'd click my heels and salute if I wasn't sitting down.' I sipped some more cognac. 'From now on, this horse is wearing blinkers and a tongue-strap.' I pointed through the windscreen. 'There's the road ahead and nothing else.' I uttered a wry little laugh as if I'd learned a hard lesson.

The Colonel seemed pleased by this admission. 'Now you're getting it,' he said. 'I'm only sorry that it cost you a shirt to find that out.'

'I can buy a new shirt, Colonel,' I said, still affecting craven acquiescence. 'A new skin is harder to come by. You won't need to warn me again. I've no desire to wind up in that morgue of yours. Speaking of which, the girl, Grete Wohlauf? I'm not sure I've found her killer, but I certainly found the man who killed those two girls in Germany. And you were right. He's living here, in Buenos Aires. As I said, I can't be sure he had anything to do with Grete Wohlauf's death. Or that he knows anything about Fabienne Von Bader. But I wouldn't be at all surprised since he's pursuing the same trade in illegal abortions he was back then. His name is Josef Mengele but he's living here as Helmut Gregor. But I expect you already knew that. Anyway, you can read all about it in a statement I persuaded him to write. I have it hidden in my hotel room.'

Colonel Montalban put his hand inside his breast pocket and took out the envelope containing Mengele's handwritten confession. 'Do you mean this statement?'

'It certainly looks like it.'

'Naturally when you were arrested we searched your room at the San Martin Hotel.'

'Naturally. And I suppose you're going to destroy that now.'

'On the contrary. I'm going to keep it in a very safe place. There may come a time when it could be very useful.'

'You mean in getting rid of Mengele.'

'He's small fry. No, I mean in getting rid of Perón. This is a very Catholic country, Herr Gunther. Even an electorate that's bought and paid for might find it hard to vote for a president who's used a Nazi war criminal to carry out illegal abortions on juvenile girls with whom he's been having sex. Of course I hope I shan't need this statement, but placed somewhere safe it becomes a very useful insurance policy. For a man such as myself, in a very uncertain profession, it's the best thing to having job security that there is. For some time now I've suspected something like this was going on, only I couldn't connect any of it with Perón. That is until you came along.'

'But how could you possibly know he was the man I was after in 1932?' I asked. 'I've only just worked it out myself.'

'A month or two after Mengele arrived in Argentina, a box of papers arrived from Germany addressed to Helmut Gregor, here in Buenos Aires. These were Mengele's own research files from his time at the Race and Resettlement Office in Berlin, and at Auschwitz. It seems that the doctor was unwilling to part with his life's work and, reasoning that he was safe here, he had all of his papers shipped on to him from someone in his hometown of Gunzburg. Not just his research files. There was also an SS file and a Gestapo file. For some reason his Gestapo file contained your KRIPO files. The ones I gave to you when you first started working for me. It would seem that someone tried to reopen the Schwarz case during the war. Tried and failed because someone higher up in the SS was protecting him. An SS Colonel called Kassner who had also worked for I.G. Farben. Anyway, Mengele never received any of his papers. He believes they were destroyed when a cargo hold in the ship bringing them from

Germany was accidentally flooded. In fact the files were intercepted by my men.

'Before they came into my hands I had had my suspicions about who Helmut Gregor really was, and that he was carrying out illegal abortions here in Buenos Aires. I suspected Perón was sending him young girls he'd impregnated, but I couldn't prove anything. I didn't dare. Not even when one of Perón's *fruta inmadura* – that's what he calls his younger girl-friends – turned up dead. Her name was Grete Wohlauf. And she had died from an infection sustained during an abortion procedure. When Mengele's papers turned up I realised that he had been the man you were looking for. And I decided to awaken your interest in the case in a way that might be to my advantage. So I had the pathologist mutilate her in order to prick your curiosity.'

'But why didn't you just level with me?'

'Because it didn't suit my purpose. Mengele is protected by Perón. You managed to sidestep that protection. I couldn't do what you have done and still keep Perón's confidence. As you said yourself, you were my gambit, Herr Gunther. When I heard that Perón's men had arrested you and taken you to Caseros, I was able to exercise some influence in another quarter and have you released. But not before teaching you a lesson. As I've told you before, asking questions about Directive Eleven is not a good idea.'

'That much I know. And Fabienne Von Bader? Is she really missing?'

'Oh yes. Have you found any trace of her?'

'No. But I'm beginning to understand why she's disappeared. Her father has part control of the Reichsbank's Swiss bank accounts and the Peróns are keen to get their hands on that money. It's my guess that the Von Baders have hidden her for her own protection, so that the Peróns can't use the girl to make her father do what they want him to do. Something like that, anyway.'

The Colonel smiled. 'As always, it's a little bit more complicated than that.'

'Oh? How much more complicated?'

'I think you're about to find out.'

SEVENTEEN

BUENOS AIRES. 1950.

The Colonel drove past the Ministry of Labour where, as usual, a long line of people was already waiting to see Evita, and went around the corner where he stopped the car in front of an anonymous-looking door.

I'd been turning over in my mind what he'd told me about Mengele. And, as we got out the car, I told him I thought I'd probably wasted a lot of time speaking to old comrades; time that, with a little careful direction from him, could have been more usefully spent elsewhere.

'We have a saying, "It takes more than one dead mouse to make a good cat".' In front of the door, he took a bunch of keys out of his pocket, unlocked it and then ushered me inside. 'When I intercepted Mengele's private papers it reminded me of how little we actually know about all the ex-Nazis who have come to Argentina. Perón may care nothing about what any of you did during the war but that could hardly be good enough for me. After all, it's my job to know about people. So I decided it was high time that we started gathering intelligence on all our "guest workers". I decided that you were our best means of obtaining it.'

He closed the door behind us and we walked up a quiet marble stairway. The handrail was sticky with wood polish and the marble floor as white and shiny as a string of fresh-water pearls. On the first floor landing was a picture of Evita. She was wearing a blue dress with white spots, a large pink tea rose on her shoulder, a ruby and diamond necklace and a matching ruby and diamond smile.

'At some stage relations with the United States will have to improve if Argentina is to recover the economic wealth we enjoyed a decade ago,' said the Colonel. 'For that to happen it may be politic, eventually, to ask some of our more notorious immigrants to go and live somewhere else. Paraguay, for example. Paraguay is a lawless, primitive country where even the worst animals can live quite openly. So you see, all this time, you have been doing this country a great service for which, one day – one day soon, I suspect – we will have cause to thank you.'

'I feel patriotic already.'

'Hold onto that feeling. You're going to need it when you meet Evita. The woman is the most patriotic person I know.'

'Is that where we're going?'

'Yes. And by the way, you remember how I mentioned that when I heard that Perón's men had arrested you and taken you to Caseros I was able to exercise some influence in another quarter and have you released? Evita is that quarter. She is your new protector. It might be a good idea to remember that.'

Colonel Montalban paused in front of a heavy wooden door. On the other side was what sounded like a beehive. He looked me up and down and then handed me a comb. I ran it quickly through my hair and then gave it back.

'If I'd known I was going to meet the President's wife tonight I'd have spent the day shopping for a new suit,' I said. 'Maybe even had a bath.'

'Believe me, she will hardly notice how you smell. Not in this place.'

He opened the door and we entered a wood-panelled room about the size of a tennis court. At the far end was another, larger painting of Evita. She was wearing a blue dress and smiling at a group of children. Behind her head was a bright light and, if I hadn't known better, I'd have said she had a husband called Joseph and a son who was a carpenter. The room was full of people and the smell of their unwashed bodies. Some of them were disabled, some were pregnant, most looked poor. All of them were quite certain that the woman they were hoping to see was nothing less than the Madonna of Buenos Aires, *la Dama de la Esperanza*. There was no pushing or jostling for position, however. Each of them had a ticket and, from time to time, an official would come into that room and announce a number. This was the cue for an unmarried mother, a homeless family, or a crippled orphan to come forward and be received into the holy presence.

I followed the Colonel into the room beyond. Here there was a long mahogany table against one wall. On it were three telephones and four vases of Calla lilies. There was a gold silk-covered sofa and three matching chairs, and four secretaries holding pads and pencils, or a telephone, or an envelope full of money. Evita herself stood next to the window, which was open to let out some of the smell of unwashed bodies. This was more noticeable than in the big antechamber because it was a smaller room.

She was wearing a dove-grey robe-style dress with a tied waist. On her lapel was a brooch made of small sapphires and diamonds in the shape and colours of the Argentine national flag. I reflected it was probably fortunate that she wasn't the wife of the President of Germany; there's not much a jeweller can do with black, yellow, and red. On the finger of her left hand was a sea anemone-sized diamond ring, with its brother and sister on her little ears. On her head was a ruby-studded grey silk beret that was more Lucrezia Borgia than Holy Mother. She didn't look particularly ill. Not nearly as ill as the skeletal woman and the skeletal child who were each kissing one of her ungloved hands. Evita handed the woman a folded wad of fifty-peso notes. If Otto Skorzeny was right, some Nazi loot had just found its way into the deserving hands of the Argentine poor and I didn't know whether to laugh or to cry. As a means of preventing the democratic overthrow of a government this touching scene lacked the symbolism of setting fire to parliament but, on the face of it, it looked every bit as effective. The Apostles themselves could not have handled this kind of charity with any greater efficiency.

A photographer from a Perónist newspaper took a picture of the scene. And it seemed unlikely he would have left out of frame the enormous painting of Christ washing the feet of his disciples that was behind Evita's shoulder. Out of the corner of his blue eye the carpenter seemed to be regarding his pupil and her good works with some approval. This is my beloved daughter, in whom I am well pleased. Don't vote for anyone else.

Evita caught the Colonel's eye. Still full of effusive thanks, the skeletal woman and child were led outside. Evita turned smartly on her heel and went through a door at the back of the room. The Colonel and I went after her. She closed the door behind us. We were in a room with a hand basin, a dressing table, a rail of clothes, and only one chair. Evita took it. Among the make-up and the many bottles of perfume and hairspray was a photograph of Perón. She picked it up and kissed it, which made me think that Otto Skorzeny was fooling himself if he thought this woman would ever risk having an affair with a scar-faced thug like him.

'Very impressive,' I said, jerking my head at the door behind me.

She sighed and shook her head. 'It is nothing. Not nearly enough. We try, but the poor are always with us.'

I'd heard this somewhere before.

'All the same your work must give you a lot of satisfaction.'

'Some, but I take no pride in it. I am nothing. A *grasa*. A common person. The work is its own reward. Besides, none of what I give is from me. It all belongs to Perón. He is the true saint, not me. You see, I don't regard this as charity. Charity humiliates. What happens out there is social aid. A welfare state. Nothing more, nothing less. I handle its dispensation personally because I know what it's like to be at the mercy of bureaucracy in this country, and I don't trust anyone else to do it. There is too much corruption in our public institutions.' She tried to stifle a yawn. 'So I come here, every night, and I do it myself. Especially important to me are the unmarried mothers of Argentina. Can you imagine why, Señor Gunther?'

I could easily imagine one reason why, but I hardly wanted to risk my new benefactor's displeasure by mentioning her own husband's efforts to procure abortions for all the underage girls he was having sex with. So I smiled patiently and shook my head.

'Because I was one myself. Before I met Perón. I was an actress then. I was not the *putita* my enemies like to paint me as. But, in 1937, when I was plain Eva Duarte and working in radio soap-opera, I met a man and gave birth to his child. That man's name was Kurt Von Bader. That's right señor, Fabienne Von Bader is my daughter.'

I glanced the Colonel's way. He nodded back at me by way of corroboration.

'When Fabienne was born, Kurt, who was married, agreed to bring her up. His own wife could not have a child of her own. And at the time, I thought I would have more children myself. Sadly, for the President and myself both love children, that has not proved to be possible. Fabienne is my only child and, as such, very precious to me.

'At first, Kurt and his wife were very generous and allowed me to see Fabienne whenever I wanted to, on condition that she was never told I was her real mother. More recently, however, all of that changed. Kurt Von Bader is one of the custodians of a large sum of money deposited in Switzerland by the former government of Germany. It is my desire to use some of that money to help lift the poor out of their poverty. Not just here, in Argentina, but throughout the Roman Catholic world. Von Bader, who still entertains some hope of restoring a Nazi government in Germany, disagreed. He and I quarrelled, violently. Much was said. Too much. Fabienne must have heard some of it and learned the truth about her origins. Soon after that she ran away from home.'

Evita sighed and sat back in her chair, as if the effort of telling me all of this had been a strain. 'There,' she said. 'I have told you everything. Are you shocked, Herr Gunther?'

'No ma'am, not shocked. A little surprised perhaps. And maybe a bit puzzled as to why you should choose to confide in me.'

'I want you to find her, of course. Is that so hard to understand?'

'No, not at all. But when you have a whole police force at your disposal ma'am, it's a little hard to understand why you should expect me to succeed where they have—'

'Failed,' she said, hearing me hesitate to complete the sentence. 'Isn't that right, Colonel? Your men have failed me, have they not?'

'So far we are without success, Señora,' said the Colonel.

'You hear that?' said Evita. She puffed out her cheeks in a scornful laugh. 'He can't even bring himself to say the word "failure". But that is what it amounts to. You, on the other hand. You are someone who has experience looking for missing persons, yes?'

'Some experience, yes, but in my own country.'

'Yes, you are a German. Like my daughter who has been brought up as a German-Argentine. Castellano is her second language. Already you move easily among these people, and I am convinced that is where you will find her. Find her. Find my daughter. If you succeed I will pay you fifty thousand dollars in cash.' She nodded with a smile. 'Yes, I thought that would make your ears move.' Evita lifted her hand, as if taking an oath. 'I'm no *chupacirios*, but I solemnly swear by the Holy Virgin that if you find her, the money is yours.'

The door opened briefly to admit one of her dogs. Evita greeted 'Canela', picked her up and kissed the dog like a favourite child. 'Well?' she asked me. 'What do you say, German?'

'I'll do my best, ma'am,' I said. 'But I can't promise anything. Not even for fifty thousand dollars. But I will do my best.'

'Yes. Yes that is a good answer.' Once again she looked accusingly at Colonel Montalban. 'You hear? He doesn't say he will find her. He says he will try his best.' She nodded at me. 'It's said throughout the world that I am a selfish and ambitious woman, but this isn't the case.'

She put down the dog and took my hand in hers. Her hands were cold, like those of a corpse. Her red fingernails were long and beautifully manicured, like the petals from some petrified flower. They were small hands but, oddly, full of power as if in her veins was some strange electricity. It was the same with her eyes which held me for a moment in their watery gaze. The effect was remarkable and I was reminded of how people had once described the experience of meeting Hitler and how they had said there was something about his eyes, too. Then, without warning, she opened the front of her dress and placed my hand between her breasts, so that my palm was directly over her heart.

'I want you to feel this,' she said, urgently. 'I want you to feel the heart of an ordinary Argentine woman. And to know that everything I do, I do for the highest motives. Do you feel it, German? Do you feel Evita's heart? Do you feel the truth of what I'm telling you?'

I wasn't sure I felt anything very much other than the swell of her breasts either side of my fingers and the cool silkiness of her perfumed flesh. I knew I only had to move my hand an inch or two to cup the whole bosom and to feel the nipple rubbing against the heel of my thumb. But of her heartbeat there was no sign. Instinctively she pressed my hand harder against her breastbone.

'Do you feel it?' she asked, insistently.

Her gaze was tearful now. And it was easy to see how she had once been such a success as an actress on radio. The woman was the personification of high emotion and melodrama. If she'd been the Duport cello she couldn't have been more highly strung. It was a risk letting her go on. She might have burst into flames, levitated or turned into a saucerful of ghee. I was getting a little excited myself. It's not every day that the President's wife forces your hand inside her brassiere. I decided to tell her what she wanted to hear. I was good at that. I'd had a lot of other women to practise on.

'Yes, Señora Perón, I can feel it,' I said trying to keep the erection out of my voice.

She let go of my hand and, to my relief, she seemed to relax a little. Then she smiled and said, 'Whenever you are ready you can take your hand off my bosom, German.'

For a split second I let it stay there. Long enough to meet her eye and let her know I liked my hand being just where it was. And then I took it away. I considered kissing my fingers, or maybe just smelling the perfume that was on them now, only that would have made me as melodramatic as her. So I put the hand in my pocket, saving it for later, like a choice cigar, or a dirty postcard.

She adjusted her dress and then opened a drawer, from which she took out a photograph and handed it to me. It was the same photograph Kurt Von Bader had given me. The reward he had mentioned was the same amount. I wondered whether, if I did manage to find Fabienne, each would pay or just one. Or neither. Neither seemed more likely. Usually, when you found a missing child the parents got angry, first with the child and then with you. Not that any of this seemed particularly relevant. They were asking me to look for her because they'd tried everything else. Since that had already failed, I figured I had next to no chance of turning up a lead on the kid. To succeed I would have to think of something that hadn't been thought of, which wasn't a good bet on anyone's *quinella*. Probably the kid was in Uruguay, or dead, and if she wasn't, then there had to be an adult who was helping her stay below the radar.

'Do you think you can find her?' asked Evita.

'I was kind of wondering that myself,' I said. 'Perhaps I might, if I had all the facts.'

'Forgive me, but isn't that a detective's job? To work without all the facts. I mean, if we had all the facts then we could probably find her ourselves. We wouldn't need you, German. And we certainly wouldn't be offering a reward of fifty thousand dollars.'

She had a point, of course. Melodramatic she might have been. Stupid she wasn't.

'What makes you think she's still in the country?' I asked. 'Could be she just got on the river boat to Montevideo. Twenty-nine dollars. End of story.'

'For one thing,' said Evita, 'I'm married to the President of Argentina. So, I know that she doesn't have a passport. And even if she did have a passport, she doesn't have a visa. We know because my husband asked Luis Berres. He's the President of Uruguay. And before you ask, he also asked Presidents Videla, Chaves, and Odría.'

'Perhaps if I spoke to her parents again,' I said. Correcting myself I added, 'I mean to her father and her stepmother.'

'If you think it would do any good,' said Montalban.

I didn't. But I hardly knew what else to suggest. All of it was a dead end. I'd known that the first time I'd met Von Bader. From everything I'd heard, his daughter and whoever she was with didn't want to be found. For a detective, when people don't want to be found, it's like looking for the meaning of life. You're not even sure that it exists. I hated taking on a job that promised so little chance of success. And normally I might have turned it down. But normal didn't even get to peek through the spyhole of this particular situation. Eva Perón wasn't the kind of president's wife you refused. Especially not so soon after my trip to Caseros.

'Well?' she asked. 'How will you go about it?'

I put a cigarette in my face and lit it. I didn't want a cigarette but it gave me time to think of something to say. Colonel Montalban cleared his throat. It sounded like a lifebelt hitting the water above my head.

'As soon as we have something to report, we'll be in touch, ma'am.'

When we were on the stairs outside the antechamber, I thanked him.

'For what?'

'For coming to my aid back there. That question she asked.'

'How will you go about it?'

'That's right.'

'And how *will* you go about it?' He grinned amiably and took a light off my cigarette.

'Oh, I don't know. I'll go and look for inspiration, probably. Stick a gun in its face. Slap it around a bit. See what happens. The forensic, judicial approach. On the other hand I might just have to hope that I get lucky. That usually works for me. I may not look like it, Colonel, but I'm quite a lucky guy. This morning I was in prison. Five minutes ago I had my hand inside the cleavage of the wife of the President of Argentina. Believe me, for a German that's as lucky as luck can buy you these days.'

'I don't doubt it.'

'Evita didn't seem ill.'

'Nor do you.'

'Not now, maybe. But I was.'

'Pack's a good doctor,' said the Colonel. 'The best there is. You were both lucky to have someone like him treating you.'

'I expect so.'

'I'll call the Von Baders and say that you want to speak to them again. Perhaps there was something we missed before.'

'There's always something that gets missed. On account of the fact that detectives are human and humans make mistakes.'

'Shall we say at midday tomorrow?'

I nodded.

'Come on,' he said. 'I'll drive you back to your hotel.'

I shook my head. 'No thanks, Colonel. I'll walk, if you don't mind. The landlady sees me arriving in that white Jaguar of yours, she's liable to put my room rate up.'

EIGHTEEN

BUENOS AIRES. 1950.

They were pleased to see me at the Hotel San Martin. Of course a lot of that was to do with the fact that the secret police had turned over my room – although not so as you would have noticed. There wasn't much to turn over. Mr and Mrs Lloyd greeted me like someone they hadn't expected ever to see again.

'One hears stories about the secret police and that kind of thing,' Mr Lloyd told me over a welcome-back glass of whisky in the hotel bar. 'But, well, it's not something we've encountered before.'

'There was a misunderstanding about my *cedula*, that's all,' I said. 'I don't suppose it will happen again.'

All the same, I went ahead and paid my monthly bill, just in case it did. It helped to put the Lloyds at their ease. Losing a guest was one thing. Losing a guest who hadn't paid was quite another. They were nice people but they were in it for the money after all. Who isn't?

I went up to my room. There was a bed, a table and chair, an armchair, a three-bar electric fire, a radio, a telephone, and a bathroom. Naturally I'd added a few personal touches of my own: a bottle, a couple of glasses, a chess set, a Spanish dictionary, a Weimar edition of Goethe I'd bought in a second-hand bookshop, a suitcase and some clothes. All my worldly possessions. I'd like to have seen young Werther cope with Gunther's sorrows. I poured myself a drink, set out the chess board, switched on the radio and then sat in the armchair.

There were some telephone messages in an envelope. All but one of these from Anna Yagubsky. The one that wasn't was from Isabel Pekerman. I didn't know anyone called Isabel Pekerman.

Augustin Magaldi came on Radio El Mundo singing *Vagabundo*. This had been a huge hit for him in the thirties. I turned off the radio and ran a bath. I thought about going out to get something to eat and had another drink instead. I was just thinking about going to bed when the telephone rang. It was Mrs Lloyd.

'A Señora Pekerman calling.'

'Who?'

'She rang before. She says you know her.'

'Thanks, Mrs Lloyd. You'd better put her through.'

I heard a couple of clicks and the tail end of another woman saying thank you.

'Señora Pekerman? This is Carlos Hausner. I don't believe we've had the pleasure.'

'Oh yes we have.'

'Then you have the advantage of me, Señora Pekerman. I'm afraid I don't remember you.'

'Are you alone, Señor Hausner?'

I glanced around the four bare, silent walls at my half-empty bottle and my hopeless game of chess. I was alone, all right. Outside my window people were walking up and down the street, but they might as well have been on Saturn for all the good it did me. Sometimes the profound silence of that room scared me because it seemed to echo something silent within myself. Across the street, at the church of Santa Catalina of Sienna, a bell began to toll.

'Yes, I'm alone, Señora Pekerman. What can I do for you?'

'They asked me to come in tomorrow afternoon, Señor Hausner,' she said, 'but I just got offered a small part in a play on Corrientes. It's a small part, but it's a good part. In a good play. Besides, things have moved on since last we met. Anna's told me all about you. About how you're helping her to look for her aunt and her uncle.'

I winced, wondering how many other people she'd told.

'When exactly did we meet, Señora Pekerman?'

'At Señor Von Bader's house. I was the woman who pretended to be his wife.'

She paused. So did I. Or rather so did my heart.

'Remember me now?'

'Yes, I remember you. The dog wouldn't stay with you. It came with me and Von Bader.'

'Well, it's not my dog, Señor Hausner,' she said, as if I still didn't quite get what she was talking about. 'To be honest, I don't think I really expected you to dig up anything about Anna's aunt and uncle. But, of course, you did. I mean it's not much but it's something. Some proof that they did at least enter this country. You see, I'm in the same boat as Anna. I'm Jewish, too. And I also had some relatives who entered the country illegally and then disappeared.'

'I don't think you should say anything else on the telephone, Señora Pekerman. Perhaps we could meet and talk this over.'

In the evenings, when she wasn't acting, Isabel Pekerman worked at a *milonga*, which was a kind of tango club, on Corrientes. I didn't know much about the tango except that it had originated in Argentine brothels. That was certainly the impression I had from the Club Seguro. It was down some steps underneath a small neon sign and at the far end of a yard lit by a single naked flame. Out of the flickering shadows a large man approached. The *vigilante* guarding the door. He had a whistle around his neck to summon the police in the event of a dispute he couldn't handle.

'Are you carrying a knife?' he asked.

'No.'

He seemed surprised at this admission. 'All the same I have to search you.'

'So why ask the question?'

'Because if you're lying then I'd figure you might be out to cause trouble,' he said, patting me down. 'And then I'll have to keep an eye on you.' When he had satisfied himself I wasn't armed he waved me to the door. Music that was mostly an accordion and some violins was edging its way into the yard.

In the doorway was a sort of coop that was home to the *casita* woman, a largish negress who sat in an easy chair, humming an altogether different tune to the one played by the tango orchestra. On her thigh was a paper serviette and a pair of lamb chops. Maybe they were her dinner, but they might just as easily have been the remains of the last man to cause trouble for the huge *vigilante*. She smiled a big uneven smile that was as white as a swathe of snowdrops and gave me a sizing-up-and-down look.

'You looking for a Stepney?'

I shrugged. My Castellano was much improved but it fell apart like a cheap suit the minute it got snagged on the local slang.

'You know. The café crème.'

'I'm looking for Isabel Pekerman,' I said.

'Where you from, honey?'

'Germany.'

'It's twenty pesos, Adolf,' said the *casita* woman. 'Don't know what you've got in mind but the lady's *cafinflero* is Blue Vincent and Vincent prefers it if you give him the bouquet before you speaks to the *gallina*.'

'I only want to speak to her.'

'Don't make no difference if you're a hunter or not. Everyone of these *creolos* is from the Centre and if you speaks to baggage you'll have to give him a bouquet. It's that kind of joint.'

'I'll bear that in mind.' I peeled off a couple of notes and pressed them into her leathery hand.

'Uh-huh.' She shifted for a moment and tucked the notes under one of her substantial buttocks. It looked as safe there as in any bank vault. 'You'll find her on the dance floor, probably.'

I breast-stroked my way through a beaded curtain into a scene from *The Four Horsemen of the Apocalypse*. The brick walls were covered in graffiti and old posters. Around a dirty wooden dance floor were lots of little marble-topped tables. The low lights on the ceiling barely illuminated the low life below. There were women in skirts slit up to their navels and men wearing trilbys pulled down low over their watchful eyes. The orchestra looked as oily as the music it was playing. The only thing that seemed to be lacking in the place was Rudolph Valentino dressed in a poncho with a whip in his hand and a pout on his lips. Nobody paid me any attention. Nobody except the taller of the two women who were dancing the tango with eyes that had done a lot more than just meet.

I hardly recognised her from before. She looked like a circus horse. Her mane was long and very blonde with just a touch of grey. Her eyes were big but not as big as her beautiful curving behind, which her skirt did nothing to conceal. She was also wearing a kind of spangled leotard that almost preserved her modesty. At least I think it was a leotard only it was a little hard to be sure the way it disappeared between her buttocks.

I stared back hard at her just to let her know I'd seen her. She stared back and then pointed at a table. I sat down. A waiter appeared. Everyone else seemed to be drinking *cubano* from large round glasses. I ordered the same and lit a cigarette.

A burly man came over to my table. He was wearing boots, black trousers, a grey jacket that was a size too small for him and a white scarf. He had pimp written all over him like the numbers on a pack of cards. He sat down, turned slowly to look at the circus horse. When she nodded at him he looked back at me, spreading his mouth into a smile that was somehow both approving and pitying at the same time. I worked it out. He approved my choice of woman but pitied me for being the kind of jerk who would even contemplate the kind of degrading transaction that was about to occur. There was no fear in his craggy features. It was a tough face. It looked like something you could have used to beat a carpet. When he spoke his breath sharpened my thirst for strong liquor. I kept my nose in my glass until he'd finished blowing his patter my way.

Silently, I tossed some notes onto the table. I wasn't in the mood for anything except information but, sometimes, information costs the same as its more intimate relations. He gathered the money in his fist and went away. Only then did she come over and sit down.

'I'm sorry about that,' she said. 'I'll get the money off him at the end of the evening and give it back to you later, but you did the right thing to pay him. Vincent's not an unreasonable man but he's my *creolo*, and *creolos* like things to look like what they're supposed to look like. In case you're wondering, he's not my pimp.'

'If you say so.'

'A *creolo* just looks out for a girl. Kind of like a bodyguard. Some of the men I dance with, they can get a little rough sometimes.'

'It's OK about the money. Keep it.'

'You mean, you want to?'

'I mean keep the money. That's all. It's information I'm after, nothing more. No offence but it's been a hell of a day.'

'Do you want to talk about it?'

'No. Let's just talk.' I sipped some of my *cubano*. 'You look different from the last time we met.'

A waiter placed a drink in front of her. She ignored it, and him.

'So who put you up to it?'

'The cop. The one who brought you. He came to my apart-ment and said he'd seen me in a show and that he had a special kind of job for me. If I did as I was told I'd make some money and keep some nice clothes into the bargain. All I had to do was play a rich, worried mother.' She shrugged. 'That was easy enough. There was a time when I had a rich, worried mother of my own.' She lit a cigarette. 'So I met Von Bader and we talked.'

'How long were you there?'

'Most of the day. We didn't really know what time you were going to show up.'

'And this was all for my benefit?'

'Ostensibly, yes. But Colonel Montalban wanted me to report on Von Bader as well.'

'Yes, that does sound like him. Two jobs for the price of one.' I nodded. 'So how was he? Von Bader?'

'Nervous. But nice. A couple of times I heard him on the telephone. I think he was planning to go abroad. He made and received several calls to Switzerland while I was there. I know that because once he asked me to answer the telephone when he was in the bathroom. I speak German, as you know. I also speak Polish and Spanish. By birth I'm a German Pole. From Danzig.' She puffed at the cigarette but seemed irritated with it and put it out only half-smoked. 'Sorry, but I'm a little bit on edge about this. That Colonel was none too pleased when I said I couldn't repeat the performance tomorrow morning. He's not the kind of man one lets down lightly.'

'So why did you?'

'When Von Bader said that you were a famous German detective and that you'd often looked for missing persons in Berlin before the war, I'm afraid I rather lost interest in their scheme. Whatever that is. You see it was me who told Anna

Yagubsky about you. And me who suggested that she might approach you for help. I thought that by helping Anna find her missing aunt and uncle you might also help me find my missing sisters. And, since you were helping me, albeit by proxy, I decided to help you. I decided to put you in the picture, as much as I'm able, concerning what the Colonel and Von Bader are up to. You see the girl, Fabienne, has gone off with her mother and nobody knows where. That's pretty much all I know. Von Bader wants to leave the country but he can't until he knows they're safe. I dunno, something like that. Either way I'm taking a big risk telling you all this.'

'So why do it at all?'

'Because Anna says she's sure that you're the man who's going to find them. And I don't mean Fabienne and her mother. I mean our relatives. Anna's and mine.'

I sighed. 'Go ahead. Tell me about them. Tell me about yourself.' I shrugged. 'Why not? I've paid for your time.'

'My mother got me out of Poland just before the war. I was twenty-five-years-old. She gave me some jewels and I managed to bribe my way into Argentina. My two sisters were too young to come with me. At the time one was ten and the other was eight. The plan was that I'd send for them when I could. I wrote to tell my mother I was well and received a letter back from a neighbour to say that she and my sisters were now in France, and in hiding. Then, in 1945, I received word that my two sisters were false weight aboard a cargo ship from Bilbao.'

'False weight?'

'It's what we used to call an illegal immigrant on a ship. When the ship docked here in Buenos Aires, however, there was no sign of either of them. My then husband made some enquiries. He was an ex-policeman. He found out that they had both been sold by the captain to a *casita*. As *franchuchas*.'

I shook my head.

'A *franchucha* is what the *porteños* call a French prostitute.

A *gallina* is what they call one from Russia. Wherever they came from they usually had one thing in common: they were Jewish. At one time half the prostitutes in this city were Jewish. Not by choice. Most of them were sold into it, like slaves. Then, my husband ran away with what was left of my money and most of Anna's. By the time he came back, he'd spent it all and I needed to make a living. So I am as you see me now. I do a little acting, some dancing. Sometimes a little bit more when the man is nice. My new life had one major advantage however. It allowed me to search for my sisters, and about two years ago I discovered they'd been arrested the previous year, in a police raid on a *casita*. They were taken to San Miguel prison. But instead of appearing before the magistrates, they disappeared from prison altogether. Since when I've heard nothing from them. Nobody has. It's like they never existed.

'It was my ex-husband, Pablo, who introduced me to the Colonel. And I really only took the job with Señor Von Bader in the hope that I might find an opportunity to ask the Colonel about my two sisters.'

'And did you?'

'No. For the simple reason that he and Von Bader made some remarks about Jews. Anti-Semitic remarks. You remember?'

'I remember.'

'As a result I didn't think it likely he was going to be very sympathetic to my situation. Then I noticed how you didn't seem comfortable with those remarks either. And what kind eyes you seemed to have. And I decided to abandon my plan to speak to the Colonel and speak to you instead. Or at least to persuade Anna to speak to you about our situation. The rest you know. She's broke, of course, but very beautiful. I hardly expected you would help us for nothing. I can assure you, nobody does anything for nothing in this country.'

'Don't count on it happening a lot that way. I pay just as

easily as the next man. Sometimes the halo slips and I get an appetite for all the usual vices and some of the unusual ones, too.'

'I'll try to bear that in mind,' she said. 'It'll give me something to think about the next time I can't get to sleep.'

'How old were your sisters when they got here?'

'Fourteen and sixteen.'

'Is there much of a white slavery racket here in Buenos Aires?'

'Listen, there's a racket in that sort of thing almost anywhere you go. Girls arrive somewhere that's a long way from home. They've no money, no papers, and there's no way back. They find they have to work to pay off the hidden costs of their passage. I'm just lucky the same thing didn't happen to me. Whatever I do, I do by choice. More or less.'

'Who does the buying and the selling?'

'You mean of the baggage? The girls?'

I nodded.

'First of all, this doesn't happen so much any more. The supply of new girls has dwindled. The sellers were usually the same men who organised passage for these girls. Ship's captains, first mates, all from places like Marseilles, Bilbao, Vigo, Oporto, Tenerife, and even Dakar. Younger girls like my sisters were "underweight". Older girls were "overweight". If they were really young the girls were called "fragile" – too young ever to see daylight during the voyage. The trade was controlled by a Pole in Montevideo called Mihanovich. Montevideo was where all the ships docked before coming on to Buenos Aires. Some stayed in Uruguay, but usually the girls were sent here, where more money could be made from their sale. Mihanovich would make a deal with the men from the Centre. That's what we call organised crime in this city. It's called the Centre because it's based on the area between Corrientes, Belgrano, the docks and San Nicolas. A lot of it is run by two French families, one from Marseilles and the other from Paris. So, the men from the Centre would buy the girls from Mihanovich, scare the hell out of them when they got here and put them to work in the *casitas* of Buenos Aires. You're a sailor with a few days leave and a cockstand? This is the place to go. There are more *casitas* in this part of Buenos Aires than in the rest of Argentina. Even the cops go carefully around here. So you can imagine how I felt, knowing my two teenage sisters were put to work there.' She shook her head, bitterly. 'This city is like something from the Last Judgment.'

I lit another cigarette and let the smoke curl into my eyes. I wanted to punish them for looking into her cleavage when what I needed most was for them to do their job and keep looking her in the eye so that I might get a better fix on whether she was telling the truth. But I guess that's how things like cleavages evolved in the first place. I shifted on my chair and looked at the room. Isabel Pekerman made Buenos Aires sound a lot like Berlin during the last days of the Weimar Republic. But, to my cynical old eyes, nothing of what I'd seen here compared with the old German capital. The girls who were dancing were still wearing their clothes and the men who were their partners were at least men, most of them, and not something in between. The band could hold a tune and there was no pretence to sophistication. I didn't doubt what Isabel Pekerman had said. But, whereas Berlin had flaunted its vice and corruption, Buenos Aires hid its appetite for depravity like an old priest sipping from a brandy bottle concealed in the pocket of a cassock.

She took my hand, opened my palm and looked closely at it. Running her forefinger over the various lines and mounds, she said, 'According to your hand, we're going to spend the night together after all.'

'Like I said, it's been a hell of a day.'

'It might look bad for me if you don't,' she said, contradicting much of what had been said earlier on. 'After all, you already paid for it. Blue Vincent will think I'm losing my touch.'

'No he won't. Not if he's got eyes in his head.'

Putting her arms around me she said, 'No? Come on. It might be fun. It's been ages since I slept with a man I really liked.'

'Small world,' I said and stood up to leave her.

As things turned out, I should have stayed.

NINETEEN

BUENOS AIRES. 1950.

The next morning I thought some more about what Isabel Pekerman had told me about Argentina's white slave traffic. I wondered if it might be connected with what Perón and Mengele were up to with young girls. None of it made much sense. I decided my brain needed a completely different kind of problem to work on. I had most of the morning before I had to go and meet Von Bader and the Colonel so, after breakfast, I went to the Richmond in search of a game of chess.

Melville was there and I played a Caro-Kann defence to a victory in just thirty-three moves that Bronstein would have been proud of. Afterwards, I let him buy me a drink and we sat outside for a while and watched the world go by. Usually I paid little or no attention to the little Scotsman's chatter. On this occasion, however, I found myself listening to him more closely.

'That was quite a peach you brought in here the other week,' he observed, full of envy.

'She is, isn't she?' I said, assuming he was talking about Anna.

'Much too tall for me, of course,' he said, laughing.

Melville couldn't have been more than five feet three. Redhaired, bearded, with a wicked gap-toothed grin, he looked like something kept to amuse the Spanish royal family.

'Me, I need them much shorter,' he added. 'And that generally means younger, too.'

I felt my ears prick up at this admission. 'How much younger?'

'The age isn't important,' he said. 'Not for a short-arse like me. I have to take what I can get.'

'Yes, but there's young and there's too young, surely?'

'Is there?' He laughed. 'I dunno.'

'Well, just how young is too young? You must have some idea.'

He thought for a moment and then shrugged, silently.

'So what's the youngest you've ever had?'

'What's it to you?'

'I'm interested, that's all. I mean, with some of these girls you meet these days, well, sometimes, it's a little hard to tell how old they are.' I was hoping to draw him out on a subject Melville was already beginning to look evasive about. 'The make-up they wear. The clothes. Some of them have experience way beyond their years. Back in Germany, for instance, I had a few close shaves, I can tell you. Of course I was a lot younger then myself. And Germany was Germany. Girls were naked in the clubs and naked in the parks. Before the Nazis, sun-worship – naturism they called it – was all the rage. Like I say, that was Germany. Sex was our national pastime. Under the Weimar Republic we were famous for it. But this? This is a Roman Catholic country. I'd have thought that things were a bit different here.'

'Then you'd be wrong, wouldn't you?' Melville uttered his manic gargoyle's laugh. 'To tell the truth, this country's a paradise for perverts like me. It's one of the reasons I live here. All the unripe fruit. You only have to reach up and pick it off the tree.'

Again I felt my ears prick up. The Castillian phrase Melville used to describe young girls was *fruta inmadura* – the very same phrase the Colonel had used to describe Perón's similar predilection.

'I don't know about Germany,' said Melville. 'I've not actually been there, but it would have to be pretty bloody good to beat the Argentine for *lecheras*.'

'Lecheras?'

'Milk maids.'

I nodded. 'Is it true, what I've heard? That the President likes them pretty young himself?'

Melville pursed his lips and looked evasive again.

'Maybe that's why you can get away with it,' I added.

'You make it sound like a crime, Hausner.'

'Isn't it? I don't know.'

'These girls know what they're doing, believe me.' He rolled an emaciated little cigarette and held the match up to his mouth. The roll-up crackled into flames like a tiny forest fire. With one chuckling puff he managed to consume almost a third of it.

'So where would I go?' I asked, affecting nonchalant curiosity. 'If I was thinking of picking it off the tree, like you describe.'

'One of the *pesar poco* joints down at the portside in La Boca,' he said. 'Of course you would have to be introduced by a member.' He lifted his whole mug in the air in a big self-satisfied grin. 'Like me.'

Restraining my first impulse, to introduce his jaw to a short uppercut, I smiled and said, 'That's a date then.'

'Mind you,' he said. 'The *fruta inmadura* scene is not what it used to be. Immediately after the war, the country was flooded with underweight baggage. That's what we used to call the really fragile fruit that was coming from Europe. Little Jewish virgins escaping to a better life, they imagined. All of them looking for the *caballero blanco*. A few found one. Some grew up and went on the game. The rest ... Who knows?'

'Who knows indeed? The way I hear it, some of those illegal Jews got themselves picked up by the secret police. And disappeared.'

Melville pulled a face and shook his head. 'Everyone disappears at one time or another in Argentina. It's a national bloody pastime. The *porteños* get depressed about all kinds of shit, and then they take off for a while. Sooner or later most of them turn up again without a word of explanation. Like nothing happened. As for the Jews. Well, it's my own experience they're an especially melancholy lot. Which, if you don't mind me saying so, is largely the fault of your own countrymen, Hausner.'

I nodded, conceding the point, which was well made.

'Now take Perón,' he said, warming to his theme. 'He was Vice-President and Secretary of War in the government of General Endelmiro Farrell. Then he disappeared. His colleagues had arrested him and put him in jail on Marin Garcia Island. Then Evita organises some mass demonstrations of popular support and, a week later, he's back. Six months after that, he's the President. He disappears. He comes back. It's a very Argentine story.'

'Not everyone has an Evita,' I said. 'And not everyone who disappears comes back, surely. You can't deny that the jails are full of Perón's political opponents.'

'You can't make an omelette without breaking a few eggs. Besides, most of those people are communists. Do you want to see this country handed over to the communists like Poland and Hungary and East Germany? Like Bolivia?'

'No, not at all.'

'Well then. You ask me, they're doing the best they can. This is a fine country. Perhaps the finest country in the whole of South America. With excellent prospects for economic growth. And I'd much rather live in Argentina than in Britain. Even without the unripe fruit.'

Melville flicked the pungent roll-up into the street. It was something I'd dearly liked to have done to him.

'What are you doing here, anyway, Melville?' I asked, trying to conceal the exasperation I felt with him. 'I mean, what is it that you do? Your work. Your job.'

'I told you before,' he said. 'Obviously you weren't listening.' He laughed. 'But there's no great mystery about what I do for a living. Unlike *some* I could mention.' He shot me a look as if to say he meant me. 'I work for Glasgow Wire. We supply a range of stock fencing and wire products to cattle ranchers all over the Argentine.'

I tried to stifle a yawn and failed. He was right, he had told me before. It was just that I'd seen no reason to think it was something I ought to remember.

'It sounds boring, I know,' he said wryly. 'But there wouldn't be a beef industry in this country without galvanised wire products. I sell it in fifty metre rolls, by the pallet. The Argie cattlemen buy miles of the stuff. They can't get enough of it. And not just the cattlemen. Wire is important to all sorts of people.'

'Really?' This time the yawn got the better of me.

Melville seemed to regard my apparent disinterest as a challenge.

'Oh yes. Why, just a few years ago, one of your own countrymen awarded me quite a large contract. He was an engineer working for the Ministry of Foreign Affairs. What was his name now? Kammler. That's right. Doctor Hans Kammler. Ever heard of him?'

The name itched a little although I couldn't think why.

'I had several meetings with your Mister Kammler at the San Martin Palace, in Arenales. An interesting man. During the war he was a General in the SS. I expect you knew him.'

'All right. I was in the SS. Satisfied?'

Melville smacked his thigh with the flat of his hand. 'I knew it,' he said triumphantly. 'I just knew it. 'Course it doesn't matter to me what you did. The war's over now. And we're going to need Germany if we're to keep the Russians out of Europe.'

'What would the Ministry of Foreign Affairs need with a large quantity of wire fencing?' I asked.

'You'd better ask your General Kammler,' said Melville. 'We met several times, he and I. The last time at a place near Tucumán, where I delivered the wire.'

'Oh right,' I said, my curiosity relaxing a little now. 'You must mean the hydro-electric plant run by the Capri Construction Company.'

'No, no. They're a client of mine, it's true. But this was something different. Something much more secret. My guess is that it was something to do with the atom bomb. Of course I could be wrong, but Perón's always wanted Argentina to be the first nuclear power in South America. Kammler used to refer to the project as memorandum something or other. A number.'

'Eleven? Directive Eleven?'

'That's right. No, wait. It was Directive Twelve.'

'You're sure about that?'

'Quite sure. Either way it was all top secret stuff. They paid well over the odds for the wire. Largely I suppose because we had to deliver the stuff to a valley in the middle of nowhere in the Sierra de Aconquija. Oh, it was easy enough as far as Tucumán itself. There's quite a reasonable railway from Buenos Aires to Tucumán, as you probably know. But from there to Dulce – that was the name of the facility they were building up there, after the river of the same name, I suppose – we had to use mules. Hundreds of mules.'

'Melville ... Do you think you could point the place out on a map?'

He smiled uncertainly. 'I think I probably said too much already. I mean, if it is a secret nuclear facility they might not care for me telling people exactly where it is.'

'You have a point there,' I admitted. 'They'd probably kill you if they found out you'd told someone like me about it. In fact, I'm quite sure of it. But on the other hand' – I lifted my jacket clear of the shoulder-holster I was wearing and let him see the Smith that was nesting there – 'On the other hand, isn't so good either. In a moment you and I are going to walk to the bookshop across the street and I'm going to buy a map. And either your brains or your finger is going to be on it by the time I leave.'

'You're joking,' he said.

'I'm German. We're not exactly famous for our sense of humour, Melville. Especially not when it comes to killing people. We take that sort of thing quite seriously. Which is why we're so good at it.'

'Suppose I don't want to go to the bookshop,' he said, looking around. The Richmond was busy. 'You wouldn't dare shoot me here, in front of all these people.'

'Why not? I've finished my coffee and you've thoughtfully taken care of the bill. It certainly won't spoil my morning to put a bullet in your head. And when the cops ask me why I did it, I'll simply tell them you resisted arrest.' I took out my SIDE credentials and showed them to him. 'You see, I'm sort of a cop myself. The secret kind that doesn't usually get held to account.'

'So that's what you do.' Melville uttered his manic laugh. Only now it was more of a nervous laugh. 'I was kind of wondering.'

'Well, now that your curiosity has been satisfied, let's go. And try to remember what I said about the German sense of humour.'

In the Figuera Bookshop on the corner of Florida and Alsina I bought a map of Argentina for a hundred pesos and, taking Melville by the arm, walked him onto Plaza de Mayo where, in full sight of the Casa Rosada, I unfolded the map on the grass.

'So, let's have it,' I said. 'Where exactly was this place? And if I find you've lied to me I'm going to come back like Banquo in that play of yours, Scotsman. And I'm going to make your hair a lot more red than it is now.'

The Scotsman moved a forefinger north from Buenos Aires, past Cordóba and Santiago del Estero, and west of La Cocha where Eichmann was now living.

'About here,' he said. 'It's not actually marked on the map. But that's where I met Kammler. Just north of Andalgala there are a couple of lagoons in a depression near the basin of the Dulce River. They were building a small railway when I saw the place. Probably to make it easier to move materials up there.'

'Yeah, probably,' I said, folding up the map and sliding it into my pocket. 'If you'll take my advice you won't mention this to anyone. Probably they'd kill you before killing me but only after torturing you first. Luckily for you they already tortured me and it didn't work, so you're in the clear from my end of this conversation. The best thing you could do now would be just to go away and forget you ever met me. Not even across a chessboard.'

'Suits me,' said Melville and walked quickly away.

I took another good look at the map and told myself Colonel Montalban would have been disappointed in me: I really wasn't much of a detective. Who would ever have thought that Melville – the bore in the Richmond bar – might turn out to hold the key to the whole case? I was almost amused at the accidental way I had managed to obtain the clue as to what Directive Twelve was, and where it had been implemented. But Melville was wrong about one thing. Directive Twelve was nothing to do with a secret nuclear facility, and everything to do with the empty file from the Ministry of Foreign Affairs Anna and I had found in the old Hotel de Inmigrantes. I was certain of that.

TWENTY

BUENOS AIRES. 1950.

I telephoned Anna and told her to meet me for lunch at around two o'clock, at the Shorthorn Grill on Corrientes. Then I drove to the house in Arenales where Von Bader and the Colonel were waiting for me. After what Isabel Pekerman had told me at the Club Seguro, I knew I was probably wasting my time but I wanted to see how the two of them behaved without her, and how their story would sound in the light of what I now knew. Not that I knew anything very much for sure. That would have been too much to expect. I supposed that Von Bader was planning to go to Switzerland and that Evita wasn't about to let him go until the real Baroness produced Fabienne.

There were a number of reasons why the real Baroness might have disappeared with Evita's daughter – always supposing that Fabienne *was* Evita's daughter. Some of it was to do with the Reichsbank's accounts in Zurich but I couldn't see how exactly. The bottom line of it was that I'd been led a merry dance by Colonel Montalban. I knew what his motives were for having me re-open a twenty-year-old murder investigation. He'd explained these to me quite clearly. But the only possible explanation for his not telling me that Fabienne had gone into hiding with her mother was that he knew for sure that they were hiding out with one of the old comrades. In any event he had a reason for arranging the charade involving Isabel Pekerman. The Colonel wasn't the kind of man who did anything without a good reason.

'Won't your wife be joining us?' I asked Von Bader as he closed the door of the drawing room behind us.

'I'm afraid not,' he answered coolly. 'She's at our weekend house, in Pilar. I'm afraid this has all been a dreadful strain for her.'

'I'm sure it must have been,' I said. 'Still, that makes it easier, I suppose.' Seeing his blank face, I added, 'To talk about Fabienne's real mother with you now.' I let him squirm for a moment and then said, 'The President's wife told me all about it.'

'Oh, I see. Yes, it does.'

'She said your daughter overheard the two of you arguing, and then ran away.'

'Yes. I'm sorry I had to mislead you a little, Herr Gunther,' said Von Bader. He was wearing a different suit but the same look of easy affluence. His grey hair had been trimmed since last we'd met. His fingernails were shorter, too, but bitten rather than manicured. And bitten down to the quick. 'But I was, still am, very worried that something might have happened to her.'

'Is Fabienne close to her stepmother would you say?'

'Yes. Very. I mean she treats my wife like she's her real mother. And to everyone who knows us that's the way it's always been. Evita has had very little to do with her daughter until comparatively recently.'

I looked at Colonel Montalban. 'What made you think she might have chosen to hide out with a German family? And in case you didn't recognise it, Colonel, that's a straight question of the kind that deserves a straight answer.'

'I think I can answer that, Herr Gunther,' said Von Bader. 'Fabienne is a very sophisticated little girl. She knows a great deal about the war and what went on and how it is that so many Germans such as yourself have chosen to live here in Argentina. You might even say that Fabienne is a National Socialist. She herself would say that she is. My wife and I sometimes argued about that.

'The reason the Colonel wanted you to search among our old comrades here in Argentina is really quite simple. It is because Fabienne herself had suggested she might run away and seek sanctuary with one of them. She was often threatening it after the discovery that Evita was her real mother. Fabienne could be cruel like that. She said, who better to hide her than one who was himself in hiding. I know this seems a strange thing for a father to say about his own daughter, but Fabienne is a very charismatic sort of girl. Her photographs don't do her justice. She is quintessentially Aryan, and among those who have met her there is general consensus that the Führer himself would have been captivated by her. If you ever saw Leni Riefenstahl in *The Blue Light*, Herr Gunther, you'll know the sort of thing I'm talking about.'

I'd seen the picture. An Alpine picture they called it. The Alps had been the best thing in it.

'To that extent she is truly Evita's daughter. Since you've met her I assume you will know what I'm talking about.'

I nodded. 'All right, I get the picture. She's everyone's little sweetheart. Geli Raubel, Leni Riefenstahl, Eva Braun, and Eva Perón all rolled into one precocious siren. Why didn't you level with me before?'

'We weren't at liberty to do so,' said the Colonel. 'Evita didn't want her secret to be told to anyone. Her enemies would use this kind of information to destroy her. However, eventually I persuaded her to talk to you about it and now you know everything.'

'Hmmm.'

'What does that mean?' asked the Colonel.

'It means maybe I do and maybe I don't and maybe I'm used to not expecting to know the difference. And besides, she's his daughter so why would he want to lie about it except that people will lie about anything, of course, and on any occasion except when there's a month with an X in it.' I lit a cigarette. 'These old comrades that she met. Did they have names?'

'About a year ago,' said Von Bader, 'my wife and I held a garden party to welcome many of the old comrades to Argentina.'

'Very hospitable of you, I'm sure.'

'One of my former colleagues was in charge of the guest list. Doctor Heinrich Dorge. Formerly he was aide to Doctor Schacht. Hitler's Finance Minister?'

I nodded.

'Fabienne was the star of the party,' said her father. 'She seemed so fresh, so captivating, that many men seemed to quite forget why they were here. I remember she sang a number of old German songs. My wife played the piano. Fabienne moved many of them to tears. She was remarkable.' He paused. 'Doctor Dorge is dead, I'm afraid. He had an accident. Which means we are unable to remember everyone who was there. Certainly there must have been as many as one hundred and fifty old comrades. Possibly even more than that.'

'And you think she's hiding with one of them, is that it?'

'I'd say it was a strong possibility.'

'One that is still worth checking,' added the Colonel. 'Which is why I would like you to keep going with your previous inquiry. There are still a great many names you haven't yet spoken to.'

'True,' I said. 'But look here, it's my guess that if she hasn't been found it's because she's no longer in Buenos Aires. The chances are she's somewhere in the country. Tucumán, perhaps. There are lots of old comrades up there, working for Capri on the dam at La Quiroga. Maybe I should go and look for her up there.'

'We already did,' said the Colonel. 'But why not. Perhaps we missed something. When can you leave?'

'I'll catch the evening train.'

*

There were only two dishes on the menu at the Shorthorn Grill: beef with vegetables, or beef on its own. There was a lot of beef displayed on skewers in the window and pictures of various beef cuts – cooked and uncooked – hung on the roast beef-coloured walls. A steer's head surveyed the restaurant and its patrons with glassy-eyed bewilderment. As fast as the beef was cooked and carried to the tables it was eaten, in companionable silence, as if beef was something much too serious to be interrupted with conversation. It was the kind of place where even your shoe leather felt a little nervous.

Anna was sitting in a corner behind a table covered with a red-checked tablecloth. Above her head was a lithograph featuring a gaucho roping a steer. There was pain in her eyes but I didn't think it was because she was a vegetarian. As soon as I sat down a waiter came over and heaped some beef sausage and red peppers onto our plates. Most of the other waiters had eyebrows that met in the middle; our waiter had eyebrows that had already mated. I ordered a bottle of red wine, the kind I knew Anna liked, made of grapes and alcohol. When he'd gone I laid my hand on top of hers.

'What's the matter? Don't you like beef?'

'Perhaps I shouldn't have come,' she said quietly. 'I've just had some bad news. About a friend of mine.'

'I'm sorry to hear that,' I said. 'Do you want to tell me about it?'

'She was an actress,' said Anna. 'Well, that's what she called herself. Frankly I had my doubts about that, but she was a good person. She'd had a hard life, I think. Much harder than she'd ever have admitted to. And now she's dead. She couldn't have been more than thirty-six.' Anna smiled ruefully. 'I guess it doesn't get much harder than that, does it?'

'Isabel Pekerman,' I said.

Anna looked shocked. 'Yes. How did you know?'

'Never you mind. Just tell me what happened.'

'After you telephoned this morning I got a call from

Hannah, a mutual friend. Hannah has the apartment upstairs from Isabel. It's in the Once. That's the *barrio* officially known as Balvanera. Historically it's where the city's Jews used to live, and quite a few of them still do. Anyway, Isabel was found dead this morning. By Hannah. She was in the bath with her wrists cut, as if she'd committed suicide.'

'As if?'

Isabel was a survivor. She wasn't the suicidal type. Not at all, not after everything she'd been through. And certainly not while there was any hope that her two sisters might still be alive. You see—'

'I know. She told me about the sisters. As a matter of fact she told me last night. She certainly didn't look like someone who was going home to cut her wrists.'

'You were with her?'

'She telephoned me at my hotel and we arranged to meet in a place called the Club Seguro. She told me everything. Your doubts about her profession were quite correct, I think, but she was a good person. I liked her anyway. I liked her just about enough to have gone to bed with her. I wish I had. Maybe she'd still be alive.'

'Why didn't you? Go to bed with her?'

'All sorts of reasons. Yesterday was a hell of a day.'

'I called you twice, but you weren't there.'

'I was arrested. Briefly.'

'Why?'

'It's a long story. Like Isabel's. Mostly I didn't go back home with her on account of you, Anna. That's what I told myself this morning, anyway. I was feeling quite proud of myself for having resisted the temptation to go to bed with her. Until you told me she was dead.'

'So you think I'm right, that she might have been murdered?'

'Yes.'

'Why would anyone kill Isabel?'

'Being the kind of actress she was is not without risk,' I said. 'But that's not why she was killed. I imagine it had something to do with me. Maybe her phone was tapped; maybe my phone is tapped. Maybe she was being followed. Maybe I'm being followed. I don't know.'

'Do you know who it was?'

'I've a very good idea who issued the orders, but it's best you don't know any more than I've told you. This is quite dangerous enough already.'

'Then we have to go to the police.'

'No, we don't.' I grinned, amused at her naivety. 'No, angel, we definitely do not go the police.'

'Are you suggesting they had something to do with it?'

'I'm not suggesting anything at all. Look, Anna, I came here to tell you that I think I might have found out something. Something important about Directive Eleven. A place on a map. I had this stupid, romantic notion that you and I might catch the night train to Tucumán and go and take a look at this place. But that was before I heard about Isabel Pekerman. Now I think it's best I don't say any more. About anything.'

'And you think that trying to shield me from something like some naïve schoolgirl doesn't make you sound stupid and romantic?' she said.

'Believe me. It's safer that I don't say any more.'

She sighed. 'Well this should be an interesting lunch. With you not saying anything.'

Lon Chaney came back with the wine. He opened it and we went through the pantomime of me tasting it and him pouring it. As absurd as a Japanese tea ceremony. As soon as he had filled Anna's glass she picked it up and drained it. He smiled awkwardly, and started to refill it. Anna took the bottle away from him, poured it herself and drank a second glass as quickly as the first.

'Well, what will we talk about now?' she asked.

'Take it easy with that,' I said.

The waiter went away. He could sense trouble coming.

'We could talk about football, I suppose,' she said. 'Or politics. Or what's on at the cinema. But you should start. You're better at avoiding certain subjects than I am. After all, I imagine you've had a lot more practise.' She poured herself some more wine. 'I know, let's talk about the war. Better than that, let's talk about *your* war. What were you anyway? Gestapo? SS? Did you work in a concentration camp? Did you kill any Jews? Did you kill lots of Jews? Are you here because you're a Nazi war criminal and because there's a price on your head? Will they hang you if they ever catch up with you?' She lit a cigarette nervously. 'How am I doing so far, not talking about what we came here to talk about? By the way, what was it that made you take me on as a client, Bernie? Guilt? Are you trying to make yourself feel better about what you did then by helping me now. Is that it? Yes, I can see how that might work.'

Her eyes narrowed and she bit her lip as if she was putting her whole body into each stroke of the verbal whip she was wielding.

'The SS man with a conscience. It's quite a story when you think about it. A little corny, but then real stories often are, don't you agree? The Jewess and the German officer. Someone should write an opera about it. One of those avant-garde ones with miserable songs, minor keys, and bum notes. Only I do think that the baritone who plays you should be someone who can't really sing. Or better still won't. That's his *leitmotif*. And hers? Something impotent, repetitive and hopeless.'

Anna picked up her glass, only this time she stood up when she had finished it. 'Thanks for lunch.'

'Sit down,' I said. 'You're behaving like a child.'

'Maybe that's because you're treating me like one.'

'Maybe I am, but I'd rather that than see your body on a slab in the police morgue. That's my only real *motif*, Anna.'

'Now you sound like my father. No wait, I think you're a little older than he is.'

And then she left.

I finished what was left of the bottle and went to the Casa Rosada to look through all the information Montalban had given me about old comrades in Argentina. There was nothing about a Hans Kammler. But then neither was there anything about Otto Skorzeny. Apparently, it seemed that some old comrades were beyond suspicion. Later on, I telephoned Geller to let him know I was coming back to Tucumán and to ask if I might borrow his Jeep.

'Are you planning to visit Ricardo again?' he asked. 'Because he still hasn't quite forgiven me for telling you where he lives.' Geller laughed. 'I don't think he likes you.'

'I'm sure of it.'

'By the way, you were asking about bastards who give us bastards a bad name. You'll never guess who showed up here the other day. Otto Skorzeny.'

'Is he working for Capri, too?'

'That's the funny thing. He's not. At least not according to my records anyway.'

'See if you can find out what he's doing there,' I said. 'And while you're at it see what you can find out about a man called Hans Kammler.'

'Kammler? Never heard of him.'

'He was a general in the SS, Pedro.'

Geller groaned.

'What's the matter?'

'Why ever did I agree to the name Pedro?' he said. 'Every time I hear it, I wince. It's a peasant's name. It makes me think I probably smell of horseshit.'

'Not so as you'd notice, Pedro. Not in Tucumán. Everything in Tucumán smells of horseshit.'

In the evening I drove to the railway station. As usual the place was full of people, many of them Indians from Paraguay and Bolivia and easily identifiable by their colourful blankets and bowler hats. At first I didn't see her standing at the head of the Mitre line platform. She was wearing a sensible, two-piece woollen suit, gloves and a scarf. By her shapely leg was a small valise and in her hand was a ticket. She appeared to be waiting for me.

'I was wondering when you were going to show up,' she said.

'What the hell are you doing here?' I asked.

'I might say that this is a free country, except that it's not,' she said.

'You really think you're coming to Tucumán?'

'That's what it says on my ticket.'

'I told you before. This is dangerous.'

'My heart is in my mouth.' She shrugged. 'Everything's dangerous when you read the small print, Gunther. Sometimes it's a good idea not to bring your glasses. Besides, these are my relatives, not yours. Always supposing you have such things as relatives.'

'Didn't I tell you? They found me under a rock.'

'It figures. You have a number of rock-like qualities.'

'Then I guess I can hardly stop you, angel.'

'It might be fun seeing you try.'

'All right.' I let out a sigh. 'I know when I'm beaten.'

'Somehow I doubt that.'

'Have you been to Tucumán before?'

'I never saw the point of spending twenty-three hours on a train just to end up in a flea-bitten dump. That's what everyone says, anyway. That there's just a couple of churches and what passes for a university.'

'That, and a couple of million acres of sugar-cane.'

'You make it sound like I've been missing something.'

'No, but I have.' I took her in my arms and kissed her. 'I hope you've got a sweet tooth. A million acres is an awful lot of sugar.'

'After what I said to you at lunchtime I could use a little sweetening, don't you think?'

'You've got twenty-three hours to make it up to me.'

'Then it's lucky I brought some cards.'

'We'd better get on the train.' I picked up her bag and we walked along the platform, past vending trolleys laden with food and drink for passengers to take on board. We bought as much as we could carry and found ourselves a compartment. Minutes later the train started to move out of the station, but after half an hour we still weren't going much faster than an old lady on a bicycle.

'It's no wonder it takes twenty-three hours, at these speeds,' I complained.

'The British built the railways,' she explained. 'Until Perón came along they owned them, too.'

'That doesn't explain why they go so slowly.'

'The railroads weren't built for people,' she said. 'They were built for the transportation of cattle.'

'And here was me thinking that it was only the Germans who had mastered the art of transporting people like cattle.'

'Hmm. Were you always this cynical?'

'No. I used to be a twinkle in my father's eye. You should have seen me then. I could light up a room from twenty feet.'

'Your father sounds like quite a man.'

'He had his turn.'

'Ruthless as well as cynical. Like all SS men.'

'How would you know? I'll bet I'm the first SS man you ever met.'

'I certainly never expected to like kissing one.'

'I never expected to be one, that's for sure. Do you want me to tell you about it? We've got plenty of time.'

'What about our no questions deal?'

'No, I think it's time you knew something about me. Just in case I get killed.'

'You're saying that just to try to scare me. Forget it. These days I even sleep with the light out.'

'Do you want me to tell you, or not?'

'I guess I can hardly walk out the door if I decide I don't like you after all. Even at this speed. Go ahead. I can always play patience if I get bored listening.'

'My brand of straight talk is strong stuff. It needs a little mixer. Like ginger ale or Indian tonic water.' I took a bottle of whisky out of my bag and poured a measure in my one small glass. 'Or some of this perhaps.'

'That's quite strong for a mixer,' she said, sipping it like it was nitro-glycerine.

I lit two cigarettes and put one in her mouth. 'It's a strong story. Come on. Drink up. I can only tell it to you when you're seeing double and I'm blowing smoke in your eyes. That way you won't notice when I grow lots of hair on my face and my teeth get longer.'

The train was leaving behind the suburbs of Buenos Aires. If only I could have left behind my own past as easily. A strong smell of sea water arrived through the open window. Gulls hovered in the blue sky close to the shore. The wheels rattled underneath the carriage floor like a six-eight march and, for a moment I remembered the bands that had marched underneath the windows of the Adlon Hotel on the night of Monday, January 30th, 1933. That was the day the world changed forever. The day Hitler was appointed Chancellor of the Reich. I remembered how, as each band had neared Pariser Platz, where both the Adlon and the French Embassy were situated, they stopped whatever they had been playing and struck up with the old Prussian war song 'We Mean to Beat the French'. That was the moment I realised that another European war was inevitable.

'All Germans carry an image of Adolf Hitler inside them,' I said. 'Even the ones like me who hated Hitler and everything he stood for. That face, with its tousled hair and postage stamp moustache haunts us all now and for evermore and, like a quiet flame that can never be extinguished, burns itself into our souls. The Nazis used to talk of a thousand-year empire. But sometimes I think that because of what we did, the name of Germany and the Germans will live in infamy for a thousand years. That it will take the rest of the world a thousand years to forget. Certainly, if I live to be a thousand years old I'll never forget some of the things I saw. And some of the things I did.'

I told Anna everything. That is everything I had done during the war and its aftermath up to the time I'd set sail for Argentina. It was the first time I'd ever spoken to anyone about it honestly, leaving nothing out and not trying to justify what I myself had done. But at the end of it all, I told her who was really to blame for it all.

'I blame the communists for calling a general strike in November 1932 that forced an election. I blame Von Hindenburg for being too old to tell Hitler where to get off. I blame six million unemployed – a third of the workforce – for wanting a job at any price, even if it meant Hitler's price. I blame the army for not putting an end to the street violence during the Weimar Republic and for backing Hitler in 1933. I blame the French. I blame Von Schleicher. I blame the British. I blame Goebbels and I blame all those rich businessmen who bankrolled the Nazis. I blame Von Papen and Rathenau and Evert and Scheidemann and Leibknecht and Rosa Luxemburg. I blame the Spartakists and I blame the Freikorps. I blame the Great War for taking away the value of human life. I blame the inflation and the Bauhaus and Dada and Max Reinhardt. I blame Himmler and Goering and Hitler and the SS and Weimar and the whores and the pimps. But most of all I blame myself. I blame myself for doing nothing. Which was less than I ought to have done. Which was all that was required for Nazism to succeed. I share the guilt. I put my survival ahead of all other considerations. That is self-evident. If I was truly innocent, then I'd be dead, Anna. And I'm not.

'For the last five years I've been letting myself off the hook.

I had to come to Argentina and see myself in the eyes of these other ex-SS men to understand that. I was a part of it. I tried not to be and failed. I was there. I wore the uniform. I share the responsibility.'

Anna Yagubsky lifted her eyebrows and looked away. 'My God,' she said. 'You've had an interesting life.'

I smiled, thinking of Hedda Adlon and her Chinese curse.

'Oh, I'm not judging you,' said Anna. 'I wouldn't say you were guilty of much. Then again, you're not entirely innocent either, are you? But it seems to me as if you've already paid a kind of price for what you did. You were a prisoner of the Russians. That must have been awful. And now you're helping me. It strikes me that you wouldn't do that if you were like the rest of your old comrades. It's not up to me forgive you. That's up to God – always supposing you believe in God – but I'll pray for him to forgive you, and maybe you could try praying yourself.'

I could hardly risk her disapproval again by telling her I didn't believe in God any more than I had believed in Adolf Hitler. A Jew who had become a Roman Catholic wasn't someone who was likely to treat the matter of my atheism lightly. After what I'd just told her I needed to earn her favour back again, so I nodded and said, 'Maybe I'll do that.' And if there was a God, I figured he'd probably understand. After all, it's easy to stop believing in God when you've stopped believing in anything else. When you've stopped believing in yourself.

TWENTY-ONE

TUCUMÁN. 1950.

We reached Tucumán the following evening. Or just about. The train was late and it was almost midnight by the time it rumbled into the local station. The place looked better at night. Government House was lit up like a Christmas tree. Under the palm trees on the Plaza Independencia, couples were dancing the tango. Argentines seemed to need little or no excuse to tango. For all I knew the dancers in the main square were really waiting for a bus. The station itself was full of children. None of them were interested in the submarine-shaped locomotive that was cooling down after our day-long journey. They wanted money. Kids were just like everyone else in that respect. I shared out a handful of coins and then found us a taxi. I told the driver to take us to the Plaza.

'Why do you want to go there?' he asked.

'Because the last time I saw it the Plaza was a hotel.'

'You should go to the Coventry. I could get you a rate there.'

'You and your brother, right?'

The driver laughed and looked around. 'That's right. You'd like my brother.'

'I'm sure I would. And I guess I couldn't like him less than I liked the Coventry. Actually I think they liked me there less than I liked them, because I was covered in bites when I left. I don't mind sharing my bed with anyone as long as they've got just two legs. When the Luftwaffe bombed Coventry in England I figure they must have been thinking of the hotel here in Tucumán.'

We drove to the Plaza.

Like most good hotels in Argentina it was trying to look like it was somewhere else. Madrid, probably. Or maybe London. There was the usual amount of oak panelling on the walls and marble on the floors. I laid an arm on the front desk like I meant business and looked across at the clerk, who wore a dark suit that matched his moustache. His face and hair were shiny with the same stuff they used on the machinery of the little elevator cage that stood at right angles to the desk. He bobbed his head at me and showed me some teeth that were heavily stained with tobacco.

'We'd like a large room,' I told him. It sounded better than asking for a large bed, but that was what we really wanted. 'With a bath. And what passes for a view in this city.'

'And not noisy either,' Anna added. 'We don't like noise except when we make it ourselves.'

'There's our bridal suite,' he said, firing a hungry glance at Anna.

I was feeling kind of hungry myself. The clerk offered to show it to us. Anna asked to see the rate instead. Then she offered to pay about half of what he was asking, in cash. This would never have worked in Germany, but in Tucumán it was normal. In Tucumán they haggled with the priest when he gave them a penance. Ten minutes later we were in the room.

The bridal suite was adequate. There was a pair of French windows that opened onto a balcony with a view of the high Sierras and a strong smell of orange blossom that made a pleasant change from horses. There was a big bathroom with a view of the rest of the suite and a strong smell of soap that made a pleasant change from drains. Most important of all there was a bed. The bed was the size of the Matto Grosso. Before long it had a view of Anna's naked body and a strong smell of her perfume, which made a pleasant change from my own bachelor smell. We made a night of it. Every time I woke I reached for her. And every time she woke she reached for me.

We certainly didn't sleep very much. The bed was too hard for sleep which was just fine by me. I certainly had not expected to enjoy Tucumán half as much as I did.

When morning finally came I took a cold bath that helped me to wake up. Then I ordered us some breakfast. We were still eating it when Pedro Geller called up and said he was waiting for me downstairs in the hotel lobby. I met him alone. The fewer people who knew about Anna's involvement the better, I told myself. Geller and I went outside, to the spot where he'd left the Jeep.

'I found out where Skorzeny is staying,' he said. 'At a big ranch in a place called Wiederhold. It's owned by a wealthy sugar farmer called Luis Freiburg. And when I say wealthy, I mean wealthy. He made millions in compensation when a couple of thousand acres of his estate were purchased by the government as part of the hydro-electric project. That land is due to be flooded when the dam at La Quiroga is finished.' Geller laughed. 'Now here's the really interesting thing. It turns out that Freiburg is none other than that SS General you told me about.'

'Hans Kammler?'

'That's right. According to Ricardo, Kammler is an engineer who oversaw all the major SS construction projects during the war. Like the Mittelwerk facility, and all the extermination camps like Auschwitz and Treblinka. Made himself a fortune in the process. Yes, he was quite a man this Kammler. Ricardo told me that Himmler regarded Kammler as one of his most capable and talented men.'

'Ricardo told you all this?'

'He can get quite talkative when he's had a few,' said Geller. 'Yesterday evening, we were coming out of Capri's technical branch office in Cadillal when we saw a big white American car driven by Skorzeny. Ricardo recognised Kammler immediately.'

'What did Kammler look like?'

'Thin, bony, hooked nose. Aged about fifty. Eagle-like you might say. Had his wife and daughter with him. From Germany, I think. That's one of the reasons Ricardo hates him. Because he's got his wife and daughter with him. Although I rather think Ricardo's jealous of anyone who got out of Germany with lots of money in his trouser pockets. That, or anyone who's made a better fist of life in Argentina than he has. You included.'

'Did Ricardo say why Skorzeny might be staying with Kammler?'

'Yes.'

Momentarily, Geller looked troubled. I offered him a cigarette. He took one, let me light him, and remained silent.

'Come on Herbert,' I said, using his real name for once, and lighting one for myself.

Geller sighed. 'This is top secret stuff, Bernie. I mean even Ricardo looked a bit shifty when he told me.'

'Ricardo always looks shifty,' I said.

'Well, naturally he worries that his past will catch up with him. We all do. Even you, probably. But this isn't past. This is now. Have you ever heard of Project Poplar?'

'Poplar? Like the tree?'

Geller nodded. 'Apparently Perón wants to build an atomic bomb. The scuttlebutt around Capri is that Kammler is the director of Perón's nuclear weapons programme, just like he was in Germany at Riesengebirge and Ebensee. And that Skorzeny is his head of security.'

'You'd need a lot of money for something like that.' Even as I said it, I remembered that Perón already seemed to have access to hundreds of millions of dollars of Nazi money; and, if Evita had her way, possibly billions more dollars in Switzerland. 'You also need a lot of scientists,' I added. 'Have you seen lots of scientists?'

'I don't know. I don't imagine they drive around wearing white coats and carrying slide rules, do you?'

'Good point.'

There was a map on the seat of the Jeep and a toolbox in the back. 'Show me where Kammler's ranch is,' I told Geller.

'Wiederhold?' Geller took the map and moved a finger south-west of Tucumán. 'It's here. Just a few miles north of the Dulce River. A few miles to the south and a little to the east and the frosts make sugar cane impossible. Cane would be impossible in Tucumán, too, if it wasn't for the Sierra de Aconquija.' He took a drag from his cigarette. 'You're not thinking of going there, are you?'

'No. I'm going here.' I pointed to one of the lagoons on the Dulce River. 'Just north of Andalgala. To a place called Dulce.'

'Never heard of it,' said Geller. 'There's the Dulce River but I've not heard of a town of that name.'

Geller's map was more detailed than the one I'd bought in Buenos Aires. But he was right: there was nowhere called Dulce. Just a couple of anonymous lagoons. All the same I didn't think Melville would have dared to mislead me. Not after the threats I had made against his miserable life.

'How accurate is this map?' I asked.

'Very. It's based on an old muleteers' map. Up until the beginning of the century mules were the only way to get around this whole area. As many as sixty thousand mules a year used to get sold in Santa, north of here. Nobody knew these trails better than those old muleteers.'

'May I borrow this?'

'Sure. Don't tell me you've found your top bastard,' he said. 'This murderer you've been after.'

'Something like that. It's best I don't tell you any more, Herbert. Not right now.'

Geller shrugged. 'Not knowing won't make me itch.' He grinned. 'While you're borrowing my Jeep I'm off to see a rather attractive girl who works for the Institute of Anthropology, here in Tucumán. I'm planning to let her study me in considerable detail.'

*

I tried to persuade Anna to stay behind at the hotel but she wasn't having it.

'I told you before, Gunther. I'm not the type who sits at home darning your socks. I didn't get to be a lawyer without outsmarting a few dumb cops.'

'For a lawyer you don't seem to have much in the way of caution.'

'I never said I was a good lawyer. But get this straight. I started this case and I intend to see it through.'

'You know something? For a lawyer, you're a pretty nice girl. I just don't want anything to happen to you.'

'Do all Germans treat women like they're made of porcelain? No wonder you lost the war. Come on, let's get in the car.'

Anna and I drove south-west out of the city. Soon we were on a narrow, pitted road that was bordered on both sides by the parted waves of a Red Sea of sugar cane. This was green on top, and an impenetrable wooden thicket below. There were miles of the stuff, almost as if imagination had failed the earth's creator.

'Sugar cane. It's just a lot of giant grass,' said Anna.

'Sure, but I'd hate to see the lawnmowers.'

From time to time I was obliged to slow down as we passed little walking thickets of cane that, on closer inspection, revealed themselves to be loads on the backs of mules, which elicited cries of pity from Anna. Every few miles we came across a shantytown of cement-block houses with corrugated iron roofs. Half-naked children, chewing lengths of sugar cane like dogs gnawing bones, observed our arrival and departure from their *villas miseria* with wild, gesticulating enthusiasm. From the metropolitan comfort of Buenos Aires, Argentina had seemed like an affluent country; but out here, on the plantations of the Humid Pampa, the eighth largest country in the world seemed like one of the poorest.

Several miles further on, the sugar cane receded and we

came to some fields of maize that led down to the River Dulce and a wooden bridge that wasn't much more than a continuation of the dirt road. On the other side I pulled over and took another look at the map. I had the Sierra rising up in front of me, the river on my right, fields of maize on my left, and the road leading down a long incline immediately ahead of us.

'There's nothing here,' said Anna. 'Just a lot of sugar and a lot more sky.' She paused. 'What exactly does this place look like, anyway?'

'I don't know exactly,' I said. 'But I'll know it when I see it.' I tossed the map onto her lap, shoved the Jeep in gear and drove on.

A few minutes later we came to the ruins of a village – a village that didn't appear on the map. Small white roofless shacks lined the road and a derelict church was home to a number of stray dogs but there was no sign of anyone living there.

'Where have all the people gone?'

'I suppose they were moved by the government. This whole area will be flooded when they dam the river.'

'I'm missing it already,' she said.

At the bottom of the street a narrow alley led off to the right and, on a wall, we saw the faintest outline of an arrow and the words Laguna Dulce – the sweet lagoon. We turned down the alley, which became a dirt track leading into a narrow valley. A thick canopy of trees covered the track and I switched on the headlights until we were in sunlight again.

'I'd hate to run out of gas here,' observed Anna, as we bounced from one pothole to another. 'The middle of nowhere has its depressing moments.'

'Any time you want to go back just say the word.'

'And miss what's just around the next corner? I don't think so.'

At last we came to a clearing and a kind of crossroads.

'Which way now?' she asked.

I drove a little further on before reversing back to the cross-roads and choosing another direction. A moment or two later I saw it.

'This is the right way,' I said.

'How do you know?'

I slowed down. In the bushes by the side of the track was an empty wooden roll labelled GLASGOW WIRE. I pointed to it. 'This is where the Scotsman delivered his wire.'

'And you think it was for a refugee camp?'

'Yes.'

That was what I had told her. But already I was beginning to realise that if a refugee camp had once existed out here, it didn't any longer. The whole valley was deserted. Any refugee camp would have needed supplies. Supplies need transport. There was no evidence that anyone had been down that red clay road in a while. Our own tyre tracks were the only ones visible.

We drove on for almost a mile until I found what we were looking for. A thick line of trees and a barbed-wire gate in front of an anonymous dirt road that led further down into the valley. Behind the tree line was an equally high barbed-wired fence. There was a sign in Spanish on the gate. Translated, it read:

PRIVATE PROPERTY OF THE CAPRI CONSTRUCTION AND HYDRO ELECTRIC COMPANY. UNAUTHORISED ENTRY STRICTLY FORBIDDEN BY ORDER OF THE FEDERAL GOVERNMENT. KEEP OUT. DANGER.

There were three padlocked chains around the gate and, at about ten feet high, I hardly saw us climbing over it. Moreover the padlocks were of a type that usually resisted picking. I steered the Jeep off the road and into a small gap in the tree line. Then I cut the engine.

'I think we're here,' I said.

'What now?' asked Anna surveying the fence.

I unlocked the toolbox in the back of the Jeep and searched it hopefully. It seemed that Geller went equipped for almost any eventuality. I found a pair of hand-sized, heavy-duty wire-cutters. We were in business.

'Now, we walk,' I said.

We walked through the trees and along the length of the fence. There was no one about. Even the birds remained silent here. All the same, I figured it was better to cut the wire about thirty or forty yards away from the Jeep in case anyone saw it and stopped to see why it was there. With the wire cutters in hand, I set about making us an entrance.

'We'll just go in and have a look and see what there is to see,' I said.

'Don't you think we should maybe come back and do this in the dark? In case anyone sees us?'

'Stand back.' As I cut another length of Melville's wire it zipped away into the trees, singing like a broken piano string.

Anna looked around nervously.

'You really quite tenacious, aren't you?' she said.

I pocketed the wire cutters. Something bit me and I slapped my neck. I almost wished it had been her. 'Tenacious?' I grinned. 'This is your search for answers. Not mine.'

'Then perhaps I just lost my appetite for them,' she said. 'Fear does that to you. I certainly haven't forgotten what happened the last time we broke into somewhere we weren't supposed to be.'

'Good point,' I said and took out my gun. I opened and closed the magazine, checked that everything was working, and slipped off the safety. Then I stepped through the gap I'd made in the fence.

Reluctantly, Anna followed. 'I suppose killing people gets easier each time that you do it. That's what they say, isn't it?'

'They usually don't know what they're talking about,' I said, treading carefully through the trees. 'The first time I killed a man was in the trenches. And it was me or him. I can't say I've ever killed anyone who didn't have it coming.'

'What about conscience?'

I let the gun lie flat on my hand for a moment. 'Maybe you'd feel better if I put this away.'

'No,' she said, quickly.

'So it's all right if I have to kill someone, just as long as your conscience is clear, is that it?'

'Maybe if I was as tough as you, I could do it. I mean, shoot someone. But I'm not.'

'Angel? If there's one thing the last war proved it's that anyone can kill anyone. All you need is a reason. And a gun.'

'I don't believe that.'

'There are no killers,' I said. 'There are just plumbers and shopkeepers and lawyers who kill people. Everyone's quite normal until they pull the trigger. That's all you need to fight a war. Lots of ordinary people to kill lots of other ordinary people. Couldn't be easier.'

'And that makes it all right?'

'No. But that's the way it is.'

She said nothing to that and for a while we walked in silence, as if the preternaturally quiet forest had affected us in some way. There was just a light breeze in the treetops and the sound of twigs cracking underneath our feet to remind us of where we were. Then, emerging from the trees we found ourselves facing a second wire fence. It was about two hundred metres long and behind it stood a number of tempo-rary-looking wooden buildings. At opposite ends of the fence were watchtowers and, fortunately for us, these were not manned. The camp, if camp this was, looked deserted. I took out the wire-cutters.

'Melville called this place Dulce,' I said, snipping one length of the little Scotsman's galvanised wire, and then another.

'Someone's idea of a joke, perhaps,' said Anna. 'There's nothing sweet about it.'

'It's my guess that this is where they held illegal Jewish immigrants like your aunt and uncle, and Isabel Pekerman's sisters. That's the assumption I've been working on, anyway.'

We ducked through the wire and into the camp.

I counted five watchtowers – one at each corner of the perimeter fence and a fifth in the centre of the camp, overlooking a kind of trench that seemed to connect one long barracks to another. Near the main gate was a small guardhouse. A road led into the camp from the main gate and onto what looked like a parade ground. In the centre of the parade ground was an empty flag pole. Nearest to the place where we had entered the camp was a large ranch house. We peered through the dusty windows. There was furniture: tables, chairs, an old radio, a picture of Juan Perón, a room with a dozen or so beds on which the mattresses had been rolled up. In a canteen-sized kitchen pots and pans hung neatly on a wall-mounted rack. I tried the door, and found it was not locked.

We went inside, breathing a musty, mildewed air. On a table we found an old copy of *La Prensa*. On the front page was a picture of Perón wearing military uniform, a white officer's cap, white gloves, a sash in the colours of the Argentine national flag, and a big generous grin. The lead story was something about Perón announcing his first five-year plan to boost the country's newly nationalised industries. I showed it to Anna, pointing out the date.

'1947,' I said. 'I guess that was the last time anyone was here,' I said.

'I certainly hope so,' she said.

I walked into another room and picked up an old helmet. Other rooms were no more enlightening.

'This must have been where the soldiers relaxed,' I said.

We went outside again, crossing the parade ground to a group of four long barracks. We went inside one. It was like a stable except that instead of stalls there were wide wooden shelves, some of which were covered with handfuls of straw

347

and almost a minute had passed before I realised that these were supposed to be beds. Probably two or three people could have been accommodated on each of the shelves.

Anna looked at me with pain in her eyes and I could tell she had arrived at the same conclusion. Neither of us spoke. She stayed close to me and eventually took my left hand. My gun was still in my right. We went into the second barracks which was much like the first. So was the third. I was reminded of the POW camp I had been held in by the Russians. Apart from the weather, this place looked almost as grim.

The fourth barracks building was just a long empty shed. The far end of the shed led down into a sort of trench that was covered with a ceiling of more barbed wire. The trench was about thirty yards long and two metres wide. We entered it and walked down into a barrack that you only knew was there when you had entered the trench. This barrack was divided into three chambers by two wooden walls. Each was about ten feet high and thirty feet wide and the inside walls were covered with sheets of zinc. On the ceiling were shower pipes. The door of each chamber was extra thick and could be closed from the outside by an iron locking bar. These doors were sealed with rubber gaskets around the edges. In each of the three chambers a copper pipe entered through a wall a few inches above a tiled floor. The pipes were all connected to a large central stove in the corridor outside the chambers. By now I had a very bad feeling about this place.

Anna was looking up at the pipes on the ceiling. 'So where did the water come from?' she asked, glancing around. 'I didn't see a water tank on the roof.'

'Perhaps they took it away,' I said.

'Why? They haven't taken anything else away.' She glanced down at the floor. 'And what are these? Tram rails? What?' She followed the tram rails to the far end of the barracks and some double doors next to a big extractor fan that was set in the wall. She pushed open the doors and went outside.

'Perhaps we should leave now,' I called out, going after her. I holstered my gun and tried to take her by the hand but she lifted it away and kept on walking.

'Not until I understand what this place is,' she said.

I tried to inject some calm into my voice. 'Come on, Anna. Let's go.' I wondered how much she knew of what had gone on at the camps in Poland. 'We've seen enough, don't you think? They're not here. Perhaps they never were.'

The rails led along the side of five grass-covered mounds that were about twenty feet wide and forty feet long. Next to these were a number of heavy duty flat-bed trolleys of the kind that might have been used in a railway yard. The trolleys were covered in rust but the design was clear enough: each trolley could be raised to tip its cargo into one of the pits. I was beginning to suspect what probably lay underneath the grass-covered mounds.

'Earthworks,' I said.

'Earthworks? No, I don't think so.'

'Yes,' I said. 'I expect they were going to build some more of these barracks and then changed their minds.'

It sounded pathetic. I knew perfectly well what I was looking at. And, by now, so did she.

Slowly, Anna bent forward to look at something that had caught her eye on the grass-covered mound. She started to crouch. Then she was on her knees, glancing around, finding a piece of wood and using it to scrape at the ground around an almost colourless plant that was growing out of the pit in front of her.

'What is it?' I asked, coming closer. 'Have you found something?'

She sat back on her haunches and I saw that it wasn't a plant at all. The plant wasn't a plant but a child's hand – a decomposed, partly skeletal human hand. Anna shook her head, whispered something and then, putting her hand up to her mouth, tried to stifle the emotion rising in her throat. Then she crossed herself.

I said nothing. There was nothing I could say. The purpose of the camp was now clear to us both. *These mounds were mass graves.*

'How many do you think?' she said, finally. 'In each one?'

It was my turn to be nervous now. I was looking around for some sign that we might have been observed. A death camp had been more than I had bargained for. Much more. 'I dunno. Maybe a thousand. Look, we really should leave. Now.'

'Yes, you're right.' She found a handkerchief and wiped her eye. 'Just give me a minute, will you? My aunt and uncle are probably buried in one of these pits.'

'You don't know that.'

'Can you honestly think of a better explanation?'

'Look,' I said. 'The people who are buried here. You don't know that they're Jewish. They could be Argentines. Political opponents of the Peróns. There's no reason to suppose—'

'That's a gas chamber in there,' she said, looking back at the barracks from which we had just emerged. 'Isn't it? Come on, Gunther. You were in the SS. You of all people should be able to recognise one.'

I said nothing.

'I never heard of Perón's political opponents being gassed,' she said. 'Shot yes. Tossed out of a plane. Yes. But not gassed. Only Jews get gassed. This place, this camp, is a place of death. That's why they were brought here. To be gassed. I can feel it. Everywhere. I could feel it in that dummy shower-barracks. I can feel it here most of all.'

'We have to leave,' I said.

'What?'

'Now. If they catch us here they'll kill us for sure,' I said. I took her arm and lifted her up. 'I never expected this, angel. Really I didn't. I'd never have brought you here if I'd even suspected that it was this kind of place. I thought it might be a concentration camp. But never a death camp. Not that. This is much more than I ever bargained for.'

I took her back to the hole in the fence.

'Christ,' she said, 'no wonder this is such a big secret. Can you imagine what might happen if people outside Argentina ever find out about this place?'

'Anna. Listen to me. You have to promise you'll never mention this. At least not so long as you remain in this country. They'd kill us both, for sure. The quicker we're away from here the better.'

Entering the trees again, I started to run. And so did she. At least now, I thought, she had grasped the true gravity of our situation. I threw away the wire-cutters. We found the hole we had made in the first, exterior fence. We started running back to where we had left the Jeep.

I smelt them first. Or rather I smelt their cigarettes. I stopped running and turned to face Anna.

'Listen,' I said, holding her by the shoulders. 'Do exactly what I say. There are men looking for us on this road.'

'How do you know?'

'Because I can smell their tobacco.'

Anna sniffed the air and then bit her lip.

'Take off your clothes.'

'What are you talking about? Are you mad?'

'Maybe they won't find the hole we made in the fence.' I was already undressing. 'Our best chance is to make them think that we stopped here to make love. That's the story we've got to stick to. If they think that's all that we were doing, they might just let us go. Come on, angel. Strip.'

She hesitated.

'No one who's just seen what we've just seen would strip and have sex in the woods, now would they?'

'I told you we should have come back and done this in darkness,' she said, and started to undress.

When we were both naked, I wrestled my way between her thighs and said, 'Now sound like you're enjoying it. As loud as you can.'

Anna moaned loudly. And then again.

I started to thrust my pelvis at her as if not just her sexual satisfaction and mine depended on this charade, but our lives as well.

TWENTY-TWO

TUCUMÁN. 1950.

I was still thrusting away between Anna's thighs when I heard a twig break on the forest floor behind me. I twisted around to see some men. None of them were wearing uniforms but two of them had rifles slung over their shoulders. That was good, I thought. At the same time I grabbed something with which to cover our nakedness.

There were three of them and they were dressed for riding. They wore blue shirts, leather vests, denim trousers, riding boots and spurs. The man without a rifle had a silver belt as big as a breastplate, an ornate-looking gun-belt, and, over his wrist was looped a short, stiff-leather whip. He was more obviously Spanish than his companions, who appeared to be *mestizos* – local Indians. His face was badly pock-marked but he had a quiet confidence in his manner that seemed to indicate his scars didn't matter to him.

'I would ask what you are doing here,' he said grinning. 'Only it seems obvious.'

'Is it any business of yours?' I said, dressing quickly.

'This is private property,' he said. 'That makes it my business.' He wasn't looking at me. He was watching Anna put on her clothes which was almost as pleasurable a sight as watching her take them off.

'I'm sorry,' I said. 'We got lost. We stopped to look at the map and then one thing led to another. You know how it is, I expect.' I glanced around. 'It seemed like a nice quiet spot. No one around.'

353

'You were wrong.'

Then, out of the trees came a fourth man riding a fine white horse and very different from the other three. He wore an immaculate white, short-sleeved shirt, a black military-style cap, a pair of grey riding-breeches, and black boots that were as shiny as the gold watch on his slim wrist. He had a head like a giant bird of prey.

'The fence has been cut,' he told the pock-marked gaucho.

'Not by us,' said Anna.

'Claims they stopped here for a quiet fuck,' said the head gaucho.

Silently the man on the white horse rode around us while we finished dressing. My holster and gun were still on the ground somewhere only I hadn't been able to find them.

He said, 'Who are you and what are you doing in this part of the country?'

His Castellano was better than mine. There was something about his mouth that made it better for speaking Spanish. The size and shape of the chin governing the mouth caused me to suspect that maybe there were a couple of Habsburgs in his family. But he was German. That much I was certain of and instinctively I knew this must be Hans Kammler.

'I work for the SIDE,' I said. 'My identification is in my coat pocket.'

I handed the coat to the head gaucho who quickly found my wallet and passed it to his boss.

'My name is Carlos Hausner. I'm German. I came here to interview old comrades so that they can be issued with the good conduct passes they'll need to obtain an Argentine passport. Colonel Montalban at the Casa Rosada will vouch for me. So will Carlos Fuldner and Pedro Geller at Capri Construction. I'm afraid we got a bit lost. As I was saying to this gentleman, we stopped to take a look at the map and I'm afraid one thing led to another.'

The German on the white horse looked through my wallet

and then tossed it back to me before turning his attention to Anna. 'And who are you?' he asked.

'His fiancée.'

The German looked at me and smiled. 'And you say you're an old comrade.'

'I was an officer in the SS. Like you Herr General.'

'It's that obvious, is it?' The German looked disappointed.

'Only to me, sir,' I said, clicking my heels together and hoping that my show of Prussian obsequiousness might excuse Anna and me.

'A job with SIDE, a fiancée.' He smiled. 'My, you have settled in here, haven't you?' The horse shifted under him and he wheeled it around so that he could keep staring down at us. 'Tell me, Hausner. Do you always bring your fiancée along when you're on police business?'

'No sir. The fact is, my Castellano is fine in Buenos Aires, but out here it lets me down sometimes. The accent is a little difficult for me to understand.'

'Most of the people in this part of the world are of Guarani stock,' he said speaking German at last. 'They are an inferior Indian race but, on a ranch, they have their uses. Herding, branding, *fence-mending*.'

I nodded toward the barbed wire fence. 'Is this your fence, Herr General?'

'No,' he said. 'But my men keep an eye on it. You see, this is a high security area. Few people ever venture this far down the valley. Which leaves me with something of a dilemma.'

'Oh? What's that, sir?'

'I should have thought that was obvious. If you didn't cut the fence, then who did? You see my problem.'

'Yes, sir.' I shook my head awkwardly. 'Well, we certainly haven't seen anyone. Mind you we haven't been here that long.'

'Perhaps. Perhaps.'

The horse lifted its tail and did what horses do. He didn't seem to believe my story either.

The General nodded sharply at the head gaucho. 'You'd better bring them along.' He spoke in Castellano and it seemed evident that neither the head man nor the two *guaranis* spoke any German.

We walked back to where we'd left the Jeep. Three horses were waiting patiently for their riders. The two *guaranis* mounted up and took the third horse's bridle while the head gaucho climbed in the back of the Jeep. I noticed that his holster was unbuttoned and decided he looked like the type who might be quick on the draw. Besides, under his belt was a knife as long as Chile.

'Just stick to the story,' I told Anna in German.

'All right. But I don't think he believed it.'

She climbed into the passenger seat, lit a nervous-looking cigarette and tried to ignore the head gaucho's brown eyes on the back of her head. 'Who was that Nazi anyway?'

'I think he's the Nazi who built that camp,' I said. 'And many others like it.' I climbed into the driver's seat, took the cigarette from her mouth, puffed it for a moment and then put it back, only it didn't stick. Her jaw was hanging down like the ramp on a truck. So I put the cigarette in my own mouth.

'You mean?'

'That's exactly what I mean.' I started the Jeep. 'Which makes him extremely dangerous. So do exactly what I say and maybe we'll live to know better than to tell the tale.'

The head gaucho tapped me impatiently on the shoulder. 'Drive,' he said in Castellano. He pointed further up the road toward the three horsemen and the high Sierras.

I put the Jeep in gear and drove slowly along the road.

'It's just one man,' said Anna. 'Why don't you throw him out or something? We could easily escape three men on horses couldn't we?'

'For one thing this man behind me is armed to the teeth. And for another so are all his friends and they know this country much better than me. Besides, I lost my gun back there in the trees.'

'That's what you think,' she said. 'It's under my bra-strap, between my shoulder blades.'

'Anna, listen to me. Promise you won't do anything stupid. You don't know what you're up against. These men are professionals, they handle guns every day. So let me deal with it. I'm sure we can talk our way out of this.'

'That man, the General,' she said. 'If he really did what you said he did, he deserves to be shot.'

'Sure he does. Only he's not going to be shot unless it's by someone who knows what they're doing.'

The head gaucho pushed his head between us. From the smell of his breath I guessed he was a stranger to a toothbrush. 'Shut up talking German and drive,' he said fiercely. For added emphasis he produced the knife and pressed the tip under my ribs. I felt like a horse who had been pricked with a spur.

'I get the point,' I said, and put my foot down.

Sitting on the edge of a mountain slope with an excellent view of the valley below, it was more like a little piece of old Heidelberg than a ranch – a mosaic of handsome wooden chalets, ivy-mailed, castle-style turrets and a small chapel complete with a bell tower. Under the arch of the main building was a huge wooden tun that, from the bottles beside it, looked like it was filled with red wine. On the cobbled courtyard in front was an ornamental circular garden with a bronze fawn leaping through a facsimile cliff-edge waterfall and I almost expected to see the student prince soaking his head under it after a night on the beer. My surprise at seeing a corner of Baden-Württemberg in Argentina was quickly overtaken by the sight of a familiar face. Walking toward me, his hand held out in front of him was my old detective sergeant, Heinrich Grund. To my relief he seemed pleased to see me.

'Bernie Gunther,' he said. 'I thought it was you. What brings you up here?'

I pointed at the head gaucho with whom Grund had been speaking just a minute or two before. 'Him,' I said.

Grund shook his head and laughed. 'Same old Bernie. Always in trouble with the powers that be.'

Even after almost two decades he looked like a boxer. A retired boxer. He was greyer than I remembered. There were deep lines in his face, and more of a stomach in front of him. But he still had a face like a welder's mask, and a fist as big as a speedball.

'Is that what he is?'

'Gonzalez? Oh, yes, he's the estate manager. Runs everything around here. He seems to think you might have been spying.'

'Spying? On what exactly?'

'Oh, I dunno.' Grund's eyes licked Anna up and down for a moment. 'Aren't you going to introduce me to your lady friend?'

'Anna? This is Heinrich Grund. We were in the Berlin police together about a thousand years ago.'

'Is it that long?'

It certainly felt that long. I hadn't seen Grund since the summer of 1938 when he was already a senior officer in the Gestapo and we'd been very much at arm's length with one another. When last I'd heard of him he'd been a major in an E.G. – a Special Action Group – in the Crimea. I didn't know what he'd done. I didn't want to know, but it wasn't difficult to imagine.

'Heinrich,' I said, continuing the formal introduction. 'This is Anna Yagubsky. According to her, she's my fiancée.'

'Then I certainly wouldn't argue with her.' Grund took her hand and, smoother than I remembered him, bowed like a proper German officer. 'Charmed, I'm sure.'

'I wish I could say the same,' said Anna. 'I don't know why we've been brought here. Really I don't.'

'I'm afraid she's not very happy with me,' I told Grund. 'I promised her a nice drive from Tucumán and I managed to get us lost. The General and his men found us somewhere down in the valley. I'm not sure but I think it was somewhere we weren't supposed to be.'

'Yes, Gonzalez told me he found you at Camp Dulce down at the Sweet Lagoon. Now that's a very secret place. And by the way, we don't call him the General. We call him the Doctor. Whom you've met of course. Anyway, he's a close friend of Perón and takes all breaches of local security very seriously.'

I shrugged. 'Occupational hazard, I suppose. I mean we all of us have to take security very seriously.'

'Not like up here you don't.' Grund turned and pointed at the tops of the Sierras behind us. 'The other side of that is Chile. There's a secret pass that was used by the Guarani Indians that only the Doctor and Gonzalez know about. The least sniff of trouble and we can all be off on our travels again.' Grund smiled. 'This place is the perfect hideout.'

'What is this place?' asked Anna. 'It looks more town than house, I think.'

'It was built by a German. A fellow named Carlos Wiederhold towards the end of the last century. But quite soon after finishing it he found an even nicer spot to the south of here. Place called Bariloche. So he went there and built a whole town in similar style. There are lots of old comrades down there. You should visit it sometime.'

'Perhaps I will,' I said. 'Always supposing I can get a clean bill of health from the Doctor.'

'Naturally, I'll see what I can do.'

'Thanks, Heinrich.'

Grund shook his head. 'Only I'm still finding it kind of hard to believe. Bernie Gunther being here in Argentina like the rest of us. I always had you pegged as a bit of a commie. What the hell happened?'

'It's a long story.'

'Isn't it always?'

'But not right now, eh?'

'Sure.' Grund started to laugh.

'What's so funny?' I asked.

'You, a fugitive war criminal. The same as me. The war made fools of us all, didn't it?'

'That's certainly been my experience.'

I heard the sound of horses and looked around to see Kammler and his men riding up the slope toward us. The SS general lifted his boots out of the stirrups and slipped off his horse like a jockey. Grund went over to speak to him. Anna was watching Kammler closely. I was watching Anna. I put my hand lightly on the small of her back. The gun wasn't there.

'Where is it?' I murmured.

'Under my belt,' she said. 'Where I can reach it.'

'If you kill him—'

'What and spoil your little Nazi reunion? I wouldn't want to do that.'

There seemed no point in arguing that one. I said, 'If you kill him they'll kill us both.'

'After what I've seen, do you really think I care?'

'Yes. And if you don't then you certainly ought to. You're still a young woman. One day you might have children. Perhaps you ought to think about them.'

'I don't think I want to bring children into a country like this.'

'Then pick another country. I did.'

'Yes, I should think you would feel quite at home here,' she said bitterly. 'For you this must seem like a real home from home.'

'Anna, please be quiet. Be quiet and let me think.'

When Kammler had finished speaking to Grund he approached us with a sort of smile on his lean face, taking his cap off, and his arm extended towards us both in a show of avuncular hospitality. Now that he had dismounted I was able to get a better look at him. He was well over six feet tall. His hair was invisibly short and grey at the sides, but longer and darker on the crown so that it looked like a yarmulke. The skull on his stick-like neck had been taken from Easter Island, probably. The eyes were set in cave-like sockets so deep and shadowy they looked almost empty, as if the bird of prey that hatched him had pecked them out. His physique was very spare but strong, like something that had been unwound from one of Melville's spools of Glasgow barbed-wire. For a moment I couldn't quite place his accent. And then I guessed he was Prussian – one of those Baltic coast Prussians who eat herrings for breakfast and keep griffins for sport.

'I've been talking to your old friend Grund,' he said, 'and I've decided not to kill you.'

'I'm sure we're very relieved to hear it,' said Anna and smiled sweetly at me. 'Aren't we dear?'

Kammler glanced uncertainly at Anna. 'Yes, Grund has vouched for you. And so did your Colonel Montalban.'

'You called Montalban?' I said.

'You seem surprised at that.'

'It's just that I don't see any telephone lines up here.'

'You're right. There are none. No, I called him from a phone down there.' He turned and pointed into the valley. 'An old service telephone from the days when the hydro-electrical people from Capri were here.'

'That's quite a view you have there, Doctor,' said Anna.

'Yes. Of course soon much of it will be under several fathoms of water.'

'Won't that be a little bit inconvenient?' she asked him. 'What will happen to your telephone? To your road?'

He smiled patiently. 'We shall build another road, of course. Workers are plentiful and cheap in this part of the world.'

'Yes,' she said, smiling thinly. 'I can imagine.'

'Besides,' he added. 'A lake will be nicer. I think it will be just like Switzerland.'

We went up to the main house. It was made of stone bricks and pale-coloured wood. I counted about twenty-five windows on the three-storey front. The central part of the house was a red-roofed turret, at the top of which was a man with a pair of binoculars and a rifle. At the lower windows were Tyrolean-style shutters and window-boxes filled with flowers. As we came up to the front door I thought we might meet the Aryan Ski Association coming the other way. Certainly the air was more Alpine-like up here than it had been down in the valley.

Inside the house we were met by German-speaking servants, including a butler wearing a white cotton jacket. A big log was burning in the fireplace. There were flowers in tall vases and pictures and bronzes of horses everywhere you looked.

'What a lovely house,' said Anna. 'It's all very, Germanic.'

'You'll both stay to dinner of course,' said Kammler. 'My chef used to cook for Hermann Goering.'

'Now there was someone who really enjoyed his food,' Anna said.

Kammler smiled at Anna, uncertain of her temperament. I knew how he felt. I was trying to think of a way of getting her to shut up without using the back of my hand.

'My dear,' he said. 'After your exertions, perhaps you'd like to go and freshen up a bit.' To a hefty-looking maid hovering in the background, he said. 'Show her to a room upstairs.'

I watched Anna go up a staircase as wide as a small road and hoped she would have the good sense not to come back with the gun in her hand. Now that Kammler was being friendly and hospitable my greatest fear was that she might turn into an avenging angel.

We went into an enormous living room. Heinrich Grund followed at a respectful distance, like a faithful aide-de-camp. He was wearing a blue shirt and tie and a grey suit that was nicely tailored although not well enough to conceal the fact that he was also wearing a shoulder-holster. None of these people looked like they were taking any chances with their security. The living room was like an art gallery with sofas. There were several old masters and quite a few new ones. I could see that Kammler had escaped from the ruins of Europe with a lot more than just his life. In a tall, free-standing oriental-style cage a canary flapped its wings and twittered like a little yellow fairy. Through a pair of French windows an immaculate lawn stretched into the distance like the green felt on some divine billiards table. It all looked a very long way from Auschwitz-Birkenau. But in case it wasn't quite far enough there was a plane parked on the lawn.

I heard a pop and turned to see Kammler opening a bottle.

'I usually have a glass of champagne about this time. Will you join me?'

I said I would.

'It's my one real luxury,' he said handing me a flute.

I almost laughed as I noticed the box of Partagas on the sideboard, the Lalique decanter and glasses and the silver bowl of roses on the coffee table.

'Deutz,' he said. 'Rather difficult to get up here.' And then, lifting his glass in a toast, he said, 'To Germany.'

'To Germany,' I said and sipped the delicious champagne. Glancing out of the window at the little silver plane on the runway-sized lawn, I said, 'What's that? A BFW?'

'Yes. A 109 Taifun. Do you fly, Herr Gunther?'

'No, sir. I finished my war working for the OKW. Military Intelligence, on the Russian front. Accurate plane-spotting was a matter of life and death.'

'I was in the Luftwaffe when the war started,' said Kammler. 'Working as an architect for the Air Ministry. After

1940 there really wasn't much opportunity for an architect with the RLM so I joined the SS. I was chief of Department C, building soap factories and new weapons facilities.'

'Soap factories?'

Kammler chuckled. 'Yes. You know. *Soap*.'

'Oh. Yes. The camps. Of course.' I drank some champagne.

'How's your champagne?'

'Excellent.' But the truth was it wasn't. Not any more. The sour taste in my mouth had made certain of that.

'Heinrich and I got out early, in May 1945,' said Kammler. 'He was my head of security at Jonastal, weren't you Heinrich?'

'Yes, Herr Doctor.' Grund raised his glass to his master. 'We just got in a staff car and drove west.'

'We were building the German bomb at Jonastal so naturally the Amis welcomed us with open arms. We went to New Mexico to work on their own bomb programme. We stayed for almost a year. By then, however, it had dawned on them that, at the end of the war, I was effectively number three in the SS hierarchy, which made my continued employment in the USA very sensitive. So I came to Argentina. And Heinrich was good enough to come with me.'

'It was my honour, sir.'

'Gradually I was able to get most of my things out of storage and shipped here. Which is how you find me now. It's a little remote but we have pretty much everything you would want. My wife and daughter are with me; they'll be joining us for dinner. Where exactly are they now, Heinrich?'

'They're looking at some new calves, sir.'

'How many cattle do you have?' I enquired.

'About thirty thousand head of cattle and about fifteen thousand sheep. In many ways the work is not so dissimilar from what I did during the war. We rear the beasts, drive them into Tucumán, and then transfer them by rail to Buenos Aires for slaughter.'

He seemed unashamed by this confession.

'We're not the biggest *estancia* in these parts. Not by a long way. But we bring a certain efficiency to the running of an estate not usually seen in Argentina.'

'*German* efficiency, sir,' added Grund.

'Precisely,' affirmed Kammler. He turned to face a little Führer shrine I hadn't noticed before. There were several photographs of Hitler, a small bronze bust of his distinctive head, a few military decorations, a Nazi armband and a pair of Sabbath candlesticks that looked as if someone used them to keep the leader's flame alight on the Nazi high holy days – January 30th, April 20th, April 30th and November 8th. Kammler nodded reverently at his shrine. 'Yes, indeed. German efficiency. German superiority. We have *him* to thank for always reminding us of that fact.'

I didn't see it that way of course but, for the moment, I kept my reservations to myself. We were a very long way from the comparative safety of Buenos Aires.

When I'd finished my champagne Kammler suggested I might go upstairs and wash. The maid showed me to a bedroom where I found Anna lying on an elaborately-carved wooden bed. She waited until the maid had gone and then sprang up.

'This is very cosy, isn't it? His own private Berghof. Just like the Führer. Who knows? Maybe he'll put in a guest appearance at dinner. Now that would be interesting. Or how about Martin Bormann? You know, I always wanted to meet him. Only I ought to tell you now, I'm a little worried about dinner. I don't know the words of the Hörst Wessel song. And, let's not beat around the burning bush. I'm a Jew. Jews and Nazis don't mix.'

'I don't mind you sticking it to me, Anna, but please try to cut the sarcasm in front of the General. He's beginning to notice. And no confessions about who and what you are. That would really cook our goose.' I looked around the room. 'Where's the gun?'

'Hidden.'

'Hidden where?'

She shook her head.

'Still thinking of shooting him?'

'I know, he should suffer more. Shooting is too quick. Gas would be better. Perhaps I can leave the oven on in the kitchen before we go to bed tonight.'

'Anna, please. Listen to me. These are very dangerous people. Even now, Heinrich is carrying a gun. And he's a professional. Before you can even cock that Smith he'll blow your head off.'

'What do you mean, "cock"?'

I shook my head. 'See what I mean? You don't even know how to shoot.'

'You could show me.'

'Look, those dead people in that camp. They could be anyone.'

'They could be, but they're not. We both know who and what they are. You said yourself. It was a camp created by order of the Ministry of Foreign Affairs. What else would they want a camp for but to imprison foreign refugees? And your friend. The Scotsman, Melville. It was him who mentioned Directive Twelve. An order for barbed wire to be delivered to a German SS general called Kammler. *Directive Twelve*, Bernie. That implies something more serious than Directive Eleven, don't you think?' She took a deep breath. 'Besides, before we left Tucumán this morning, you told me it was Kammler who built the big death camps. Auschwitz. Birkenau. Treblinka. Surely you must agree that he deserves to be shot for that alone.'

'Perhaps. Yes, of course. But I can promise you, shooting Kammler here, today, isn't the answer. There has to be another way.'

'I don't see how we can arrest him. Not in Argentina. Do you?'

I shook my head.

'Then shooting him is best.'

I smiled. 'See what I mean? There's no such thing as a murderer. There's just a plumber or shopkeeper, or a lawyer who kills someone else. Ordinary people. People like you, Anna.'

'This isn't murder. This will be an execution.'

'Don't you think that's what those SS men used to tell themselves when they started shooting pits full of Jews?'

'All I know is that he can't be allowed to get away with it.'

'Anna, I promise you I will think of something. Just don't do anything rash. All right?'

She remained silent. I took her hand but she snatched it away again, angrily.

'All right?'

She let out a long sigh. 'All right.'

A little later on the maid brought us some evening clothes. A black, beaded gown that looked stunning on Anna; a dinner jacket, dress shirt and bow tie that somehow managed to fit me.

'Well, what do you know, we look almost civilised,' said Anna, and straightened my tie. There was some perfume on the dressing table. She put some on. 'Smells like dead flowers,' she observed.

'Actually, I rather like it,' I said.

'It figures. Anything dead probably smells good to a Nazi.'

'I wish you'd lay off that Nazi jibe.'

'I rather thought that was the point, Gunther. To make them think you're one of them so we can save our skins.' She got up and paused in front of the full-length cheval mirror. 'Well, I'm ready for anything. Maybe even a killing, or two.'

We went down to dinner. As well as Kammler, Grund, Anna and me, there were three other guests.

'This is my wife, Pilar, and my daughter, Mercedes,' said Kammler.

'Welcome to Wiederhold,' said Frau Kammler.

She was tall and thin and elegant with perfect semi-circular eyebrows that looked like they'd been drawn by Giotto and lots of wavy fair hair either side of her face that lent her a spaniel look. She belonged in the Cologne Prize winner's enclosure at Weidenpesch racecourse. But I wouldn't have raced her; I'd have put her out to stud at a million dollars a time. Frau Kammler's daughter was no less beautiful and no less charming. She looked about sixteen, but was perhaps younger. Her hair was more Titian than red because as soon as you saw her you thought she belonged on a velvet couch in the studio of a great painter with an eye for beauty. When I saw her I was sorry I didn't paint myself. Her own eyes were a peculiar shade of green, like an emerald with a trace of lapis lazuli, but quietly knowing, too, like she was about to check your King and you were just too dumb to know it yet.

All of us did our best to be civilised and polite. Even Anna, who responded to the thrown-down gauntlet of so much unexpected beauty by finding a little bit of extra beauty inside herself and switching it on like an electric light. But it was difficult to maintain this genteel atmosphere when the last guest was Otto Skorzeny. Especially as he had been drinking.

'What are you doing here?' he asked, when he saw me.

'Having dinner, I hope.'

Skorzeny draped a big arm around my shoulder. It felt as heavy as an iron-bar. 'This fellow is all right, Hans,' he told Kammler. 'He's my confidant. He's going to help me to make sure those grease balls never get their hands on the Reichsbank's money.'

Anna shot me a look.

'How's the hand, Otto?' I asked him, anxious to change the subject.

Skorzeny inspected his big mitt. It was covered in some livid looking scars from when he had punched King George's picture. It was clear he had forgotten how the scars had come to be there at all. 'My hand? Yes. I remember now. How's your in-growing toenail, or whatever it was?'

'He's fine,' said Anna putting her arm through mine.

'Who are you?' he asked her.

'His nurse. Only somehow he manages to look after himself very well without me. I wonder why I came at all.'

'Have you known each other for long?' asked Frau Kammler.

'They're engaged to be married,' said Heinrich Grund.

'Really?' said Frau Kammler.

'It's for his own good,' said Anna.

'Do you have any friends as good-looking as you?' Skorzeny asked her.

'No, but you seem to have plenty of friends of your own.'

Skorzeny looked at me, then at Kammler and Grund. 'You're right,' he said. 'My old comrades.'

Anna shot me another look. I hoped she didn't have the gun on her. The way things were going I thought she might shoot everyone, including me.

'But I need a good woman,' he complained.

'What about Evita?' I asked. 'How's it coming along with her?'

Skorzeny pulled a face. 'Not a chance. Bitch.'

'Otto, please,' said Frau Kammler. 'There are children present.'

Skorzeny looked at Mercedes and grinned with open admiration. She was grinning back at him. 'Mercedes? She's hardly that.'

'Thank you, Otto,' said Mercedes. 'At least there's someone here who's prepared to treat me like a grown-up. Anyway, he's right, Daddy. Eva Perón *is* a bitch.'

'That will do, Mercedes.' Her mother lit a cigarette in a

holder the length of a blow-pipe. Scolding Skorzeny gently, she took him over to the most comfortable-looking sofa and sat down with him. Evidently she had experience of his behaviour because a minute later the hero of Gran Sasso was asleep and snoring loudly.

We dined without him.

As promised, the dinner prepared by Goering's chef was excellent. And very German. I ate things I hadn't tasted since before the war. Even Anna was impressed.

'Tell your chef that I'm in love with him,' she said, full of charm now.

Kammler took his wife's hand. 'And I am in love with my wife,' he said, bringing the long slender hand to his lips.

She smiled back at him and taking his hand back to her mouth, nuzzled it tenderly like a favourite pet.

'Tell me, Anna,' said Kammler. 'Did you ever see two people who were so much in love as us?'

'No. I can't say I ever did.' Anna smiled politely and looked at me. 'I do hope that I'm as lucky as you are.'

'I can't tell you how happy this woman makes me,' said Kammler. 'I think that I would die if she left me. Really I would. I'd just die without her.'

'So, Anna,' said Grund. 'When are you and Bernie planning to get married?'

'That all depends,' she said, treating me to one of her most saccharine smiles.

'On what?' asked Grund.

'He has a small quest to perform for me first.'

'So he's a true knight,' said Mercedes. 'How romantic. Just like Parsifal.'

'Actually, he's more like Don Quixote,' said Anna, taking my hand and squeezing it playfully. 'My knight is a little older than most knights errant. Aren't you darling?'

Grund laughed. 'I like her Bernie,' he said. 'I like her a lot. But she's much too clever for you.'

'I hope not, Heinrich.'

'And what is this quest?' asked Mercedes.

'I want him to slay a dragon for me,' said Anna, with eyes widening. 'In a manner of speaking.'

When dinner was over, we returned to the living room and found Skorzeny was gone, to everyone's relief. A little after that Mercedes went to bed, followed closely by her mother and then Anna, who mischievously blew me a kiss as she went up. I breathed a sigh of relief that we had managed to get through the evening without her shooting anyone. I said I needed some night air and having taken one of the cigars offered me by my host, I went outside.

There's nothing like staring at a night sky to make you feel a long way from home. Especially when that sky is in South America and home was in Germany. The sky above the Sierras was bigger than any I'd ever seen, which made me feel smaller than the smallest point of silvery light on that great black vault. Perhaps that was why it was there. To make us feel small. To stop us from thinking that any of us is at all important enough to be a member of a master race and nonsense like that.

After a moment I heard a match scrape and, looking around, I saw Heinrich Grund lighting a cigarette. He stared up the heavens, took a deep drag on the cigarette and said, 'You're a lucky fellow, Bernie. She's really very lovely. And a bit of a handful, I imagine.'

'Yes, she is.'

'Do you ever think of that kid in Berlin? The crippled one who got herself murdered back in thirty-two? Anita Schwarz, wasn't it?'

'Yes. Yes, I do.'

'And you remember the arguments we used to have about her? Me saying it was all for the best that people like her died and you saying that mercy killing was wrong.' He shrugged. 'Something like that, anyway. The fact is, Bernie, I really had

371

no idea what I was talking about. No idea at all. It's one thing saying it, but it's quite another doing it.' He was silent for a while. Then he asked, 'Do you think there's a God, Bernie?'

'No. How could there be? If there was you wouldn't be here now. Neither of us would.'

Grund nodded. 'I was glad when we lost the war,' he said. 'I expect that surprises you, but I was glad it was all over. The killing, I mean. And when we came here it seemed like a fresh start.' He shook his head sadly as if weighed down by something monumentally heavy. 'Only it wasn't.'

When he had been silent for almost a minute, I said, 'Do you want to talk about it, Heinrich?'

He let out an unsteady, tremulous sort of breath and shook his head. 'Words don't help. They only seem to make it worse. For me, at any rate. I don't have Kammler's strength. His sense of absolute certainty.'

'I expect it helps having his family around,' I said, trying to change the subject. 'How long have they been here?'

'I dunno. A few months, I suppose.' Grund clapped himself on the chest. 'For him, Hitler still lives, in here. Always will, probably. For him and a lot of other Germans. But not me. Not any more.'

There was nothing I could say to this. There was nothing I wanted to say. We had both made our choices and were living with the consequences of those, good or bad. I wasn't sure I'd come off any better than Grund but at least, thanks to Anna, I still had some hope for the future. Grund didn't seem to have hope left in anything at all.

I left him on the terrace, with his thoughts and his fears and whatever else a man like him goes to bed with impaled on the shards of his conscience.

Anna sat up in bed as I came through our bedroom door. The bedside light was on. I sat down on the edge of the mattress and started to unlace my shoes. I wanted to say something tender to her but there was still something else on her mind.

'Well?' she said. 'Did you think of something? Some sort of punishment for that bastard Kammler?'

'Yes,' I said. 'Oh, yes.'

'Something terrible?'

'Yes. I think it will be. For him.'

TWENTY-THREE

BUENOS AIRES. 1950.

Two days later we arrived back in Buenos Aires. Since it seemed unlikely that the Colonel would have heard Kammler's news – that his men had picked me up next to the secret camp at Dulce – with any equanimity, I told Anna I needed some time to straighten things out with him before we could count ourselves safe. For now, I told her, she should go home and stay indoors until I called her. Better still, she should go and stay with a friend.

I had no way of knowing if Anna was likely to take my advice since, for most of the journey back from Tucumán, she hadn't really been speaking to me. She didn't like my idea as to what we were going to do about Hans Kammler. She didn't think it was enough of a punishment and told me that, as far as she was concerned, our relationship was over.

Maybe she meant that. And maybe she didn't. There was no time to make sure. I was coming out of the Richmond when they picked me up a second time. It might have been the same three men, only it was a little hard to tell with the dark glasses and the matching moustaches. The car was another black Ford sedan but not the same one that had driven me to Caseros. This car had a cigarette burn on the rear seat and a large blood stain on the carpet. Of course, it might have been coffee, or it might have been molasses. But over the years you get to recognise a blood stain when you see one on a car floor. I tried to keep calm but this time it wasn't working. Only I wasn't worried for myself as much as I was worried for Anna.

This was the moment I realised I was in love with her. That's usually the way, of course. It's only when you have something taken away that you realise how important it was to you. I was worried about her because, after all, I'd been warned, and in no uncertain terms. Naturally the Colonel would have guessed what I was up to when Kammler telephoned him; that I was sticking my nose into Argentina's biggest secret. Not the Pulqui II jet fighter aircraft, not even an atom bomb, but the fate of several thousand illegal Jewish refugees. The puzzle was why the Colonel hadn't just told Kammler to kill us both. I guessed I was about to find out. Only this time we sped past Caseros.

'Where are we going?' I asked.

'You'll find out soon enough,' growled one of my chaperones.

'Mystery tour, huh? I like surprises.'

'You won't like this one,' he said ominously. And everyone else laughed.

'You know I've been trying to get in touch with your boss, Colonel Montalban. I called him several times last night. I need to speak with him very urgently. I have some important information for him. Will he be where we're going?' I glanced out of the window and saw that we were driving south-west. 'I know he'll want to speak to me.'

I nodded, almost as if I was trying to convince myself of this. But, struggling for the right Spanish vocabulary to find something else that would convince them of my need to see the Colonel, I found myself unable to say anything much at all. There was a hole in the pit of my stomach the size of the football stadium at La Boca. My greatest worry was that this metaphorical hole might soon become a real one.

'Anyone got a Spanish dictionary?' I asked. No one answered. 'How about a cigarette?'

One of the thugs sandwiching me shifted on his backside squeezing me for a moment as he reached for a packet of smokes. I caught the smell of sweat on his jacket and the oil in his hair and saw a little blackjack poking out of his breast-pocket. I hoped it was going to stay there. I'd been black-jacked before and I wasn't keen to repeat the experience. He turned back with the packet in his hands and pushed open the little cardboard drawer. My fingers reached for one. The cigarettes looked like little white heads tucked up in bed, which was where I wished I was now. I put the cigarette in my mouth and waited while he found his lighter.

'Thanks,' I muttered and bent my head down to the flame. Too late I remembered it had been an old Gestapo trick. Straight out of the unofficial manual, Part III. How to silence a talkative suspect in the back of a black car. One fist holds the lighter. The other comes across from the other side of the car as the suspect ducks down to the flame, and knocks him out cold. At least, that's what I suppose must have happened. It was that, or the Argies really did have an atom bomb and someone had accidentally pressed the fire button instead of the bezel on a cigarette lighter.

For me the effect was pretty much the same, however. One minute it was a nice sunny day. The next, darkness all over the land until the ninth hour. And the sensation that I was humming like a very sick bee, as if someone had just put twenty thousand volts through a metal cap and a brine-soaked sponge attached to my cranium. For a moment or two I thought I heard laughter. The same kind of laughter you get when you're a cat in a sack full of stones and someone drops you down a well. I hit the water without so much as a splash and disappeared below the surface. It was a deep well and the water was very cold. The laughter went away. I stopped mewing. That was the general idea. I was pacified, the way the Gestapo liked. For some reason I remembered Rudolf Diels, the first head of the Gestapo. He only lasted until 1934, when Goering lost control of the Prussian police. He ended up as a local government official

in Cologne or Hanover, and found himself dismissed altogether when he refused to arrest the city's Jews. What
happened to him after that? A sucker punch and a trip to a
concentration camp no doubt. Like poor Frieda Bamberger
who died in the middle of nowhere with rubber seals on the
shower doors. I couldn't see where I was going but I felt like
I was already under the earth. I felt my hand poking up
through the ground. Reaching for life ...

Someone wrestled my arms around behind my back and
tied my wrists together. I was blindfolded now. I was standing
up and leaning across the warm bonnet of the Ford. I could
hear the sound of aeroplanes. We were at an airport. I thought
it must be Ezeira.

Two men lifted me under the arms and dragged me across
the tarmac. My feet weren't coming with me. It didn't seem to
hinder our progress. The noise of the aircraft engine grew
louder. A metallic, oily smell filled the air and I felt the wind
of the propeller in my face. It seemed to revive me a little.

'I feel I should warn you,' I said. 'I'm not a good air trav-
eller.'

They hauled me up a short flight of metal steps and then
flung me down on a hard floor. There was something else on
the floor besides me; something else that shifted and groaned
and I realised there were others in the same boat as me. Except
that it wasn't a boat. It might have been better if it had been.
Either way I had now guessed what lay ahead of us: a river
trip. The River Plate. Perhaps it was better this way after all.
At least we wouldn't drown. The fall would kill us.

The door closed and the aircraft began to move. Someone,
a man a few feet away, was reciting a prayer. Someone else
was retching with fear. There was a strong smell of vomit and
human incontinence and gasoline.

'So the rumours are true, then?' I said. 'There are no para-
chutes in the Argentine air force.'

A woman started crying. I hoped it wasn't Anna.

The plane engines roared. Just two of them I thought. A C-47 Dakota, most likely. You often saw them heading out over the Rio Plata. People sitting outside the Richmond would look up from their newspapers and their coffees and make jokes about these aeroplanes. 'There goes the opposition', or 'Why can't communists swim in the River Plate? Because their hands are tied together'. The floor underneath me began vibrating loudly. I felt the plane accelerate and we started our take-off. A few seconds later there was a lurch and we were airborne. The vibration settled into a steady, droning rhythm and the plane began to climb. The woman crying was almost hysterical by now.

'Anna?' I called. Is that you? It's me—'

Someone slapped me hard across the face. 'No talking,' said a man's voice. He lit a cigarette and suddenly I remembered why I was a smoker. The smell of tobacco is the most wonderful smell in the universe when you're facing death. I remember being shelled in 1916 and how a cigarette had got me through without losing my nerve or my bowels.

'I wouldn't mind a smoke,' I said. 'Under the circumstances.'

I heard a man's voice murmur something from the opposite end of the aircraft and, a few seconds later and much to my surprise, some fingers pushed a cigarette between my lips. It was already alight. I rolled it into the corner of my mouth and let my lungs go to work on it.

'Thanks,' I said.

I tried to make myself more comfortable. It wasn't easy but I hadn't expected it would be. The cord around my wrists was as tight as the skin on a fat snake. My hands felt like balloons. I managed to straighten my legs, which weren't tied and kicked someone else. Maybe I would kick a shark in the eye before I drowned. Always supposing I hit the sea and lived. I wondered how high the pilot was planning to go before they started baling us out.

Minutes passed. I was down to the filter. I spat the cigarette out of my mouth and it burned my shoulder before ending up on the deck. I hoped it might hit a pool of gasoline and cause a small fire. That would teach them. Then, what sounded like a handful of gravel hit the fuselage. It was raining. I took a deep breath and tried to steady myself. To make peace with myself. Negotiations opened slowly. I told Gunther he should think of himself as one of the lucky ones. How many others had ever managed to escape from the Russians? I was still telling myself how lucky I was when someone interrupted my winning streak and opened the door. Cold air and rain blasted through the guts of the plane with a sound like the roaring of some terrible cloud monster. A minotaur of the skies that needed to be served with regular human sacrifice.

It was impossible to guess how many human sacrifices were planned. I thought there were at least six or seven of us on that plane. With the door open now, the engines seemed to throttle back a little. There was movement all around me but, so far, no one had tried to move me towards the door. There was some sort of commotion and then a naked woman fell on me. I could tell she was naked because her breast squashed against my face and she was screaming. As they hauled her off me I decided I had to say something or I'd be telling it to the seagulls.

'Colonel Montalban? If you're there speak to me, you bastard.'

The woman who was screaming started begging them not to kill her. It wasn't Anna. The voice was older, more mature, huskier, not well-educated. It was hard to say more about her voice because, suddenly, it was not there and I sensed she wasn't there either.

Behind me a man was praying the same prayer over and over again, as if the repetition might make it count for more in the long line of prayers that were already winging their way

ahead of us to the divine waiting room. From the speed of his
prayers and his breathing and the way his position changed, I
guessed he was next in line to the door. And even as I was
thinking this he was gone, too, his final scream as he was
bundled out of the plane lost forever in the slipstream of eter-
nity.

I tried to shake the blindfold off my eyes but it was useless.
I might as well have had no eyes at all. Only I could have
wished that they had also stopped up my ears as, one by one,
they deported the other men and women through the open
door of the plane. It was like having a front row seat in the
dress circle of hell.

I bellowed like a man roasting on a spit, and cursed their
mothers and their fathers and their bastard children. I told the
Colonel what I thought of him and his country and his president and his president's cancerous wife and how I was going
to have the last laugh because only I knew what he and she
had dearly wanted to know and that I wasn't going to tell him
anything now, not even if they did throw me out of the plane.
I told them that I was spitting in all their faces in the knowledge that at least I was going to die knowing that I'd thwarted
their stupid schemes. Someone slapped me. I ignored it and
kept on talking.

'A month from now. A week. Maybe even tomorrow, you
and that dumb blonde whore are going to ask yourself if
Gunther really knew what he said he knew. If he really could
have told you what you wanted to find out most in the world.
Where you can find her. Where she's been hiding all this time.
Don't you want to find out Colonel?'

I heard a woman scream several times before the open door
silenced her permanently. Some sadistic part of my brain tried
to persuade me that there had been something about her
scream that had seemed familiar. Her perfume, too. But I
wasn't buying it. I hadn't any more reason for thinking Anna
was on the plane than for believing the Colonel was. If she

had done as I had told her and gone to stay with a friend, there was every reason to suppose she was all right.

Someone snatched off my blindfold. I was just in time to see two of my moustachioed friends carrying a man to the open door behind the wing. Mercifully the man was unconscious. He was wearing just underpants. His hands and his feet were tied and he looked like he'd been badly beaten. Either that or his face had been stung by a whole jungle full of bees. The less said about his toes the better. The two who threw him out of the plane probably thought they were doing him a favour. One of them pulled a filthy handkerchief out of his trouser pocket and wiped his brow. It was hard work. Then they looked at me.

'What did you expect?' said a voice behind me. 'I warned you to leave it alone.'

My neck was painful from when I'd been slugged but, gritting my teeth, I turned my head into the pain to meet the Colonel's eye.

'I didn't expect to find what I found,' I said. 'I didn't expect the unthinkable. Not again. Not here. This is supposed to be a new world. I didn't expect it would be just like the old one. But, you know? Now that I've seen your national airline and how it handles double-booked passengers, suddenly it doesn't seem quite so surprising.'

'This?' He shrugged. 'It's easier this way. There's no evidence. No camps. No bodies. No graves. Nothing. No one can ever prove anything. It's a one-way ticket. No one comes back to tell the tale.'

'Who were they, anyway? Those people who disappeared just now.'

'People like you, Gunther. People who asked too many questions.'

'Is that all you've got against me?' I got a grin going and tried to make my mouth hang on to it, like I still had an ace up my sleeve. It didn't feel right. My lips were trembling too much but, from here on in, show and tell was all I had going for me. If he decided I was bluffing I was in for a flying lesson. He knew it. I knew it. The two stooges by the still open door of the Dakota knew it. 'Hell, I'm a detective, Colonel. It's my job to ask too many questions, stick my nose in where it's not wanted. You of all people should know that. Everything's my business until I find out what I've been hired to find out. That's the way this racket works.'

'Nevertheless you were warned not to ask questions about Directive Eleven. I couldn't have been more specific. I thought, after your trip to Caseros, you might appreciate that a little more keenly.' He sighed. 'I was wrong, of course, and now you're in a tight spot. Truly, I regret having to kill you, Gunther. I meant all I said when we first met. You really were a hero of mine.'

'Well then, let's get to it,' I said.

'You're forgetting something, surely?'

'I don't pray so well these days, if that's what you mean. And my memory is not so good at altitude. How high are we anyway?'

'About five thousand feet.'

'That explains why it's so damned draughty in here. Perhaps if those two altar boys were to close the door I might warm up a little. I'm like a lizard that way. You'll be surprised just what I can do for you if you just let me sit for a while on a nice warm rock.'

The Colonel jerked his head at the door and with a weary look of disappointment, like two French Catholic noblemen denied the pleasure of defenestrating a big-mouthed Huguenot, they closed it. 'There,' he said. 'How's your memory now?'

'Improving all the time. Perhaps when we're on the ground again I'll remember Evita's daughter's name. That's assuming she really is Evita's daughter. To my untutored, cynical eye she and the President's wife looked very unalike.'

'You're bluffing Gunther.'

'Maybe. But you can't afford to take a chance on that, can you? If you knew any different, Colonel, I'd be in the river, looking for my old comrades from the *Graf Spee*.'

'So why not tell me?'

'Don't make me laugh. As soon as I've spilled my guts there's nothing to stop you from spilling me out the door.'

'Maybe. But look at it this way. If you tell me when we're on the ground there's nothing to stop me killing you in a day or two, or a week from now.'

'You're right. I never looked at it that way. You'd better think of something to put my mind at ease about that possibility or you'll wind up not knowing anything at all.'

'So what are we going to do?'

'I don't know. Really I don't. You work it out, you're the Colonel. Perhaps if I had another cigarette and my hands free we might reach some sort of understanding.'

The Colonel put his hand in the pocket of his suit. It came out with a switchblade as big as a drumstick. He turned me around and sawed at the cord binding my wrists. While I was rubbing some pain back into my hands he put the knife away and took out his cigarettes. He shook one loose from the pack, put it into my mouth, and then tossed me a book of matches. If I'd had any feeling in my hands I might have caught them. One of the Colonel's thugs picked up the matches and got my cigarette going for me. Meanwhile the Colonel leaned through the open cockpit door and spoke to the pilot. A moment later the plane began to turn back toward the city.

I was desperate to know if Anna had been one of those poor people thrown out of the aircraft, but I hardly knew how to ask the Colonel. If I didn't ask about Anna he might get the idea there was no one important in my life who might be used against me. If I did ask, I'd be putting her in grave danger.

'We're going back to Ezeira,' he said.

'I feel better already. Never was one for air travel.'

I glanced around the inside of the plane. There was a large pool of blood and something worse on the floor. Now that the door was closed I could smell the lingering stench of fear inside the Dakota. There were some seats up front. The Colonel sat in one. I got up off the floor and went and sat beside him. I leaned across his lap and glanced out of the window at the grey river beneath us.

'The people you just murdered,' I said. 'I suppose they were communists?'

'Some were.'

'And the others? There were women, weren't there?'

'These are enlightened times we live in, Gunther. Women can be communists, too. Sometimes – no, usually – they're more fanatical than the men. More courageous, also. I wonder if you could take as much torture as one of the women we just dumped.'

I said nothing.

'You know, I could always take you back to Caseros. Have my men go to work on you with that electric cattle-prod. Then you'd tell me what I want to know.'

'I know a little bit more about torture than you think, Colonel. I know that if you torture a man to make him tell you lots of things then gradually he'll give them up, one by one. But if you torture a man to make him tell you one thing, the chances are he'll clam up and take it. Make it a contest of wills. Now that I know how important this is to you, Colonel, I'd make it my life's last mission to say nothing.'

'A tough guy, huh?'

'Only when I have to be.'

'I believe you are. I suppose that's one of the reasons I like you.'

'Sure you like me. That's why you wanted to throw me out of a plane at five thousand feet.'

'You don't think I enjoy this sort of thing, do you? But it has to be done. If the communists were in power, they'd do the same thing to us, I can assure you.'

'That's what Hitler used to say.'

'Wasn't he right? Look what Stalin has done.'

'It's the politics of the cemetery, Colonel. I should know. I just crawled out of the one called Germany.'

The Colonel sighed. 'Perhaps you're right. But I think it's better to live without principles than be righteous and dead. That's what I've learned in the cemetery. There's this too, that I've learned. If my father leaves me a gold watch I want my son to have it after me, not some *paisano* carrying a copy of Marx he's never read. They want my watch? They'd better kill me first. Or it's out the door they go. They better know that in Argentina we practise the redistribution of health. Anyone goes around thinking that all property is theft soon finds out that all killing is not murder. The last communist we hang will be the one who helped himself to our rope.'

'I don't want to take anything from anyone, Colonel. When I came here I wanted a quiet life, remember? Nothing made your business my business except you. For all I care you can hang all the communists in South America on your Christmas tree. All the Nazis, too. But when you hire me to be your dog and sniff around you shouldn't be surprised if I bark a bit and piss on your flowerbed. That may be embarrassing to you but that's the way it is. I embarrass myself sometimes.'

'Fair enough.'

'Fair enough, he says. You haven't played fair with me since I got off the damn boat, Colonel. I want to know everything. And when I know everything I'm going to get off this plane and I'm going back to my hotel and I'm going to take a bath. And when I've had some dinner and I'm good and ready and I've understood how everything works, I'm going to tell you what you want to know. And when you find that I'm telling the truth you, and Von Bader and Evita are going to be so damned grateful you're even going to pay me like you all said you would.'

'As you wish, Gunther.'

'No. Just what I said. What I wish would be too much to expect.'

TWENTY-FOUR

BUENOS AIRES. 1950.

By the time we landed at Ezeira I knew almost everything.
Almost. I still didn't know if Anna Yagubsky was dead or alive.
I found a pay phone and called Anna's parents, who told me
they hadn't seen her since the trip to Tucumán but that she'd
left them a note saying she was going to stay with a friend.

'Do you know who this friend is?' I asked Roman
Yagubsky.

'As a matter of fact I thought it might be you.'

'If she comes back or calls, tell her I need to speak to her,
urgently.'

'Always in a hurry,' he said.

'It's the business I'm in.'

'Did you find my brother yet?'

'Not exactly.'

'What kind of an answer is that?'

'Not much of an answer but I won't lose any sleep over it.
If you think I've done an unsatisfactory job you can refuse to
pay me. I won't argue about that. But when I say not exactly
that's exactly what I mean. There are rarely any definite
answers in the private detective business. There are only
probabilities and maybes and not exactlys. They're the kind
of answers that are to be found in the crevices of what we're
allowed to know for sure. I have no evidence for saying your
brother and your sister-in-law are dead. I didn't see their
bodies. I didn't see their death certificates. I didn't speak to
anyone who saw them die. All the same, I know they're both

dead, sir. It's not an exact kind of knowing but there it is. Fact is, it's best I don't say any more. For your sake and mine.'

There was a silence. Then Señor Yagubsky said quietly, 'Thank you, young man. Of course, I've known they were dead for a while. If they were alive they'd have got in touch, but a brother is a brother and a twin is a twin and you feel an obligation to find out what you can. To have someone independent tell you what you think you know already. And you're right, of course, that isn't an exact kind of knowing but it's better than nothing, right? So thank you again. I appreciate your candour. Not to mention your discretion. I know what kind of people are in this government. But I'm a Jew, Señor Hausner, I'm used to it. Maybe if I had more money and I was ten years younger I'd go and live in Israel, but I don't and I'm not. So I say may God bless and keep the Peróns a long way from me and mine.'

'Don't forget, sir. Tell Anna to call me. I'll be at my hotel.'

'I know, I know. Urgently. Germans. Every time you people open your mouths I hear a clock ticking. Hitler might still be in power if he hadn't been in such a hurry to do things.'

The next morning I went to meet the Colonel at the Jockey Club, as arranged.

The Jockey Club of Buenos Aires would have shamed any Berlin or London club for luxury. Inside there was a great, empire-style rotunda, a fine marble statue of the goddess Diana, and a magnificent staircase that looked like the eighth wonder of the world. There were Corinthian columns everywhere and these were ornamented with onyx, ivory, and more lapis lazuli than a Russian Orthodox cathedral. I found the Colonel in the library – although calling the library at the Jockey Club a library was like calling Rita Hayworth an actor. There were plenty of books, it was true, but nearly all of their bindings were tooled with a little bit of gold so that it was like entering a long-lost burial chamber in the Valley of the Kings. And there were some club members who clearly belonged in a tomb: old men with profiles that you might have seen on a thousand-peso note. There were no women in that club, however. They wouldn't have known what to do with a woman in the Buenos Aires Jockey Club. Try and saddle her probably or, in the Colonel's case, defenestrate her.

He put down the book he was reading. I sat in the chair opposite and, curious, picked it up. I'm always interested in what mass-murderers are reading.

'*Martin Fierro*, by Jose Hernandez,' he said. 'Our national poet. Are you familiar with this book?'

'No.'

'Then I give it to you. I think you'll enjoy it. It's somewhat romanticised but I'm sure there are elements that will appeal to you. The hero is an impoverished gaucho whose house, farm, wife and family are all gone. Destroyed. He gets himself into one scrape after another. Knife fights and other brutal combats, and various affairs of honour. Eventually, Martin Fiero becomes an outlaw, pursued by the police militia.' The Colonel smiled. 'Perhaps this is a familiar tale to a man like you, Gunther. Certainly this book is very popular here in Argentina. Most children grow up able to quote a few stanzas from *Martin Fierro*. Myself, I know most of it by heart.'

'Assuming you have one.'

The Colonel smiled almost imperceptibly. 'To business,' he said.

There was a briefcase beside his leg. He laid his hand on it for a moment. 'In here is one hundred thousand American dollars. Fifty from Evita and fifty from Von Bader. There is also an Argentine passport in the name of Carlos Hausner. This bag is yours if you tell me what I want to know. The true whereabouts of Fabienne Von Bader.'

'Let's not forget her mother,' I said. 'Ilse Von Bader. Her real mother. Not Evita Perón. And certainly not Isabel Pekerman. Beats me why you went to all that trouble.'

'Originally we thought it might add to the sense of urgency if you believed that only the girl had disappeared. A girl who merely goes away with her mother hardly needs to be found with any great urgency.'

'True. But why the Evita story as well?'

'Evita is a woman who believes in the personal touch. As I'm sure you remember. She thought that an appeal to you from her, in person, would encourage you to find Fabienne.'

'She was very good,' I said. 'But then she is an actress, after all. What will happen to them? To Ilse. To Fabienne?'

'They will be kept here, in Buenos Aires. Kept safe. No harm will come to them, I can assure you. As I told you on the plane, Von Bader is the only one of the three remaining trustees of the Reich bank accounts with a family. Therefore he is the only one who can be trusted to go to Zurich and do what we require him to do, which is to sign over the Reich bank accounts to the Peróns. Ilse Von Bader feared allowing herself and her daughter to become a hostage for her husband's safe return. That is why they disappeared. Which left our plans in obvious disarray, since we could hardly let Von Bader go to Zurich without some guarantee that he would come back again.' The Colonel lit a cigarette. 'So, as soon as you tell me where they are hiding we can pick them up and he can be on his way.'

'How much is there?' I asked. 'In the Zurich account?'

'No one knows for sure. Not even the trustees. But in all likelihood it's several billion dollars.'

I whistled. In the Jockey Club it sounded like a bomb falling out of a Junkers 88.

'Stolen, of course,' I said. 'From millions of murdered Jews.'

The Colonel shrugged. 'Perhaps so. However, you've seen

390

what she does with the money. She gives it away to the sick and the poor. Can you think of a better thing to do with it?'

'She's buying an electorate.'

'Don't be so naïve. All electorates are bought in one way or another. Promises to reduce unemployment. Promises to reduce taxes. Promises to raise public spending. There's not much difference between that and what Evita does. And who's to say her way isn't less wasteful, with no money used up by a bureaucracy.' He smoked patiently. 'So. Where are they?'

I had little desire to help the Peróns, but it was that or the plane ride to the bottom of the river.

'They're living with your friend Hans Kammler,' I said. 'At Wiederhold, his ranch near Tucumán. Posing as his wife and daughter.'

'That's impossible,' said the Colonel.

'No, it's not.'

'You must have made a mistake. His wife and daughter are living at Ingenios. It was me who arranged their visas to come here from Germany. More than a year ago. I think I'd know if it wasn't them.'

'Perhaps I didn't make myself clear. I didn't say they *were* his wife and daughter. I said they were posing as his wife and daughter. It took me a while to recognise Fabienne. She calls herself Mercedes now and has dyed her hair red. But her father, Von Bader, was right. She's still a real beauty. Only it wasn't she who captivated Kammler. It was Ilse. She's a beauty, too. Kammler is very much in love with her.'

'So where are his real wife and daughter?'

'Kammler's a rich man, Colonel. He's got a plane in his back garden. My guess is that he paid the real wife off with a nice piece of change, and then flew her and his real daughter to Chile. Set them up somewhere else. Maybe they're already back in Germany.'

'I didn't know he had a plane up there.'

'He's got it all up there. Wealth. A beautiful home. A beautiful mistress. I almost envied him.'

'Kammler.' The Colonel frowned. 'How very ungrateful of him.' His frown deepened. 'You're sure of this.'

'Of course, I'm sure. I always remember a face, especially a pretty face. It's names I have a problem with.'

'Yes, I think I believe you.' The Colonel shrugged. 'In which case, this is yours.' He patted the briefcase. 'You know, it's nice to be proved right about someone. I was right about you. In your own haphazard way you're a hell of a detective, Gunther.' He nodded thoughtfully. 'Yes, perhaps that was it. You were the random factor that was needed in this case.'

'If you say so, Colonel.'

'Incidentally, the passport contains visas to a number of foreign countries including Uruguay, Brazil, Cuba, and Spain. There's also a first class ticket for tonight's river boat service to Montevideo. Leaving at twenty-one hundred hours. I know how much you dislike air travel. Anyway, I strongly suggest you're on that boat. Very strongly. You can leave the car in the CNFA office at the ferry station.'

'Getting rid of me, is that it?'

'As I said to you before, many times, in Argentina it is better to know everything than to know too much. I'm afraid that now you know too much. Like Isabel Pekerman, for example. Leaving the country, for good, is the only possible solution for a man who won't disappear.' He smiled his infernal smile. 'I hope I've made myself very clear this time.'

'Very. I was thinking of leaving anyway.'

'Don't judge us too harshly. What happened at Dulce was regrettable, I agree, but that was several years ago. Directive Eleven was judged necessary to stop the country from being swamped with Jews, but still they came. And the question soon arose as to what we should do with all those we had arrested and interned. Finally it was decided that it might be easier just to get rid of them as quickly and quietly as possible.'

'So Kammler built Argentina its own death camp.'

'Yes, but on a very much smaller scale than anything that he had built in Poland. There were no more than fifteen or twenty thousand Jews at most. And since then things have changed for the better. An amnesty for all foreigners who entered the country illegally was granted last year. There are no illegal Jews held in camps like Dulce anymore. And the people who implemented Directives Eleven and Twelve have now been removed. So there is even less anti-Semitism than there was. Many Jews are now Perónists. Perón himself now believes that the Jews can actually help Argentina, that their money and enterprise can help our economy to grow. After all, what is it you Germans say? Why slaughter the chicken that lays the golden eggs? Jews are welcome in Argentina.'

The Colonel pointed a salutary finger in the air. 'All Jews except one. There is one Jew who ought to be on that boat with you perhaps. Anna Yagubsky.'

'Never heard of her.'

'Yes, it might be a good idea,' continued the Colonel ignoring me, 'if she accompanied you tonight. Things might be difficult for her if she stayed here in Argentina.'

'I don't know where she is.'

'Well, she can't have disappeared, can she? If she had, I'd know about it, wouldn't I? And if she hasn't disappeared she won't be hard to find. Not for a detective like you, Gunther. For her sake I hope not. And who knows? Perhaps the two of you can find happiness somewhere. You're a little old for her, perhaps, but I believe some women like the older man.'

'What if she won't come with me? Her parents are here. They're old. She won't want to leave them.'

'That would be unfortunate for you, of course – after all, she is very beautiful – but for her, especially.' The Colonel stood up. 'I hope you enjoy your trip to Uruguay. Its government is stable, democratic and politically mature. There's even a welfare state. Of course, the people are entirely European in origin. I believe they exterminated all the Indians. As a German you should feel very much at home there.'

TWENTY-FIVE

BUENOS AIRES. 1950.

It took me three hours to find Anna. Her father was no help. I might just as well have asked where Martin Bormann was hiding. Eventually I remembered that the person who lived upstairs from Isabel Pekerman and who had reported her 'suicide' had also been a friend of Anna's. All I knew was that her name was Hannah and that she lived in Once.

Bisected by Calle Corrientes and the Jewish Quarter, Once was an ugly area with an ugly railway station, an ugly plaza out front of it and, in the centre of this ugly plaza a rather ugly monument. At an ugly police station known to locals as the *Miserere* I showed my SIDE identification to an ugly-looking desk sergeant and asked about the Pekerman case. He told me the address and I went to an ugly building on Calle Paso. It was full of ugly smells and ugly music. There was no getting away from it: Argentina had lost some its charm for me.

A dark and coarse-featured woman came to the door of the apartment above Isabel Pekerman's. She had hair like the tail of a Noriker mare, much of it on her cheeks, and a complexion like the inside of a coffee pot.

'Is Anna here?' I asked.

The woman rubbed her Cro-Magnon chin with vaguely hominid fingers and smiled an uncertain smile that revealed gaps in her teeth as big as the keys on a typewriter. She seemed like the living proof not just of some improbable palaeontological theory but, more importantly, Durkheim's first law of sisterhood, which states that every beautiful woman shall have a really ugly best friend.

'Who wants to know?'

'It's all right, Hannah,' said a voice.

Holding the door, the friend stepped back into the apartment to reveal Anna standing a few feet behind her. She was wearing a gabardine dress in a blue hound's tooth print with a nipped-in waist. Her arms were folded defensively in front of her, the way women do when they're aching to hit you with a rolling-pin.

'How did you find me?' she asked as the friend went back to her stall.

'I'm a detective, remember. It's what I do. Find people. Sometimes I can even find people who don't want to be found.'

'Well you got that part right, Gunther.'

I shut the door behind me and glanced around the ugly little hallway. There was a hat stand, a doormat, an empty dog-basket that had seen many better days, the ubiquitous picture of Martel the tango-singer, and the bag that had accompanied Anna to Tucumán.

'So, did you tell your friends in the secret police about your friends in the SS?'

'That's a nice way of putting it. But yes, I did.'

'And?'

'I imagine they're on their way there now. As I tried to explain on the train, Kammler's wife and child are really someone else's wife and child. And whatever domestic happiness they once enjoyed is now over.'

'And you think that's punishment enough?'

I shrugged. 'Punishment is a little like beauty, sometimes. Subjective. True, lasting punishment at any rate.'

'I prefer the kind of punishment that everyone can understand.'

'Oh, you mean like a public execution.'

'Isn't that what he really deserves?'

'Probably, but we both know that isn't going to happen. In the long run I suspect he'll get what's coming to him. We all do, eventually.'

'I wish I could believe that.'

'Take it from someone who knows.'

'Hmm. I wonder.'

'You're a hard woman, Anna.'

'It's a hard world.'

'Isn't it? That's why I'm here. Now that the police know what I know I've been told to leave the country. And just to make sure I got the message they took me for a ride in a plane with the door open and showed me the River Plate from five thousand feet. The bottom line is that I can be on tonight's boat to Montevideo, or I can be underneath it.'

'They actually threatened you?'

I laughed. 'You make it sound so much nicer than it was, Anna. I was blindfolded, punched in the head, with my hands tied and allowed a last cigarette. For good measure, they threw six people out of the plane ahead of me. For a moment, I thought one of them was you. Then it was my turn. If I hadn't been able to trade the information about Kammler's wife and daughter, I'd be tomorrow's shark shit.' I sighed. 'Look, can we sit down? I still get kind of wobbly thinking about it.'

'Yes, of course. Please. Come through.'

We went into an arty-farty sort of living room that was probably more farty than arty. Everything had been painted with an Italian filigree: the walls, the furniture, the doors, the electric fan, a piano, even a typewriter. There was an artist's palette and some brushes on a filigreed table.

'Hannah's an artist,' explained Anna.

I nodded, and told myself I probably had about ten minutes before Hannah came and started painting a design on my forehead. Maybe it needed one, too. You can grow tired of seeing the same face in the mirror every day. That's why people get married.

'So what are you going to do?' she asked sitting down.

'I'm not much of a swimmer,' I said. 'Especially when my hands are tied behind my back. It's been made clear to me that I can spend the rest of my life dead, or I can go. So, I'm going. To Montevideo. Tonight.'

'I'm sorry about that,' she said, and kissed my hand. 'Really I am.' Then she let out a sigh. 'I don't know why I'm surprised. Most men who are good to me – and you have been good to me Bernie, don't think I don't appreciate what you've done – most of them end up leaving. My father says it's because I don't know how to hang on to a man.'

'With respect to your father it's very simple, angel. Especially in this case. You don't have to say anything. You don't have do anything. Not a thing. Oh, maybe just thread your arm through mine and come with me.'

'To Montevideo?'

'Why not? That's where I'm going.'

'I can't leave, Bernie. This is my home. My father and mother live here.'

'They left Russia because of persecution, didn't they?'

'Yes, but that was different.'

'Somehow I don't think your aunt and your uncle would agree.'

'You said you weren't sure about that. You said we don't know who those people were. That they could have been anyone.'

'We both know I only told you that to stop you from getting us both killed.'

'Yes. Only I do wish I'd listened to you in the first place. You were right. Sometimes it's better not to know. I thought dead was dead and that was as bad as it could get. Well, now I know different, but maybe I want to forget about it now.'

'I'm not asking you to leave on my account,' I said. 'But

your own. The secret police told me that, given you know what I know, it would be advisable for you to leave the country, too. I'm really sorry to have you tell you this, Anna, but I worry about what will happen to you if you stay. It could easily be you that's thrown out of the next plane over the River Plate.'

'Is this another lie? To make me come with you?' She pushed her long tangle of hair out of her eyes and shook her head. 'I can't leave. I won't.'

I put my hands on her shoulders and shook her gently.

'Listen to me, Anna, I'd like you to come with me. But if you don't want to, I can understand that. Only – with or without me – you have to leave, tonight. It doesn't have to be Uruguay. If you like I'll buy you an air ticket to wherever you want to go. There's a PLUNA office around the corner. We'll go there now and I'll get you a ticket to Asuncion. La Paz. Wherever you want. I'll even give you some money to get yourself started somewhere else. Ten thousand American dollars. Twenty. But you *have* to leave the country.'

'I can't leave my parents,' she said. 'They're old.'

'Then I'll pay for them, too. We can send for them when we get to Montevideo. It's not so far. I'll buy us a big house where we can all live. I promise you. It will be fine, we'll manage. Only you do have to believe me. The police know about you. They know your name. Almost certainly they know where you live and where you work. This is serious, Anna. One morning soon, you'll be on your way to work and they'll pick you up and take you to Caseros. They'll strip you naked and abuse you. Torture you. And when they're finished torturing you they'll put you on a plane and they'll throw you out of the door. If you stay here, angel, there's nothing left for you but prayer. I heard one on the plane, yesterday, over and over again. And guess what? It didn't work. They threw him out anyway. These people, they're immune to prayer. They'll listen to your prayers and they'll laugh and then they'll throw you out.'

'No.' There were tears in her eyes, but she was shaking her head with disbelief. 'This is just another lie of convenience. Like telling me those people in the burial pits at Dulce were not Jews. You're just saying all this because you can't bear the idea of going away on your own. I can't blame you for wanting me along. If I was you I'd probably say the same thing. I like you a lot, Bernie, but I'll get over it. We both will. Only I do wish you'd stop trying to scare me. That's pretty low of you.'

'You can't believe I'm making this up surely?'

'Why not? Bernie, everything about you is made up. I really don't know anything about you.'

'I told you everything there was to know on the train.'

'How do I know that? All I know for sure is that you're here on a false passport. Even the real name you're supposed to have given to your old comrades – the ones who brought you here – even that's not yours. That man at the ranch. Heinrich Grund. You told me he was a murderer, but you knew him. He greeted you like he was an old friend.'

'He was, once. Before the war. Before Hitler. I had lots of friends before Hitler.'

'For all I know, you're one of them, too. How can I possibly trust you? How can I believe a word you say? I'm a Jew, and you're an ex SS-officer. What kind of trust could there ever be between us?'

'You came to me for help,' I reminded her. 'I helped you as best I could. I'm trying to help you now. I asked for nothing in return. Whatever you gave you gave because you wanted to. I saved your life once before and I'm trying to save it again. I put my own life in peril for you. I have to leave the country because of you. Maybe that doesn't mean so much to you. But I'm still glad I did. I'd have done anything for you. I suppose what I'm trying to say is that I love you, Anna. Well what of it? There's just this. If there's any small part of you that feels the same way I do then forget everything else. Forget everything your head tells you and listen to your heart, because that's all that matters between two people. I know I'm not much of a catch for a girl like you. You could do a lot better, I know, and if you weren't standing in an aeroplane doorway I'd probably tell you to go and do a lot better, too. But you're there. I can see the bruises on your face and the wind in your hair, angel.'

I pulled her toward me and kissed her hard as if I was trying to breathe some sense into her body. She put her arms around me and kissed me back so that, for a minute or two, I almost thought it might be working.

Then she said, 'I suppose I do love you, but I won't leave the country for you. I won't. I can't. Every time I see you it reminds me. Of what happened to my aunt and uncle.'

I wanted to slap her hard on both cheeks, the way you're supposed to when you've been in the SS. That might have worked, too. With anyone but Anna. Hitting her would have been like giving the Hitler salute. It would only have confirmed what she already suspected. That I was a Nazi.

I let her go. 'Listen, angel. This probably isn't going to work but I'll try it once more and then I'll leave you alone. When two people are in love they're supposed to look out for each other.'

'Being in love doesn't make any difference,' she said. 'It's not enough of a reason.'

'Let me finish. When you get a little older – maybe too old – you'll understand that it makes all the difference to everything and anything.'

Even as I said it, I knew it wasn't going to happen. She wasn't going to get any older. Not if Colonel Montalban was as bad as his word.

'Love is all the reason you need, angel. It's the only reason in the world that exists for you to trust me. That might not be the kind of reason that would satisfy a Greek in a toga. I don't know that you could ever use that kind of reason as the basis for a truth that exists outside of ourselves. All I know is that you have to give it a chance if you're to know if someone is what we want or what we think we want. It needs a little time. Let's just make it this. Come with me for just a few days. As if we were just going back on the train to Tucumán. And then, if it doesn't work out, you can say to hell with you Gunther, I'm going back to Buenos Aires because I'd rather die than be with a man like you. So, don't say another word just now. Think carefully about what I've said. Speak to your father. I did. He'll give you some good advice. Fathers usually do. I'll buy you a ticket for tonight's boat. We can be in Montevideo in less time than it takes to say that I'll wait for you at the Cia de Navegacio Fluvial Argentina office.'

And then I left.

TWENTY-SIX

BUENOS AIRES. 1950.

That night it rained heavily. The river was calm. The tide and the moon were full. Somewhere, on the other side of the Plate was Uruguay. I stood in the office of the CNFA, staring out of the window at the pier and the boat and the waves lapping at the jetty. Half an eye was on the clock. With each shuddering movement of the second hand I felt my hopes ebbing away. I wasn't the first man to be stood up by a woman. I wouldn't be the last. That's how poetry gets written.

What are you supposed to do when you know you'll be murdered if you stay behind to be with a girl you love? Meet death together like you were both in some crummy movie? It doesn't work that way. You don't get to walk out of the picture, hand in hand, to the sound of some invisible choir heralding your joint arrival in Paradise. When death comes it's usually nasty and brutish and sharp. I should know. I'd seen it often enough.

A voice came over the tannoy loudspeaker. The last call for passengers on the twenty-one hundred to Montevideo.

She wasn't coming.

I walked along the pier and felt it move under my feet as if I had been standing on the breathing chest of some enormous giant. Rain sprayed my face. A melancholy rain like the tears of the night wind that stirred my hair. I stepped off Argentina and into the boat. There were other passengers but I didn't notice them. Instead I remained on deck, waiting for the miracle that wasn't going to happen. I even started to hope that the Colonel might show up to see me off so that I could beg for Anna's life. But he didn't come either.

The rumbling engines roared into life. They were casting off our ties. Water stirred in a maelstrom underneath the boat and we lurched away from the pier. Away from Buenos Aires. From her. We retreated into darkness like some abandoned, pagan thing, cast adrift from the world of men. Overwhelmed with self-pity and confusion and struggle and flight, I almost threw myself over the side and into the sea in the hope of swimming to the vast edges of the shore. Instead I went below.

In the galley, a steward lit a little gas ring to boil some water for coffee. The blue flame girdling the pot tickled it quietly. And I pictured that other flame: the small, quiet flame inside of me that burned with neither joy, nor peace, nor hope, nor help from lonely pain. Not for Adolf Hitler. But for her. It burned for her.

AUTHOR'S NOTE

I am indebted to Uki Goni's excellent book *The Real Odessa* for much of my information about Nazis in Argentina. For anyone writing about this subject it is the one indispensable source.

Directive Eleven was signed into existence by the Argentine Foreign Minister, José Maria Cantilo, on July 12th 1938, thus condemning as many as 200,000 European Jews to death. Its existence is still denied to this day.

Throughout the war, rumours persisted of the existence of an Argentine concentration camp for Jews in Argentina's remote forests. According to Goni there were some Argentine government ministers who demanded 'a solution to the Jewish problem' in Argentina. No such camp has ever been confirmed as having existed.

According to Gerald Posner and John Ware's authoritative biography *Mengele*, huge quantities of Nazi loot almost certainly fell under the control of the Peróns. Four of the Argentine-German trustees of the Nazi money were murdered between 1949 and 1952.

Eva Perón developed uterine cancer in 1950. Despite having undergone a hysterectomy by the eminent American surgeon, George T. Pack, Evita's cancer returned rapidly. She developed lung metastasis and was the first Argentinian to undergo chemotherapy (a novel treatment at that time). Despite all available treatment, she died at the age of thirty-three, on July 26th, 1952.

Eva's brother, Juan Duarte, was dispatched by Juan Perón to Zurich in early 1953, ostensibly to persuade the Swiss authorities to sign over Eva's personal fortune into Perón's own name. Following Duarte's return to Buenos Aires in April 1953, he committed suicide. But most people believed he was murdered.

The fifty-eight-year-old Perón took a fourteen-year-old mistress, Nelly Rivas, in October 1953. She was one of many young girls the President dallied with openly. Perón himself was excommunicated from the Roman Catholic Church by the Vatican on June 16th, 1955. He was deposed not long afterwards.

After eighteen years in exile, Perón returned as President in June 1973. His wife Isabel, succeeded her husband to the presidency and was herself deposed by a military coup in March 1976. A military junta took control and combined a widespread persecution of political dissidents with the use of state terrorism. As many as thirty thousand Argentine people 'disappeared'.

Josef Mengele was one of several thousand Nazi war criminals who went to live in Argentina after the war. In 1958 Mengele was arrested by Buenos Aires police and accused of being an illegal abortionist. After bribing a detective to release him, Mengele fled to Paraguay. He probably drowned in Sao Paulo, in Brazil, in 1979.

Adolf Eichmann was kidnapped from Argentina in May 1960, put on trial in Israel, and hanged in Jerusalem on May 31st, 1962.

General Doctor Hans Kammler was an engineer who oversaw numerous SS construction projects. He designed and built the extermination camps and oversaw the destruction of the Warsaw ghetto. From January 1945 he was number three in the SS and in charge of all Nazi missile projects. He disappeared in May 1945 and, it is strongly suspected, was taken to the USA as part of the 'Paperclip' programme. There is no further information on Kammler after this. But Kammler is, perhaps, the highest ranking Nazi war criminal who, even today, no one has ever heard of.

Uki Goni reports that most of the documentation on Argentina's Nazi past, including the still denied Directive Eleven, was destroyed by Perón in 1955; and in 1996, when the burning of confidential immigration dossiers containing the landing papers of Nazi war criminals was ordered.